# I Choose
## TO Live Bravely
### A NOVEL

BRAVELY TRILOGY
BOOK TWO

NICOLE DWIGANS

Inked Paper Press
Beaverton, Oregon

Published 2019 by Inked Paper Press
Beaverton, OR 97008

ISBN: 978-1-7321386-3-6 (hardcover edition)
ISBN: 978-1-7321386-4-3 (paperback edition)
ISBN: 978-1-7321386-5-0 (ebook edition)

LCCN: 2019907304

02010919

Edited by Emily Mulica
Cover model photography by JW Photography & Covers
Cover model Wade Hayes
Cover and interior design by Inked Paper Press

## Books By Nicole Dwigans

### Bravely Trilogy

*I Choose to Love Bravely*
*I Choose to Live Bravely*
*I Choose to Dream Bravely*

Thank you for choosing this book.
It is for you that I write.
Love,
Nicole

For my husband, Sean, and all who have been
diagnosed with cancer.

# CHAPTER 1

## GAVIN

On the living room at the end of the hall, Gavin paces like a guard dog. The only sound is the tap-tap of his wingtips as he wears a groove in the old wood floor. He pulls at the collar of his shirt to loosen an invisible tie as an animal-like "arrgghhh" rips through his clenched teeth.

Gavin strides across the living room to the back of the house. He crosses his arms tightly over his chest and stares out the window. One of Gavin's favorite things about their home here on the hill is the vast view. Skyscrapers jet up from the earth and sparkle under the sun like jewels. Bridges stretch across the thick, blue Willamette River and unite the east and west sides of the city. Lush trees blanket the landscape as far as the eye can see. To him, it's an evolving piece of art. As an architect, he dreams of how he'll enhance the view with new buildings and improve older ones.

Now, though, with what the nurse told Gavin today, he fears he won't get that chance. Even worse, he's scared the life he envisioned with Nyla has been stolen not only from him, but from her as well.

Pressure builds behind Gavin's eyes, then, like a dam pushed to its limits, tears escape. He wipes them away with a rough hand, then squeezes his eyes shut. "Get it together," he says under his breath.

When at last Gavin thinks he's regained control, he opens his eyes and looks straight into those of an emerald-headed hummingbird. A sense of familiarity comes over him. Stepping closer to the window, he tilts his head to the side, and says, "Hi," then laughs at himself. "Now I know I've gone insane. I'm talking to a damn bird. Though," he glances over his shoulder, to be sure he's still alone, "if you can help me—"

"Gavin?" Nyla says.

He spins and moves toward her, but she widens her stance like a warrior halting him. She stretches her neck, exposing the most vulnerable part of herself as if to say she can and will defend herself against anything, even him.

Despite the unspoken message which pierces Gavin's heart, his desire to be close to her swells. He's in love with her fierce I-don't-need-anyone side, as well as the fragile one, all of which he's promised to protect no matter what it costs him.

"We're all supposed to be at the restaurant in a couple hours," Nyla says. "Do you want to tell them in person, or start making calls?"

Though he knows the answer, Gavin asks, "Do you love me?"

Nyla's eyes narrow. "What is it with you? Do I love *you*? Do you love *me*?"

"I love you more than anything."

"You've got a funny way of showing it."

Gavin's knee begins to bounce. He's unsure of where to start, or how to explain why he went completely insane in their bedroom. Finally, he blurts, "Sue called me this afternoon."

Nyla's eyes narrow as she says, "I don't know who Sue is."

"She's a nurse at my oncologist's office. I had an appointment earlier this week. A scan, blood work, fertility testing. Something is off. They need a biopsy."

The nurse told Gavin they only need a few cells, but the tumor is on his thyroid, and there is only one way to get them. Gavin's hand goes to his neck. He can almost feel the puncture of a large needle as it rips deep into his throat.

"You never said anything about an appointment," Nyla says dryly.

Gavin tosses a hand in her direction. "You had this last-minute trip and the wedding. I didn't want to worry you."

Nyla's strong stance doesn't falter. An onlooker would assume she's unfazed, but Gavin knows she's gone into "race mode." This mental state allows her to shut everything out so she can focus on one thing. It helped her become a successful sports reporter and before that a world-class runner. Unfortunately, in times like this, it makes her almost impossible to work with.

Gavin's shoulders sink as he says, "I can't do what he did to you."

Nyla's face softens as she says, "Lorenzo," but then she clenches her jaw, and her eyes harden.

The tender way she says her departed husband's name feels like a dagger slipping between Gavin's ribs. He doesn't want to admit it, but he's accepted he'll always be second. What he hasn't accepted is the possibility of hurting her like Lorenzo did.

He balls his hands at his side, and though he doesn't want to say it, he bites out, "I can't do what he did to you. I will not be a man that shatters you."

"Fine. We'll tell everyone at dinner that the wedding is off. That you're afraid you have cancer—"

"Don't tell them! I don't want them to know!"

Nyla's race mode glitches as she tosses her arms into the air. "What do you want from me? I don't care. You can tell them whatever you want. Tell them you don't love me, that I was just some lapse in judgment and you don't want to marry me. Does that make you happy?"

Her shirt works its way up over her hourglass hips as she talks with animated arms. Gavin watches as it goes, little by little, revealing angry red welts and smearing blood. He's overwhelmed with a desire to bring vengeance to the person who hurt her. Then he realizes, it's him who's done this, and he says, "What have I done? Heaven help me. What have I done?" He moves toward her, but she squares her shoulders and yanks her shirt down. "Are you all right?" he asks.

"I think it's time for you to get going," Nyla says.

"Do you hate me?"

"Do you actually want me to answer that right now?"

"I want to marry you, more than anything. But I need to know when I stand up there and say I do, that I'm able to offer myself to you whole. I don't want you to worry that you're marrying a man who will make you a widow again."

He reaches for her, but she shakes her head like a queen delivering a sentence to a man on death row.

"I'm fine on my own," she says.

"I'll fix it," Gavin replies.

"You need to go."

"Do you understand that I do want to marry you? I just can't right now, Nyla. I need to know for sure."

There is a tiny tremble in Nyla's chin that tightens before she says, "You'll be late."

"Let's go to this dinner tonight," Gavin says. "Talk after when we've both had time to think, and we'll go from there."

"Pretend like everything is as it was?"

"Yes."

"I'm not a very good actress."

"Could have fooled me. Or maybe you just don't care that I might have cancer again."

Nyla's shoulders shutter, but she doesn't move.

"You're so damn stubborn!" Gavin snaps. "Can't you get mad sometimes? I'm not the media, the outside world that you have to shield yourself from."

"I think to some degree I need to shield myself from everyone. Clearly."

Though Nyla's feet stay planted like a fortress that will not be breached, her eyes follow Gavin who's begun to pace back and forth again.

"It was wrong, Nyla. I've never felt fear like this. Never have I had so much to lose and at the same time felt the—"

Nyla abruptly turns to the hall of their bedroom.

Gavin says, "Where are you going?"

She turns on her heel and with emotion leaking, she says, "I cannot listen to all the reasons you can't marry me. You've had hours to process this, and I'm trying to sort through everything right now. I'm trying to keep myself together, to simply stay upright, because I have family on the way over."

Nyla begins to turn away again but stops and looks back at Gavin. Her hard eyes dissolve into anguish. Her eyelashes flutter as she takes a deep breath. Then in a tone that yields a knife, she says, "You might have worried about making me a widow, but do you realize I would have preferred that to you willingly breaking my heart? You didn't do what Lorenzo did to me. What you have done is much, much worse. He didn't have a choice."

Gavin's mouth unhinges. As his eyes fall to his feet, his shoulders slump. He doesn't see the regret on Nyla's face. For a moment it looks as if she's going to reach for him, but instead she turns and leaves the room.

# CHAPTER 2

$\mathcal{G}$avin walks down the hall to Nyla and his closed bedroom door. He wraps his hand around the cold metal doorknob and twists. It's locked, and despite his efforts it doesn't budge.

He slams his fist against the door, and shouts, "Nyla! Nyla? Love?" Gavin presses his ear to the door, and while he doesn't hear a response from Nyla there is the distant sound of running water. It conjures an image of her naked with pink-ribboned water swirling around her feet.

Bile burns up Gavin's throat. He rushes back through the living room to the back window again. He searches for the hummingbird, but there isn't a single one. "What do I do? Help me," he says as he leans his head against the glass. Then he's struck with an idea and hurries out of the front door.

Their house is at the end of a private road called Appleton Way. It's a rare piece of property with several acres and no neighbors in sight. Aside from the house, which looks like a small Timberline Lodge, there are two structures. One is a four-bay garage. The other, which

Gavin rushes to, looks like an average family home. Inside, though, is his large open shop.

Gavin opens the door, and the familiar scent of fresh-cut wood calms him. He spends time out here at least four days a week working on projects and repairing things. It's a stress relief for him much in the same way running is for Nyla.

There are numerous tools of all shapes and sizes, meticulously organized shelves, and a workbench. In the back corner below a window is a metal desk. Next to it is a large fireproof safe with a keypad. Gavin enters the code, then opens it. From the top shelf he grabs a key.

The house was built in the early 1900s. When Gavin renovated it he did his best to retain its natural charm and save the original hardware. He was able to keep all of the interior doorknobs which share this skeleton key.

Knowing he can get to Nyla now, Gavin strides back across the property toward the house with renewed determination.

Ten feet from the front door a hummingbird zips past Gavin, so close he hears the hum of its wings. Gavin slows and watches the bird fly up to the top of the roof where it turns and looks down to him. The blur of its emerald wings hypnotizes Gavin to stillness. His ragged breath steadies, jaw relaxes, and color returns to the knuckles of his hand gripping the key.

Gavin slips the key into the pocket of his trousers, and says to the bird, "I'll give her space."

He gets into his black truck which is parked in front of the house. As if it's a chore he doesn't want to do, Gavin starts the engine and puts it in drive. He slows as he passes a window of their bedroom. It's obscured by a bush when you drive into the property, but you can see it on the way out. Nyla rushes by the window, her amber skin a blur and hair fluttering like a flag on weak wind. The sight of her stirs Gavin's anguished heart and another place he ignores.

At the end of their gravel road is a newly paved city street. Its inky-black surface looks naked without any lines. Gavin stops here and puts the truck in park. He closes his eyes as his head drops back.

As a teenager, Gavin stood a head above all the other boys, and his shoulders were as broad as a grown man's. He joined the football team because that's what big guys do. He loved the game but hated to play. He wasn't afraid to take a hit, but he was not willing to give them. It was his size that kept him on the team, but he mostly warmed the bench.

Football taught Gavin that he isn't aggressive, but he is competitive. He's a man who gets what he wants and exceeds every goal set. He also likes to be in control, but with Nyla he's not. It's something he both relishes and hates.

If Gavin were to do things his way right now, he'd return to the house, make her sit down, and talk. It's not that he likes to talk things out, it's that he doesn't want to leave things messy. And what he wouldn't give to hear her say I love you and feel her protective arms around him.

Knowing that Nyla needs space, and trusting that they'll be okay, Gavin puts the car in drive and turns onto the inky-black road.

•••

At the Portland Airport, Gavin pulls into the short-term parking garage and takes the spiral ramp to the top level. He parks near the elevator and checks his watch. Somehow he's right on schedule.

As Gavin moves to get out of his truck, the skeleton key in his trousers pokes his leg. He digs into his pocket and pulls it out. It doesn't fit on his key ring, so he places it in the center console.

Outside the truck, the concrete parking structure amplifies the heat of the August day. Gavin shields his eyes from the sun and watches a small commuter jet take off. It's like the one he was aboard the first time Nyla spoke to him. The memory of how she smiled and said, "Nice shoes," melts through him.

Before that day Gavin knew who Nyla was. He'd seen her on TV, in photographs at Samuel Tripple's office, on the cover of magazines, and even in micro-sized photos at the end of her articles. From watching how Nyla grabs peoples' attention and holds it, Gavin expected her to be a vibrant woman. However, in person, he found her energy even more enthralling than he expected.

At the elevator Gavin presses the call button. At the same time his phone vibrates with a message from his father, Richard. "We'll be at baggage claim in five minutes."

Richard and Kathy, Gavin's parents, are flying in from his hometown of Seattle. Jax, his brother, and his girlfriend Brooke are flying in from Boulder, Colorado. Their flights are scheduled to arrive twenty minutes apart.

Gavin rides the elevator down to the second floor. As he enters the skybridge that goes between the parking structure and the airport, his phone buzzes again. This time it's a message from Jax. "We're pulling up to the gate. See you soon."

Halfway across the bridge, Gavin steps out of the flow of people and stops next to the window. He takes his phone back out and taps the text message string with Nyla. The little round photo of her smiling face stares back at him. He quickly types a new message. "I love you. Meet me outside the restaurant, please." When he's about to send it, uncertainty floods him. Are the words sufficient?

Before he can decide, his phone rings replacing the message screen with a photo of Richard.

"Hey, Gavin. Where are you?"

"Headed your way," Gavin says.

"We're at carousel two."

"Be right there."

His father's voice brings Gavin back to reality and makes the last few hours seem like a hazy nightmare. He can hardly relate to the desperate, out of control version of himself that fumbled the very important conversation with Nyla at home.

With a clearer head, Gavin brings his message to Nyla back up and amends it. "I am sorry. I love you more than anything. Meet me outside the restaurant, please." He presses send and then continues across the bridge to meet his family.

•••

Kathy spots her son riding down the escalator to baggage claim and waves an excited hand at him. When he waves back, she clasps her hands in front of her chest hardly able to contain herself. Behind her, Richard wraps his arms around her and kisses the top of her head.

The only thing Gavin inherited from his mother is her coffee-bean color hair, though hers is now threaded by white. Everything else comes from his father whom he looks like a younger version of, plus five inches: almond-shaped eyes, strong brow, fuller bottom lip.

"The handsome groom," Kathy says proudly.

"Thanks, Mom," Gavin says.

"Where is Nyla?" she asks.

"There's been a change in plans. Her family is picking her up. They'll meet us at Mix."

Kathy runs a gentle hand along Gavin's forearm and tilts her head. "Are you okay, Gavin?"

"Yeah, Mom, I'm fine."

"He looks just fine to me," Richard says with a firm pat on Gavin's back. "You've gotten a little sun?"

"A little."

"It's too bad Nyla couldn't come with you," Kathy says.

She picks up a small gift from the top of her carry-on. It's wrapped in silver paper with a mini, ivory bow.

"Don't mind your mother," Richard says. "She's just more excited to see Nyla than you."

Gavin smiles with a tinge of sadness. "I see that."

Kathy cradles the gift like a treasure. "I'm not more excited to see her than you. But I have been excited to give this to her."

"What is it?"

Kathy beams as she says, "It's the necklace that the last three women to join the Boston ranks wore."

Gavin recalls his mother talking about this necklace from when he was younger. The oval mother-of-pearl has been worn by Kathy, his grandmother, and great-grandma. All three women had sons. There's a running joke that boys are all Boston men know how to make.

"Well ... um ..." Kathy looks anxiously to Richard, then back to her son. "I guess not all women. You see, I didn't want Pandora to wear it because I never felt good about her."

"I know you didn't, Mom."

"Even from the beginning. I had a bad feeling. Not with Nyla, though. You two are a perfect match. Do you think she'd wear it too? Or does she already have jewelry picked out?"

Gavin shrugs. "I don't know."

"No, of course not. The groom isn't supposed to know the bride's clothes. Maybe I should have talked with her sooner. It's just so hard to pin her down. I wanted to ask her in person, but the last few times we've visited, she's been gone. But you don't mind if I ask her?"

With his eyes stuck on the box, Gavin replies, "Of course not."

Kathy reaches for the collar of Gavin's shirt and smooths a side that rolled under. "It's a little wrinkled. That's not like you. You're sure—"

Richard takes her hand and kisses the back of it, then holds it between his own. "Kathy, I think he's too old for his mother to be fixing his clothes."

"Never," she says.

Gavin's always admired his parent's perfect relationship. It's the one you see in shows and movies, but it's as common as a twenty-carat diamond. Kathy stayed home with the boys until they were in school, then she returned to her profession as a third-grade teacher. Her family, though, has always been first.

A long and loud buzz signals the start of the luggage carousel.

"May I get your bags for you?" Gavin asks.

"No," Richard says and leans in close to his son. "Do go check a mirror, or Jax will be asking you more questions than your mother."

Gavin finds a full-length mirror in the restroom. He is shocked by his reflection. His freshly cut hair—short on the sides and longer on top, just like Nyla likes—looks like he drove here in a convertible with the top down. He does his best to smooth it, though it's a far cry from its usual perfection. Then he fixes his collar, smooths the shirt, and neatly re-rolls the sleeves to just below his elbow. His bloodshot eyes are something he can't fix. He also can't right the strained pull of the muscles below the contours of his face. Only Nyla can do that.

When Gavin returns to his parents, Jax and Brooke are there.

The two brothers share little resemblance, though their facial expressions are similar. Jax's boy-next-door look no doubt helped his rise to pop-stardom.

For ten years, Jax struggled. He played dive bars, lived on a shoestring budget, and gained little recognition. But when "Mystery Girl" was released, it blew up the charts and catapulted him into stardom.

Gavin, inspired by a dream, wrote the lyrics to the song. He shared them with Jax and hummed the chords he heard in his head. Within two hours, Jax wrote the music and pulled the whole song together. With the stipulation that Gavin's name appears nowhere, he gave Jax permission to record it.

Jax extends his hand to Gavin and pulls him into a hug. "Brother, brother. How are you?"

"Great," Gavin says as he turns to Brooke for a hug.

Though Brooke and Jax got back together only a year ago, she entered their lives at the very beginning of Jax's career.

She tucks her blond hair back behind her ear and turns her big, brown eyes up to Gavin like a proud little sister. "The dashing groom."

Jax points to the other end of baggage claim, and as he begins to walk backward, he says, "Our luggage is coming out on the belt, down there. I'll be right back."

"May I help you?" Gavin offers.

"No. I got it."

"Where is Nyla?" Brooke asks.

"We're meeting her at the restaurant with her family," Kathy replies.

When Jax returns with two medium-sized suitcases, Gavin turns to the ladies and asks, "May I get your carry-ons?" Gavin picks up Brooke's oversized pink bag and puts it on his shoulder. Then he grabs the handle of his mom's rolling bag. "We have everything?"

"Looks like it," Richard says. He leads the way as if this is his hometown.

The two women walk alongside each other chatting like an adoring mother-daughter duo.

So that no one ahead of them can hear, Jax asks Gavin, "Are you okay? Not getting cold feet, are you?"

"What? No. Not at all."

With a squinted right eye, Jax scans his brother's face as if he can see something no one else can.

"Is she?"

"No," Gavin snaps under his breath.

"You just look, I don't know, concerned."

"It was a stressful day at work. I've taken a few days off here and there over the years, but not a real vacation like this. Even when I was sick, I worked. Planning to be offline for three weeks isn't easy."

"You actually got Nyla to agree to this offline thing?"

Gavin nods proudly, but it quickly fades.

Jax says, "Three whole weeks? Wow, she must love you or something." They are quiet as they make their way back across the skybridge. Then, just before they reach the parking lot elevator, Jax lightly pats his brother's shoulder and says, "It's okay to be nervous."

# CHAPTER 3

$O$ver the last year, it's been impossible to bring Gavin and Nyla's entire families together. They're busy people and scattered over three states. Still, Nyla and Gavin thought it was important for everyone to meet before the wedding festivities began. That's why they planned this dinner tonight at Mix.

Gavin steps into the restaurant, his family close behind. He scans the room for Nyla but doesn't see her. There is, however, an empty barstool that catches his eye. It's the exact spot Nyla was last year when he arrived here, and everything began to change. Seeing this empty space, as if it's being held for her, he remembers that pivotal day.

Nearly a year ago now, Gavin found a note on his desk. Neatly written in Linda's hand, it read, "Six at Mix. I promise it will be worth your time." He tossed the note back onto his desk and immediately decided he wasn't going to go.

At a quarter to six, though, Trace came into his office and said, "Ready?"

Gavin shook his head. "I'm not going. How many times have I told Linda not to set me up? But she keeps pushing."

Trace collapsed into a chair across from Gavin, picked up the note, read it, then tossed it back onto the desk. "Look, I don't know if my wife is setting you up. But she told me you have to come. We both know it's not good to piss her off, and I live with her. So if you don't want to do this for her, do it for me. It's just a drink. You can be gone in thirty minutes."

Gavin, not wanting to put his friend and business partner in a difficult place, reluctantly packed up for the day and went with him.

When Gavin walked into Mix, Nyla looked up to him from under the sparkling chandelier, and her inviting smile gave him hope.

What he wouldn't give now to see her perched on that barstool with her long legs crossed and shiny hair cascading over her shoulder.

A woman at the hostess stand says, "Good evening. Five for dinner tonight?"

"Actually," Gavin says, "we have a reservation. The Tripple-Boston party."

"Yes. Welcome. I'm Maria. And you are Gavin I presume?"

"Yes."

"Wonderful to meet you, and congratulations on your upcoming nuptials. We have everything ready in the private dining room upstairs. This way."

As Gavin follows Maria, his family behind him, he asks, "Are we the first to arrive?"

"You are," Maria replies. "I'm not sure if you heard, but there was a terrible accident on Burnside. The road is closed, so people have to take detours. We've been getting calls for the last half hour with people telling us they'll be late."

"Oh, dear," Kathy says.

"No worries, though," Maria says brightly. "I held the appetizers Nyla ordered just in case you all were delayed. I'll get them out quickly, and we can get drinks started."

"That would be great," Gavin says.

They walk up the stairway to a large mezzanine. There's a long, wooden table with cream napkins and mismatched place settings.

"Lisa," Maria says to a woman who's come up the stairs behind them. "This is Gavin, the groom, and his family. The rest of the party will be along soon, but I think they're ready for a drink."

Gavin says, "Yes, let's get those going. I'll have a whiskey sour, please." Then he turns to his family. "You all order and get settled. I'm going to meet Nyla out front."

The anticipation of seeing her begins to rattle his cells. He hopes he can atone for the stress he caused, and that despite everything, she'll still want him.

Outside of the restaurant, Gavin works his way through the crowd of people. Northwest 23rd is a popular district lined with trendy restaurants, coffees shops, and boutiques. Today, he thinks it's even busier than usual.

Gavin finds the shade of a tree and checks his phone. Five missed calls from business associates and a text from his assistant, Alvis. No reply from Nyla. He listens to his voicemails, then replies to Alvis's text.

Jax throws his arm around Gavin's neck, and says, "There you are."

Gavin, a tall, handsome guy, usually catches people's eyes, but with his brother's presence, even more are looking. Some even openly stare. Right now, Gavin would prefer people didn't notice him because when Nyla gets here, he'd like to talk with her alone. Though he knows that's hard because she draws just as much attention as Jax, possibly more.

When Gavin tries to shrug Jax's arm off, he says, "Lighten up, Gavin." Then he licks three of his fingers and reaches for Gavin's hair.

Gavin leans back and shuffles quickly away. "Don't you dare."

"The top is messed up," Jax says.

Gavin turns to the window and uses the reflection to check himself. From behind it, two beautiful women watch him. When he finally notices them, one licks her lips, the other flashes a come-hither grin.

"Careful," Jax says.

Embarrassed, Gavin smiles cautiously and turns away. "You don't have to worry about me." He checks his watch and shakes his head.

"She's only five minutes late," Jax says. "She probably wants to make sure you'll appreciate her when she finally gets here."

"Nyla isn't like that."

"I know, I do. I was kidding. I was trying to get you to laugh because you look way too serious for a man that's about to marry the woman of his dreams."

Gavin glances back at the restaurant door to ensure that no one else has followed Jax out.

"You can tell me what's up," Jax says.

"Like I said, work. It's been stressful. And Nyla . . . I haven't really had a chance to talk with her. She's been traveling the last few days. And she missed her flight last night."

"I don't know if it's good or bad that you found a woman who's married to work more than you. Well, not you, but you know, married to work more than you are. You know what I mean."

"Yeah, I do. I just need a hug from her. What a wuss. Right?

"Nah. I actually understand. It's okay to need your lady."

Up the street Emma, Linda and Trace's six-year-old daughter, spots Gavin. She pulls her hand from her mother's and runs as fast as her tiny legs will carry her.

"Uncle Gavin!" Emma hollers.

Gavin turns, kneels down, and catches Emma as she jumps into his arms with complete trust. He lifts her up and spins her around while she giggles. When he comes to a stop, she wraps one arm around his neck.

"Mommy wouldn't let me wear my flower girl dress," Emma says.

"No? Well, that's because it's for Saturday," Gavin replies.

She has on a skirt made of several layers of purple tulle. She lifts one of them, and asks, "Do you like my skirt?"

"I do. It's very fancy."

"Mommy said Nyla will love it! It matches her running shoes."

"It matches her favorite pair. Nyla will love it."

Alex, Emma's older brother, stops next to Gavin and looks up at him. He has floppy hair and bright, blue eyes like his mother's. His jeans paired with a nice, navy blazer make him look older than his ten years.

"Hey there, Alex," Gavin says. "Looking sharp."

"Where is Nyla?" Alex asks.

"What about me?" asks Gavin.

"Sorry, Uncle Gavin. Hi." He looks to Jax then back to Gavin. "Where is Nyla?"

"Man." Gavin shakes his head and ruffles Alex's hair. "Everyone wants to know where Nyla is."

Linda, finally catching up with her kids, says, "She's the bride. Star of the show." She winks at Jax. "And here is another star. Kids, do you remember Jax?"

Alex and Emma shake their heads no.

"Jax is Gavin's little brother. We all grew up together."

"Oh," Alex replies, then looks back to Gavin, clearly still waiting for his answer.

"Nyla is on her way," Gavin says. "She rode with her family."

"If she came up over Burnside," Linda says. "She probably got stuck. We came from Washington Square, and it was so backed up that we had to jog over to twenty-six and come in that way. That's why we're late. Sorry."

"Yes, I heard it's a mess," Gavin says. "You all head in. We're upstairs. Drinks and apps are out."

"Can I stay with you?" Emma asks.

"No silly," Gavin says as he sets her down.

Trace takes her hand. "Come on, Em. Let's get you a juice."

After the Smiths go inside, Jax says, "Maybe you should call her."

Gavin takes a couple of steps away from his brother as he pulls out his phone. It goes straight to voicemail. "Hello, love. I'm waiting outside of the restaurant. I really need to kiss your lips. See you soon."

From down the street, Kevin booms, "My man, the groom!"

Kevin, though not as large and imposing as his father Samuel, carries an air of confidence. He still has the athletic build and boyish good looks from his quarterback days in college.

Next to him, his wife Mia looks even more petite with her six-month-old daughter in a carrier on her chest.

Gavin shoulders ease. "Finally!"

"Sorry. Traffic was a mess," Mia says. "And it's never easy to get anywhere on time with a baby."

"You don't slow them down, do you?" Gavin says to Rania as he tickles her neck. She giggles at her soon-to-be uncle whom she's very fond of. "Jax, this is Kevin, his wonderful wife Mia, and this bundle of joy is Rania."

Jax shakes their hands, then reaches out to the baby who grips his offered finger. "Oh aren't you cute," he says to her.

Gavin looks beyond Kevin and Mia to the parking lot where they came from.

"What's wrong?" Kevin asks, looking in the direction Gavin is.

"Where are Nyla and Samuel?"

"I thought they would have beaten us here," Kevin says. "On the way out the door, this little one had an explosion."

Mia makes a bomb sound which makes Rania look up at her with rounded eyes. "Huge. So we had to put her in the bath and clean things up."

"Dad went on ahead and picked up Nyla," Kevin says. "He was going to take her out for a drink and then meet us here."

"Where?" Gavin asks.

"Six-Four-Three," Mia says. "It's a few blocks up."

Jax scrunches the side of his face confused, and asks, "That's the name of it?"

Kevin replies, "It's a baseball reference. It's a—"

"They're still there?" Gavin says as if this explanation isn't needed.

With a dismissive eye roll, Mia says, "They probably lost track of time watching sports. Have you tried to call her?"

"Yes, but it went straight to voicemail."

"I'll run down and get them," Kevin says.

"No, I got it," Gavin says already beginning to walk away. "You head in. We're upstairs. Drinks and apps are out."

"I'll go with you," Jax says.

"You don't have to. Go enjoy yourself."

"Come on, you look like you need company, and I'm pretty sure you need to get something off your chest."

Gavin leads his brother up the street quickly, barely pausing at crosswalks.

"So?" Jax says.

"So what?"

"Are you going to get it off your chest."

"I'm fine. Everything will be fine."

# CHAPTER 4

$\mathcal{G}$avin pulls open the door to Six-Four-Three and goes to the hostess stand. A short, in-charge-looking woman says, "Welcome, gentlemen. How can I help you?"

"Good afternoon," Gavin says. "I'm meeting my fiancée."

"I don't have a note of anyone waiting for additional people, but you're welcome to look around." She points to the left, "I'd check the bar first, and if she's not in there," she points over her shoulder, "check the restaurant."

"Thank you."

Gavin and Jax turn into the bar where flat-screen televisions hang from the ceiling, and sports memorabilia in shadowboxes cover the walls. All of the tables are taken, and every inch of standing space is full.

"The two of them should be easy enough to spot," Gavin says.

"If it weren't so packed, maybe," Jax replies.

The brothers work their way through to the back. There is no sign of Nyla or Samuel.

"Let's check the restaurant?" Jax says.

Gavin nods in agreement and walks through a small passage that leads into the restaurant. Like the bar, every table is full. However, everyone is seated, making it easier to look around. They scan the large, rectangular-shaped room from the periphery.

In the center of the room, a table of determined-looking women jumps up and head toward Jax. One holds her phone up like she's about to ask Gavin if he'll take a photo.

Gavin backs away, as he says to Jax, "While you deal with that. I'll go check the bathrooms."

"Thanks a lot," Jax says.

Gavin walks to the back of the restaurant where it's lined with display cases filled with trophies, baseballs, and more. On a pedestal, in a large square case is a pair of running shoes which stops Gavin in his tracks. They're a worn, bright-purple pair signed in thick, black ink. Seeing Nyla's strong, looping signature accented with an oversized N and T squeezes Gavin's belly.

"Excuse me," a woman says. She looks past Gavin to the hallway that leads to the bathrooms which he's blocking.

"Sorry," Gavin says and slides over. "Actually, are you going to the restroom?"

The woman recoils and eyes him skeptically.

"I'm sorry, ma'am. That sounded creepy." He presses his hand to his chest like an honest man and says, "I'm not creepy, really. I'm looking for my fiancée. Would you holler 'Nyla' while you're in there?"

"You think she's hiding in the bathroom? Wouldn't that indicate she doesn't want to be found?"

"She does, I assure you. I just came by to get her. You see, her phone is off, and we're late for dinner with our family, so I'd—"

The woman holds her hand up. "Okay, okay. Hang on." A few minutes later, the woman returns and shakes her head no. "I hope you find her, though."

"Me too."

Gavin goes into the men's restroom, does a quick check for Samuel, then goes back to where he left Jax. He's finished with the signature-request frenzy of women.

"No luck?" Jax says.

"No."

"Well, what's next?"

Gavin leads him back to the front, where the hostess asks, "Didn't find her?

"No," Gavin says. "I'm wondering if you've seen her."

The hostess leans on her stand, and says, "I see a lot of people, and I don't remember everyone."

"I know, but her name is Nyla Tripple. She's a gorgeous, tall woman. Long bl—"

The woman stands up straight. "I know who Nyla Tripple is. We've got a pair of her shoes, but no, unfortunately, I've never seen her in person. You're her fiancé?"

Jax claps his brother's shoulder, and proudly says, "They're getting married Saturday."

Gavin nods in agreement. "Yes. Perhaps you could ask the bartender if he's seen her."

She shrugs, sets her grease pen down on the stand, and says, "Sure."

"What does it matter if she was here if she isn't now?" Jax asks.

"I don't—" Gavin turns, his attention grabbed by the largest TV in the bar. Darren Dryer, Nyla's co-host of Thursday football, fills the screen. He's intimidating with his bald head and square jaw, but when he smiles he looks like a real charmer. If it weren't for the wedding, Nyla would be there with Darren doing preseason guest spots on sports shows.

The hostess returns to her station, and says, "The bartender hasn't seen her either."

With his eyes still on the TV, Gavin replies, "Thanks for checking."

"Sure. Can I get you a drink while you wait?"

On TV a man wearing headphones hands Darren a piece of paper. His open mouth laugh drains away as he reads it. Then he looks straight into the camera as if looking directly at Gavin.

"We're good," Jax says to the woman, then to his brother, "You okay?"

Even if one isn't good at lipreading, it's easy to see Nyla's name form on Darren's lips, but what comes after is hard to decipher. When he's done talking, he stands abruptly and walks off camera.

Gavin turns, grabs for the hostess and catches her sleeve. "Sorry," he says. "Could you please turn up the volume?" He points to the large TV as Darren returns to the screen.

"You wouldn't be able to hear it over the noise in here," she says.

Jax grips Gavin's arm and points to the TV. Along the bottom of the screen, a ticker displays up-to-date sports scores and news. It's there Gavin reads, "Nyla Tripple involved in a head-on collision in Portland, Oregon. Status unknown."

"Status unknown?" Gavin snaps.

Gavin's size seems to grow uncontrollably causing people to turn and stare. Even the in-charge-looking hostess takes a step back.

"Gavin," Jax says in a pacifying tone.

"Sir?" the hostess says.

Gavin looks at her and commands, "Turn it up!"

"I don't have the remote, and it wouldn't matter be—"

"Fuck! Turn it up! Someone!"

Silence ripples through the bar and into the restaurant.

Gavin, in an effort not to explode, grits his teeth, and says, "Please."

"I'll try to find a remote," she says.

"Thank you," Jax replies, and takes his brother by the shoulders.

Gavin twists away from him. "The wreck on Burnside!"

"I'm sure that isn't her. She's fine. Try to call her again."

Gavin fumbles for his phone in his pocket and nearly drops it when he gets it out. His hand shakes as he enters his code, then taps Nyla's smiling circle photo.

"No answer," Gavin says.

"Her dad?"

Gavin calls Samuel, but it goes straight to voicemail as well.

The hostess returns with a remote and points it to the TV. Darren rips his mic off, tosses it aside, and leaves the screen again. The camera cuts to another man who looks blankly at the camera.

Gavin's phone vibrates in his hand, Darren Dryer's name lit up on it.

"What's going on?" Gavin says so loud the entire bar hears. Aware of the attention, he moves through the lobby where people part like the sea.

"Is Nyla with you?" Darren asks.

"No."

"Where is she?"

"I can't find her."

Darren draws in a sharp breath. "Damn."

Gavin pushes the door open so hard it rattles on its hinges, then he turns up the street.

"I saw you on TV just now. What did the report say?"

"Hang on," Darren says. "Hey, you, where did this report on Nyla come from? Local news? Gavin, hold on a minute. The kid is getting me footage of something."

Gavin grunts approval, and his walk turns to a jog. As he hurries up the sidewalk people jump out of his way as if frightened by him. Jax however, seems to run into almost everyone, and he falls farther and farther behind.

"You still there?" Darren says.

"Yes."

"This story has to be wrong. It shows a red sports car getting smashed by an old piece-of-shit, blue pickup. The damn thing flies into the air. Nyla still has that old SUV, doesn't she?"

"It's her dad's," Gavin whimpers.

"Damn, Gavin. That is all the information I have. I'll try and get more."

"Okay."

"Call me, or text me, something, once you know. Please. She's like my baby sister."

"Yeah."

Gavin's thoughts collide, what comes first or third doesn't make sense. But he keeps moving as if he's slipped into a primal state where the only objective is to survive.

Quickly, Gavin reaches the corner where Mix is, but before he gets to the door, it flies open and out comes Kevin as if the building is ejecting him.

"Gavin!" Kevin says. He hinges over, puts his hands on his knees, then presses one of his palms to the side of his head.

Gavin grabs his elbow to help him stand up again. "What did you hear?" he asks.

Kevin's jaw works up and down until he finally sputters, "There's been an accident. Dad's been taken up the hill."

"Up the hill?" Jax says.

"The hospital, on the hill," Gavin says as his voice fades like he's afraid to ask, "What about Nyla?"

"I'm sorry. My ears and mouth weren't working right. I just listened, and they didn't say anything about her. I didn't ask."

"You didn't?" Gavin's nostrils flare, and he roughly drops Kevin's elbow.

"Calm down," Jax says. "We have to keep our heads straight here."

Gavin puts his hand's onto his hips and begins to pace, just like he'd done at home earlier when everything with Nyla went sideways.

Gavin's family, the Smiths, and Mia with Rania still strapped to her chest come out of the restaurant.

"What is wrong?" Mia asks when she catches sight of her husband who looks like a snowman in the hot August sun.

"According to Darren," Gavin says, "that accident on Burnside may be them."

Kevin nods frantically, and says, "No, it is. That much I did get from the officer. He said, 'accident on Burnside.'"

Mia's shoulders pull back, her face sets with commanding authority. "Trace, you take Gavin and Kevin to the hospital. Jax, you go too. We'll...," she turns to everyone behind her, then back to them, "be in touch." She puts her hand on Trace's shoulder. "You call as soon as possible with where to meet."

"I will," Trace says.

Mia cups the side of her husband's face and draws it closer to hers. "It will be okay. Do you hear me? Let me get Rania to my parents, and then I'll be up there."

"Yes, okay." He kisses Mia's lips, then the top of Rania's head.

The four men head to the parking lot up the street. They climb into the truck like men on a mission. Trace turns onto the street where the cars creep along slower than the people walking on the sidewalk. Trace taps the steering wheel with an impatient index finger.

At the intersection of NW 23rd and Burnside, despite having a green light, they can't go any farther. A police barricade blocks right-turning traffic, and to the left is gridlock with horns blaring like it's New York City.

Even though Trace has the air conditioner on full blast, the heat in the car rises until Gavin can no longer stand it. He opens the door and gets out. Like a dog escaping from an animal control van, he looks right and left, then he takes off up the hill.

"Oh come on, Gavin!" Trace slams Gavin's empty seat. "Well, fuck!"

Gavin runs across a parking lot at a speed that would impress Nyla, past the police barricade without notice, and up Burnside. Several hundred feet up, after a bend in the road, the scene of the accident is before him, and he slows.

Emergency personnel rush about. Police, black vans, ambulances, firetrucks. There is an old blue pickup that's collided head-on with the blunt, rocky hillside. In the center of the greatest commotion is Samuel's red sports car; upside down and molded into a new shape.

A police officer, spotting Gavin, takes off after him as he yells, "Stop! Halt!" When he's within arm's reach, he lunges and takes Gavin down like a quarterback still in possession of the ball.

Gavin slips from the officer's grip, scrambles to his feet, and says, "It's my wife!"

"Sir, no!" the officer yells. "Calm down!"

The crowd in front of Samuel's car shifts, and now with the direct line of sight, Gavin sces the door has been removed, airbags deflated liked old party balloons, and it's empty.

Gavin's knees go soft, his foot scraping along the pavement as the cry of a grieving bear rips from his chest, then he begins to melt toward the earth.

The officer's arm goes around his ribs, not to restrain him, but to support him, as he says, "Sir, we've got you. We'll take care of you."

# CHAPTER 5

Gavin doesn't look up when Jax enters the hospital room. Jax drags a chair up to the side of Nyla's bed across from Gavin, and takes a seat.

"You look like shit," Jax says.

"Good morning to you too," Gavin mumbles as he slumps further into the mint-green armchair.

For the last four days Gavin has been sitting here, both when he's awake and asleep. He refuses to use the window bench that doubles as a bed even though the nurse supplied sheets and a pillow. He's afraid if he leaves Nyla's side, he'll miss something despite her being in a medically induced coma.

"On my way in," Jax says, "I saw the doctor leave. Any news?"

Gavin's knee begins to bounce. He presses his hand to it, but it keeps moving.

"What did she say?" Jax asks.

"Tomorrow," Gavin says, then stands from the chair like he's carrying a thousand extra pounds. He walks to the window, eyes still on Nyla, and leans against the corner. A heavy sigh falls from him. "They'll wake her up tomorrow."

"That's good news!"

With great effort, Gavin pulls his eyes away from Nyla and gazes out the window. The hospital's view here on the hill is similar to the one at their home, only a slightly different angle. There's also the tram, a pill-shaped gondola that travels from the river's edge, up the steep slope to the hospital.

"Gavin?" Jax says. "What else did the doctor say?"

"Not much, other than her warning that it isn't like the movies."

"What does that mean?"

"Apparently in real life, people don't necessarily wake up thankful to be alive and ready to jump right back into life."

"What did she say to expect?"

"Almost anything. She says there can be confusion. And there's no telling what, if any, permanent . . . "

Jax walks across the room and puts an arm around Gavin's shoulders. "You do realize we're talking about Nyla here. A woman that exceeds every expectation."

A smile tugs a corner of Gavin's mouth up. While he hears the doctor's warning, there's a part of him that knows his stubborn and determined Nyla can do anything. He knows she'll heal quickly from the cuts, bruises, and broken leg. The doctors have already been amazed by how well she's rebounded from the brain swelling and collapsed lung.

What concerns Gavin most is how she'll recover from the news of her father. Part of him dreads tomorrow because it will break her heart.

Jax pats his brother's back, and says, "Four days caged in this room makes me wonder if you're trying to torture yourself. Get out of here, for a little bit at least."

"No. I can't leave——"

"Go home. Shower." Jax runs his hand roughly over Gavin's beard. "Shave, or at least clean this mess up. When she wakes up tomorrow, you want her to see you. Not this shell. What do you think Nyla would say to you?"

"I know what she'd say."

"Exactly. Mom, Dad, and Brooke went out for breakfast, so you'll have the house to yourself. I promise not to leave Nyla's side, and if there is anything, I'll call you right away."

"Her brother will be here in an hour."

"We'll take good care of her."

Gavin goes back to the armchair and sits on the edge. He lovingly lifts Nyla's hand and kisses the back of it. He'd prefer to kiss her lips, but they're swollen like over-ripe tomatoes after a downpour, and they're cut. There's also a gash on her cheek. It was glued back together by a plastic surgeon who said there will be a long, clean scar.

"She looks better today," Jax says.

"Yeah."

"Go," Jax says. "Take care of yourself, because your real work begins tomorrow when she wakes up."

•••

Gavin turns onto Appleton Way where he stops his truck and gets out to check the mail. The box is the color of angry clouds and wrapped in old, gnarled vines which appear to hold it up. Gavin breaks back a few tendrils of green leaves growing over the flap. Then with a small key, he unlocks it.

One of the first responsibilities Gavin had as a kid was to get the mail and sort it into piles: junk mail, bills, letters, coupons. Every day he looked forward to the mailman's arrival. Now, getting the mail isn't quite as exciting, but every day he's home, he does it without fail.

At the house, Gavin carries the thick stack of mail into his office where he sits at his desk and sorts through it. There are two bills. He puts them into a vertical folio on the cabinet behind his desk marked, "To be paid." Once a month he pays them all. There are also at least fifteen white, and pastel-colored envelopes addressed to Nyla, obviously cards. He starts a stack on the top corner of his desk that will undoubtedly continue to grow.

While Gavin typically looks forward to the silence of the house, today it is painful. Without Nyla and the constant, reassuring beep of her heart monitor, there is a void.

Gavin pushes back from his desk and goes to the living room. Once there, he notices a floral scent. He follows his nose, the smell intensifying as he goes, to the dining room. On the table, floor, and windowsill are dozens of floral arrangements. Some are sweet bunches no larger than a fist. Others are grand, three-foot displays that fan like peacock feathers. There are enough to start a floral shop.

Dotted throughout the arrangements is a rainbow of miniature envelopes on plastic sticks. Gavin begins to pluck them. Then thinking Nyla will want to see who sent each arrangement, so she can properly thank them, he does his best to return each one to its original spot.

Not at all hungry, but not ready to go into their bedroom, Gavin goes to the kitchen and opens the fridge. It's full of takeout boxes and new groceries. Whenever his mom is here, she stocks everything like he's a college kid who needs help.

While Gavin hasn't seen his family much, as visitors are limited at the hospital, they refuse to leave town. Jax and Brooke, who flew out for the wedding in the middle of a tour, have rescheduled concert dates and plan to stay through the month. His parents haven't said how long they'll be here, but it will probably be even longer. Although Gavin has insisted they don't have to stay, he appreciates that they're still here.

Gavin grabs a green, glass bottle of sparkling water, one of his mother's staples, and opens it. He takes it out to the back deck where he collapses on their new outdoor couch. The view is perfect, but it makes him think of the one from the hospital, and that makes him miss Nyla.

He can't delay it any longer.

Gavin pushes open their bedroom door and stands at the threshold for a moment before he walks in. The bed is made, drapes open. It smells of Nyla's mingled lotions and oils, the strongest of which is lavender.

In the closet, he sits on the narrow bench and looks at her clothes. Caught on the edge of the dirty laundry basket is one of Nyla's shirts; it's the last one Gavin saw her wearing. The bottom is spotted with red. As if the shirt offends Gavin, he snatches it and carries it into the bathroom where he throws it in the trash.

Gavin strips the clothes from his body, tossing them on the floor, and gets into the shower. He turns on the water and places his hands against the stone wall. As the warm water runs over him, he tries to relax and clear his mind. It's no use, though. All he can think about is the last time he and Nyla were in here together happy.

A week ago, the night before her business trip, they had sex on the desk in her office. Then she pulled him naked through the house and into the shower. With her arms wrapped around his neck, her soft breasts pressed to his chest, her backside in his hands, she asked, "Does it get better than this?"

Nyla first asked Gavin that question after he proposed to her in Maui. Now she asks it as if it's her way to say, "you make me the happiest woman in the world." Every time she says it, Gavin can hardly believe the life they have, the love she shares.

"Tell me, does it?" she urged.

Gavin replied, as he always does, "Yes, but right now, it doesn't get any better than this."

Alone now in the shower, Gavin ignores the growing length of himself. Quickly he washes, gets out, dries his head roughly with a towel, and wraps it around his waist.

In the bedroom, he grabs his phone and sits in his single club chair. He dials his oncologist's office and asks for Sue.

"I'm sorry," the receptionist says, "she isn't available right now."

"Look," Gavin says harshly, "I have to talk with her now because I won't be available later. Put me on hold, and find her. Tell her it's Gavin Boston."

His knee begins to bounce faster and faster the longer he waits. He's nearly given up when a sweet, sympathetic voice comes on the line. "Hello, Gavin. I was going to call you today. I heard."

"Yeah."

"I'm very sorry." There is a slight pause before she continues, "I have a feeling you're calling to tell me that you aren't going to make your biopsy today."

"No, I have no one to take me."

"No family? Your mom? I'm sure she would."

"I'm not ready to talk with them about it. Besides I can't right now. One thing at a time." Gavin takes a deep breath, afraid to ask, but he must. "How long can I wait?"

"The cancer you had was very aggressive, and while we don't even know if it's anything yet . . . look, time can be our friend or our enemy here. I wouldn't wait too long. Let things settle there, but ask a family member to take you soon. Please. You call anytime, and I'll find a way to get you in."

"Okay."

"Sooner than later, Gavin."

"Got it."

He ends the call, slams his phone on the table next to him, and thunders, "Ffffuuuucccckkkk."

Gavin can't do this without Nyla. Determined to get his fiancée healthy, he knows he needs to look strong and healthy for her tomorrow. With great care, Gavin shapes up his beard, packs a new bag of clothes, and then heads back to the hospital.

# CHAPTER 6

## NYLA

*My* eyelids seem to have been sealed shut, but after much effort, I'm finally able to pull them open. Everything is blurry, like looking out a window being pounded by a storm. The brightness of the light around me burns my eyes.

A hand touches the top of my head, and a soothing voice says, "It's all right."

I don't know much, but I do know what she's said is a lie. Nothing is all right.

Though I want to move, I can't, so I lay here. Gradually, my vision comes into focus, and the pain in my eyes ebbs to a tolerable dullness. I'm in a hospital room, one that's familiar in a déjà vu way, which is also how I feel about myself.

A large man leans over me. His bright-green eyes begin to tear, which makes them sparkle like a gem. Cautiously, he touches the side of my face. Desperate for his warmth, I lean into him. I'd like to touch him too. I lift my arm, but it's like moving a rusty piece of metal, and as I do, pain splinters through my body. When my hand makes it to his chest, though, the thump of his heart is reassuring.

The man says, "I love you," as if he may never get to say it again.

My arm grows weak and falls back onto my chest.

"Everything hurts," I tell him.

He smiles at me the way you would a scared kitten, and says, "You're okay. I love you."

"You love me?"

"I love you more than anything, Nyla."

"Nyla?"

"That's . . . " His head drops, stealing his eyes from me.

The woman, who I now see is a nurse in sun-colored scrubs, touches my shoulder, and says to him, "Remember, this may take time. But we need her to stay calm."

He nods as if he understands, then asks me, "May I kiss you?"

My lungs tighten, making it hard to breathe. His full lips, though, make me believe he can supply all the air I need.

I nod yes.

He touches the side of my mouth, and says, "I'm going to kiss you here because there's a cut on the other side."

I'm lost in the pleasant pressure of his lips. As the seconds pass, it intensifies. It feels good, but at the same time, I want to scramble away from him. It's as if I have a threshold for not just pain, but pleasure.

Suddenly my chest begins to collapse. It feels as if this man has crawled on top of me, and I can't bear his weight. Unable to pull away, I try to form words to say what's happening, but before I am able to, an alarm sounds. I try to take another breath, but my lungs won't open. The last pockets of air bleed from me, and with them, I manage, "Help."

"She has to stay calm," the nurse says.

I want to tell her I am calm; however, something won't let me speak, and that same thing is going to kill me. My helplessness is such a foreign sensation that I stop and try to understand it. While I should be able to save myself, I can't.

Everything around me slows, and my eyes close without permission. I'm weightless. No pain. Nothing.

"Nyla, you've got to relax," his deep voice says. "Remember, deep breaths?"

I do remember . . . slow and steady breaths win the race. Control the breath, control the mind.

Something is shoved against my nose, then there's a steady stream of air which gives me a bit of strength. When my eyes open, the first thing I see is him. He parts his mouth and makes exaggerated movements, as if showing me how to breathe. With great effort, I emulate him even though it hurts.

"There you are," he says encouragingly. "You got it."

"Everything hurts," I squeak.

"Everything?"

Desperate to touch him, I trail my hand along his jaw covered in soft hair, then run my knuckles below his chin and down his neck. "Yes, everything except my hand."

"Nyla," the nurse says quickly.

My heart thumps faster, harder until it reaches a pace that could shake me open, like an earthquake does a fault line. Something isn't right.

The woman's calm face sets firm.

His beautiful eyes turn down at the corners.

Alarms go off again, and this time people flood into the room. All around me things slam and crash.

"She has to relax," the woman says urgently.

"Look at me!" he shouts. "Nyla! Breathe!"

An odd memory rushes to me. Someone—a beautiful woman with dark hair and knowing eyes—told me that everything can be fixed, anything undone. But then one afternoon, I sat in a field of green grass. Water poured from the gray, billowing clouds above me, and I learned she was wrong. Once the clouds release the rain, it can't be stopped, it can't be undone.

That's what this feels like, now. Something has started that can't be fixed or undone.

With my last drop of energy, I whisper, "Let me go."

"You have to stay!" he says.

A surge of pain, so intense that it alone can kill, overtakes me. Then a fluttering reaches into my core, and with a violent crack, I am ripped from my physical body.

All pain stops . . . everything dissolves into darkness so pure it promises comfort. I've been here before, and I'll happily stay.

I'm aware that I am a part of something larger than me, like a brick in a wall, or a star in the cosmos. From the source higher than me comes things I don't understand—images, feelings, sounds . . . a life. They dissipate through me in search of the spaces and crevices they're meant for. I want to sort through it, to understand it. But before I can, there's a thump that hurls me through the darkness, and I collide back into my body.

Something isn't right, though, because still, I'm flying as I did in that car where there was no gravity. I cling to the fight, to this body and life. Like a person trying to reclaim their land, I struggle for the control of myself. It's mine, they can't have it. It's a painful fight, but if I remember one thing now, it's that I'm a winner.

I remember who told me that everything can be fixed, anything undone. It was my mother, the beauty who graced the covers of magazines. I'd asked her about the rain when I was a tiny girl, barely to her waist. She told me, some things aren't met to be fixed or undone. But those things we can do something with too. The way raindrops revive dead grass or join to form the ocean, we can learn to use what can't be undone for something else.

The memory of my mother falls away, and a numbness descends on my body. But at last, I can see again. His emerald irises look deep into me. They're the eyes of a man who's seen unspeakable crimes. Isn't it strange that sadness can be beautiful?

"What's wrong?" I ask.

"Don't leave me," he says.

"I won't."

All of my memories find the spaces they're meant for, like grains of sand filtering into place.

"You're my husband," I say.

"Yes. Well, no … not yet. Almost."

"Not yet. Almost. Gavin?"

He shakes his head fast, and says, "Yes."

The room is packed with serious faces, doubtful ones too. Doctors in white coats, nurses in colorful scrubs. Behind them, against the wall with his fist tucked below his chin, is Pop.

"Pop," falls from me in relief.

People snap warnings at him not to get too close, to give me space, but Pop, like me, doesn't listen well. He pushes past them and sits into the chair that Gavin vacates.

"Everything will be okay, Nyla," Pop says.

His voice tells me something is wrong. It lacks the baritone depth and the slow easy draw of his words.

Like movie magic, his mature face morphs—the creases around his mouth smooth, the sag around his jaw tightens, and the creases along his forehead fade—into the version of him I remember as a child. Kevin is an exact replica of our youthful father.

"Nyla, you have to breathe," Gavin says. He presses his finger to my lips and parts them. "Breathe."

The nurse pushes a mask over my mouth and nose. I fuss to remove it, but she presses harder and says, "We have to."

"Where is Pop?" I ask Kevin.

His nostrils puff, and he bursts into tears.

Gavin sorrowful face confirms my brother's unspoken answer.

"No," I moan.

Gavin shakes his head. "Love, I'm so sorry."

"I want Pop."

Teardrops slip down Gavin's face, into his beard.

"Tell me," I say to Kevin who can't even lift his head, let alone answer me, so I plead to Gavin, "Tell me."

With his knuckles pressed to his lips, Gavin whispers, "He's gone."

In an overwhelming rush, I see and experience the accident all over again. When the car stilled, I looked over to Pop, blood dripping from his nose, and I knew he was gone.

A chill ripples through me as I say, "So was I . . . I was gone too."

My eyes close, breath steadies, and I'm taken off to dreamland.

At least I hope that's where I go.

# CHAPTER 7

*I*'m not sure how long I've been asleep, but it feels like an eternity. The hazy memories of the last few days make no sense. It's like I've had too much to drink over and over. Perhaps the drugs were too strong.

Now, though, my head feels clear, light almost. My body, however, doesn't.

The room is quiet except for the breathy sounds from Gavin, who's asleep on the window bench. He's upright, legs stretched out and back against the wall. Aside from his head hanging from his neck like a rag doll, he looks peaceful. A shuttered snore wakes him, then with a moan, he squeezes his neck and lifts his head.

"That didn't look like the most comfortable way to sleep," I say.

His eyes move to me first, then his head. He looks at me as if he thinks I might not be real, and says, "No."

He sets the tented book on his knee aside and stands. Next to my bed, he sits in a green chair and rests his elbows on his knees.

"The most important question is, are you all right?" he asks. "I mean, I know you aren't all right, but how do you feel?"

"Like Sleeping Beauty," I say.

"You definitely are." He drops his cheek into his hand and begins to smile. "I tried kissing you, though, and you didn't wake up."

"Perhaps it was a delayed reaction. It doesn't always happen like they show in the movies."

"Are we really talking right now, or am I dreaming?"

I run my fingers through Gavin's soft, wiry beard. He still looks like himself, but something is different and it's not just the new hairs.

"Gavin, you—"

"I know. Jax tells me I look like shit."

"No, it's . . . I've never seen you with a beard. I like it."

Gavin takes my hand and nuzzles the side of his face into my palm. "I don't know that I like it," he says, "But I don't have the energy to shave." He places his other hand on the side of my face and draws it down my temple. "Your eyes . . . they look like you again."

I sense, like me, he has a lot to say, but he doesn't know where to start.

"Really, are you okay?" I ask.

He turns his face and kisses my palm. "Don't worry about me."

I don't worry about Gavin, but I've always had a desire to protect him and keep him happy. I know, though, that he doesn't like to be fussed over, so I bite my tongue. "A lot has happened," I say.

"Yeah," he says with a flat laugh, and settles back into his chair.

It's clear he doesn't want to talk about what's happened. To be honest, I don't want to either. My current condition, what happened with Gavin, and worse of all, Pop, are boulder-sized problems I can't lift yet. "What day is it?" I ask.

"Thursday," he says perplexed.

"Where's the remote," I say.

"What?"

"For the TV. There should be a preseason game on."

"You can't be serious," he says. "All right. Fine."

He reaches for a corded remote on the side table and then points it at the TV mounted in the corner of the room. The game between Seattle and San Diego has just kicked off. The familiar rhythm of the event is relaxing. Much to my relief, all those heavy worries empty from my head.

There's a quick knock at the door, and Gavin says, "Come in."

A woman in blue scrubs covered with unicorns enters the room. She beams a bright smile at me as she unloads the things in her arms onto a nearby table.

"Well, look who we have here!" She taps her badge, looks at it and sees it's backward, then flips it over. "I'm your nurse, Abigail. I've been taking care of you since you arrived, minus my days off."

"That was my grandmother's name," I say. "And her hair was curly too."

"Was it going white as well?" she asks.

"As far back as I can remember, it was white as snow."

She pats her head. "I'm not there yet. But I suspect time will do it."

"It was beautiful."

She nods as if it's something to look forward to, then looks at Gavin. "And don't you have a beaming groom here this morning. It's good to see your handsome smile finally."

"You haven't seen his smile?"

"Nope, just a—" She pulls the corners of her mouth down with her fingers. "That's understandable, though. I take it these new meds feel better for you, Nyla?"

"Yes, I guess so."

"That's a step in the right direction. How about the rest of you?"

"It feels like I'm wooden and nothing will actually move. Except this." I wiggle my fingers.

"Everything will move," she says. "I'll chat with the doctors about getting you up soon. How does that sound?"

"Sounds painful."

Her head lolls side to side, then reluctantly, she says, "It will be."

"But worth it," Gavin adds cheerily.

Abigail points at him like he got the right answer. Then she goes to her computer. "Nyla, on a scale of one to ten, how's your pain?"

"That's Gavin's favorite question," I say.

"You've spent time in the hospital too?"

Gavin shifts in his chair, and hesitates before he finally admits, "I had stage four lymphoma a few years back."

He put extra emphasis on the word had. It makes my belly churn because I have to wonder, is that the correct tense? Did he go to his appointment? Does he have results? I have so many questions for Gavin, but I think any bad news might crack me.

Abigail gives Gavin a thumbs up and a wink, like a mother on the sideline of her kid's basketball game. "Glad to see you're still kicking." Then she says to me, "How about it, Nyla? A one? Ten?

"Eight?" I say, then amend, "Seven?"

"Seven point five maybe?" Abigail says playfully.

It's such an ambiguous scale. In all the times Lorenzo answered this question, I never considered how difficult it is to answer. The thought of him steals my breath and makes me desperately want him.

Thankfully Abigail taps away at her computer, then puts the items she brought in with her away. This gives me time to stuff away my uncomfortable desire for Lorenzo.

"We have a few swap outs to make here," Abigail says as she begins to unhook my IV from one of the hanging bags that's empty. "And we're going to turn down the pain medications."

"Sounds good," I say, even though I'm not sure that it does. What will it feel like with the pain medication turned down?

"Also," she says, "You need to eat something. We'll start light. Like toast. Or better yet, let me bring you a few saltine crackers first. Let's see how that goes."

"Yes, saltines. That sounds good. Gavin, would you sit me up further?"

He presses a button on the corded remote. It accesses not just the TV, but bed adjustments and lights.

Even from the slight movement, things shift in me. My blood sloshes around and makes me feel dizzy. "That's good," I say.

He stops and quickly stands. "Are you all right, Nyla?"

"Yes. Right there is fine."

Abigail looks me over and nods as if she agrees with me. Then she says, "How about you, Gavin? Can I get you to eat some saltines too?"

"Sure," he says.

Abigail moves down the bed to my feet and takes the blanket in her hands. "I'm just going to take a look, if that's okay?"

"That's fine," I say.

Abigail turns back the covers. I barely manage not to hurl when I see my leg in a cast. How did I not notice it? It's no small thing, starting just below my knee and going all the way to my toes.

"Can you feel this?" Abigail says, and squeezes both of my big toes.

"Umhum," I managed through pressed lips.

"Good."

"My leg?"

"Broken," she says.

"I'll be able to walk again, right?"

She covers my feet back up and pats the calf of my other leg.

"Yes," Gavin says confidently. "You only have two fractures."

"Two?"

"One in the fibula and the other in the tibia. You managed to escape the accident with no other broken bones."

"It's purple," I say.

"To match your running shoes."

"You can't run in it, though." My skin breaks out in a cool sweat, and my words fumble as I say, "I'll be able to run?"

"Yes, I'm sure you will in time."

My whole body begins to itch. I reach up to scratch my cheek, but Gavin grabs my hand.

"You have a gash there that is healing," he says.

"It will probably be itchy," Abigail says. "Don't itch it. You don't want it to scar any worse. Such a pretty face."

I'm not a vain woman. I've never worried about people thinking I'm pretty. Perhaps that's because I am. Or was. My shallow concern feels dirty, but I still ask, "Is it still pretty?"

Gavin's eyes, with a touch of wonder, fall over my face. "Very. You're still the most beautiful woman I've ever seen."

"You two are cute," Abigail says. "I can already tell. Okay. Do you have what you need? Oh! Crackers. I'll be back. How about a juice too? Do you like apple?"

"Yes," I say.

As soon as we're alone, Gavin pulls his chair closer to my bed. The warmth of his breath flows over my cheek, and the scent of mint scurries out the sterile stench of the hospital.

"I know it's selfish to ask," he says. "But your lip is mostly healed. May I kiss you? I'll be gentle."

"Yes."

His lips barely touch mine before he pulls away.

"Harder," I beg.

"You're sure?"

He closes his eyes and lowers his lips to mine again, but I keep mine open because I want to drink him in. He gives me what I ask for, but still not as much as I want.

"Oh, you two," Abigail says, startling us both. "Give her some time." On the table next to me, she sets down a tower of crackers that tips to the side and falls over. Then she unloads three small containers of apple juice from her pockets. She winks at me. "Men."

"I've missed her," Gavin says.

"Gentle, though. Think of her as a delicate flower. You have everything now?"

"Yes," Gavin says.

"Once I've had a chance to talk with the doctors, I'll be back. But don't be surprised if you see one of them come in shortly without me."

As soon as Abigail closes the door behind her, I say, "I'm not a delicate flower."

"No, you're not," Gavin says. "A warrior, through and through."

"I'm tired again, though."

Gavin strokes his hand over the top of my head. "Sleep."

My eyes, the only part of me that has no pain or stiffness, close easily. Just as I begin to fall asleep, I manage to say, "I love you, Gavin. That's why I wanted to live, so you'd know that."

# CHAPTER 8

$\mathcal{O}$ver the last few days, I've moved through the motions of hospital life: nurse and doctor visits, pain meds, a visitor or two, occupational therapy, and mostly, sleep.

Every time my eyes close the same nightmare finds me: the accident, beginning to end. What's odd, though, is I see it happen from different points of view. There are times I'm a disembodied figure outside of the car. Others I'm in the back seat where I see my long hair lift around my face, and Gavin's unanswered text on my phone. However, no matter what view I see it from, it always ends the same; cold death beckoning me like a drug pusher with a taste of euphoria. Each time the price—my life—is too steep, and, while it hurts, I choose to live.

Like now, when I wake, tears are leaking from my eyes.

Gavin leans over me, wipes my eye with a tissue, and asks, "Are you in pain?"

"Yes."

He puts my pain button, a narrow, silver cylinder with a button on top, into my hand and closes my fingers around it. When it's pressed, an extra bump of pain medication is delivered through my IV. I've pushed it every chance I get since regaining consciousness. But it, too, comes at a price: foggy brain, a desire to lay here inert, a sense of separation from all around me.

"All you have to do is press it, love," he says.

I kiss Gavin's chin, the hair of his beard rough on my lips, and say, "There isn't medicine for this kind of pain."

"Oh, dear," Abigail says. "Do you need something?"

This nurse, she's a ninja. I never know she's here until she speaks or when I hear her tap away at the keyboard.

"She's processing," Gavin says.

"It is a lot to take in," Abigail says as she places two fingers on my wrist to check my pulse. "It's all going to be okay."

Everyone keeps saying, "it's okay," but what does this mean? Is okay an acknowledgment that the bare minimum has been met? Do they think I'm okay only because I'm alive?

Abigail turns to my IV bags, pulls a piece of paper from her pocket, and jots something down. "I forgot to bring this new bag in. I just need to see to another patient, and then I'll be back with it."

She disappears behind the striped curtain that hangs from the ceiling all the way down to the floor. It separates the door from the room, offering a bit more privacy when the door is open.

Alone again with Gavin, who yet again turns to stare out the window, I let my head fall back. I'm continually haunted not only by the memory of the accident, but by that text message Gavin sent me. "I am sorry. I love you more than anything. Meet me outside the restaurant, please." I've wanted to talk with Gavin about it, and every-thing that happened that day. But I haven't found the strength to do so, and he hasn't brought it up.

Having forgone the extra pain medication, my head feels more clear, and finally, I gather the courage. "Have you had your test, Gavin?"

Gavin's shoulder blades pinch together like he's been stabbed in the back. "No."

"Why did you want me to meet you outside of the restaurant?" I ask.

Gavin turns, presses the heel of his palms to his eye sockets, then as they fall away, he says, "It's complicated."

"Please tell me, Gavin?"

He sits onto the window bench, drops his chin into his hand, and now watches me as if I'm as complicated as the landscape of buildings outside.

"Gavin?"

Into his hand, he mumbles, "I thought you'd forgotten."

"Forgotten what?"

"You haven't mentioned anything about that day. The doctor said it's possible you'd forget things."

"I remember everything. I've been too scared to bring it up."

He presses his hands onto his knees and stands, then at the foot of my bed, he paces back and forth.

"Everything?" he asks.

"I think so. Should we go over the entire day to be sure."

His tongue jets out and swipes over his lips. "No, we shouldn't."

"Please stop moving back and forth, you're making me dizzy."

He plants his feet at the end of my bed and crosses his arms.

"Your test?" I ask.

"It was supposed to be last Monday. I couldn't do it."

"You didn't go?"

"I can't go alone."

"I'm sure your mom will go with you."

Gavin shakes his head. "No. I mean yes she would, but no. I need to deal with one thing at a time. Having you like this has been all I can handle. I know it's selfish to say, especially right now, but I need you to go with me."

"Noooo, please. Waiting doesn't do you any good. If . . . "

Gavin presses a hand to his stomach and lifts his other up to stop me. "I need to wait. The tests will be there, and if I have cancer, it will still be here in a couple weeks too."

I told myself the last couple of days that everything had to be okay. We've been through so much, both together and individually, that fate couldn't possibly do that to us. But now, I feel as sick as I did the day Lorenzo told me. If I were one to believe in karma, I'd have to wonder if I did something really horrible in a previous life.

With a shaking voice, I say, "You cannot wait, Gavin. You need to get whatever tests they need to be done now. Time matters. Weeks matter when it comes to treatment."

He sits on the edge of my bed, runs his hand over my leg, and says, "I need you to go with me. Sue said it can wait."

"I don't know when I can go with you, Gavin. I'm probably a week or two from getting out of here. It does neither of us any good if you wait. Reschedule your test."

"No."

There's a gentle rap on the door behind the curtain.

Gavin gives me a curt nod that says no is his final decision, then says, "Come in."

My eyes are still on Gavin's when Kathy's sweet voice says, "Are you seeing visitors?"

Yesterday, the doctors eased up on my visitor restrictions. Today is the first time I get to see not only Richard and Kathy, but Jax and Brooke later this afternoon.

"Yes, please, come in," I say.

Kathy sets her purse down on the floor while Richard pulls two chairs up next to my bed.

As Kathy takes a seat, she pats my hand, and says, "You look wonderful. Why, you wouldn't even know all you've been through."

She reaches over and pats Gavin's knee. "You look good, too, Gavin."

"Thanks, Mom."

"Your eyes are clear," Kathy says, as she strokes her hand over my hair.

"Thank you," I say.

"How are you today?" Richard asks.

"Good. Getting reacquainted with the living world."

"You have lots of people rooting for you. There have been at least a hundred cards delivered to the house. And so many bouquets of flowers. Your dining room table looks like a floral shop."

Kathy's head drops, and her face pinches like she's trying to hold something back. Finally, she lifts her head, and says to Gavin, "I'm sorry. I wasn't trying to eavesdrop, but the door was open, and as we came in—"

"Now isn't the time, Kathy," Richard says.

"Gavin?" Kathy says.

"Mom?"

"What tests?"

"Can we talk about this later?"

"Another time would be better," Richard says.

"No, it wouldn't. Gavin, do you have cancer again?" Kathy asks.

Gavin looks at me, as he says, "I don't know. Look, Nyla and I haven't had a chance to talk about this fully, so I'd appreciate it if we wait."

"You don't think we," she presses her splayed palm against her chest and leans down to catch Gavin's eye, "have a right to know? I should be the first call you make."

"That isn't—"

"What?"

"Yes, you should know right away," Gavin says. "But I found out the day of the accident. I didn't want to talk about it with everything else going on." Gavin takes my offered hand. "There's a growth on my thyroid they need to check."

"You have a tumor?" Kathy asks.

"I guess."

"Cancer?"

"It could be benign. That's why they need to biopsy it."

"And when is this?"

"I haven't rescheduled it."

"Rescheduled?"

"It was supposed to be last Monday, but I couldn't go."

Kathy smiles tightly like a teacher restraining the real thing she wants to say. "Gavin, I'm sure Nyla will agree, you should go now, tomorrow at the latest, and get this looked at. They said if it came back—"

"I know what they said." Gavin looks to me. "But I need Nyla to go with me."

"I'd be happy to take you," Richard offers.

Gavin shakes his head no. "Thanks, though. Nyla's a rock star. She'll be out of here in no time."

All three of them look at me as if what I say is important. I'm torn between both sides, each of which has merit. Gavin, however, is who I'll always support. Even if I don't entirely agree with him.

"I'll be out of here in no time," I say. "And I'll be happy to take you."

"Well," Richard says, "since Nyla is here, why not have it done now? Perhaps they can wheel her down to the test area."

"It's at a different hospital," Gavin says.

"I'm sure they have the same equipment here," Kathy urges.

"I need to do one thing at a time. This is all I can handle right now." Gavin lifts my knuckles to his lips. "One thing at a time. I just need you all to understand that, and I don't want to talk about it anymore right now."

Richard sets a hand on the back of his wife's neck, gently rubs it, then says, "We respect that."

Kathy's posture tightens.

"Nyla?" Abigail says as she pulls back the curtain and enters with a man alongside her. "I forgot to tell you earlier that you had another visitor coming."

He's a foot and a half taller than Abigail and as wide as a linebacker. But it isn't his size that captures me, it's the fact that he looks exactly like Lorenzo. Black curly hair, dark golden skin, and those eyes—both shape and color.

My throat tightens. I can't look away from the man. Even though I know this isn't Lorenzo, I want to throw my arms around him. Thank goodness I'm not able to move quickly, or I might just do it.

"You forgot to tell her about me?" the man says with exaggerated surprise.

Even his voice, thick and smooth, sounds like Lorenzo.

"I know, how could I forget?" Abigail bumps her shoulder to his arm like a cool aunt. "I'd like to introduce you to Oliver. You are one lucky woman, Nyla."

"Abbi is far too kind," Oliver says.

"Lucky?" I ask like I'm out of breath.

"He doesn't work in the hospitals much," Abigail says, "but apparently someone has some pull. He's the best though."

Kathy and Richard stand from their chairs and step back for Oliver. He moves closer to me, extends his hand, and says, "Oliver Buckle, at your service."

I try to keep my hand steady, but it still shakes a little.

"Nyla Tripple. But you already know that. What is it that you're the best at?"

He claps his hands together then pulls them apart like a man trying to be modest. "It's not me that says the best."

"He is," Abigail says as she types away on the computer.

He laughs and it, too, reminds me of Lorenzo.

"Perry sent me. I'm your physical therapist. If you want me, of course."

Abigail comes back to stand next to Oliver. She sets her hands on her hips, and says, "He's the PT for the Portland Soccer Club."

"Really?" Richard says, impressed.

"Sports recovery is my specialty," Oliver says.

Abigail says, "I'm sorry, I meant to tell you earlier he was on the way, but I hurried out to take care of another patient and forgot."

I really should stop looking at Oliver, even if just for a second, but I can't. Is someone about to tell me this is a joke?

"Are you ready?" Oliver asks.

"For what?" I reply.

"To run again. No, I'm kidding. Well, not really. We'll get you running again. For now, though, walking and getting some strength back."

Abigail pats my shoulder. "She's already moving around well. Exceeding everyone's expectations."

"Well listen to that," Oliver says. "You're gonna make my job easy, aren't you?"

"I'll try."

"Great. If you're up for it, I'd like to go on a walk. We can see how you feel, get a general gauge of where you're at. And if there is anything you can't handle, we'll back off."

"Hang on there," I say. "Was that a challenge? You best be careful."

He half snorts and laughs. "Careful. Noted."

"Should we leave?" Kathy asks, pointing to Richard and herself.

Oliver turns and holds out his hand to her. "I'm sorry, I didn't properly meet everyone."

Kathy introduces herself and Richard. Then Oliver turns to Gavin, who stands from my bed with his I-get-anything-I-want business smile on. "Gavin, Nyla's fiancé."

"It's good to meet you all. Our session shouldn't take too long today. An hour or so. You're welcome to wait in the room, Gavin perhaps you'd be able to join us? I'm sure Nyla would appreciate your help."

"Absolutely," Gavin says.

"Why don't we go grab a bite in the cafeteria," Richard says to Kathy. "Can we bring anything back for anyone?"

"No, thanks, Dad," Gavin says.

I pull back the covers, roll onto my side, and sit up. Oliver crouches down, so his eyes are level with mine. He cradles my elbows with his hands and helps me stand.

"Very strong," he says. "Perry was right."

"Don't tell him that, he always thinks he's right. But, what is he right about?"

"That you can be running six-minute miles in no time with the right therapist."

"The right therapist?"

"Yep, that's why he called me. We really will have you running in no time."

# CHAPTER 9

"That's the last page," Abigail says. "You're officially free. Shall I cut that band off of your wrist?"

I hold my arm out, and say, "Free me, please."

Gavin watches over Abigail's shoulder as she takes a pair of scissors from her pocket and cuts the hospital band off.

She holds it up and asks, "Do you want to keep it?"

I shake my head no, and she tosses it in the trash.

Abigail grabs a stack of papers, and says, "These are copies of your discharge instructions we went over earlier." She flips to the last page and points to a phone number. "If you need anything, call. Fever, call. New pains, call."

With an amused giggle, I say, "Okay."

"I'm serious, Nyla. I know you like to tough it out, but you need to listen to your body."

"I understand."

"Don't worry," Gavin says, and kisses the top of my head. "I'll keep a good eye on her."

Gavin slips the papers into the front zippered pocket on my bag. Then he lifts it onto the top of a packed, two-tier cart. Neither of us realized how much stuff we'd amassed here until Gavin loaded it all up this morning. Thanks to a Tetris skill I didn't know he has, he was able to get it all in one trip.

"I'll run this stuff out to the truck, and be back to get you."

"You'd think we'd moved in or something," I say.

Gavin looks around the room, which emptied of all of our things, is bare. Then he looks at me, winks, and says, "I'm happy to move out. Be right back."

"I can meet you down there," I offer.

"No," he smiles softly, "I'll be right back."

As Gavin pushes the cart from the room, I watch him. He looks more like himself now. The worry in his face has eased, his hair is styled, and while he's kept the beard, it's clipped and well-groomed.

"He's a good man," Abigail says.

"He's actually an amazing guy. I'm lucky."

"Yes, but so is he. And you remember to listen to Oliver too."

"Did I hear my name?" Oliver says.

"As if by magic," Abigail waves her hand like a fairy godmother, "he appears." She pats Oliver's shoulder and points to me. "You keep an eye on that feisty one."

"Me?" I say in mocked offense. "I'm not feisty."

She narrows one eye at me, and says, "No, not at all."

Oliver and her smile as if they've figured me out. I suppose, after all they've done for me, they might know me better than some.

"I passed Gavin on the way in here," Oliver says. "I told him we'd walk down and meet him out front."

Abigail places her hands on her hip, head inclining. "I'm never sad to see my patients off because I'm glad you don't need me anymore. But still, I'll miss you."

"I feel the same," I say.

"Anything, you call."

"Got it. I will."

Oliver holds my crutches out for me. As I stand, pain zaps through my bones, tendons, and muscles. I conceal all discomfort because I don't want them to keep me longer or offer me more medication. Neither of which I want.

What I do want is to get back to life. To be back home where I can sleep in my own bed next to Gavin. To walk and run again in a few weeks when I get this cast off. And to get back to work.

"Looking good, Tripple," Oliver says, coach-like.

Self consciously I adjust my jean shorts and T-shirt. They used to fit perfectly, but now with all the weight I've lost, they are a couple sizes too large.

Oliver lifts his chin at my University of Oregon shirt. "Have I told you my girlfriend met you there once?"

"I don't think so."

"She attended a clinic there when she was a senior in high school. You'd just returned from the games. She said it was the highlight of her high school days."

"I genuinely hope that isn't true."

"If I'd met a gold medalist when I was in high school, it would have been a highlight for me too."

"I'd love to meet her sometime."

Oliver flashes his crooked grin, and says, "She'd like that too."

After working with Oliver every day for the last two weeks, the initial Lorenzo-look-alike shock has worn off. Sure, they still look alike, but after getting to know him better, both during therapy and after when he stayed to visit, I see him as just Oliver.

Abigail returns pushing a wheelchair. She stops and puts the brakes on it.

"What's that for?" I ask.

"You're supposed to leave the hospital in it."

"No way," I say.

Oliver takes the handles. "I'll push it next to her, that way if she needs it."

"I won't need it."

Abigail winks at Oliver. "Take care of her."

On my crutches, I make my way through the long hall, ride down on the elevator, and then outside. At the front entrance, Oliver leaves the wheelchair with several others. Then he comes to sit next to me on a concrete bench.

"You okay?" Oliver asks.

"Perfect."

"You're pale."

I lift my face to the sky and close my eyes. Though I've been outside a lot, it feels even better now with the freshness of freedom on the warm summer air.

"I just need more sun," I say, "I'll have to make up for lost time."

"You're one of the most stubborn people I've ever met. And that's saying a lot, considering the kinds of people I've worked with."

"Thanks."

"That wasn't a compliment."

I glare at him.

"I see it hurts to stand, and it was painful to make it here. I know why you didn't say anything back there," he tips his head in the direction of the entrance, "but out here, now, between you and me, you have to be honest. It's the only way I'll be able to help get you running again."

I'm not sure what to say, so I look away from him to Gavin's truck as it pulls up.

Hopping out, Gavin asks, "All ready?"

"Yes," I say.

Gavin shakes Oliver's hand. "Thanks for walking her down. Would you like a lift to where you're parked."

"No, I'm good. Thank you for the offer, though."

I'm thankful Oliver and Gavin get along so well, especially since Oliver will continue to work with me until I'm fully recovered.

Oliver opens my door, and Gavin helps me in.

When the door closes, the silence of the cab hurts my ears. I pull at the belt across my chest which feels like a trap. Then when Gavin starts the engine, my teeth grit.

"Ready?" Gavin asks with an excited pat on my knee.

"Humum" I manage through tight lips as I grip the door handle.

Usually, Gavin drives above the speed limit and makes quick, decisive movements like a race car driver. Today, however, he drives like a man with precious cargo aboard. He checks his speedometer like it's a ticking bomb, quadruple checks the mirrors before lane changes, and stops at yellow lights.

"Are you all right?" he asks.

"Yes," I say.

"Your knuckles are white."

Sometimes no matter how careful we are, or how much we trust someone, things happen. Pop was a good driver. His brand-new sports car was equipped with every bell, whistle, and safety feature. The drunk driver—a day drinker leaving the bar at rush hour—crossed the double-yellow line driving an old-hunk-of-metal pickup. We didn't have a chance.

"You are a good driver," I say. "I trust you, Gavin, but this is scary."

"I promise, we'll be all right."

I know he means well, but it's a promise he can't keep.

Gavin takes a roundabout way home, probably to avoid the roads I last traveled with Pop. However, we can't avoid the neighborhood streets to get to ours. Finally, when I see the familiar Appleton Way sign atop its wooden post, my anxiety eases.

We turn onto our gravel road, and Gavin stops at the mailbox. He puts the truck into park, and asks, "Do you mind if I get the mail? It's been overflowing."

"Not at all."

As Gavin hops out and goes to the mailbox, I roll down my window. I've missed the smell of the woods around our house: sweet pine, earth, and fresh air. Already these familiar surroundings, and seeing Gavin go about a regular routine, is comforting.

Beaming at me, Gavin gets back into the truck and sets a thick stack of mail on my lap. "People love you," he says.

"They do, do they?" I reply.

As we drive through the tunnel of deciduous trees toward the house, I thumb through the mail. Most are cards—bright envelopes in a variety of sizes. There are a few white, business-sized envelopes that, compared with the others, look serious. One has a return address marked from "Trusted Medical Transport and Ambulance."

"No time wasted getting the bills out," I say.

"Everyone wants their money," Gavin says. "I'll take care of it."

"I can pay it. I didn't mean anything by it."

"I know, but leave the bills to me. You focus on getting better."

Gavin and I already combined our checking account. Since I travel so much, he's taken on the role of paying the bills. I'll admit, it is a responsibility I was happy to turn over.

With Lorenzo, we paid the bills together. When he got sick, though, I took on the role of household CFO so that he could focus on getting better. Medical bills came at a dizzying pace. Occasionally I lost track of what I had and hadn't paid. Sometimes we'd get a second notice, while other times I received a check saying I'd paid twice. I arranged payment plans to keep us afloat, and sometimes Pop helped us out. I don't think Lorenzo ever knew that.

After Lorenzo passed, the bills kept coming; each one a punch in the gut. I stopped paying them. Second and third notices piled up on my counter like a growing pyramid.

Then, one day, Pop showed up unannounced. "I was worried, you haven't been returning anyone's calls," he said. When he saw the pyramid of envelopes, I broke down into a tearful confession.

We spent hours sorting through the bills, and one by one, paid them all. It should have felt good, but instead, it left me depressed. With his funeral already a month past then, and all the loose ends resolved, the book of Lorenzo's life had closed. The problem was, I didn't know how to let go of him. I decided to leave Bainbridge and the life we'd lived together. Starting over seemed like the only way I'd be able to live again.

Out front of our house, Kathy, Richard, Brooke, and Jax hold a string of signs that read, "Welcome Home Tripple Threat Nyla."

"Welcome home," Gavin says as he turns the truck off. "Your brother wanted to be here, too, but since you were discharged early, they weren't able to make it in time. They'll be here for dinner, though."

"Dinner?"

"Yes. The Smiths are coming too. Linda's bringing most of the food."

"It's going to be a good dinner, then."

Gavin gets out and runs around the front of the truck. He grabs my crutches from the back, then opens my door and helps me out.

"Welcome home!" Brooke hollers like we're at a rock concert.

The family descends on me with warm hugs. They act as if they haven't seen me many times at the hospital. Although I'll agree, it feels different to see them here too.

As I walk into the house, the wispy breeze of my past departure whooshes by, and on it is Pop's cologne. His passing has left an empty space in my heart, and being here fuels its growth like a black hole. Though I want to turn back, to run away from this feeling and anything that makes it worse, I force myself to keep moving.

Across the living room through the back window, a hummingbird with an emerald head is watching me. I cross the room and press my fingers to the glass.

Gavin's hand wraps my upper arm, then he kisses the top of my head. "It's always here."

I bite the inside of my cheek to keep from crying. The bird's surreal presence makes me miss Lorenzo so much that I feel guilty. As this feeling swells, the scent of Pop's cologne fades, giving way to the mingled scent of flowers.

I go into the dining room and find more flowers than I've ever seen in one place: roses, lilies, carnations, sunflowers, and more.

"They keep coming," Kathy says. "People love you."

"Mom has made it her personal mission to keep every-thing alive," Jax says.

"I haven't been able to, unfortunately. There were so many more than this. I took pictures of all of them, though. So you could at least see them." She picks up her phone from the table.

"Mom," Gavin says, "you can show her later."

I steady myself on one crutch and take her hand. "Thank you," I say.

"It's the least I could do."

"If you all don't mind," Gavin says. "Nyla and I need a few minutes."

"We do?" I ask.

"Yes," he says sweeping his hand toward the hall that leads to our bedroom.

The closer I get to our bedroom, the slower I move.

"I can only imagine how hard it all is," Gavin says.

He steps ahead of me and opens our door.

I have thousands of positive memories in that room, and only one horrible one. Why is it that one bad experi-ence seems to override all the good?

Gavin reaches his hand out to me, but on crutches, I can't take it. I hated these things before, but now I despise them.

"I'm okay," I lie.

I make my way to the single club chair where I sit and take in the room: midnight-blue walls, the bed Gavin made from wood he salvaged during the house remodel, matte wood floors which glow from the lights above. As usual, it's clean. Not a speck of dust.

As the day I'd get to go home drew closer, I wondered what it would be like to return. Perhaps foolishly, I hoped things would snap back into place, and I'd feel normal once I got here. Instead, I'm outta place, and I miss Pop more by the second.

After Gavin sets my bag in the closet, he comes to stand at the foot of the bed. He stuffs his hands into his pockets and, uncharacteristically, looks down to his shoes.

We've spent a lot of time together these last few weeks. Even so, we haven't broached the subject of what happened that day in here. And we've only talked once about those tests Gavin needs to have done.

"I'm so sorry," I say.

Gavin comes to me and squats down. "No—"

I press my hand over his heart and the thoughts in my head fumble. What do I say? Where do I start?

"I should have held onto you that day, Gavin. I don't know why I reacted so selfishly. But I am sorry. I'd never leave you or let you go. I hope you know that."

Gavin's chest pumps below my hand. "I was . . . I went . . . crazy, Nyla. It won't ever happen again."

I lift a shoulder. "Eh? I don't know. I think we all have a bit of crazy in us that surfaces now and then. I'm not sure that's something you, or anyone, can promise."

"I'm sorry for touching and hurting you like I did."

"If I hadn't pushed you away, you wouldn't have hurt me."

He snorts and shakes his head. "No. It is my fault."

"I forgive you," I say. "Do you forgive me?"

"Yes."

Gavin goes to his nightstand and grabs something from the drawer. He comes back to me, gets down on one knee, then takes my left hand. He opens his fist, and there in his large palm is my engagement ring: a gold band inset with a row of sparkling emeralds.

"I thought maybe it was lost in the accident," I say.

Startled, Gavin says, "What? No. No. They cut it off in the emergency room, and it was damaged. But I've had it all fixed. Better than new."

I shake my head in acknowledgment, unable to say anything.

"Will you still marry me?" Gavin asks.

It's not like the first time Gavin proposed. The blind belief that we can survive anything has been shaken.

"Do you want to marry me and this mess I am?" I ask.

Gavin slips the ring onto my finger. "I still want to marry you more than anything." He kisses me very softly, then he pulls back. "Can I kiss you?"

"I think you just did."

"No. I want to really kiss you." He brushes his finger down the center of my lips. "It's been so long. Too long."

Our lips touch, then part, inviting one another. We're both stiff. It's like we didn't at one point know each other's body as well as our own. If it had been our first kiss, I'd question if we have any chemistry. I wonder if it has any hope of coming back.

When I pull away from Gavin, his eyes are still closed. He presses his forehead hard to mine; it's warm enough that he could have a fever.

"I want to keep you forever, Nyla."

His words are full of honesty. Perhaps, like me, he's hopeful.

# CHAPTER 10

$\mathcal{L}$inda Smith is the kind of woman who shows people how much she cares for them through her food. As she and her family lay out a feast fit for a photo shoot, I feel very loved.

I peek over her shoulder as she removes foil from two glass baking dishes, and ask, "Is that eggplant parm?"

Her big, blue eyes beam as she says, "It is."

"That is my favorite thing you make," I say.

She puts her arm around me. "I know. I'm hoping you'll like it."

"I'll admit I haven't had much of an appetite, but I think it just returned in full force."

As Trace sets down a bowl, he says, "Here's the salad."

"And rolls," Alex says, setting a bag onto the table. He walks over to me, eyes cautious. "Can I hug you?"

Linda and Trace visited me in the hospital several times, but I haven't seen Alex or Emma since before the accident. Trace told Gavin that they didn't feel it was a good place for the kids.

"Yes, you can," I say. "I'm all better."

He keeps his wary eyes on me as he circles his arms around my waist, but barely touches me. Then, quickly, he pulls away. "When do you get the cast off?" he asks.

"In a few weeks."

"My friend has a cast too. Everyone in my class signed it with a black marker."

"Should I find a marker so you can sign mine?"

"That sounds fun," Linda says, setting her hand on Alex's shoulder.

Gavin comes out of the house galloping like a horse with Emma in his arms. She giggles with pure delight, head tossed back and her blond hair floating over her shoulders. When she sees me, her eyes go wide as if she's seen a unicorn, and she falls silent. Scrambling from Gavin's arms, she waves a paper around. Then, when she gets to the ground, she comes running my way. Unlike her cautious brother, she throws herself at my right leg.

"Emma!" Trace snaps.

"It's fine," I say, then mouth to him, *she can't hurt me*.

Emma's skirt has several layers of sparkly-purple tulle. Delicately she lifts one, and asks, "Do you like it?"

"I do! Purple is my favorite color."

She shakes her head enthusiastically and hands me the paper in her hand. The pink card stock is folded in half, and on the front, she's drawn a bear. Inside, carefully written yet still hard to decipher, it reads, "I want you to feel better soon. Emma."

"Thank you," I say. "This makes me feel much better."

My brother and Mia's arrival draws my attention away from Emma. She happily skips along over to Kathy, who exclaims, "Well, don't you look like a princess."

Kevin, still in his navy work suit, hesitates in the doorway looking at me. I've seen him every day. He knows the extent of my injuries and that I've lost weight, yet he seems surprised by the sight of me.

Mia pats Kevin's back, propelling him in my direction.

"Hey, Ny," Kevin says and kisses my cheek. Stress has etched deep into his face: bags under his eyes, carved lines over his brow and around his mouth. "Sorry we're late. Things went sideways at the office."

I wish I could do something to help him. Aside from a few short summer internships where I mostly made copies and ran errands, I don't know anything about Tripple Properties.

Kevin has worked there since he graduated from college. He spent his first ten years here in Portland learning everything from Pop. Then, a couple of years ago, he opened their new office in Chicago. The plan had always been for Kevin to take over the company when Pop retired, but it wasn't supposed to happen this soon, or so suddenly.

"Double F was it?" I ask elbowing him.

When we were kids, my mother joked that there was always a fire to be put out on Fridays near the end of the day. Over time, she began to call these a double F."

Kevin digs a finger and thumb of his right hand into his eyes and pinches the bridge of his nose. Then he looks at me amused. "It was a triple F."

"That bad?"

"Yes, but only because it's me trying to fill Pop's shoes. I'm sure it would have been nothing for him."

"You're doing a great job," I say.

Kevin looks away from me, then sadly says, "Thank you."

Pop was a cut to the chase kind of guy, and honest even if it stung. He thought the world of Kevin, not just as a son, but as an executive at the company. I'm sure with Pop gone, Kevin is the best at what he does.

Gavin gently caresses my elbow and says, "I made you a plate."

"Grab some food, a beer, and relax," I say to Kevin. "It's Friday after all."

I sit down to a heaping plate of food, way more than I'll ever be able to eat.

"It looks and smells good," I say to Linda.

"I helped," Alex says.

"Really?" I reply.

"He's taken an interest in the kitchen," Linda says.

"You get to learn from the best," I say. "Pay close attention."

I take a bite of the tasty eggplant parm, then pull apart a roll that is crusty on the outside, but soft and fluffy inside. The salad, laden with carrots, cucumber, and Kalamata olives, is refreshing. Even though this the best food I've eaten in weeks, my stomach protests after a few bites.

I set my fork down and place my napkin on the table. "It's delicious, really, but I'm already stuffed."

"You hardly ate anything," Linda says. "I understand, though. I'll wrap it up so you can have it later."

"Thank you."

Gavin helps me up from the table, then leads me across the deck to our new outdoor furniture. We ordered the espresso-brown wicker set at the beginning of July. It was delivered the day before my accident when I was away on a business trip.

"What do you think?" Gavin asks.

"It looks even better than I expected."

"Have you tried it out?"

"No. I just saw it through the window."

"Try it out."

I sit down on the couch that faces out to the valley. To one side is the oversized armchair, to the other is a love seat. In the middle is a rectangular table with a gas firepit in the center.

"May I join you?" Gavin asks.

Patting the spot next to me, I say, "Please do."

He sits so close that the sides of our bodies touch. Usually, I'd snuggle into his side and lay my head on his shoulder. But we haven't been this close in so long that it feels strange.

"I love the colors," I say and run my hands over the leaf-green cushion. "Do you like it?"

"I do. A lot." Gavin reaches his foot out, and with his big toe taps a button igniting the fire. "First time."

I look up to him with a smile, and my heart grips when I see his soft gaze on me. A kiss would be appropriate, even I can see he wants one. But it was so awkward in the bedroom that I can't bring myself to repeat it out here. Thankfully, Kevin joins us taking a seat in the armchair.

"I think you two have the best view in the entire city," Kevin says.

"I won't deny it," I say. "It's true."

"I'll be right back," Gavin says. "I'll help Linda clean up and get dessert out."

I press my hand to my belly at the word dessert, feeling its silent protest.

"Don't worry," Gavin says. "You don't have to eat any-thing else." He kisses my cheek, and as he stands, whispers, "I love you."

Kevin watches me as Gavin walks away. Once we're alone, he says, "Dad, he really likes him. Liked. Actually, I'm sure he still does. Even before you two started dating."

Kevin runs his pinky down the side of his beer bottle, clearing a line in the condensation. "Let me know when you're ready to talk about the funeral and everything."

"I'd prefer never to talk about it," I say.

"We have to, though."

"Then I'd rather do it sooner than later."

"Are you sure?"

"I can't imagine how complicated this is going to be. The business, and all of Mom and Pop's stuff. They have so much. I never asked Pop what he wanted. Did you?"

"No, but we don't have to guess. Dad left detailed instructions. I set copies of everything on your desk."

"Did he leave instructions about his funeral?"

"Yes, actually. But he doesn't want a funeral, he wants a party."

"A party?"

"No funeral, no church, no preacher."

"You know, after Mom's funeral, he told me he'd never do that again. He said the whole thing was too depressing and didn't represent Mom. Funny thing was, that's how I felt about Lorenzo's. It wasn't fun to plan, and it wasn't fun to attend."

"Is it supposed to be fun?"

I pull at the hem of my jean shorts as I try to decide what a funeral is supposed to be. "I'd like it to offer closure, at least. If it's supposed to be a celebration of the person, shouldn't it reflect them? Maybe I should have hosted a football game in honor of Lorenzo."

Kevin laughs. "A scrimmage?"

"Yeah."

He takes a deep breath, lifting his chest near his chin, then lets it go in an exhausted groan.

"You had him cremated though, right?" I ask.

"Yes. He wants his ashes spread at Mom and his favorite spot."

Their spot is on the edge of Lost Lake on Mount Hood. It's where Pop proposed to Mom, and also where we scattered her ashes.

"There's something else," Kevin says as he sets his bottle down on the table and shifts in his chair. "Mia and I, we're moving back. Here. I'm running the company now, and it's much easier to do from the Portland office. Besides, we'd rather be here near you and Mia's family."

The thought of having my brother around fills a small space in my empty heart. And Mia, she and I used to be inseparable when I was in town. Of course, there is little Rania. I want to see her grow up and to be an active part of her life.

"That is the best news I've heard all month," I say.

"Yeah?"

A wave of emotion steals my voice, but I'm able to shake my head vigorously yes.

"I'd like to ask you a favor," Kevin says.

"Anything."

"We don't have time to house shop right now, and we've settled into the house. Do you mind if we stay in it for a while?"

"No, stay as long as you want. Really. I'll help you clean out someday, although it will be while. But clean out as you want and need. Settle in."

"Thanks."

"It will be nice to have you all around. To see Rania grow up."

"Yes, then she can play with her cousins someday."

I laugh.

"What's that," he imitates my laugh, "for?"

"What?"

He gives me the don't-bullshit-me eye.

"I just don't think we'll be having kids. My career, his, we don't have time. And all of this." I gesture to the mess I am.

"Please, you'll be fine in no time. And family is more important than your career. I bet Gavin would agree with me on that."

Gavin sits down next to me and sets Rania on his lap, so she faces out to the view. "Agree with what?" he asks.

"That family is more important than a career," Kevin says.

"This is really not the time for such a discussion," I say. "A lot is going on."

"There is," Gavin says. "But I still agree."

"Yeah. Guys think that when it comes to the woman's career, but it doesn't apply to the guy."

"What are we talking about?" Mia asks as she sits down on Kevin's knee.

"Kevin says that kids are more important than a career, but I say that statement only applies to the female."

She bobs her head considering. "I don't know. I mean, I'm working less because I want to. But, I bet if I wanted to return to work full time, we would make it work."

"That's true," Kevin says.

"Have you worked less?" I ask him.

"Well, a little."

"No," Mia says with an eye roll.

"Women want to stay home a lot of the time," Gavin says.

"Oh, please," I say.

"My mom did. Maybe you wouldn't want to, but each family has to adjust to what they want."

Rania twists to the side, as if searching for something, then sticks Gavin's finger in her mouth.

"She's hungry," Kevin says.

"Ouch," Gavin says with a hiss. "She bites hard. I feel sorry for you, Mia."

"Yes, my nipples hurt permanently," Mia says as she picks Rania up. "That is something the guys can't help with."

I laugh, a full, deep laugh that I can't stop. It's like a bubble of happiness is slowly escaping.

Kevin smirks at me as he gets up and follows Mia offering help to her as he walks away.

"Was it that funny?" Gavin asks.

"I don't know. I just can't stop laughing. I don't know why."

"Don't stop. I'd like to hear you laugh forever."

Kathy sits on the love seat and asks, "What's so funny?"

"She's in a fit of laughter," Gavin says, "Though I'm not sure of its exact source, I'm not stopping it."

When at last my laughter fades into a big smile, Kathy says, "Someone has a big birthday coming up."

"Mom," Gavin says.

"The big four-o," she says. "Come now, you said you wouldn't talk about it until Nyla was out of the hospital. Look at her now. Bright, laughing, and ready to celebrate I bet."

"I don't like birthdays," Gavin says.

"Gavin," I say. "Remember what we talked about last year?"

Gavin looks down to me, a soft smile pulling at his mouth, and puts his arm around me. "I remember my last birthday very well," he says. "And the week later too."

"What happened on your last birthday?" Kathy asks.

"Well," Gavin pulls me tight to him, and I can't resist laying my head on his chest. "I met this beautiful woman for the first time on a flight home from Seattle. Then a week later, Linda's sneaky planning had me meet her again."

"And what did I tell you that night?" I ask.

"Something about every year has to be celebrated." He plants a quick kiss on my lips. "Fine. Something small and family only."

Kathy grins.

"I'm serious," Gavin says. "I hate people looking at me."

"You never have liked the spotlight. Not like our star Nyla."

"I actually don't like the spotlight either," I say. "But I quickly learned that if I wanted to be a professional athlete, I'd have to get used to it. And at some point, you have to embrace it."

"You look good in the spotlight," Gavin says.

"Thanks."

"Okay," Kathy says. "No spotlight, keep it simple. I could make your favorite birthday dinner. Or, maybe you'd like to go out. How about we find a nice place for dinner, and we'll get you a cake. I won't even tell the restaurant that it's your birthday, so no embarrassment."

"Sounds good," Gavin says.

"Kathy," Richard hollers from the back door.

"Coming," she says and stands. "And perhaps now, we could start to talk about that other thing you wouldn't talk about until Nyla was out of the hospital."

Gavin shakes his head at his mother as she walks away.

"She likes to poke things," Gavin says.

"She's worried about you. Can you blame her?"

He groans in an answer.

I suppressed bringing up his tests every single day. I could have, maybe should have, talked about it on the way home from the hospital today. But I was too nervous about being in a car to do it. However, I plan to broach the subject tonight, once things calm down, and we're alone. So long as I can muster the courage.

"What's your favorite birthday dinner?" I ask.

"I don't know that it's my favorite now, but when I was a kid, I loved spaghetti with Alfredo sauce."

"I had no idea. Still full of mystery, aren't you?"

"Mystery? Not a very exciting one. Besides, don't tell Mom, because I don't want to hurt her feelings, but I have a new birthday favorite. A new tradition I want to keep."

"What's that?" I ask.

"Pancakes."

Our first official date was nearly a year ago. It began with me making him pancakes as a belated birthday celebration. It ended with me realizing he made me feel things I never thought I would again.

"I was so nervous that day," I whisper.

Below my cheek, his chest vibrates with silent laughter, then he says, "Me too. But it turned out to be one of my favorite days. That was the sweetest thing anyone had ever done for me."

"I seriously doubt that," I say.

"You have no idea, Nyla, even after all we've been through, what you do to me."

Silence settles comfortably between us. The breeze rustles the leaves above. Behind me, Kathy laughs lightly. In the distance, perhaps from the house, Rania's coo earns a collective, "Ahhhh." Then from the grass below, I hear my brother's voice which reminds me of Pop.

"It's so good to have you back," Gavin says. "Soon, we'll get things back to normal."

"I'm not sure it ever will be," I say.

"Well, no, not like it was. But a new normal. Maybe?"

"Maybe . . . Gavin?"

"Love."

"Will you make your appointment now?"

"I need a few days to settle back in, to be away from hospitals."

"I can respect that. But I need you, Gavin. Please, make the appointment."

I never thought I'd survive Lorenzo's passing. With losing Pop, I know I'll survive because as a child we're prepared to outlive our parents. But Gavin, dear God, if Gavin . . . I don't know what I'd do. There is no way I could survive losing him.

# CHAPTER 11

$\mathcal{M}$ia holds tight to Rania as she arches her back, and her mouth opens with the loudest scream of the night. She has alternated between this and moments of silence for the last thirty minutes.

Standing, Mia says, "I think we'd better get going."

Kevin, with an exhausted huff of air, says, "I've been saying that for the last twenty minutes."

Mia rolls her eyes and hands Rania to him. Then she leans down to hug me. "I'm so glad you're home."

Kevin kisses the top of my head. "Love you, Ny. Let me know in the morning when it's a good time to stop by. Then we can go over the papers I left on your desk."

"I will. Although I can't say I'm looking forward to it."

"No kidding," Mia says. "She just got out of the hospital, Kevin."

"I'd rather deal with it than put it off," I say.

Mia lifts her shoulder dismissively. "You're a stubborn bunch, but have it your way. We'll see you tomorrow."

Gavin and his family are inside cleaning up, and the Smiths left a while ago. In this gift of space, I sink deeper into the leaf-green cushions.

For the first time in weeks, I'm alone. It's a relief to be free of heavy eyes constantly analyzing my movements, breaths, and words.

For so many weeks now I've put on the face people wanted to see, answering questions in a way that would please others. I never realized how easily I fib, or perhaps I should say outright lie, until recently. Now, absent of others to keep happy, I'm not sure how I actually feel.

The air is warm as the evening claims that day, but there's a nip in the air that shows fall is around the corner. Crickets, one by one, join in nature's symphony, and some-place farther off is the croak of bullfrogs.

The sky has turned dark, and my body has become stiff. To prevent myself from becoming a permanent fixture on this couch, I scoot to the edge and get up.

As I approach the back door, Gavin springs from his club chair in front of the window and rushes toward me. I shake my head and open the door on my own.

With a proud smile, Gavin says, "Well, look at you."

I close the door behind me, and with a wink, say, "I'm not helpless."

"Helpless and Nyla doesn't go in the same sentence," Jax says from the chair next to Gavin's.

"Thanks," I say.

The living room is quiet, and all the lights except the one between the two chairs are off.

"Where is everyone?"

"Mom and Dad went to bed a while ago, and Brooke just turned in herself," Jax says.

"I think I'll follow their lead. I'm exhausted."

"I'm right behind you," Gavin says.

In our bedroom, I turn on my bedside light, pull back the covers, and draw the drapes. As I go into the closet to put on my pajamas, I smell the hospital. I sniff my shirt, then my arm, and find it's not only my clothes, but me. There is no way I'll be able to sleep smelling like this, so I head for the shower.

Inside the large bathroom, I squeeze my eyes shut and try to ignore the memory of pushing Gavin away in here. Every day I live with oppressive guilt of how I reacted that day. If I'd been stronger, if I'd held onto Gavin and shown him the unconditional love he deserves, this wouldn't be our reality. I'd have two working legs, a fiancé who trusted me completely, and Pop.

"What'cha doing?" Gavin asks from behind me.

"Nothing," I say to the floor.

Gavin comes to stand in front of me, and then he gently lifts my chin. "Sometimes when I'm in here, I think about that day too."

"I'm sorry, Gavin."

"We agreed, no more apologies. Remember? Or we'll spend our whole lives stuck in the past. I want to move forward with you."

"Okay," I whisper.

Gavin's face lights with excitement. "I have a surprise for you."

"Oh?" My eyes flick down to his shorts and up to his eyes. "Don't look so petrified."

"Gavin, I'm not ready," I say in a rush. "It wouldn't be a good idea."

He takes my shoulders, then softly says, "Calm down, love. Don't worry, that's the furthest thing from my mind. But I do have a surprise for you. Wait here."

Although I'm relieved to hear him say that's the furthest thing from my mind, it also feels like an insult. While I'm not ready to be intimate, I still want to feel desired.

"Close your eyes," Gavin says from behind me. "Are they closed?"

"Yes," I say.

"Okay," Gavin says, his voice now in front of me. "Open them."

I open my eyes to his handsome face. He has a strong brow with perfectly shaped eyebrows which take him no work. Unlike mine which requires daily maintenance.

"What do you think?" Gavin asks.

Between us is a bamboo shower seat that's contoured to fit the bottom.

"You hate it?" he says.

"No. Of course not. I need one."

"Yes, you'll need it for a while. You'll probably need help too."

Our shower, while great for mobile bodies, is not great for a woman on crutches. With practice, I'll figure it out and be able to take care of myself on my own. Today, though, I do need help.

"If you don't mind?" I say.

"I'm more than happy to help in any way you need me." Gavin pulls a package out of his back pocket. "You also need these."

I take the shower cast covers, and say, "You think of everything."

"I try to."

Gavin takes the things into the shower, which reminds me of a cavern. A natural, uneven stone forms the ceiling and walls. The floor is made of the same stone, only smooth, though not slippery. There is a showerhead in the ceiling, three in the walls, and also a handheld one where the controls are.

He returns to me, stuffing his hands into his pockets, and asks, "Do you want to undress here, or the shower?"

In the hospital, I never changed in front of Gavin. I waited until he stepped out. At first, I was embarrassed by the bruises that clouded my golden skin like a stormy day. Then, weight shrunk from me, taking my hourglass figure and thick, powerful thighs that I loved. As it melted away, so has my confidence.

Swallowing the lump in my throat, I hand him my crutches, and say, "Here is fine."

As I begin to pull my shirt off, Gavin's eyes dart away like a guy caught peeking. He turns his back to me, and says, "Sorry! It's all so . . . different." He glances back as I unsnap my bra, then away again.

Naked and embarrassed, I take my crutches from Gavin. He turns back to me, eyes bouncing all over the place.

"I feel like I'm not supposed to look. That's stupid, right? I'm allowed to?"

I manage little more than a sad smile before I go into the shower. On the cool bamboo bench, I slip the shower bag over my cast, then sit up straight facing the stone wall. I've never felt so exposed or ashamed.

I turn to tell Gavin that I'll do it on my own, but the sight of him arrests my eyes. His back is to me again, shoulders rounded like a man who's done manual labor all day. Slowly, as if he's sore, he peels his clothes off. He folds each article as he goes, and stacks them in a neat pile next to the door. Naked, he picks up my discarded clothes, folds them, and adds them to his stack.

I look away to the rough stone of the shower, sit up as straight as I possibly can, and pull my arms together.

Gavin sets his fire-hot hand onto my shoulder, and asks, "Comfortable?"

His hip brushes my arm as he moves next to me, adjusts several knobs, and starts the water. Then he holds out the showerhead, and asks, "How's this temperature?"

I put my fingers into the stream and say, "Fine."

Gavin moves behind me, tips my chin up, and then wets my hair. When he picks up my shampoo, I say, "I can do most of it on my own."

The snap of the cap echoes, and then his words, "I'll take care of everything."

He massages my scalp as he cleans my hair, he's gentle with the ends as he conditions them, and softly he washes my body with an ivory washcloth. He does it all with the utmost care, as if it's the first time he's ever touched me, or perhaps the last time he ever will.

As Gavin moves around me, I admire how gorgeous he is. I notice the way his muscles move below his skin, the way his jaw is clenched but his lips soft. I also notice that his cock hasn't even begun to stiffen.

Kneeling in front of me, Gavin's hand caresses my knees, and he asks, "Are you all right, love?"

He used to always get hard when he saw me naked, that's why the silent rejection of his flaccid state crushes what little confidence I have left. I tighten my arms to my body as if the water has gone cold.

The cast on my leg will come off. The final bruise on my hip will fade. Someday soon the curves of my body will fill back out, and the muscles will return. I will be beautiful again. Still, something in me whispers a desperate question: will his body respond to me again?

"Nyla?" Gavin says.

I can't say a word, so I nod yes and close my eyes so that I don't have to look at him. As I do, I hear Lorenzo's past words, "I miss the way you used to look at me, Nyla. The way you used to touch me, and how your body would respond to me."

•••

Today, after thirty-nine days, Lorenzo was discharged from the hospital. We've been home an hour, and already I miss the comfort of the nurses who checked on him regularly, and assured me all is okay. I'm afraid here alone that I'll fail him. What if I hurt him or miss a crucial sign about his health?

As I go into the kitchen, a man walking through the back of our property startles me, but then I realize it's Lorenzo. Before all of this, he was enormous and solid. Now everything—treatments, drugs, and the transplant—have transformed him into a man I hardly recognize. He's shrunk, and his sharp bones look as if they might pop through his skin.

Through the open window, I watch Lorenzo go to our favorite spot. It's a bench tucked into a thick of trees on the edge of the island.

When he disappears from sight, I go to the fridge and grab a couple of beers. I don't think it's a good idea for him to drink, but he insists his doctor said it's okay. Since I don't want to argue with him, I try to do anything to make him happy.

I find Lorenzo exactly where I expect on our bench, arms stretched across the back. He's at ease and appears nearly as big as he used to be.

The glorious orange sun is tumbling behind the mountains spraying rays of yellow, and lighting the sky with pinks and purples.

The doctors say there's still hope, but I'm afraid. Not just of him leaving, but how this experience is changing us; individually and together. Constantly I replay old memories because I'm scared they, too, could leave me. I try to catalog and cherish every moment we have now. Sometimes (though I'll never tell anyone) I'm afraid someday all I'll have left are memories.

"Here you are," I say as I hand Lorenzo his beer.

He takes a long drink, eyes on me as I sit, then says, "I've missed this." He looks at the bottle, swipes a thumb over the label. "It tastes even better. So much better. You brought me two, right?"

"Of course," I hold mine out to him.

"Nyla, I was kidding." He puts his arm around me and tries to draw me tighter to him. "Sit closer."

Carefully I slide next to him. As I do, the bench squeaks and creaks.

"This old thing," I say.

It was here when we moved in, and, while I never thought much about it before, I suddenly want to reinforce it with extra brackets and nails.

"It's fine," Lorenzo says. He wiggles the bench back and forth causing it to snap and pop.

He threads his fingers into mine, then squeezes firmly. I try to squeeze back, but I am barely able to.

"Are you afraid I might break?" Lorenzo asks.

"No!" I say.

"There are a lot of things I miss. But nothing as much as I do your touch."

"I'm touching you."

His sad, blue eyes bore into mine. "No, you're not. You haven't touched me in months."

My voice cracks when I say, "I don't want to hurt you."

"I might be dying, but I am not dead yet. I'd like you, my wife, to touch me like you still have hope too."

"I have hope."

He licks his lips, then kisses mine. "Show me."

I've been more alone in these last few months next to Lorenzo than I ever have in my life. I'm isolated by grief for him, for our life, and myself; though I won't tell him or anyone else. I want to be more hopeful, but I'm afraid to get my hopes up.

Lorenzo's eyes travel over my face, down my neck, and to the V of my T-shirt. "You're beautiful, Nyla."

"So are you."

His lips flatten as he shakes his head no, and turns back to the sunset.

He used to be my best friend. We'd tell each other everything. But this disease is trying to kill not only him, but us. I don't want it to win.

I look at him from the corner of my eye. It's been a least two, maybe four, months, since we've had sex. I'm desperate for his touch. Have I underestimated all that he can handle? Can he still take me?

Slowly I stand up and step in front of the sun. "Do you want me?" I ask.

"More than anything."

"I'm scared that I'm too much, too heavy for you now."

"Never."

My hands shake as I unzip my shorts and slip them to the grass. Then I take my shirt off, my bra, and lay them on the bench. The wind off the ocean swirls my hair up like I'm submerged in water.

The biggest smile I've seen in months transforms Lorenzo's face to the man I fell in love with. "How on earth did I manage to find you?" he asks. "You're what keeps me here."

My chin shakes. "I'm afraid you'll leave me."

He runs his hand along the curve of my hip and up the inside of my thigh. Then he works himself free and pats his lap.

I've never been afraid to have sex before. But as I set my knees on the bench and slowly take the girth of him, I am petrified. His sounds that used to be sexy—grunts, moans, and compliments of how good I feel—scare me.

I ride him how he's always liked until I bring him to his edge where greedily, I keep him. I don't want these moments to become a memory. I want to keep him. How do I suspend time?

"Nyla," Lorenzo bites out as his fingers dig into my ass. "You're killing me, beautiful."

All I ever wanted was to share my whole life with him. I wanted to have our family, to read the book he wanted to write, to win more gold for him. All I ever wanted was to make him happy.

I'll remember how this feels as he goes: the way his arms tighten like he can still protect me, the way his teeth dig into my shoulder, the way he lifts his head and his blue eyes look at me like I'm all he'll ever want.

"You're not even close," Lorenzo says.

"Yes. I'm close," I lie.

He pulls my face to his and kisses me hard, then slaps my backside just how I like it.

"You forget how well I know you," he says, "I know what you feel like outside, and in. I know what you feel like when you're close."

"I'm sorry," I say and cover my face so he won't see the tears.

When I try to slip off him, he draws me tight to his chest, and says, "I miss the way you used to look at me, Nyla. The way you used to touch me, and how your body would respond to me. I also miss the way you always told me the truth."

# CHAPTER 12

In the living room, Gavin sits in his favorite chair, gazing out the window. His hands are laced behind his head, and with no shirt on, his arms and shoulders are on full display.

"Happy birthday," I say.

Gavin twists to look over his shoulder at me, his arms releasing as he does. "Good morning," one side of his mouth lifts, "beautiful."

The way "beautiful" rolls off his tongue reminds me of better times; when I felt it was true and not an attempt at flattery.

As I lower myself into the chair next to his, I ask, "Where is everyone?"

This was the first time since I've been home that I didn't wake up to the sounds of Gavin's family moving about.

"Probably plotting treachery," Gavin says. "You're not in on it, are you?"

"You know better. I would never conspire against you." I pump my fist. "Team Gavin, all the way."

"You're moving well this morning," Gavin says.

I adjust my oversized cardigan, smooth back my hair, and smile as brightly as I can. It's his day, and I want to do everything in my power to make it a good one.

"Thanks, I'm feeling good. So, birthday boy, the big four-o. Do you feel any different?"

"Yes, I do."

"How so?"

"Luckier."

"Luckier?"

Gavin reaches across the space between our chairs and brushes his knuckles along the top of my hand. "I was thinking about my last birthday when I met you. Then the next week at Mix, when you actually noticed me."

"Have you seen how handsome you are? It's impossible not to notice you."

"Really? On my birthday at the airport, you didn't notice me."

"Sure I did. In fact, I talked to you first."

"You know what I mean. You didn't notice me, notice me."

I look away from Gavin, his gaze imploring too much honesty. "That wasn't an easy day for me. I was leaving my house on Bainbridge. All kinds of stuff was stirred up. But I was glad to have met you, although I was happier the week later, the second time."

Wanting a change in subject, I dig into the pocket of my oversized, cream-colored cardigan, and say, "I have something for you."

"Oh, yeah? What?"

Last year, before Gavin and I spent our first Christmas together, we made a pact not to give each other physical gifts. Instead, we would make or do something for one another.

"This is the one and only time we're allowed to break this rule," I say. "And I had to. You'll see. Open it, birthday boy."

With reserved excitement, Gavin rips the paper. He pulls the lid off, and says, "Nyla."

Gavin has dozens of tailored suits, numerous cuff links, rows of handmade shoes. But he's only ever owned one watch, and he wore it every day. It was a graduation gift from his parents.

While I was in the hospital, I noticed Gavin wasn't wearing his watch. I asked him about it, but he dismissed my question and said he hadn't needed it. Jax, however, told me what really happened. On the day of the accident, on the way from Mix to the hospital, Gavin got out of the car and ran to the accident. The police stopped him, but in a struggle fueled by rage and grief, his watch was broken.

This new one isn't exactly like his old one, but it was as close as I could find. It is two-toned silver and gold with a blue face with white hash marks for the hours.

"Jax told me what happened to your old one."

"Yes," he says quietly.

"I know the watch meant a lot to you. I can't replace it, but hopefully, you'll enjoy this one now."

"It's perfect," Gavin says as he removes it from the box. He turns it over, and reads the inscription, "Time is on our side. Eternally yours, Nyla." He kisses it. "Thank you."

"I hope you'll enjoy it."

"I'll treasure it. And always think of you when I look at the time." He holds the watch out to me. "Would you put it on me?"

I slip it over his hand and clasp it shut. It's a perfect fit.

"It looks good on you," I say. "Now how about some pancakes?"

Gavin follows me into the kitchen and asks, "May I help?"

"While I'd love to refuse your offer, I think I'll have to take you up on it. Will the family be back for breakfast?"

Gavin's eyes soften with desire as he moves towards me. "No. I asked them if we could have the morning alone together. I wanted some time with just you."

I should want Gavin, and perhaps in a way I do. But I don't believe he really wants me. For the last couple of days, he's helped me shower and never shown any indication that he's attracted to me.

Gavin's hand cups my cheek, slides down my neck, along the back of my arm, and settles onto my hip. All the bruises from my accident have gone. However, I have a few new ones from clumsy moves on crutches. One of which is directly below Gavin's hand. He jerks his hand away like he's touched a hot stove.

"Damn, Nyla. I'm very, very sorry. I forgot."

"It is okay, Gavin. It's almost healed."

"I don't know. That bruise still looked pretty angry last night." Turning away from me, he says, "I'll get the griddle out."

My happy mood plummets, but I put on a happy face, and say, "Thanks."

Together we gather all of the ingredients, a mixing bowl, whisk, and ladle. Then I say, "I've got it from here."

"I'll—"

"No. Sit or go read. I've got it."

He moves to me again and kisses my cheek. "Are you sure?"

"Yes."

Gavin sits on the barstool across from me and sips his coffee. After several minutes of silence, he picks up his phone. From it, he plays music over the wireless speakers. I recognize the tune of "Mystery Girl" right away, but the voice that comes on is not Jax's, it's Gavin's. I watch him as his gravel-rock voice pours over the speakers. It's so different from his brother's version, but somehow it seems like this is the real, original version.

Hearing it makes me think of our lives before each other, what we've experienced together, and the challenges that lay ahead. I want to be his Mystery Girl, but there have been so many moments this last month that make me wonder if I really am.

When the song ends, Gavin stands and reaches over the counter to brush a tear from my cheek.

"It was supposed to be your wedding present," he says. "I couldn't wait any longer to give it to you."

I press my hand to my heart. "I love it, Gavin. When did you record it?"

"This summer."

"Thank you."

He holds up his watch and says, "Thank you."

A gift like this deserves a physical reward; a hug, a kiss. Really, it deserves an even deeper connection. But I can't, and to keep from crying tears of frustration, I return to my task of pancake making.

He's proposed again, so I think he still wants to marry me. But neither of us has talked about rescheduling it. I'd like to, though first I need to be myself again.

With precision, I cook golden-brown, silver-dollar pancakes. Then I stack six of them on a plate. From the pocket of my cardigan, I pull out a box of gold candles. Just like last year, I put a single one in the center.

Gavin looks over my cardigan as if he expects for more things to appear. Then with a chuckle, he says, "Where did you get those? What else do you have in that magic sweater?"

"I'll admit that I've had some help."

I light the candle and slide the plate to him.

"Make a wish," I say.

He looks at the burning candle, and says, "Do you want to know what I wished for last year?"

"If you tell me, it might not come true."

"It already has. I wanted to spend my next birthday with you."

Even though I'm choked up, I manage to say, "Do you know what you're going to wish for this year?"

Gavin watches as a drop of wax slips down the gold candle and pools on the pancake. Then he closes his eyes, says, "Yes," and blows out the flame.

•••

Soon after breakfast, the family returns and informs us they've made reservations for dinner. Gavin, clearly excited by the prospect of a night out, quickly turns to me and asks if it would be all right.

The idea of leaving the safe fortress walls of our house, and getting ready for a night out is daunting. However, since it's Gavin's birthday, I say, "Of course!"

I endure another shower session with him—even though I insisted I could do it on my own—with conflicting emotions. I want our bodies to return to our natural responses, but despite the day, nothing has changed in that department.

I blow-dry my hair and curl the ends. It takes a lot of make-up for me to look alive, but I apply and apply until I do. In the closet, I try on twenty dresses. Nothing fits right on my shrunken frame. Finally, I settle on an old, black dress with a wide belt.

We all pile into Gavin's truck, which snugly fits six. I find myself in the front seat next to Gavin. I squeeze my eyes shut and pinch my hands between my knees the entire way. Will I ever be able to ride in a car again and breathe normally?

Finally, we arrive at a hotel near Pioneer Square. Above it, on the fifteenth floor, is a restaurant called Flight. Large white tiles cover the floor, walls, and ceiling. The lighting is just right, making everyone look perfect and the place sparkly.

We're seated at a table tucked in the corner near a window overlooking downtown. Across from me, Brooke slides into the white leather bench. She says, "This place is romantic. Don't you think, Nyla?"

"Very," I say. "I haven't been here in years."

Our waiter arrives at our table just as we've all settled into our seats. After rattling off a list of specials, he asks what we'd all like to drink.

"Wine or cocktails?" Richard asks Gavin.

"Wine sounds good to me. What do you think, Nyla?" Gavin says.

"That sounds great."

"Would you like to order a bottle or glasses?" the waiter asks.

"A bottle, please," Richards says. "Gavin, do you have a preference?"

"Nope. You choose, Dad. You're the wine expert."

A rare and genuine smile lightens my cheeks as I remember the afternoon of our first date. Gavin and I went to a winery where I learned more about wine in an afternoon than I had in my entire life.

Richard lifts his chin to look through his reading glasses, his finger running down the lengthy wine list. "The tempranillo sounds good. Gavin, what do you think?"

Tempranillo was Pop's favorite wine. If there were one on the menu, no matter what he was eating, he'd order it. The good mood that I've worked so hard to maintain sputters.

"Is that all right?" Gavin asks me. "I know. I remember too."

"It's okay. It would be a good way to remember him."

"That sounds good, Dad, thank you." Gavin puts his arm around me and lowers his lips close to my ear. "Nyla, I'll do anything to see your smile. I've missed it so much, and I'm desperate to keep it there."

He takes my hand, turns it over, and kisses the inside of my wrist. Deep inside me, I feel all those little flowers he used to make bloom. A few may still be alive, but even this sweet and intimate gesture does nothing to rouse them from their wilting state.

I'm not a very good actress, but I try to grin shyly at Gavin as if what he's done feels sublime. He looks at my lips like he's going to kiss me, and to avoid this, I nuzzle the side of his neck with my nose. He smells so good, like standing on the edge of the flowing river. This familiar scent makes me long for the way we used to be. When I didn't have to play up my attraction to him, and I knew I turned him on. When I believed I would be strong enough to protect him.

The waiter returns and fills our glasses.

"I'd like to make a toast," Richard says, lifting his wine. "To our son. Your mom and I are so proud of the man you've become, and everything you've accomplished in your forty years. We can't wait to see what you do with your next forty."

I take a sip of my wine and lay my hand on Gavin's thigh. "I'm proud of you, too, Gavin."

He squeezes me gently and says, "I love you more than I've ever loved anyone in my forty years."

His tender words remind me that the greatest gift I can give him tonight is my full presence. For a few short hours, I'll focus only on Gavin and allow myself to believe that all will be okay.

# CHAPTER 13

$\mathcal{I}$ open the front door to a man dressed in a black suit with a white shirt. "Good morning, Nyla," Frank says.

He's someone you'd mistake for a bodyguard instead of a driver, but he's as gentle as they come. Anytime Pop needed a town car or limo, he called Frank. Now, on the rare occasion I need one, I always call him too.

"Are you ready?" Frank asks.

"I am," I say, then holler down the hall, "Gavin. Frank is here. I'll meet you in the car."

"All right. Five minutes," Gavin calls back.

After Gavin's family left Sunday, I asked him to call the doctor when he returned to work the following day. Reluctantly, he agreed. Even though his family knows he needed to make this appointment, he made me swear not to tell anyone. Since I still can't drive, and he isn't supposed to after the procedure, I called Frank.

I settle into the town car and begin to work through a few emails. While I haven't officially returned to work, I've started to make my way through the thousands of emails I have. The progress is slow since most of my time has been dedicated to planning Pop's celebration of life this weekend.

Gavin gets into the car and puts his seat belt on. He closes his eyes as he lays his head back against the headrest.

"What time did you get up?" I ask.

"About five. I didn't sleep much."

I unlatch my seatbelt, slide over to the middle seat, and weave my arm around his. "Are you okay?"

"Mmm-hmm."

"Are you sure?"

"Completely," he says as if there are no syllables in the word. He looks at me with tired eyes, takes my hand, and kisses my knuckles. "Nyla, I'm fine."

In the two days since Gavin returned to work, I haven't seen him. He's gotten up early and been out the door before I'm awake. At night, exhausted from all of the planning, I turn into bed before he gets home.

At the hospital, Frank helps me out of the car. We stand in awkward silence for a minute. Then he leans down, looks in the car, and asks Gavin, who is still seated and buckled, "Is this the right place?"

"Yes, it is," I answer for him. "Gavin, are you coming?"

Gavin unbuckles his seatbelt, and as he slides out, he asks, "Do I have to?"

Frank winks at me and closes the door behind Gavin. "I'll be waiting for your call."

"Thank you very much, Frank," I say.

Gavin, walking as if we have nowhere important to be, takes a couple of steps, then says, "Yep, thanks, Frank."

I shrug apologetically to Frank, then follow after Gavin. "Are you sure you're okay, Gavin?"

Eyes open, but glassy, he says, "Yeah, right as rain."

"Right as rain? What's up? Seriously. You're walking funny, your speech is slurry, and your eyes do not look right."

"Oh, ah, well, you see . . . " He leans very close to me, wavering. "The prospect of having a needle stabbed into my throat for a biopsy had me a little concerned."

"Yes, I can imagine why."

"So when I talked with Sue, you know the nurse at my oncologist's office."

"Yes."

"I asked her how on earth a man was expected to lay still while someone shoved a needle in his throat. It's insane they won't just knock me out for it."

I urge him to continue with a head nod.

"So she called me in a prescription."

"A prescription of what?"

"Stuff to keep me calm, which is usually not a problem, by the way. Nothing gets to me. Well, except for you." He leans forward and plants a firm kiss on my lips. "I like your lips."

"Thanks, Gavin. What meds?"

He shrugs and pulls out an orange pill container.

I quickly read the label; it's nothing that I recognize.

"How many did you take?" I ask.

"Two," he says. He settles his hands onto my waist, presses his chest to mine, and kisses my lips again.

"You took two pills?" I hold the bottle up in front of his eyes. "This says to take one before the procedure. Why did you take two?"

"You take two of everything."

"No, you don't!"

"Don't be mad at me. Beautiful, I love you. You're sexy too."

"Are you really hitting on me right now?"

He grins lazily. "Is it working?"

"No."

"Then I'll keep trying."

I roll my eyes at him.

"Thank you for coming today," he says.

"You're welcome. Come on, before you're late."

After Gavin checks in at the reception desk, he flops down into the chair next to me. He lays his head on my shoulder and says, "This is why I wanted you here."

"So you had a place to put your head?" I ask.

"Which one are you referring to?" He laughs at his own joke like it is the best he's heard in a year. Then it trails off to a chuckle, and then silence. "No. When I look at you, I feel hopeful that things might be okay. That it's just a scare. When I don't see you, and I think about it, I get scared. Tell me it will be okay."

I lean my head against his. "It will be okay."

"Nyla, once we're done with this crap and life starts up again . . ."

I wait a few seconds, but when he doesn't continue, I say, "Gavin?"

"I want to slow down. Even just a little."

"Hmm?"

"I lived so fast when it was just me. And since we've been together, it's been even faster. I want more days like we had in the hospital."

"I don't."

"I mean. Where we don't have to go anywhere. More time to talk. To read together. To tell stories."

"Gavin Boston," a strong female voice calls.

"That's me," Gavin says. He kisses me with his loose, warm lips, and then stands. "I love you."

"I love you, Gavin. More than anything in this entire universe."

He leans down, his face so close to mine I smell the mint in his mouth. "More than the sun?"

"More than. You're also much hotter."

"Are you hitting on me?" he asks.

I quickly plant a kiss on his lips. "Trying."

"Gavin Boston!" the woman calls again.

He stands up straight, and with a hint of fear in his voice, he says to me, "Don't ever stop doing that."

•••

Two hours later Gavin returns to me. His legs are solid, eyes no longer glazed, and he definitely looks relieved.

"How was it?" I ask.

He points at his throat. "They put a needle in it."

"You're alive, though."

"Very, and I'm starving now. How about I take you on a date to the hospital cafeteria?"

"Wow, you really know how to win a woman's heart."

He helps me up then says, "I'm trying. Every day."

It's true. I never give Gavin enough credit for all the effort he puts into us. He flies out to meet me in random cities, even if he only has a night to spare. There's always half-and-half for me in the fridge even though he never uses it, and he knows just how much I like in my coffee. Even these last two days when he's left before I've gotten up, there have been sweet notes left on my bedside table.

As we walk down the hall to the cafeteria, Gavin says, "I remember I told you once we'd go to the hospital and make happy memories. And look at us now."

"This is a happy memory."

"Yeah?"

"You're here."

"Do you know what I like least about you being on crutches?"

"What?"

"That I can't hold your hand while we walk, or put my arm around you when you say sweet things."

"Soon," I say. "Soon."

In the cafeteria, Gavin and I go separate ways. I head for the grill where I order a veggie burger. From the drinking fountain, I get a cup and fill it with ice tea. Just as I realize it will be impossible to carry it on my crutches, Gavin is at my side.

"I'll get that," he says and sets my drink on a tray next to a small pint of ice cream.

"That's all your eating?"

"Be it real or imagined, my throat feels funny."

He snaps a plastic lid onto my drink, puts a straw in it, and holds it up for me to take a sip.

Since we've been home from my extended hospital stay, Gavin's skin has regained its natural glow, and his eyes have brightened. It makes me believe that this is just a cancer scare because he looks really healthy.

In the months that led up to Lorenzo's diagnosis, he'd changed. His dark skin paled. Each day his eyelids grew heavier, and his eyes seemed to withdraw into his sockets. "It's just exhaustion," he kept saying. When I finally convinced him to get a checkup, he returned with a diagnosis of chronic fatigue; at least that was what he told me. I look back on that time and wish I'd pushed harder and insisted he return to the doctor sooner. Maybe then . . . life would have been different.

I'm faced with memories like this often. Of Lorenzo, of a life well-lived, and still, I'm overwhelmed with what-ifs, thoughts of what I should have done differently. Then I look at Gavin, someone I love with all I am and wouldn't change a moment with, and I feel guilty for still wishing I could have saved Lorenzo.

In the cafeteria, we find two spots across from each at the end of a communal table. Gavin sets our tray down, helps me get situated, and then sits across from me. I take the top off his ice cream and stick a spoon in it.

"Not sure this plastic spoon will work all that well," I say. "We should have gotten a metal one."

"Easily solved," he says and hops up.

I tear open a ketchup packet and squirt it onto the hamburger bun, then I add mustard. Gavin returns with his metal spoon and takes a huge bite of ice cream.

"Can I ask you some things?" I say.

"Anything."

Gavin and I haven't talked much about his illness. Instead, we focus on what's ahead, and what's happened since we have been together. I do know he had Large-B Cell Lymphoma and was treated with chemo, a transplant, and radiation.

"Will you tell me about it?" I ask.

"The procedure? Well, I mean, you—"

"No." I shake my head. "I don't want to know about that."

"Oh good. Too soon. My skin was crawling thinking about it. You mean when I was sick?"

"Yes. How'd you feel before you were diagnosed?"

I hold my breath, petrified he'll tell me that he had no idea. Could he have looked as healthy as he does now and not known it? Have I missed something? Am I failing him too?

"I thought it was stress. My stomach hurt a lot." He gnaws at his lower lip a moment before he sets down his ice cream, and says, "Pandora suggested I get it checked out."

A shiver of revulsion shakes my core.

"I know, her name makes me feel the same way. And actually, let me put it this way. She said, 'go get it checked out or stop bitching.'"

"That sounds like her."

"I walked away with a prescription for an antacid. Doc said it was an ulcer, not too shocked that I had one. I mean I was married to her, and she was pregnant with a child she already hated. Then she lost the baby. My stomach got worse, and I was tired all the time. Actually, I thought she'd sucked the life from me."

With his fingers, he makes fangs from his upper lip. We laugh. He picks up his spoon again.

"I went to visit my parents one weekend when Pandora said she needed a break from me. Mom said, 'You look like shit.' To which I replied, 'Thanks a lot.' But she was right. I was pale, and I'd lost about forty pounds. Anything I ate upset my stomach. I told my mom a divorce would cure me, but she insisted on a doctor visit. Actually, it took daily reminders for two weeks before I finally booked the appointment. And . . . the rest is history."

I reach across the table and lay my hand on his.

"I feel good now, love. Really. Aside from the stress the last month, which has been hard, I feel good. It isn't like before. The doctor just wants to check anything that might develop or be of concern. What I had was aggressive."

"I'm glad your doctor is careful."

"I promise, I won't leave you."

If every promise that had been made were kept, I wouldn't be here today. Everything in life would be different. I wouldn't be a sports reporter. I'd have set more records and won more gold. Lorenzo and I would have a child with blue eyes and another with nearly black hair.

Are we responsible for promises we break if forces greater than us break them?

"Good," I say, "because we have a lot of things still to do."

"Like . . . ?"

"Get married for one. Travel. Read."

He grins and leans forward, takes my hand and turns it over. As he softly runs his finger along the inside of my wrist, he says, "And things we need to make up for missing these last few weeks. It's been torture."

Moments like this, when Gavin looks at me like he still wants me, my desire for him swells. In these fractions of time I feel like myself again, the woman I'd transformed into over the last year with him. It's who I want to be all the time.

Somehow, though, shackles of sadness and despair yank me back.

# CHAPTER 14

$\mathcal{G}$avin's truck comes up our road; the engine's hum and the crunch of the gravel below the tires I know well. Usually, I'm excited to hear those sounds. But the closer he gets, the harder my heart beats, until it nearly leaps from my chest when the door of his truck slams closed.

On Fridays, Gavin rarely comes home early; if he does, he tells me. What makes this more concerning is that he's only returned to work this week, and he took Wednesday off for his biopsy. There is no way he should be here already . . . unless something is wrong. He's not supposed to have his test results back yet, but what if they've already called? It can't be good. If they were, he'd have called me.

From here on the couch, I have a direct line of sight into the foyer. Through the windows that run along the side of the front door, I see Gavin walking like his shoes are full of sand. Outside the door, he stops and pulls his shoulders back before he comes in.

Although I'm looking right at him, Gavin doesn't see me when he hollers, "Hello, love." He bends and unties his wingtips, then sets them on a mat below the entry table. When he finally notices me, his face softens with relief. "I didn't see you nestled into the couch below all those blankets."

"It's kinda cold today," I say.

He collapses on the couch next to me. "It's that time of year when things begin to change. Summer and fall battle for control of the thermostat."

"You're home early," I say.

"Don't look so worried. I couldn't concentrate at work anymore, so I asked Alvis to cancel my afternoon meetings and left."

"You haven't heard anything?"

"No." Gavin scoots closer to me, slumps down, and stretches his legs out to the coffee table. "I know they said it would take a week, but I was really hoping they'd see right away that it's nothing, and call to let us know. I didn't want this question mark looming with your dad's service tomorrow. I'm so sorry."

Setting aside my laptop, I lift my blankets and drape them over Gavin too. Then I wrap my arms around him, pull him to my chest, and hug him tight. "We'll make it through, Gavin. I love you."

He nestles his head onto my breasts and replies, "I love you more than anything, Nyla."

My phone vibrates across the table, ringing a horrid tune I don't remember setting. It shatters the silence in the house and breaks the peace I felt with Gavin in my arms.

With a groan, Gavin reaches for it, and says, "You probably need to take that, don't you?"

I check the name on the caller ID; it's Perry Tacklin. "I don't have to."

Gavin pulls back the blankets and stands. "Go ahead. While you take that, I'm going to go call Sue at my doctor's office and beg her for peace of mind."

I press the green accept button on my phone, but I wait to say anything until Gavin turns the corner down the hall toward his office.

"Good afternoon, Perry."

"Kid," he says like a parent who has missed their child. "You sound much brighter than last time when we talked. How are you?"

"Never better," I say.

"Oh, come now. I'm sure you've been better."

"Well, perhaps that's true. But I'm working with the idea of fake-it-till-you-make-it. How about you?"

He makes a drawn-out, "Hmmmm," before he says, "I'm fine. Though I was surprised when a little birdie informed me of the email you sent today."

This morning, I woke up early and wasn't able to get back to sleep. Without disturbing Gavin, I got up and went to my office. I needed to do something, so I checked and rechecked the to-do list for Pop's service tomorrow. Every single thing was already checked off not just once, but twice.

Pop's funeral is the last thing I ever wanted to plan, but it's given me something to focus on. Full, busy days made it easy to ignore not just the pain I feel in my body, but in my mind and heart too.

With nothing to do or think about, pain crashed down on me. In my office, lit only by the single lamp on my desk and darkness pressing the window panes, the slime of depression began to seep in. It's swirled around me since the moment I woke up from the accident.

I lost myself to it once, and I refuse to do it again. So I turned my attention to what saved me before: work. I emailed my editor at *American Sports Journal*, letting him know I was ready and available to write.

"I didn't think such simple editorial things pass your desk," I say.

"You know me," Perry says, "I hear everything."

"The all great and powerful."

He chuckles. "You are a funny one, kid. You are. Really, though. I thought we'd talked about a return in December."

"Yes, to TV. But writing, I can do that from here."

"It's too soon."

"Please, allow me to be the judge of that. I love the game, Perry. And I love my work. It's a part of me that I want to get back to."

Perry groans, "Okay. I can relate. But this can't in any way negatively impact you. And if you need anything, you call me."

"Deal."

"Promise me."

"Perry, I promise. You know I never let you down."

"I know. Alright, kid. Welcome back."

"Thanks, Perry," I say.

"And you're sure that deadline next week isn't too soon with your father's funeral tomorrow."

"Not at all. I've got this. Thank you, Perry, for all that you've done for me. Everything."

"I'm the one who should be thanking you. Thank you. I'll touch base with you next week."

"Sounds great. Goodbye, Perry."

I open my laptop and begin to draft my article. This is the first real excitement I've felt since the accident. It's almost intoxicating, like a good run. Oh, how I miss my runs. Once I can do that, I'll really feel like myself again.

Gavin returns to the room, his face even longer than when he returned home. He shakes his fist up at the gods. "Nothing! They got nothing. In fact, according to some woman they're running behind." He stops. "You look deep in concentration."

"I'm working," I say.

"Working?"

"I'm writing an article for the website, and hopefully I can get one in the magazine next month."

"Is that what Perry called about? You know, I like the guy, but we told him December. He should not push you."

"It was me, actually, Gavin. I sent my editor an email this morning asking if he'd do me a favor and give me an article or two to write."

"Really?" Gavin sinks slowly onto the couch next to me. The center of his forehead wrinkles down the middle. This happens when he's thinking hard about something he's not happy with.

"You've just been through so much, and you finally seem happier, Nyla. I'm worried that pressure might . . ."

"When have I ever cracked under pressure?" I say and elbow him playfully.

"It wasn't a challenge," he says.

"I'll be fine. Actually, it will make me happy."

"If it makes you happy, I won't object."

He falls silent, his eyes staring off into space.

"What did they say?" I ask.

He swings his legs onto the couch. "Can you move your laptop so I can lay on you?"

"Please." I pat my thigh.

"Mid next week." He lifts his head, and asks, "Is this alright? Is my head too heavy?"

"It's perfect."

"I'm not preventing you from working, am I?"

"No. It can wait."

I stroke my thumb across his forehead to smooth the worry lines.

"That feels good," Gavin says, as his eyes drift down.

From Gavin's closed eyes, a tear escapes which I swipe away with my thumb. He rolls over onto his side and presses his face into my belly. Then he wraps his arms around me and holds on desperately. He cries like I've never seen him do before, loud and heavy sobs. I wrap him in my arms and hold on tight. While tears stream down my face, I stay silent to ensure Gavin doesn't know.

•••

The next day, as we get ready for the funeral, I ask Gavin, "What are you going to wear?"

Gavin organizes his side of the closet not only by type of clothing, but color as well. From the top row of dress shirts, he picks out a dark-gray one. Then from the row below, he grabs a pair of black pants. He holds them up to me in question.

"I think Pop would hate it if we wore all black. Maybe a blue shirt? Pop's favorite color."

Gavin puts them back. Then he looks through his blue shirts of varying shades and subtle patterns. He picks one that reminds me of beach glass, and asks, "What about this one with charcoal pants?"

"I think he'd like that one," I say.

I turn to my side of the closet. It isn't messy, but it has no real organization. Near the back is a gray garment bag which contains the vintage, ivory-lace dress I wore to the gala last year. Behind it, in a clear bag, is a navy, chiffon dress printed with sunflowers. At the waist is a thick, white satin belt.

As I take it out of the bag, Gavin says, "I've never seen that dress before."

"Mom picked it out for my college graduation, and Pop loved it. I haven't worn it in years."

Gavin takes the dress from me and says, "Hands up." He guides it down my arms and into place over my body. The tips of his fingers brush my neck as he moves my hair to the side, then zips me in. The front of his body brushes my backside as he reaches around to put the white belt on me.

"Is it too tight?" he asks.

"No," I say, unable to hide the smile of appreciation which I quickly remove.

"It's okay to smile sometimes," Gavin says.

"Maybe, but not today."

Gavin turns back to his side of the closet. He opens the top drawer of his dresser, which is filled with what I call man jewelry: an assortment of cuff links, pocket squares neatly folded, and his watch. He removes a pair of gold cuff links and holds them out to me. He's been putting these on himself most of, if not all of, his adult life. But when I'm in here, he always hands them to me in silent question. It's good to know he doesn't need me, but he'd prefer me to help if I'm here.

He kisses my cheek. "Thanks, beautiful." Gavin lifts my chin with a crooked finger. "You are beautiful."

"Thank you. You are handsome."

"One more thing," he says. He takes the watch I gave him for his birthday out of the drawer and hands it to me. "Please?"

"Of course."

After I fasten it on him, I say, "I'll be just a few more minutes," and head for the bathroom.

I usually don't wear much makeup unless I'm on TV, but today calls for damage control. A thick layer of concealer to hide the dark circles around my eyes. Blush, far more than I usually need, to give a hint of blood flow in my body. Bronzer not just on my face, but my chest too. Eyeliner and eyeshadow to brighten and lift my eyes. Waterproof mascara. Pink lip gloss to bring color to my pale lips.

I'm not beautiful as Gavin said. In fact, I look only a little better than death dressed up.

•••

I slide out of the truck at the curb of my childhood home. Frank gets out of his limo parked in front of the driveway.

"Good morning, Frank," I say.

"Morning, Nyla. I just got here. Haven't even made it up to the door to let Kevin know."

"I'll get him, and we will be ready to go in a few minutes."

"There is no rush," Frank says.

As I walk the S-shaped pathway toward the house, I notice flowers along the path and in pots on the porch. Annual flowers haven't been planted there since my mother passed away. The dots of color make the house seem lively. It's strange because I expected the house to feel empty, sad even, without both of my parents here.

The front door swings open, and Mia says, "Hey, NyNy," like her bright, usual self. She stretches every inch of her petite frame and hugs me carefully, then Gavin.

"The limo is here," I say.

Mia peeks her head out of the door and waves at Frank. "We're just about ready." She closes the door behind us. "I like that you two didn't wear black." Mia looks down at her black dress, then tucks her dark wavy hair behind her ear. "In fact, I'm going to change. Your dad would be furious if we all wore black. It would be opposite of the celebration he requested."

"Hey, Ny," Kevin says, as he comes down the hall from the kitchen, Rania in his arms.

My little niece has on a blue dress a few shades darker than Gavin's shirt. It matches her eyes perfectly, which are just like her father's, whose are just like Pop's.

As Mia goes back up the stairs, Kevin asks, "Hey, where are you going? I thought you were ready."

Over her shoulder, she says, "To change. The black we're wearing is too stuffy. Look at Nyla and Gavin."

Kevin hands Rania to Gavin, and says, "I suppose that was her way of saying I need to change too."

In front of the window in the living room, Gavin slowly bounces Rania. He talks to her in an octave above his normal tone about the cute little doll in her hand.

When at last I've had all the cuteness I can handle from the Gavin and Rania interaction, I go down the hall. It leads to a large open space divided between a kitchen, and a family room where Pop's favorite chair is. Against mom's design wishes it survived several remodels and new sets of furniture. Only once did she talk him into reuphol-stering it. She used light brown leather that, to me, looked identical, minus the rips that had come from overuse. Pop, however, swore it was too red. For a man that had never spoken of color or design before, it was amusing the way he insisted it was the wrong color. "I'll go sit in my red chair," he'd say. I've missed mom a lot since she passed, but now with Pop gone, I miss her even more.

I sit into Pop's "red" chair and settle into the indents he's left behind.

"Where is Nyla?" I hear Kevin ask from the front living room.

"I'll get her," Gavin replies.

I wrap my hands around the arms of the chair, then reach down to the old wooden lever and pull it. The footrest pops out. For something so old, it still works perfectly. There isn't anything I really need in this house, but this I want. I have no idea where it would go, and honestly, it's a little homely looking and could do with another reupholstering.

"Nyla," Gavin says. "They are dressed in bright colors and ready to go."

"I want this," I say.

"The chair?"

"Yes."

"Hmm, all right. Does Kevin know that?"

"No."

"I bet he'll be fine with that, but how about we bring it up another time."

I push the footrest down, pat the arm a few times as if Pop were in it, then I get up. I can't believe it's really time to say good-bye.

# CHAPTER 15

*I* never asked Lorenzo what he wanted after he passed. He never brought it up, either. Even in the days leading up, when it was all but imminent, I couldn't broach the subject.

After he passed, I switched onto auto-pilot and planned a typical funeral. It didn't offer me any closure and left me depressed.

When Mom passed, it was unexpected. My family and I repeated the cycle and planned another depressing funeral.

Pop, thankfully, learned something from all of this. In his precise instructions, he said exactly how to handle the business, to divide all possessions fifty-fifty, and to skip the funeral and have a party. He outlined nearly all aspects of the celebration, from the brand of Champagne to the setlist for a live band.

"Well," Kevin says to me, "what do you think? Is it what he'd asked for?"

"I think we did a good job. Not bad for pulling a party together in a week and a half."

"Pretty good, I think."

There are at least a thousand people along the water's edge here to honor Pop. Five large tents shield them from the warm afternoon sun. The buffet of Pop's favorite foods is guaranteed to fill everyone's belly. On a small stage is the cover band he wanted.

"I wish I'd done something like this for Lorenzo. I'd never planned a funeral before then. It was depressing."

"It was nice," Kevin says.

I fix him with a challenging oh-really eye.

"I don't know, Ny, unless you do something like this, I think all funerals are depressing. Even this, with all the upbeat aspects, is a little sad."

"It's not the same without Pop. He made the room . . . change."

"So do you," Kevin says. "You've got his charisma times three."

"No."

"I'm serious. I always wanted to be half the man Pop is, or was."

I link my arm into Kevin's and lean against him. "I see him every time I look at you."

"Thanks."

A small hand slips around my waist, and I look over to see Ms. Marshall's big smile. What I miss most about my old bungalow in Portland is living next door to her.

"Hello, Nyla. You're looking much better than the last time I saw you."

The comforting presence of her solid energy shakes loose a shuttered breath, and my eyes well. "I've missed you," I say.

"My damn sister," Ms. Marshall says in mocked annoyance. "I told her not to have a heart attack. The timing was so inconvenient."

"How is she?"

"Much better. She's got a few more years in her old bones yet."

"I'm happy to hear that."

"Well, except now that I'm back in town, you may not be able to get rid of me. I've got all of my get-better recipes I must unleash on you."

"I'm ready."

"I make a cure-all chicken noodle soup."

"Noooo," I say. "You know better."

"What if I just take out the chicken."

"No chicken broth."

"But there is no chicken in it."

She looks at Kevin for a rally against my vegetarianism, but all she gets is a hearty laugh from him.

"Fine, I'll use vegetable broth, no chicken, but it won't be the same."

Gavin joins us, and says to Ms. Marshall, "You found her."

"Sure did."

"I made you a plate," Gavin says to me. "And Walter is saving spots at a table."

"Walter?" I ask.

Gavin looks to Ms. Marshall, and the apples of her cheeks flush the colors of her lips. She lifts one shoulder, and says, "What? I haven't told you about Walter?"

"Noooo, I'd remember a Walter," I say.

"Maybe you hit your head harder than you thought in that accident."

We all laugh and follow Gavin's lead toward a tent.

"I don't think I'd forget a detail like that," I say. "You told me you didn't date because you didn't plan to be on this earth much longer."

"Eh, so I decided differently, you clearly need me to stick around. And with Gavin now, I might actually get something as close as I'll ever have to grandbabies."

"Keep wishing," I say, playfully.

"I didn't plan on him," she says in a moment of raw honesty. "But we don't always get a say, do we?"

"No."

A man with a bald head stands to kiss Ms. Marshall and greets me warmly. There are deep lines around his mouth and between his brow, but everywhere else is smooth youthfulness. His energy is much like Ms. Marshall's, and as with her, it's impossible to guess his age.

Ms. Marshall sits in a chair that Walter pulls out for her. "This is one hell of a party," she says.

"Pop planned it," I reply.

"I bet he did." She nods her head, and repeats, "I bet he did."

Ms. Marshall came to see me several times in the hospital when I was drugged beyond belief, so I remember little of her visits. Gavin told me she was his favorite visitor. She never said the trite things others would, and it was easy for him to be with her in silence. These are things I've always loved about her too.

"You need to eat more," she says and pokes my arm with her finger. "You're too skinny."

"I keep telling her the same thing," Gavin says.

"It's hard when I'm never hungry, and my belly fills immediately," I say.

"Too much sitting around," Ms. Marshall says. She knocks on my cast three times. "Get this sucker off and then you," she points to Gavin, "can help her work up an appetite."

"Ah, yes ma'am," he says.

"That's what the doctor is prescribing."

"Are you a doctor?" I ask, in jest.

"I was a long time ago."

My mouth drops open, and then I say, "Wait, are you kidding?"

"When you live as long as me, there can be a million lives led. Or just one. It's up to you, really. And yes I was. Speaking of new lives." She pats the arm of the man seated next to her. "This is Walter. The guy who is helping me work up an appetite."

Gavin coughs, sending a few drops of his whiskey from his mouth. I dab the back of my hand on my cheek where one landed.

"Sorry," he whispers.

"Walter, this is my unofficial niece, Nyla Tripple."

"I've heard so much about you," he says.

Kevin taps me on the shoulder. "Sorry to interrupt." He nods toward the stage.

"Okay," I say.

Ms. Marshall takes my hand and looks at my eyes as if reading a critical sign. "You're okay. Don't forget that. Samuel knows it too." She looks at Gavin. "You take care of her."

"I'm trying," he says.

"And you," she looks at me more seriously than I've ever seen, "take care of him."

"I'll do better," I say sincerely.

"I know you will." She slaps my hip like you would your favorite horse as you send it out to pasture. "Head up."

I've found these last few weeks that keeping my head up is sometimes the hardest thing to do. But I lift my chin, take Gavin's hand, and stand. "I'll do better at that too," I say.

Kevin puts his hand lightly between my shoulder blades, and together we walk to the stage. People flood toward the stage, some with plates of food in hand. Waiters begin to circle with glasses of Champagne—the real stuff, as Pop instructed.

"Hello," Kevin says into the microphone. "Nyla and I would like to thank you for joining us to celebrate Dad's life. This entire party was his idea." Kevin holds up a white business envelope. "He also asked if we'd read this today."

Kevin runs a finger below the envelope flap and pulls the paper out. He clears his throat, then says, "Welcome to my last party. Who knows how I went. I hope it was painless, and in some ways, I hope it was epic. Then again, in my sleep would be good.

"I asked my kids to throw this party because after my wife passed, I realized funerals are depressing. And, let's be honest, they're not for the dead, who are already gone. They are for the ones who are lucky enough to still be living. And while yes, there is sadness, I don't think we should punctuate the memory of anyone with a sad event, with everyone dressed in black. Should I be lucky enough for you to shed a tear over me, I ask it not be in sadness, but as you laugh and remember something happy. And if still, you feel sad, have another damn whiskey.

"I'm sure you are waiting for some grand last words since I bothered to write this. But I'm not the writer in the family. So I'll leave you with my life's motto: love hard and live fast."

•••

We return to my childhood home, unload from the limo, and say goodbye to Frank. Mia packs a small cooler with snacks, while Kevin puts Rania's car seat into the back center seat of Gavin's truck.

As we all get into the truck, Kevin says, "We forgot something." He runs into the house and returns with a small rosewood box that he sets in my lap. "How about you hold Dad."

The burnt red hue of the rosewood reminds me of that moment when the sun sets and gives its final flare with the darkening sky behind it.

"Thanks for agreeing to do this today," I say to Kevin.

"To be honest, I didn't want to put it off either."

The massive weekend traffic makes it stop and go all the way through Portland. Once we get to I-84, which travels up the Columbia River Gorge, there are still a lot of cars, but it flows.

In the back seat, Kevin, Mia, and Rania have fallen asleep. The silence in the truck's cab allows my mind to begin to slow. I've been thinking nonstop for the last few weeks. Between my health, the questions marks about Gavin's, house guests, planning a funeral, and deciding to return to work, I haven't let myself breathe. With Pop's party now behind us, there is space, as unpleasant as it might be for now.

Two and a half hours later we pull into the main area of Lost Lake. We continue past the lodge where people rent boats and stand-up paddleboards, as well as purchase drinks and snacks.

"Do we need anything?" Gavin asks as he stops the truck to let people clad in swimsuits cross the small road.

"I'm still full," Kevin says sleepily from the back.

Gavin looks to me, and I say, "I'll pass on kayaking today."

"Another time then," Gavin says.

"Yes, another time."

"We've never done that together," Gavin says. "We need to add that to our list."

"We have a list?" I ask.

"I do, of all the things I want to do, especially with you. Don't you have a list?"

I shrug. "I guess we've all got things we want to do. I've just never thought of it as a list."

"What about as a bucket?" Kevin says.

"Maybe," I reply. "There's a spot."

I point to the only empty space I've seen between all three parking lots, and while it's a tight fit, Gavin makes it work. At least three-quarters of the cars are being loaded up as people finish their day of fun in the sun.

"Should we have changed?" Kevin asks as he squats down so Mia can put Rania into a hiking pack.

"Naw. A man in a suit and polished shoes with a hiking pack on is perfectly normal," I say.

"I think you look handsome, babe," Mia says.

"Thanks, babe," Kevin says. "I remember where the spot is that Pop asked us to do this, but it's on the other side of the lake almost." Kevin looks at my leg. "What are your thoughts on that?"

"I can do it," I say.

Kevin, Mia, Pop, and I were here over two years ago when we spread Mom's ashes. It's where Pop proposed to Mom. We also came here as kids to play in the lake. We'd paddle around on inflatable kayaks, and often times mom would watch from the edge perched on a log, looking at peace.

"Here?" Kevin asks. He steps off the path and walks toward the edge of the lake. "It's the best spot I've seen so far."

"Is this legal?" Mia asks.

"Who knows," Kevin says. "But it's a man's dying request. What are we supposed to do?"

"I don't know, when we spread your mom's ashes, there weren't as many people around, so I didn't think anything of it."

"There is hardly anyone left now since they're all heading out. Besides animals die in this water every day."

"That makes me not want to get in the water like this ever again," Mia says with her nose wrinkled in disgust.

"I could carry you," Gavin says to me.

"Thanks, but that could result in us both being injured."

"Hey, I can carry you. You know that. Right?"

"Yes, but with my bum leg, on uneven ground in your fancy black wingtips, it sounds like a recipe for disaster."

I work my way from the main path on my crutches through a narrow opening in the brush. The ground is stable, though tree roots line the surface like an abstract drawing. At the lake's edge is a foot and a half drop-off to the water's surface which mirrors the glorious peak of Mt. Hood. Its very tip is still covered in white, as it is all year round.

Kevin holds the box out to me. "You're sure?" I ask. As I take it, Gavin steadies me with his hands on my waist and elbow.

I hold the box tightly to my chest and lean back into Gavin's support. With my hand shaking, I open the box with an irrational hope that it will be empty and none of this is real. But inside is a clear bag with powdery ashes. I set the box on Kevin's offered hands, take the bag out, and undo the loose knot at the top. After a few deep breaths, I scatter the ashes as if they are delicate seeds that contain the secret of life.

•••

Back at the house, Kevin and Mia begin to unload their things.

"Do you want to come in?" Kevin asks.

"I can make dinner," Mia says.

"No, but thank you," I reply. "I'm tired, and afraid if I go into the house I might fall asleep."

"That would be okay," Mia says.

I shake my head no. "But thank you."

"I'll help you unload," Gavin says and gets out of the truck.

Mia comes to my door and reaches her hand through the open window to give my shoulder a gentle squeeze. "Love you."

"Love you too," I say. "By the way, the house and the flowers look great."

"Thank you. I found your mom's old tools in the garage. It seemed like it was time to bring a little color back to it. See you tomorrow, maybe?" she says.

"Okay."

Gavin follows Mia into the house while Kevin leans his folded arms onto my open window and rests his chin on them.

"Great funeral, brother."

"No kidding. Damn, I am so tired."

"Me too."

He kisses my cheek. "Love you, sis."

"Love you." He taps the door three times and pushes off.

"Hey, Kevin. Do you think you'll stay?"

"In Portland?"

"No, I know you're staying in Portland. I mean do you think you'll stay here, in the house."

"I don't have time right now to look for a new place, and honestly I love this house. Would you mind?"

"It doesn't make you sad to think of them?"

He shakes his head no. "It feels good to have some life in it again. Would you care if we kept it? I'd buy you out."

I wave him off. "Please, don't even. I do have one thing I want."

"What's that?"

"Pop's chair."

"That old thing," he says with a snort. "It's yours."

"You can keep the house then."

He winks at me and turns back to the house. When he and Gavin pass by each other, they stop to hug, then talk for a moment. I make no attempt to hear what they say. In fact, I do my best to block it out.

Gavin gets into the truck, and as we pull away from the house, he says, "You know how I said my parents may end up staying?"

"Yes," I say.

"Do you mind if they do? Mom sent me a text while we were driving that I just got."

"You know I love your parents. I never mind them staying."

"I know, but it doesn't mean you may not need space after everything today."

"It's fine, really. It's good because I didn't get a chance to talk with them at the celebration. Actually, I didn't get a chance to talk with Jax and Brooke, either. It was kind of them to fly in this morning, even though they had to get back for the concert tonight."

"We all love you," Gavin says.

"And I love you all."

# CHAPTER 16

*T*his dream is nothing like I've experienced before. I'm in the dark, unable to see anything. A pressure in my ears accompanies the silence. My weightless body touches nothing. The only sensation is the bite of cold that pierces my skin. Perhaps it's a nightmare. I have no urgency to escape it, in fact, I want to stay here.

•••

"There you are," Gavin says, and squats down next to the bed. He slips the sheet down from my shoulder and traces it with his thumb. "It's three."

"Three?" I ask.

"In the afternoon."

"Hmm."

"My parents are heading out, do you want to say goodbye?"

"I'll be right there."

After the bedroom door closes, I press myself up from my side and sit on the edge of the bed. My armpits hurt from the long walk yesterday, and I think my shoulder joints are out of place. Everything else—legs, core, arms—aches too. There have been many times I've pushed through grueling workouts and raced despite being injured. It's this experience that allows me to keep moving despite the pain. I clench my teeth to keep from screaming as I stand.

I work a smile onto my face, open my eyes all the way, and go out to the foyer. Richard and Kathy's packed bags are at their feet, and they look ready for a drive in the open countryside.

"There she is," Kathy says.

"How'd you sleep?" Richard asks.

"Good," I say with a smile.

"We're off," Kathy says, "but if you need anything, anytime, you call."

"Thank you," I say, "We will."

After they leave, the smile on my face melts off. For the first time, I'm grateful for my crutches; otherwise, I might liquefy into a puddle on the floor.

There's work I need to do, but I can't rouse myself to think of anything right now. I go out to the couch on the back deck and lie down. I'm not sure if I'm exhausted from the events of yesterday, or if something is wrong with me.

Gavin sits at my feet and gently begins to work my foot. I don't want to be touched right now, but if I say something, he'll only worry.

"You know," Gavin says, "You don't have to tell people you feel good when you don't. And people don't always expect a smile."

I tip my chin down so that I can see him as I contemplate his words. There are a million smart-ass retorts I could make because he's not one to talk about sharing what he feels. But I don't have the energy, and for some reason, though I'm aware that I should, I don't care.

"Okay."

"It gets exhausting when you try and be happy for everyone, and it isn't genuine. Eventually, you find there's no more energy."

My nostrils flare, my eyes sting, and I work hard to keep myself from even breathing because I'm afraid if I do, I might cry.

"When I was sick," Gavin says.

"Don't," I snap.

"I want you to listen."

"You're going to make me cry."

"Just listen, Nyla."

"When I was sick everyone kept asking those questions. How are you doing? Are you feeling good? What's your pain level on a scale of one to ten? But the worst was when people would say, 'you look great,' when behind their tone and in their eyes, I could see they were shocked I was alive."

An acknowledging-snorty-laugh-cry escapes me, and then it's no use. The waterworks begin to stream from my eyes, across the bridge of my nose, down the side of my face, and onto the pillow.

"Sometimes," Gavin goes on, "I wanted to tell people what I really thought. I wanted to say I felt like shit. I'm shocked I'm still here too. And sometimes I wanted to tell the doctor my pain was a ten, but I was afraid I wouldn't be much of a man then. There were times, too, when I wanted to tell people I couldn't put on a happy face for them, that I was all out of fake smiles."

"Are you scared?" I ask.

"No."

I look down to him, swipe away the tears from my eyes so I can see him clearly.

"Yes," he says. "Why do you think I balled like a baby the other day?"

I hear the embarrassment in his voice.

"It's okay to cry," I say.

"Is it?"

"I'm crying, okay. You got me. Nothing else seems to make me cry, except you."

"I'm not sure, love, if that is a compliment or an insult."

As I lay here, Gavin's hand still working my foot, silence descends on us.

Even though it's been hard to smile and answer people's questions cheerfully, it was for me as much as it was for them. A fake-it-till-you-make-it attempt to eradicate the sadness. "Happiness comes from within," I hear my old therapist's voice chime.

Now, though, it isn't just a sadness I feel. It's deeper than that, and it's consuming me from inside out.

"Nyla," Gavin says.

"What?"

"It's all right to be sad. You just can't let the sadness keep you."

•••

The mattress shifts as Gavin tosses and turns before he finally gets up. I watch his bare ass as he walks across our bedroom and to the bathroom, but when he turns to look at me, I close my eyes. When the shower finally turns on, I open them again. The irregular pattern of water hitting the smooth stone floor tells me he is washing his hair and body. The very thought of him in there used to be enough to invoke some feeling in me, if not a need for immediate satisfaction. But now an uncomfortable numbness smothers my desire to live.

Gavin opens the bathroom door as he pulls a fluffy, white and blue striped towel around his hips. I don't have the energy to close my eyes this time, so we just look at each other. He tucks the corner of the towel, flashes a disappointed smile, and goes into the closet.

When he comes out, he's dressed in dark slacks, a white shirt, and a striped vest. He lays something on the comforter over my hips, and says, "If you do nothing else today, please get out of bed and change. I think you've been wearing those sweats for two days."

I try to nod, but nothing moves.

Gavin turns and leaves the bedroom, his footsteps heavier than usual.

Something in the very back of my brain whispers to do this for him. I prepare myself for the pain of moving my body and push myself up.

I pick up the emerald silk shorts and tank Gavin set out. He bought them for me one random day. They used to make me feel sexy, but after I've dressed in them, I feel nothing of the sort.

In the kitchen, I sit at the bar and watch as Gavin fries eggs. He slips them onto a plate, turns to me, and sets them on the bar.

"Could you eat two eggs?"

"No."

"You love eggs, Nyla."

"Loved, maybe."

Gavin shifts his weight like an irritated teacher and pushes the eggs under my nose. "I don't know whether to be pissed at you or feel sorry for you. Which will reach you? I've tried to talk nicely to you, but you ignore me. I tried yelling at you yesterday, and you still ignored me." He shakes his head, balls a fist, and thumps the counter. "Wake up! What is wrong with you? Oliver called me yesterday very concerned about you. He said you canceled PT."

I sniff the egg and push it away. "I don't have the energy."

"For what?"

"Physical therapy."

"Nyla, that's because you aren't eating. You've hardly eaten anything in the last month, but you've not eaten a thing in the last three days."

Gavin pushes the plate back to me. I push it away. He slides it across the bar again, this time until it touches my chest that's leaned against the edge of the island holding me up.

"Jesus, Nyla. Eat something. It's like you want to shrivel up and die suddenly. What happened to my fighter?"

"I thought you said it was okay to be sad."

"I said it was all right to be sad, yes, but I said it can't keep you. And this isn't sad. This is, maybe it's depression. Do you want me to see if I can get the therapist you saw in Seattle to make a house call and help you?"

"No." I lower my nose to the eggs again and sniff like a picky cat.

Gavin leans down so that our eyes meet. "Here is the deal. I'm going to work. All I ask is you eat that. I won't even watch you. I'll trust that you do. Plus, I won't ask you to eat another thing the entire week." He kisses the crown of my head. "I hate to be selfish here, but I really need you right now. The stress of everything is getting to me."

I lift my head to look at him as my mind skitters around a dozen thoughts, but I can't say anything.

"I'll see you tonight," Gavin says, and leaves the room, then I hear the front door open and close.

The two fried eggs on the white plate look like an insurmountable challenge. Actually, the idea of anything right now seems impossible. I used to love eggs. I used to love wearing this outfit for Gavin. I used to love the way he couldn't resist me in it.

"Nyla!" Gavin shouts as he snaps his fingers in front of my eyes. "You've got to wake up, you are scaring me. Someone could walk in here, and you won't even know it."

"I thought you left," I say.

"I did, got all the way down to the end of our driveway when Perry called me. He, like everyone else, is worried about you. You missed your deadline, and he can't seem to get ahold of you."

Like a match has been struck, I feel something light in me, right behind my belly button, but just as quickly it goes out.

"Tell him I'm sorry. My phone is off."

"Oh, no," Gavin says. "You have to call him back."

"I will. Today."

"No, in the next hour. And the damn eggs. Eat 'em, Nyla. Do you hear me? Eat."

The front door slams shut shaking the windows, which seems to vibrate the air around me, and then something right behind my belly button again.

With the tip of my finger and my thumb, I rip a small piece of egg off and set it on my tongue. Cautiously I chew the rubbery bit. Gavin even broke the yolk; the best part is a runny yolk. I snort at the fact that I'm irritated by Gavin's poor egg cooking skills. It's good to feel something.

Two eggs consumed—though bland because I didn't have the energy to get up and add salt—I go into the living room and lie down. I can't close my eyes because I'm not tired. Actually, I have more energy than I've felt in weeks. Still, I don't want to do anything.

With superpowers I've never developed, I try to mentally will the TV remote to my hand. Nothing happens, so I settle for staring at a black screen.

I'm sure I won't make Gavin's required deadline to call Perry back within an hour, but at last, I get up from the couch and go in search of my phone. I check my purse, my office, the kitchen, the bedroom, and my nightstand. It's not in the bathroom either. I start to check odd places I may have set it: the fridge, freezer, in my makeup drawer. With no success, I start from the beginning again, this time dumping my purse onto the couch. My phone thumps out, screen dark. I curse and snatch it up as if it's done something wrong.

In my office, I dig a charger out from the top drawer and plug the phone it in. Since It will take a few minutes for it to charge up enough to be turned on, I look around the room for something to do. There is a fresh spark of exhilaration pumping through me, perhaps from the thrill of the hunt and the success of finding what I was looking for. I wonder out of my room, down the hall, and into the living room. I go to the back doors and prop them open because it's a nice day and the house could do with some fresh air.

The fuchsia-flower-shaped hummingbird feeder Ms. Marshall gave me catches my eye. There isn't a single bird around it, and I can't recall the last time I saw one here. It probably hasn't been cleaned or filled since before my accident.

I go into the kitchen to get the stepladder, but then I realize there isn't a way for me to carry it with my crutches. Besides, it probably isn't a wise idea to try and use it right now.

Back out on the deck, I stare up at the bird feeder which hangs from a long brass chain. I've never tried to get it down, Gavin's always done it. But now I think perhaps it's not as high up as I thought. Below it, I press down on my right crutch and stretch my left arm up. My ligaments and muscles protest with zaps of pain and sounds that remind me of popcorn popping.

With my fingers cradling the bottom of the feeder, it slips from the chain. A thrill of accomplishment floods me. Abandoning one of my crutches I creatively make my way back into the house holding the feeder like a prized jewel.

In the kitchen, I make the sugar water mixture. While it cools, I clean the feeder. Then I fill it halfway, so it isn't too heavy to hang again. Taking it down proved to be the easy part, but after two side cramps, I manage to get it back up.

The doorbell rings. I ignore it because I'm not expecting anyone, and I'm in my silk tank and shorts. It's not an appropriate thing to answer the door in.

Just as I go to sit on the outdoor couch, there's a rapid knock on my door, followed by Ms. Marshall's distinctive voice, "Nyla, it's me. Are you okay in there? Nyla? If you don't answer in the next ten seconds, I'm going to assume something is wrong and call 911."

"I'm coming!" I holler as I work my way through the house. "Don't call 911."

When I open the door, I'm met with Ms. Marshall's whistle. "Was I not the company you were expecting?"

"I wasn't expecting anyone."

"Good girl. Every woman should dance alone in her pretty things. We can certainly take care of ourselves," she elbows me as she walks by, "can't we?"

"We can. But it wasn't like that."

She sets her purse on the coffee table and sits down on the oversized couch. It looks obscenely large with little Ms. Marshall on it.

"You look nice," she says.

I sit on the chair opposite her. "Thanks."

"But sad."

"Thanks."

She looks around the room, then back to me. "You know, it's okay to be sad. Someone who loves you called me."

"Did he?"

"He's worried about you."

"Trust me, I know."

"He said you aren't moving around much."

"I've actually moved a lot this morning, and I ate eggs Gavin made for me."

"See, I told him there was nothing to worry about. Gray clouds come, but they pass too. Just because you're sad, doesn't mean you have to stop living. Movement, doing good things, is what shakes it loose."

"Oh yeah?"

She nods as if she knows just how brilliant she is. "You should go shower, you know."

"Yes, I do."

"Your hair has become a solid mat in the back."

"Thanks for pointing that out."

"Means you've been lying about too much. Go jump in." She stands, holds her hand out to me, and wiggles her fingers. "Look, you can either do it on your own, or I'll drag you in there."

"I'll do it myself."

"Go shower. You'll probably need a big handful of conditioner if you want any chance of getting these," she lifts the matted mass of my hair, "snarls out. If you need help, I'll be happy to brush it out for you. I used to love playing with my daughter's hair." A nostalgic smile turns her serious face into something light. "Then let's go out. Oh, and wear something that makes you feel pretty. Because it looks like you forgot how beautiful you are."

# CHAPTER 17

*E*ven though I tell Ms. Marshall I can get the car door, she rushes ahead of me and opens it. Her old, brown station wagon has fake wood paneling along the side. There isn't a scratch on it, and the tan fabric still looks brand new. It reminds me of my childhood. My parents didn't have one like this, but my best friend's parents did.

"Well," Ms. Marshall says. "Where should we go?"

We slow to a stop behind a long line of cars at the traffic light. It's here we have to turn right or left onto Burnside. While I've been in a car many times since the accident, we've managed to avoid this light, this road, and this choice.

"Hmm?" she says as the car begins to roll again, and she gets into the right-turn lane. "Are you hungry?

Nervous panic makes me reach for the door handle and squeeze it hard. "Where are we going?"

"I'm just driving at the moment because you haven't answered my question, Nyla. Where would you like to go?"

We turn right onto Burnside, and suddenly, I feel Pop's presence.

Ms. Marshall pats my forearm. "You're okay, sweetheart. I didn't realize that being in a car bothered you."

"I haven't been on this road."

"Oh, dear, I should have asked."

I pull the seatbelt across my chest tighter. As we go through the tunnel, I hold my breath, only letting it go once we reach the other side.

"This is good," I say. "I mean, I'd have to do it at some point, right? No use skirting around the long way anymore."

"There's my can-do girl. You know, it's lunchtime. Maybe we could find something that sounds good to you in this food town of ours."

"Sure," I say, not because I want to eat, but because I can't possibly have a conversation right now with what's ahead on this road.

We descend the hill, momentum provided by the steep slope. Images of the last time I was here flicker through my vision as if two separate times are blending. Pop's final moments of life were a gift because he used them to do what he'd always done—lift me up. "The question is," I hear Pop say, "can you tell him you love him, for better for worse, in sickness and in health?"

Already, Gavin has held up his side of the promise we have yet to make, but me, I've continued to fail him like I did that day. Loving someone in sickness isn't just about the healthy one loving the sick.

The traffic on this road is unusually thin for a weekday. Every light is green. As we fly past the spot where Pop's life came to an end, I press my hand to the window, and softly say, "I love you."

When the forest of trees yields to the concrete landscape of downtown, relief ripples through my body. Finally able to breathe again, I press my hand to my heart.

"Should we warn him?" Ms. Marshall says.

"Who?" I ask.

"Gavin."

"Warn him about what?"

"That we're taking him to lunch. You just said that was a good idea."

"Did I?"

"I said, 'shouldn't we invite Gavin,' and you said, 'Uhuh. He'll be thrilled.'"

"No, yeah. Of course. Sounds like a good idea."

Ms. Marshall drives the scenic route to Gavin's office. We turn onto NW 23rd and pass by Mix, where everything began to change. Then, two blocks up, the parking lot where my SUV windows were shattered. It's there, vulnerable and uncertain, I accepted Gavin's help.

We weave through the neighborhood of Victorian homes until we come to a business district. The Boston Smith Company building—bright white brick, windows trimmed in black steel, and fresh wood accents—is the polished jewel of the area. I'm so proud that the Boston in this company is mine; not that I had anything to do with this business, but I'm always proud of him.

Ms. Marshall pulls into the parking space next to Gavin's truck. "There's that secret service truck," she says.

That first night, after my windows were shattered, Gavin insisted we take my SUV up to his house for safekeeping in his garage. He drove me home where Ms. Marshall, sitting on her porch next door and smoking Mary Jane, said his truck looked like secret service. She's right, it does.

Ms. Marshal puts the car into park. "Look at that smile."

I lift my fingers to the rounded apples of my cheeks, and for a moment I marvel at the feeling of a genuine smile. I'd forgotten how easily it can come from inside.

Ms. Marshall hops out of the car, grabs my crutches from the back, and brings them to me.

"I could have gotten them," I say to her.

"Hey, an old lady can help you. You got it there?"

"Solid and steady."

"As ever." Ms. Marshall looks up and down the street. "You know, I'm not all that hungry. I ate lunch before I came."

"We could get coffee."

"No, you look like you need lunch." She looks over her shoulder at the Boston Smith building. "And I'm willing to bet there's a guy in there who could use a date." With a wink, she turns and walks down the sidewalk. Then she calls back over her shoulder, "There's no rush. I'll find a nice spot and watch people stroll past. You know how much I love to do that."

I make my way to the front where Pat, the receptionist, opens the door for me. "Nyla!" she says with a sweep of her hand inviting me in.

"Hello, Pat."

"Do you need any help?"

"No, thank you. I've got it."

Inside, every detail from the fixtures and furniture to the art is done with the greatest taste. My favorite part of the lobby, though, is the blue-glazed cement floors which look like the swirling ocean. As usual, it's bustling with people moving in all directions, and every waiting chair is taken.

"What a wonderful surprise," Pat says. "Gavin didn't mention you were coming.

"It's a surprise," I reply.

She claps her hands like a proper Southern woman, and says, "He'll be tickled to see you. Do you know where the elevator is? Back of the building."

"No, actually I don't. But that's okay." I look to the stairs made of thick wood planks that appear to be floating. A marvel designed by Gavin. "I'll take the stairs."

"On crutches?"

Determination, something I haven't felt in a while, swells in me.

"Yeah, on crutches."

After the first floor, I pause at the landing, twist my hair into a long rope, and pull it over one shoulder so that my neck can get some air. Then I begin again. Step by step, floor by floor, I make my way up. My muscles burn as I go, but I won't give up. Finally, I make it to the fourth floor. I stop and wipe the sweat from my forehead and nose.

It's unusually quiet up here. The usual hum of voices from the high-walled cubicles in the center is absent. All of the office doors around the perimeter are open. At the far end, though, the glass-walled conference room is packed, perhaps everyone is in there.

I'm not surprised to find Gavin's office empty, but I am shocked by the state that it's in. Blueprints everywhere: leaned against walls (several of which have fallen over), open on his desk, and several rolled up on the table in front of the couch. Stacks of binders and papers, not only on his desk but on the floor. His usually pristine office doesn't seem like it belongs to my Gavin; instead, it looks like the space of a mad professor.

"Why, hello, beautiful," Gavin whispers in my ear.

Startled, I nearly fall, but he steadies me with his strong hands.

"Surprise!" I say, nervously.

"Indeed, you are."

"I stopped by . . . to see . . . " Why am I nervous to ask him to have lunch with me? It's like I've never asked him out, like I'm some woman five rungs below him hoping he'll consider me. "Lunch? Have you had any?"

"No. Did you eat breakfast?"

"You said you weren't going to ask." He raises a challenging eyebrow. "I ate it," I say.

"Thank you."

Gavin shoves his hands into the pockets of his navy trousers and takes a few steps back, then leans against the edge of his desk.

Embroiled in my own dark place over these last few days, no weeks actually, I haven't stopped and truly looked at Gavin. His beard is unkempt, and while some could consider it sexy, it's not him. His skin is pale, and under his eyes, it's dark. The bit of softness that used to pad his body, and made him look healthy, has shrunk; he almost looks sickly.

Is it cancer? Have I done this to him? Have I failed him?

Overwhelmed with guilt, I want to take him in my arms and hold him tight. I want to promise him I'll make everything better, that I'll make him better, that I'll get better.

"You look a bit winded," Gavin says.

"I took the stairs," I reply.

Small crinkles form at the corners of his eyes like there is a smile that wants to break free.

"It was hard," I say. "I was sweating after the first flight."

"You? Really?" he asks disbelievingly.

"I haven't been working out much."

He nods in agreement.

"Lunch, though," I say. "Do you want to go? Together?"

"Did Ms. Marshall put you up to this?"

"No! Well, she drove me here, and maybe before I knew it, we'd decided to take you to lunch. Then she ditched me. But, Gavin, I'm happy I'm here. And I'd like to go to lunch with you. If you have time."

His eyes fall down my body like a floating feather. "You look beautiful."

"Thank you. I showered and brushed my hair. Not enough energy for makeup or anything fancy."

"You don't need makeup, and you're fancy on your own."

His full lips pull into a smile I haven't seen in a while.

"Will you eat?" he asks.

As if on cue, my stomach growls like a monster waking from a long winter sleep. "Is that answer enough for you?"

Gavin's phone rings. "I don't want to ruin the moment but let me check this. I left a message with my doctor's office. They're a day late with my results." He grabs his phone from his desk and looks at the screen. His shoulders fall. "It's still not them."

"Gavin, I have a feeling everything is okay. They probably get backed up this time of year."

"September is a big month for tests, is it?"

"Must be. I look at it like this. If it were horrible news, they would have called you the first day."

"Or perhaps I just got at the bottom of a pile. Feels like my luck has gone a little sideways lately."

I'll never understand why the universe throws horrible things at terrific people. It's as if it wants to test them and absorb their good energy. Which sounds like me . . . No matter how much he tries, I keep testing the limits of his love, and I, too, keep taking from him.

"Your luck hasn't run out, Gavin. I promise it's going to be okay. And no matter what, I'll take care of you."

Gavin steps to me, hope in his eyes. I begin to set my crutches aside. "I'll take those," he says and leans them against the chair.

"I want to be able to hug you, without those things in the way," I say.

He opens his arms. "Please, hug away."

As we hold each other, I feel Gavin's body strengthen yet his muscles relax. I inhale the familiar scent of his cologne; standing on a river's edge. Against my cheek, his heart thumps, and I can't imagine it will ever stop. In Gavin's arms, I feel once again, as if this is the safest place in the world.

Thankfully, some things never change.

# CHAPTER 18

$\mathcal{B}$ack at the house, with a little more wind in my lungs, I get out of Ms. Marshall's wood-paneled station wagon all on my own.

Ms. Marshall rolls down her car window. "Are you sure you're okay?"

"I'm fine. Really."

"Are you sure? Because when I got here this morning you looked like death warmed over, but now, I dare say, you're flushed. Do you have a fever?"

"You still enjoy teasing me, don't you?"

She grins. "Is it Gavin fever, perhaps?"

I roll my eyes at her.

"Okay, okay, legs. I'll leave you to it," Ms. Marshall says.

I unlock the front door and head for my office to power up my laptop. Last week after Perry okayed my return to work, I wrote my assigned article. All I had left to do was put a few finishing touches on it, which on Friday I'd told myself could wait until Sunday. Quickly, I finish it then write an apologetic email to my editor, assuming full responsibility for my late assignment. I attach the article and hit send.

My knee bounces like a kid waiting outside the principal's office as I call Perry. I have never been late for an assignment, and I've always been the team player everyone counts on. I don't want that to change.

"I've been worried about you, kid," Perry says in greeting. "Thankfully Gavin assured me that you were alive, just having a rough go of it."

"Perry, I'm sorry. I've already submitted the article to my editor, and I assure you it will never happen again."

"Nyla, it's not the article I'm worried about, it's you. You know, players that push through physical injuries often end up hurting themselves even more. It's the same for mental injuries. You need to give yourself time to heal there too."

"I did, I took it. I've spent the last few days healing. I'm healed."

"Nyla."

"Healing, I'm healing. But, as I told you on Friday, I need this. A reason, a purpose to get up in the morning. I swear I'll never let you down again."

"How about you take one more week."

"I need this work. It's everything to me."

"I hope that isn't true," Perry says with a laugh. "Don't let it be everything to you. Let yourself and your relationships be everything to you."

What he says makes sense, I get it, really I do. But he doesn't understand how integral this work is for me.

"Okay," I agree because I want him to agree with me.

Perry groans, "All right, kid. Get back to work. Your editor will send you another assignment this afternoon."

"Thank you. I'm ready. This was just a small stumble and something that will never happen again."

"I trust you."

My bouncing leg settles, I lean back in my chair and look out of my office window. Seized by spontaneity, I say, "Perry, there's something else. I'll be in Minnesota the week after next."

"Nyla Tripple, no way. You must be joking."

I turn to my computer and bring up the airline website where I begin to make my travel arrangements. "I've already booked my travel." Fibbing doesn't feel good, but I think right now I have to.

"You are still on crutches."

"People on crutches can fly you know. But it's a moot point because I get my cast off Monday morning before I head to the airport."

"You, you are . . . crazy. Do you know that?"

"I'd prefer determined. I just want to get back to my life."

"And what does Gavin think? Have you talked with Oliver?"

"Perry, Perry, Perry. Since when do I need anyone's, especially a man's, permission to work?"

"Well, sounds like you've got your heels dug in. And, like always, I'll trust your judgment."

"Thank you."

"What about running? Has the doctor said when you can start that again?"

"Not exactly, but soon, I hope, because without two feet on the ground, I feel like a bird with clipped wings."

•••

A softly spoken "love" and the gentle caress of a warm hand on my shoulder pulls me from sleep. Fogginess clears as I open my eyes. The living room is dusted in evening's purple hue, and there's a chill in the air.

"I was going to let you sleep." Gavin kneels in front of me. "But you were making funny sounds. Bad dream?"

"Aren't dreams supposed to be happy?"

"A nightmare?"

"I don't remember."

I cup Gavin's cheek which is rounded with an enormous smile. "What?" I ask.

"I have news."

I sit up so fast my head smacks his chin and we both curse.

"Sorry," I say, and kiss his chin. "Tell me."

"The doctor called."

"And?"

"It's benign."

My whole body sags with relief as if I've finished a marathon I didn't want to run. "Gavin!"

"Of course they'll continue to keep a close eye on everything, including that tumor, but she said not to worry at all."

"At all?"

"Not at all. We're not going to think about or worry about it again. Go back to sleep. It's been a full day for you. But still, I had to tell you."

I toss the blanket back, and say, "Go back to sleep? Are you kidding me? We have to uphold tradition and celebrate."

"It's too late to make pizza," Gavin says.

"Then we can go pick it up or have it delivered. There is ice cream in the freezer, and we have lots of wine."

"Then how about we order in," Gavin says. "How about you call it in. I'll go change and then open a bottle."

After I place the pizza order, I hurry about tossing pillows and blankets onto the floor to re-create the indoor picnic Gavin and I shared after his last healthy checkup.

This afternoon, after lunch with Gavin and talking my way back into my job, I was exhausted. I didn't think I could do another thing today. Now, though, with this great news, I'm refueled and feel that the universe might finally be on our side again.

Gavin returns, now in lounge pants and a sleeveless shirt, with a bottle of wine and two glasses. He appears both happier and more relaxed than I've seen in a long time.

"Wow, you did this?" Gavin says as he looks over everything on the floor.

"Yep."

"You're moving well all of a sudden."

My arms and legs feel looser, and for the first time in a very long time, there is no pain. Not in my body or my heart. For a brief moment I feel guilty. Shouldn't I still be in mourning for Pop? But something in me pushes the thought away and hones my attention back to Gavin—the one who's here with me and who I need to take care of.

Gavin sits onto the floor then guides me down next to him. I watch the hypnotic flames in the fireplace as Gavin trails soothing patterns along my thigh with his fingers.

"I love this time of year when the nights are cool enough to use the fireplace," Gavin says.

"Me too," I say and snuggle into his side. "I can't believe how much better I suddenly feel, Gavin. It's like someone flipped a switch in me."

"It happened slowly, but suddenly. It's kind of like an overnight success. Nothing is overnight, they've been working at it for years but then something aligns, and it changes so quickly it seems like overnight. You've been healing for weeks, Nyla. I'm glad to see this, though. It's a complete change. Thank you for coming to see me today."

"You're welcome. Thanks for going on a date with me."

"Anytime. I want to toss an idea at you."

"What's that?" I say.

"My shop is way more than I need. We could easily split it in two and turn half into a gym so you can work out here. Who knows, maybe you'd convince me to join you sometime."

"You'd give up half of your shop for me?"

"I'd give it all up for you."

"Now that's love. A man willing to give up some of his shop space."

"Pure love, yes."

"It would be nice to have one here. I could drop my gym membership, which I've never really liked, anyways. Also, it would save time. More I could spend with you."

"Done!" Gavin says like a proclamation. "Construction starts in the morning."

I run my hand below Gavin's shirt and gently work the muscles along the side of his spine until they soften.

"I don't think I deserve you," I say. "You give and give. I have no idea how to match what you do for me."

"Funny, because I think the same thing about you."

"No, Gavin. You're always bending over backward for us, always taking care of me."

"Have you ever read a book in the first person?"

"Yes."

"When you read a book like that you get to feel and experience the world through that character, see the world through their eyes. It's only one view, though. You don't get a chance to see through other people's eyes. In a way, you don't get the full picture. You live in the first person, as do I, yes. But if you were to see life as I do, you'd get an entirely different story." Gavin cups my cheek. "And wow, what a view it is, Nyla. I see a woman who gives me everything, who's willing to risk her heart on me, who makes me feel better about myself than I ever have, and . . ." He runs his hand up my leg below my shorts and slides a finger below the edge of my thong. "With you, I feel things I'd never get to otherwise. Seriously, I'd give up my whole shop for you, and more."

My whole body goes weak, and while I do want him, I can't do it yet. There is this cast, and for some reason, I need it off before I can. I'm about to explain this to Gavin when the doorbell rings.

"What timing the delivery guy has." Gavin springs up from the floor and hurries to the door. A couple of minutes later, he's back on the floor next to me opening the pizza box.

"Your office was covered in blueprints," I say.

"Messy, I know," Gavin says as if irritated with himself.

"Why so many?"

"We have a lot of projects going, and I haven't been as tidy as normal." He scratches the side of his beard. "Actually, I didn't notice how bad it was until you were in there today. Embarrassing."

"Never be embarrassed with me. How's the Yamhill project coming along?"

He dabs his mouth with a napkin, takes a drink of his wine. "Good. Getting close to breaking ground. The next few weeks will be crazy. Late nights, there's so much I have to catch up on."

"I support you in whatever you need to do."

I should probably tell him that he doesn't need to worry about the late nights because I'll be on the road again. But I don't want anything to dampen the mood right now.

"But, Yamhill, it's coming along nicely," Gavin says. "Next time you come to the office, remind me, and I'll show you the final model of it. I'll bore you with architect stuff about why I've gone with certain pillars and the properties of the glass I chose."

"I love to hear you talk about your work, you're so happy when you do. Go on, tell me all about it."

# CHAPTER 19

The Smiths live in the Eastmoreland neighborhood, not far from my old house in Woodstock. The yellow house has a roof which rounds at the edges; it reminds me of a hobbit-like home, though it's much more substantial in size.

Gavin and I walk up the brick steps lined by boxwoods. Before we've even knocked on the front door, it's yanked open, and Emma throws herself at my good leg.

Linda gently draws her back and says, "Emma, remember what we said?"

Emma looks at me with apologetic eyes. "Nyla has an owie. Be gentle."

"It's okay." I smile. "I really needed that hug."

Gavin swoops Emma up, and she says, "Mom told me I was too rough on Nyla last time."

"She's fine, look at her," Gavin says. "She'll even have her cast off soon."

"Really?" Emma asks.

"Just over a week." Catching the scent of something yummy, my belly rumbles. "Oh, Linda, you outdid yourself again, didn't you? Is that lasagna I smell? Please tell me it is."

"Complete with garlic bread," Linda replies. "Come on in."

We follow Linda through the front door, down the hall, past the living room, and into the kitchen. Inside the renovated home there's no hint of its hobbit-like exterior. It's modern with white walls, clean lines, and silver fixtures.

Without asking, Linda hands me a glass, and says, "Pinot. Gavin, wine or beer?"

"Beer," Trace answers as he closes the garage door behind him.

He's still in his suit—a proper one with a black jacket that matches his black slacks, and a white shirt with a bright blue tie, and a brown leather briefcase in hand— he looks to have just come from the office.

Trace thumps Gavin's back, and says, "Everything is a go on that one. What a rough Thursday."

Linda hands them each a beer, and says, "You're always late because of a rough day. Isn't that the truth, Nyla?"

"She wouldn't notice," Gavin says. "If she does manage to make it home before me, she goes right to work in her home office where she stays long after I get home. It's me prying her away from work."

I bump Gavin with my shoulder, though I don't say anything because he's right.

Trace pulls at his tie. "If you'll excuse me, I'm going to change."

Alex throws open the back door, catching it only after it thuds against the doorstop. With round oh-no eyes, he says to Linda, "Sorry, it just flies open."

"Mmm-hmm."

"What?" he replies as he walks over to me, football under his arm and clothes a patchwork of green grass stains and brown dirt.

"Practicing?" I ask.

"Yeah, Dad got me a net that catches the ball, for drills."

"He's a starter tomorrow," Linda says.

I hold my hand up for a high five, and he slaps it as if trying to prove he is a big kid. "Wow! That's exciting."

"Can you come to watch?" Alex asks.

"Of course. I haven't seen you play yet."

He bumps his fist in the air, then snags a cracker from the cheese platter.

"Hey," Linda says, swatting his hand away. "You go shower and put on clothes that aren't filthy."

Alex darts around Linda to get a slice of cheese, and with an innocent face says, "Okay, Mom."

Linda waits until Alex leaves the room before she says, "I swear that kid is gonna drive me bonkers. Suddenly in fifth grade, big man on campus and quarterback, you'd think he's a star."

"It's good for you, Lin," Gavin says. "Remember what you were like when you were ten, almost eleven."

She gives him a death stare. "I was an angel."

Gavin snorts as he brings his beer to his lips, and under his breath says, "Yeah, just like now."

"Best be careful, Gavy," Linda says as if she's got the real dirt on him. Then she scoops up the cheese tray and says like a proper hostess, "Okay, let's turn on the game."

The TV room off the kitchen is equipped with three large, gray couches shaped like a horseshoe and an enormous projection screen TV.

"Should we plan to eat dinner at halftime?" Linda asks.

"Whenever it's good for you," Gavin says as he takes a seat on one of the couches, pats the spot next to him indicating for me to sit there, and picks up the remote from the table. "Or we can pause it whenever you need."

I make a strangled sound. I hate pausing a game, it should be watched in real time.

"We can pause it for lasagna and garlic bread," Gavin says.

Emma bounds into the room and hands me a drawing. I have no idea what it is, but I think a fair guess would be a rainbow.

"I made it at school for you," she says.

"For me?"

She crawls onto the couch next to me. "My teacher said it's really good."

"It is."

I can't believe how much Alex and Emma have changed in the year I've known them. Emma is in kindergarten now, and already she's as articulate as some adults I know. Alex is shifting from a child to something more teenage like; preteen I think they call it.

Once we're adults, we don't often talk about how much people change. We assume the person we knew last year is exactly the same today. But I think, for some of us, just like kids and teens, we change, shift, and evolve almost daily. Looking back on the last twelve months—the same amount of time I've known the Smiths—I see how much I've changed, and especially how much Gavin has changed me. I can only imagine where I'll be a year from now.

On the enormous television screen is a familiar face I've missed, Darren Dryer. Even though he's a retired running back, he looks like he still plays. He's bald, half by nature and half by choice, and has dark brown eyes that make women swoon. In his post-football career, he coached at the collegiate level before getting into commentating. For his first three and a half seasons, Darren co-hosted with another man who, mid last season, was let go for inappropriate conduct. That made room for my promotion from sideline reporter to co-host.

Darren and I have always had a great relationship, he's like a brother to me. We've talked regularly since the accident, but I haven't had a chance to tell him about my impending return.

Actually, I haven't told anyone about my plans. Last night, after hearing Gavin's results, I wanted to keep the focus on his great news. I was going to tell him on the way here tonight, but he was venting about a situation at work, and I didn't want to interrupt him. Tonight though, on the way home I plan to tell him.

"Hello and welcome," Darren begins in his robust, rouse-them-up-for-the-game voice. "I'm your host, Darren Dryer." He leans onto the anchor desk, and in a slightly calmer manner continues. "Now, before we get into the game, I have some exciting news to share with you. Our favorite host, Nyla Tripple, has recovered quickly, and she'll be back here," he taps my usual spot next to him, "in just two weeks."

"Ahhhhhhh!" Linda's squeal drowns Darren out. "That's great news! Why am I just finding out? I'd have made a cake. Or bought one. Oh heck, we can go pick one up!"

Gavin, eyes still on the TV, says, "Yeah. Why are we just now hearing this?"

I place my hand on top of his, but he doesn't turn his over to take mine as he usually does.

"I just talked to Perry yesterday—"

Gavin slides his hand from mine and stands. He picks up my empty wine glass and his bottle. "Anyone else need a refill?"

"Sure," Linda says. "You can open the other bottle on the back counter. It's the same thing."

When he leaves the room no one needs to say a thing, but innocently Emma says, "Uncle is mad. Why?"

I grab my crutches and go after him. In the kitchen, Gavin is opening the wine bottle with the swift efficiency of a wine sommelier.

"I'm sorry," I say.

"For what?" he replies.

"Not telling you. It was an accident."

"Accident? How on earth can that be?"

"It wasn't, you're right."

"When did you decide this?"

"I talked with Perry after we had lunch."

Gavin sets the open bottle on the counter. "Perry knows you're not ready. Why on earth would he put that pressure on you?"

I tap my finger on the rail of my crutch and look down at my foot.

"Nyla?" Gavin says. "Look at me."

"It wasn't his idea or request, rather, it was mine."

He shakes his head, then pinches the bridge of his nose.

"I didn't want to bring it up during your celebration," I say.

"The entire drive over?" he asks.

"You talked about work, your Yamhill project."

"This would have been something to interrupt me about."

"I knew you'd be mad, Gavin. I didn't want to rock the boat that's just steadied. And you've got so much going on right now."

He leans heavily on the counter. "What is your plan then?"

"I leave after my appointment a week from Monday," I say, abashed.

He snaps his fingers. "Cast off, and then," he makes a mock plane with his hand like it's taking off, "whoosh. You're off again. Like nothing happened."

"Not like nothing happened." I move closer to him and take his hand. "But I need to get back to life, living it again. Doing what makes me happy, Gavin. This is my purpose, just like building things is yours. Imagine living and breathing, but not being able to do the work you love."

He laces our fingers together, and calmly says, "For the record, I think it's too soon. And why wouldn't you tell me you were thinking about this?"

"Because I hadn't been thinking about it. When I called Perry about my missed deadline I suddenly decided, or I realized, I had to get back to work."

"This is what I've talked about before. I want to be a part of your life decisions, especially the decisions that affect our life."

"I'm not a part of your work decisions."

"But my work decisions do not impact my presence in the relationship like yours do. Your work changes the landscape of life, the way we live our days. Did you stop to think that while you might be ready to go, I'm not ready? Damn, Nyla, I almost lost you. I'd like just a few days with you while you're healthy and happy again before you're gone all the time. Did you think about that?"

"You don't understand. I need this to be happy again."

He clenches his jaw, then as though he's afraid to ask, says, "Are we still getting married?"

"Of course!"

"When?"

"I don't know. After the season is done. I bet I can push back the production start on *Behind the Sport* to make room for it."

He laughs in a disbelieving way, shaking his head, and takes his hand from mine. As he fills Linda's and my wine glasses, he says, "You're gonna squeeze me in, are you?"

"I didn't mean it that way," I say.

Alex appears at the door of the kitchen and looks between us.

"Hey, buddy," Gavin says with no hint in his voice of the frustration that rolls from his body. "Need something?"

"The game is just about to kick off," he says. "Nyla said she wanted to see kick off."

Gavin picks up the two wine glasses and his beer bottle with his broad hands. "Of course, we can't miss kick off, can we," Gavin says, artificially upbeat. "Ready, love?"

Back in the living room, Gavin and I sit back alongside each other. Where his body was soft and yielding to me before, it's now stiff, his hands folded in his lap. Nervously, I reach over and place my hand on his, this time, thankfully, he turns his over and squeezes mine tightly.

We all turn our attention to the game as the two teams take their positions. After kick off, Gavin's entire body relaxes. He leans into me, his lips so close to my ear that his warm breath rushes down my neck, and whispers, "I love you. Sorry for wanting to keep you to myself."

Our lives are like two partially overlapping circles of color. One is blue, the other yellow, but where they touch it's green. Gavin and I are two distinct individuals, and yet we are not. I'm not sure I'll ever think to talk to Gavin about every decision I make. Part of my success in life, especially my career, is because I make quick and decisive decisions on my own.

Still, Gavin is right, I need to talk to him more.

# CHAPTER 20

$\mathcal{I}$ used to declare myself the world's fastest packer, but I won't be setting any records today. The crux of my situation is that I need Gavin's help to pack, and he's not exactly happy that I'm leaving. Though reluctantly he's agreed.

Gavin follows me into our closet, and as I point to my purple suitcase, I say, "I appreciate your help with this. Really."

With a forced smile, he moves slowly to get it. "Going with the medium-sized one, are you?"

"The weather in Minnesota is all over the place. There's possible snow a couple of the days, in the forties a few others, and like sixty-five one day in the middle of it all. So I need to pack for all possibilities. Rain jackets to snow coats."

Gavin picks up my suitcase like it's filled with lead and sets it on the bench. "Sounds miserable. Are you sure you don't want to stay home?"

"I can get the rest of it," I say.

"No, I'll help. May as well enjoy that you need me to do something for you for the next couple of hours. Point and I'll retrieve."

Over the last week and a half, I've followed Oliver's training regime as if it were doctrine. Not only the exercise, but the eating. I've started to put on weight, thankfully, and definition has begun to return to my body. However, many of my clothes still don't fit right and some not at all. This means I have to pack more strategically. I select dresses that tie or belt, pants which used to be snug (though in a good way) but now fit loosely, and form-fitting workout wear, which always fits.

Gavin folds my clothes more neatly than I ever have, then stacks them into organized piles of shirts, pants, skirts, workout clothes. I blush, though I shouldn't, when he insists on neatly folding my lace undies, and slips them into the netting of the top flap. It's been so long since he's touched those panties on me.

"I'll need shoes as well," I say.

"Soon you'll need two, instead of one."

Gavin packs the five pairs of shoes I'll use for work. Then, with excitement bubbling over, I point to my favorite pair of runners. They're purple at the toe and fade to black at the heel.

"Will you be able to start running again?" Gavin asks as he packs them.

I squeeze my hands together, pressing them to my lips, I'm hardly able to contain myself. "I don't care what the doctor says, I'm running."

Swiftly, Gavin moves to me, presses his body to mine suggestively, then kisses as if begging for something.

"I'm very excited for you, love," Gavin says, threading his hands into my hair. "Although I'm much more excited for other activities."

Lightheaded from the rush of endorphins flooding my body, I breathe, "Really?"

"What do you mean, really? Of course, I am."

I turn my eyes up to his confused ones, and reply, "It just didn't seem like you've been . . ."

"Been?"

"Interested."

"Nyla, you've been bruised up until a couple of weeks ago. What kind of man would I have been if I'd . . . and since then I didn't want to pressure you. I've wanted you to make the first move, to show me I've got the all clear."

"Soon," I say.

"Any chance we could before you go? There's time to spare between your appointment and getting you to the airport."

"There might be, at best, ten minutes," I say.

"That's all the time I need."

"In your truck?"

"It would be a first for me."

I shake my head regretfully. "We can't."

"Come on. What's stopping us?"

"That time of the month," I say. When Gavin rolls his eyes at me, I add, "Sorry. You chose to date a woman, and that's part of it."

"I chose to not just date you, but to marry you. And I really, really don't care." He presses his forehead to mine. "I desperately need to feel you."

"How about we rent a cabin for the weekend or a house at the beach. And we can escape phone calls, computers . . ."

Gavin nibbles my ear lobe making my toes curl.

"And," I say, "I'll wear nothing for the entire weekend."

"Don't say anything else," he warns as his cock begins to harden against my thigh.

"This weekend," I say.

"You better have an early flight home Friday. I'm taking you directly to a secluded place, and you are 100 hundred percent mine for the weekend. Promise me."

"Okay."

"Promise."

"I promise you."

"Actually, I don't think I'll be able to make it all the way to this beach house. We'll have to stop on the way, someplace where no one can see, and experience truck sex."

"I've never done that."

"Good. We can have that first together."

•••

At my orthopedic surgeon's office, Gavin and I follow a nurse named Melody down the hall to a patient room. She offers us both a seat, and while I take one, Gavin politely declines. He keeps moving: bouncing knee, pacing, hands in and out of his pockets. I'm just about to ask him to stop because he's making me anxious when Dr. Abernathy enters.

I've attached a lot of weight to this appointment by telling myself it will be easier when . . . I'll be happier when . . . Gavin will be happier when the cast comes off. The elusiveness of this date made it easy to assume this and, perhaps in a way, not really deal with everything I should have.

"There she is," the doctor says.

Many would describe Dr. Abernathy as ordinary looking: five-ten, at best, with a medium build, dark brown hair parted on the side, brown eyes. He walks across the room to a stool on wheels, sits, and then slides across to me. Behind him, Melody is busy arranging things on a silver tray lined with a paper towel: small circular saw, scissors, cloths.

"Big, big day," the doctor says. "Let's get this cast off and be sure your leg still works."

I sit up straight. "Is that an actual concern?"

Gavin folds his arms and widens his stance as he looks over the doctor's shoulder at my leg.

Laughing as if what I said was a joke, Dr. Abernathy takes the small saw from Melody, and says, "This won't even touch you, and it if did it would be fine it's just—"

"I know how it works," I say. "My brother broke his leg when we were teens. Can we just get this off?"

The doctor turns the saw on; the high pitched sound makes me shiver. Even though I know this won't hurt, I squeeze my eyes shut. When at last the cast is pulled off, air rushes around my newly revealed skin.

"Oh good," Dr. Abernathy says. "It's still there. Come on now, open your eyes. While the rest of you escaped with bruising and scratches, this leg got chewed up."

Peeling my eyes open, I finally see my leg. The angry scars look like a ravenous creature took an enormous bite out of me. I run my fingers the length of my shin, feeling the jagged lines that have changed my once smooth leg to something that I can't even register as my own.

When the doctor stands, Gavin takes a step in his direction, and as if I'm not in the room, he says, "Nyla is expecting to get on a plane in a couple of hours. Do you think this is a good idea?"

Dr. Abernathy folds his arms and leans back against the wall. "Eh," he replies, waving a hand side to side. "I have a feeling what you or I think won't deter her. It should be fine, but be careful with these million-dollar legs. Now, how about you test it out and be sure I put the bones back together right."

Performance anxiety descends on me like it did when I tried drama in seventh grade, but I'm so eager to stand on my own two feet that I push through it.

"You're lucky," the doctor says. "Clean, simple break."

"Clean and simple?" I say.

"Your other injuries were much more concerning." He points to his head. "That swelling can be dangerous stuff."

"Running is my life."

"Retired, though. At least you don't have to worry about getting back into the starting blocks, and it can heal. You may limp like that for a while. You could use a crutch if there is discomfort. But, take it slow."

"Slow is foreign to Nyla," Gavin says.

"Slow," the doctor says seriously. "You need to take this with you." He looks around the room and grabs a cane. "Here."

"I don't need this."

"For longer walks, like through an airport, you might. Go on, start walking around."

Slowly, I begin to move. My leg feels funny, sort of like when you sit too long and it falls asleep. Though I feel an urge to sit back down, I keep moving.

"Your limp will fade over time," the doctor says. "Any discomfort?"

"No," I say quickly.

"Really?" He bunches his lips and looks at me like he wants another answer. "Okay. I spoke with Oliver this morning. He said you have a training regimen in place. Do you feel comfortable with everything?"

"Yes, we do," I say.

"Okay. Training is important and vital to your recovery."

"You don't have to convince me."

"I didn't think so. But I do think I need to convince you to not overdo it, and listen to the pain. This isn't something to push through blindly. With travel, today, be sure you have help. You shouldn't be carrying bags, and you might find walking through the airport a challenge." He turns to Melody. "Let's get the leg cleaned up before she goes." He shakes Gavin's hand and then mine. "You take care and work hard with Oliver. In no time, Tripple Threat Nyla, you'll be running again."

With my leg cleaned up, I walk out of the doctor's office on my own. Without crutches I'm free and restless, like I want to move faster, faster . . . to run.

Gavin walks alongside me, shoulders bunched and carrying my cane as if he might use it to destroy something. As we get closer to the truck, he lengthens his stride and reaches my door before me. He yanks it open.

"I could get it," I say.

"Hey, this is just me doing things for you, like I love."

When Gavin gets into the driver seat, he turns the truck on, then leans his head on the steering wheel. "I'm not comfortable with you going today," he mumbles.

"You thought the doctor would stop me, didn't you?" I snap and cross my arms over my chest. "I thought you'd been almost too helpful. Backfire."

He sits up and tries to shake the steering wheel, but it doesn't budge. "Now I'm an ass of a husband for not dropping everything to go with you on this trip. I'm not able to, though. I have a meeting with the mayor this afternoon, another with the city planner tomorrow, we're so close to breaking ground."

"Husband?" I ask.

With a bamboozled expression, Gavin asks, "Is that all you heard?"

I pat his thigh. "I got distracted."

He grits his teeth.

"I'm kidding, Gavin. Mayor, city planner, groundbreaking. You're a big man, you've got things to do, just as I do. I can take care of myself, you don't need to worry."

He lets out a loud breath and backs out of the parking spot. The truck is quiet as we work our way down the hill from the hospital and onto the highway. The longer we drive, the more Gavin's face bunches like a grumpy old man.

"I'll be fine. I'll walk very slowly and carefully through the airport, my bag is on wheels, and I'll call a cab instead of renting a car. Does that make you feel better?"

"No! No, it doesn't make me feel better! I love you, Nyla. More than anything. I hate that this experience keeps reminding me that I can't protect you from everything. That's it. I'll cancel my appointments and go with you."

"Absolutely not. You need to make those meetings, we both know it. This project is your baby, take care of it." I slip my hand suggestively up his thigh, its solid curve sends an electric pulse through my body. How could I have wondered if we'd find our chemistry again? "I'll be back Friday, Gavin, and I'll help you release all that pent up energy."

"I have a lot of pent up energy," he grumbles. "Now I'm worried about you in a totally different way."

"Trust me, I can handle you."

His face relaxes, and he settles back in his seat. He takes my hand, turns it over, and kisses the inside of my wrist.

Suddenly, leaving Gavin is much harder than I expected.

# CHAPTER 21

At the Minneapolis–Saint Paul Airport, I exit the jetway where a man says, "Ms. Tripple? I am Marcus. I'm here to help you."

His shiny, gold name badge is engraved with black letters that read "Marcus, Passenger Assistance." While he's tall and lean like a distance runner, his company-issued, black-polyester vest and slacks with deep creases along the front are a bit snug.

"I apologize, Marcus," I say, "but I'm confused. I didn't arrange for passenger assistance."

He pulls a paper folded like an accordion from his back pocket, smooths it against his chest, and reads, "Nyla Tripple, transport to taxi service. Arranged by a G. Boston."

"He did, did he?"

"Yes, and when I saw your name I was certain it had to be you. There can't be another Nyla Tripple in the world, can there? May I?" Gently he lifts the bag from my shoulder then takes the handle of my carry-on. "Shall I take that as well?" He asks of the cane in my hand.

"Sure," I say and happily hand it over. I only brought it with me because it made Gavin feel better, but I haven't used it, and still refuse to.

Marcus loads my items onto a little-motorized car. I hop into the front seat next to him.

"I'm a big fan, Ms. Tripple," Marcus says.

"You like football?"

"Well sure, yeah," he says with a shoulder lift. "But I'm a runner. I go to the junior college here in town, but I'm hoping to transfer soon." He points at my leg. "I had an accident, too, a year ago. My leg is still healing."

"I just got the cast off today."

"Congratulations!"

"What events do you run?"

"Anything 3,000 and up. I'm not a good sprinter like you."

"Well, I'm not a good distance runner like you. I mean, I love to run nonstop for myself, but I never raced long distance."

Marcus weaves us through the airport around people, other little vehicles, and straight for the exit.

"I have a bag that I need to pick up," I say.

"Actually, there was an arrangement made for the bag. It's being delivered."

"Delivered? To where?"

"When we get to the spot, I'll read over the instructions."

"What spot?"

He points up ahead near the windows, and says, "No way," like a child seeing a superhero.

Darren Dryer is there with a sign that has my name scrawled across it in his challenging-to-read handwriting. He's in his standard casual attire of loose-fit, dark jeans and an untucked button-down shirt.

Next to him is my friend and cameraman, Tate. Tall and wiry, his sharp cheekbones and long nose make him appear more serious than he is. One of his shoulders sits lower than the other as if he's lugging a heavy camera. In his hand is a bunch of balloons, and at his feet is my purple suitcase.

I can't imagine how long it took Gavin to arrange all of this. While the overabundance of caution is unnecessary, I'm humbled by his thoughtfulness and care, even far away.

"Well look who it is," I say.

"Miss us?" Darren asks.

The two men swallow me with their arms in a happy, family-reunion-like hug. I melt into their caring embrace and feel a whole new calm wash over me. I've told myself, and others, that I wanted to get back to work for the focus and to have a purpose to my days. But, it's also been for these guys and everyone else that I work with. They are like family, and I like to be around people.

"Gavin called, apparently?" I say when they finally let me go.

"He doesn't have all the good ideas," Darren says. "We were going to pick you up anyways. But yes, he did call, and was insistent and specific about things."

"What things?"

Darren lifts his hand with one extended finger, and says, "We were to be here to get your bag and pick you up." He extends a second finger. "You are not to drive."

"I can drive."

He holds up a third finger. "You are to have someone with you at all times."

"No way."

"I'm not done." Fourth finger. "You are not to exert yourself."

"Come on."

Fifth finger. "You're to use your cane. Where is it?"

"I'm not using it."

Marcus gives my two bags to Tate, then holds the cane between the three of us.

"You take it," I say to Darren.

"Look, I'm not sure which is scarier, an irate Gavin for not following orders or an irritated Nyla."

"It's me," I say with a squinted eye. "I assure you."

Darren takes the cane. "For some reason, I think that's true."

"Good men worry about their ladies," Tate says. "I worry about mine all the time even though she says I don't need to."

"Is that everything you'll be needing today, Ms. Tripple?" Marcus asks.

"Yes, sorry. Let me introduce you. I think by the looks of it you know Darren. And this is Tate, he's the best cameraman in the business, and you wouldn't see us if it weren't for him."

Marcus is young enough that he probably only saw Darren play near the end of his career. He's one of those football stars, though, that people will always talk about and compare young players too. Everyone knows who he is, regardless of age.

Darren, Tate, and I go outside into the cold Minnesota air. I follow them to a white Mercedes SUV that is parked with the hazard lights flashing. This is the area where passengers are typically dropped off, not picked up.

"Parked illegally?" I say to Darren.

"I told the security man I was picking up an injured woman, and he didn't ask any questions."

There are some things people wouldn't even think to do or ask for. But for Darren, if it makes sense to him, he just does it. If it requires permission, he asks in a way that people seem incapable of saying no.

Darren loads my bags into the back. Then Tate tries to stuff the balloons in, but each time he goes to close the hatch, one pops out. It takes six tries and Darren's help before they can finally shut it with one still hanging out.

"It's just going to have to stay there," Tate says, setting his hands on his hips.

"It will be fine," Darren says.

"We might lose it," Tate says.

"If we do," I say, "that's okay. I always love to see balloons floating in the sky. They're like little happy messages."

Tate nods in agreement, then he rushes ahead of me to open my door. After I'm in, he gets into the back where he scoots into the middle seat.

"I can't see a damn thing," Darren says, checking all his mirrors. "Between those balloons and your head, Tate."

"Neither of which I can do a thing about," Tate replies.

"You've got an enormous head, man."

"Why, thank you for noticing. My mom said it's because I'm smart."

"It's true," I say.

Tate squeezes my shoulder. "I've missed you. I'm tired of staring at this guy's ugly mug."

"I don't know," Darren taps his cheek, "my wife claims I'm quite handsome. Maybe you have the best job in the world."

"Like I said," Tate adds, "it's good to have you back, Nyla."

"You have no idea how happy I am to be here."

•••

The upscale hotel room has crisp, fluffy bedding, dark wood furnishings, and a marble desk with a gold lamp. Plus, I have a great view of downtown Minneapolis.

When I stay in a hotel, the first thing I do is settle in. Going about my usual routine, I put my clothes away in the drawers and on hangers in the closet, then I unload my toiletries in the bathroom. The next thing I usually do is head out to meet someone for dinner. Tonight, though, I'm too tired.

I order a sandwich and salad from room service and eat it while I watch AST. After I get ready for bed, I pull back the covers and collapse into the luxurious bedding.

I grab my phone from the nightstand, and just as I'm about to call Gavin, it rings.

"Handsome," I say, "I was about to call you."

"Good to know we were thinking about each other," Gavin says.

"I'm always thinking of you."

"I bet you are. How's Minnesota?" he says with an exaggerated accent. "Are you all settled?"

"Yes. And I was welcomed to the great state by Marcus, Darren, and Tate."

"Who's Marcus?"

"Airport assistance. A very unnecessary thing."

"Well, I had to be sure you weren't pushing yourself there."

"How'd the meeting with the mayor go?"

"Great. He and his wife will be at the groundbreaking. She's a piece of work, by the way."

"Oh, really?"

"Yes."

"If there's already an enormous hole in the ground, why are you groundbreaking? Hasn't the ground already been broken?"

The lot Gavin purchased on Yamhill Street in downtown Portland already has a deep, one-block by one-block hole in the ground. It's sat there with rusting rebar, bordered by chain-link fence covered in plyboard for years. Once, it was someone's dream, but the money ran out. No one wanted it until Gavin came along.

"We're starting over, in a lot of ways," Gavin says. "New digging will have to be done. But really, the groundbreaking ceremony is to mark the beginning of the project."

"I know. I was only kidding."

"I'm wondering, love, if there is any way you could make it. I know you're busy with work and travel. But it would mean the world to have you by my side with a shovel in your hand."

"I'd get a shovel?"

"I'll get you a gold one."

I laugh at that, but it fades into, "Gavin, I don't know, I mean . . . I just, or am just, getting back to work. When is it?"

"We're working on a date. But I thought if we did it on a Tuesday, that it could work for you. I mean, it's not like missing a couple practice games would be the end of the world."

"That's also when I do player interviews and talk with coaches. I don't just—"

"I know, I know. I wasn't trying to be rude. I'd just really appreciate it. But I also don't want to impact your work."

I smack my palm against my forehead and inwardly reprimand myself. "Send me the date, and I'll do my best."

"In some ways, this project makes me think of us. I was starting it when we met. It's also the last thing I closed with Samuel."

Pop worked with Gavin on all of his commercial real estate purchases, and they sat on a few boards together. They knew each other for years before Gavin and I met. Pop gently encouraged me to consider Gavin when he learned that we'd met at the airport. Then he strongly encouraged me not to give up on Gavin when I learned he was a cancer survivor. Of course, there was the day of the accident when Pop, yet again, reminded me to be the partner Gavin deserved.

"I'm sorry, Gavin. Of course, I'll make it."

"Thank you, love. As soon as it's scheduled, I'll send you the date. There are many moving parts to bring together, but we're hoping in the next couple of months. How's the hotel?"

"Really nice."

"The way you said that makes me doubt that it's nice."

"No, it is. It's a very nice hotel."

"What, did they put you next to the elevator or the ice maker room?"

"They know not to do that." I run my hand over the empty space next to me in this king-sized bed. "It just isn't home, and I miss it a little already. See, I was off the road too long, and I got too comfortable at home."

"It's okay to miss your bed. I always do when I travel."

"I miss that, but really, handsome, it's you I already miss. Even though we've seen each other more in the last month than we probably have in our entire relationship."

"That can't be true, and if it is, what a depressing thought. Friday will come quickly."

"Maybe I'll find a red-eye out Thursday."

"Don't do that to yourself."

"You're right. I'll survive the torture of an empty bed and just have to fill my head with thoughts of football."

"You know, you could still fill your head with thoughts of me when you're gone. I'd prefer that over you thinking about football and, well, the players when you're in bed."

"The only problem is when I think of you, it turns me on."

"Love," he purrs, "that isn't a problem. That's what happens when I think about you alone in bed too."

# CHAPTER 22

The next morning, I open my eyes alert and ready for the day. I roll out of bed and put on my leggings, sports bra, and shirt that I set out last night. Then I drink a bottle of water as I roll out my yoga mat. This is how I always start my days on the road. I've missed this pattern in the same way you miss an old friend who's vital to the happiness of your life.

As I move through my sun salutations—ligaments tighter and muscles weaker than I'd like—I am grateful for all of the work Oliver has done with me. Without him, I'm not sure I'd be able to do this much.

Stretched and ready to get outside, I put on socks then lace up my running shoes. My heart beats like a child being let out early for summer break as I step out of the hotel and into the new day. It's warmer than yesterday, nearly fifty-five already. This should be the warmest day of my visit. I'm not sure how the snow they're calling for will be here in just two days. Though I know a change in the wind can bring a whole new weather system, and with it unseasonable occurrences.

I walk east until I reach the Mississippi River, then continue along the waterfront a short distance before I come to Stone Arch Bridge. I take the thoroughfare along with a steady flow of people, some on foot and others on bikes.

The sound of the rushing river below and having walked a whole mile brings me a new sense of calm. My lungs open and the muscles in my chest, tight from weeks on crutches, ease.

A man bumps my shoulder as he runs past, and he doesn't turn back to apologize. Instantly I'm irritated, and not because he was rude, but because he passed me. A slow jogger passed me! I increase my speed from that of a casual walk to that of a speed walker. Then I'm jogging. I run faster and my limp fades until it's gone entirely.

With each foot strike on the brick bridge, the stress that accumulated over the last few weeks shakes loose. A new excitement about life blooms, making me feel euphoric. I want to share this great feeling with someone. I nearly stop a woman in pink pants running the opposite direction, but not wanting to sound like a crazy woman, I resist. I'll call Gavin as soon as I return to my hotel room. Even though I don't usually bother him in the middle of the day, I'm sure he'll be happy to hear my good news. I won't tell him I ran, though, maybe that I jogged.

A tap on my shoulder catches me by surprise. As I turn to see who it is, a bolt of pain shoots through me and steals my breath. The side of my foot drags along the pavement, tripping me.

As I fall, everything slows, just like it did in the car accident. Does this happen to give us more time to react, to save ourselves? I should brace to protect my face, but I only want to save my legs.

A hand slips around my waist, and for a fraction of a second, I'm yanked back into something hard and hot as fire. The person's grip falters, and I hear a deep curse, then he says, "I got you." He regains control of me; one hand cups the back of my head nestling my face into a silver shirt, while the other one tightens around my back. He's a warm cocoon, and I feel safe even though together we fall.

On impact, I bounce in his arms as if they're made of bungee cords, then something sharp strikes my head. Slowly I float to the ground, and the heavy weight of him lays over me. His chest pressed to my face blocks all light. I recognize the scent of him, ocean-like, yet I can't place it.

The man scrambles off of me. For a second I see the blue sky patched by gray clouds above me, then Blake's face fills my vision. I can see every one of his impossibly long eyelashes that frame his eyes, blue as the sky above, like Lorenzo's. I never noticed that before.

"Nyla? Nyla?" He cradles the side of my face. "Nyla. Say something."

My breath eludes me.

"Please say something," he begs.

I shake my head yes. "I'm okay."

I lift my hand and cup his red chin. "Are you okay?"

His body eases as if a weight has been removed from him, and his eyes close as he works to regain control of his breath.

His eyes open again and he looks down the length of our bodies—my thighs between his, private areas intimately aligned—and seems to just notice where he is. "I'm so sorry," he says and presses quickly away from me.

"Are you two okay?" the woman in pink pants asks, kneeling down next to me. "Do you need an ambulance?" she asks me.

"No," I reply. "I'm okay. Thank you."

Blake helps me to my feet. He brushes the hair away from my face, his fingers stilling as they sweep over the scar on my cheek. The tightness around his eyes makes me think he's about to say something important, but the woman says, "I have some tissues." She holds out a crumpled wad to Blake. "It's all I have. You're bleeding badly. Do you want me to see if I can find someone?"

Blake's dark blue athletic shorts stop just above his knees, leaving them completely exposed. Blood trickles down his shins, through his thick hair, turning the tops of his socks from white to red.

"I'm okay, thank you," Blake says.

"How about you, sweetie?" she asks me.

"I am fine, thanks to Blake here."

"Actually it isn't thanks to me, it's my fault." To the woman in pink pants, Blake says, "We'll be okay. Thank you, ma'am."

I begin to dig into my pocket in search of a tissue I may have, while lowering to my knees to help Blake, but he catches my elbow to stop me.

"I'm fine, Nyla," he says. He cups my face and makes me look at him. "You're sure you're okay? You don't sound okay. Look at me."

I look into his blue eyes and say, "I am."

"You didn't hit your head, did you?"

I touch the top of my head which feels like it's bleeding, but it isn't.

"That was my chin," Blake says. "Sorry."

"Really, I'm okay. Don't worry about me. You, on the other hand."

Blake bends down and picks up a pair of white earbuds, then hands them to me. "I think these are yours."

I stuff them into my pocket. "Your knees are oozing blood, and you're picking up my earbuds." I grab the tissues the woman gave him from his hand and kneel, this time too quick for him to catch me.

"Stop, you don't have to take care of me," Blake says.

"This is my fault." I try to clean the trail of blood, but it only smears into the hair of his leg. "There are rocks in your knees."

"I feel it."

I stand quickly, jog to a garbage can where I throw away the used tissues, then go back to him.

"Where are you staying?" I ask.

"The Skywalk Hotel," he replies.

"Me, too, but that's a mile back if I'm guessing right. Can you walk that far? Or I could call someone."

"No, let's walk. I'll be fine."

"I have a small first aid kit in my bag at the hotel, but it won't have everything to take care of this. There's a drugstore on the way, we'll stop there."

Blake looks at me and takes a deep breath. As he releases it, he says, "I'd appreciate the help," as if he doesn't want to admit it.

My limp returns on the walk back to the hotel. About a block from the drugstore, Blake begins to slow, and he walks more gingerly. I cup his elbow and wrap my other arm around his ribs to take a little of his weight.

"We're probably comical to see helping each other," I say.

He snorts a laugh. "I'm an ass. I kept calling your name. I didn't see you had earbuds in. I'm really sorry. I didn't mean to scare you."

"No apologies, all is fine. We'll dig out those rocks and get you bandaged up. I'm fine, really."

"You're limping."

"I was limping before."

"No, you weren't actually. I was stunned to see you going so fast. I barely caught up to you, and it took all I had."

"It disappeared when I was running."

At the drug store, Blake elects to stay outside while I go in. I always carry a twenty and my ID when I go for a run. It's enough to purchase a pack of large bandages, packets of alcohol swabs, and gauze. As I wait in line to pay, I watch him through the window, and it's clear he's in pain.

Many years ago, at the first football game I sideline reported at, I met Blake. Being a well-known sportswriter, I knew who he was before he introduced himself.

Our professional paths cross at least a dozen times each year. When we find ourselves in the same city, we often get together, though usually with other colleagues.

There was a time last year, though, when the two of us hung out alone. Embarrassingly, I didn't realize until the third night that he thought we were on dates. He's sweet, handsome, and a sports expert—any woman would be fortunate to date him—but I wasn't sure what, if any, feelings I had for him. Things with Blake never went anywhere because it was about the time I met Gavin.

On the morning of my accident, I learned that Blake joined our Thursday crew. He took over my old post as the sideline reporter. I haven't had a chance to talk with him, but I did text him a congratulatory message that day.

With my bag of first aid items in hand, I return to Blake outside. "Doctor Tripple at your service."

"Doctor? Does that mean you're going to charge me?"

I wave him off, and say, "Nah," then place my hand below his elbow to help him walk again.

"You've been doing a great job, Blake," I say.

"Have you been watching the games?"

"Nothing stops me from watching football. Well, except a medically induced coma."

"Yeah, that'll do it."

Walking through the hotel lobby, we get several funny looks. A man at the front desk offers us help, but I tell him that we've got it.

Once inside my hotel room, I point to the bathroom. "I think it will be best if you get in the shower and wash your legs off. Then let them air dry, and we'll see where we're at."

Ten minutes later I have Blake sitting on the bathroom counter. His knees are skinned up, and already there is dark bruising. I pick out the rocks with the crappy, plastic tweezers that came in my little first aid kit.

"Gauze, please," I say.

Blake hands me a square of gauze, and humorously says, "Blood and wounds apparently don't bother you at all."

I remove the last rock and drop it in the trash. "Nah. My brother and I learned early on that if we took care of each other's cuts and bruises we wouldn't have to tell our mom what happened. Thus it would save us an earful about how we got them."

"How would you get them?"

"Roughhousing, playing sports, doing stupid things we shouldn't."

Once Blake is bandaged up, he slides off the counter, and we tidy up. Two washcloths have too much blood on them to be left for housekeeping, so I toss them in the trash.

"You know," I say, "I was actually going to give you a call today and ask if I could buy you a drink."

"I'd have a drink with you anytime, but is there an occasion?"

"Two really. First to congratulate you on joining our team. Second, I know this is outa left field, but do you remember a while back when my mom passed, and you helped me?"

His eyes drop from mine to the floor. "Yes."

"I don't think I thanked you."

"You did, that day."

"I cried on your shoulder and made a mess of your shirt with my mascara, then you drove me to the airport, and returned my rental car. I owe you more than a 'thank you.'"

"I don't think you do, but I'll be happy to have a drink with you if that makes you feel better."

"It would make me feel better. I have a dinner meeting tonight, meet me in the hotel bar, say eight?"

"That sounds good."

I put the rest of the large bandages and alcohol pads, plus the antibiotic ointment, in the plastic bag and hand it to him.

"If you need any more help with those knees, just let me know. And again, thanks for catching me. Now I've got to kick you out so I can get ready. I've got a player interview soon."

•••

I'd planned to wear a charcoal-gray skirt today, but it isn't in my bag. I do, however, find my royal-blue skirt, Gavin's favorite. Whenever he sees me in it, his eyes look as if they're going to fall out of his head. Of course, then, it never stays on me long. I put the skirt on and pair it with a rose color blouse. It's the first professional outfit I've worn in weeks, and it feels good. Confidence fills me as I slip on a pair of cream flats and head out.

I take a cab to Minnesota's training facility to meet Pete Monroe. He and I have something in common: on

Thursday we return from nearly career-ending injuries. Okay, so mine wouldn't have been a career-ending, more of a life-changing one. But still, at the same time, we are returning.

Pete's cocky nature is well known. He frequently interrupts people before they've fully asked their questions, and his grand effort at verbose descriptions are rarely understood. To me, though, he's always been kind and accepted my interview requests.

"Looking strong," I say as I shake his hand.

Pete waves me off like a shy guy and sits down in the chair next to me. He straightens his suit jacket—something I've never seen him wear—and says, "I'm not physically as strong as I was, but I'm mentally stronger. The second is actually more dangerous."

He looks down to his hands folded in his lap.

"Are you ready?" I ask.

"Ms. Tripple, you have no idea how ready I am. I need this. I need to get back on the field like I need a heartbeat."

The man I interview for the next hour is not the one I knew. He waits patiently while I talk, as if he's genuinely interested in what I'm going to say. Then his answers are concise and articulate. While he still weaves in a few poetic lines, they work.

Once we wrap and the camera turns off. I stand as Pete does, and say, "You're different."

"Like a man who's found Jesus," he replies playfully. "The injury was the best thing that ever happened to me." He snaps his fingers. "Changed everything."

"Everything?"

"You have no idea."

"I might, actually."

"Touché, Tripple Threat. The leg by the way, and I say this with the strictest professional manners, looks good. You know, those gnarly scars," he runs his hand along his cheek as if indicating mine and then points at my leg, "take you from a badass looking woman to one who looks prepared to conquer the world."

I worried that the weight I'd lost would make me look weak, but I'd never considered that my scars might make me look strong.

"Thanks, Pete."

He places his enormous hand on my shoulder, and says, "My condolences for your father, though. I lost mine a few years back just as I was entering the league. He was my guiding light, you know. I'd have been a better man before, if he were still around."

I think about Pop constantly. I often wonder what would be different if he'd survived. And since I boarded the plane yesterday, I keep wondering what he'd think about my return to work this quickly. Part of me knows he wouldn't have approved, that he would have insisted I spend more time actually getting better. The very last thing I'd ever want in life, is to disappoint him.

Quite unexpectedly two tears fall from my eyes, something about them further softens Pete's enormous body. He opens his arms and wraps me in a big bear hug that reminds me of how Pop hugged me. Without hesitation, I hug him back, and quietly, I say, "Thank you."

# CHAPTER 23

*D*arren pats his full belly, and says, "I just don't get it, Tripple. How can I not be a cool dad? How is it possible that they are embarrassed to be seen with me?"

He's had me in stitches this entire meal with stories of raising his thirteen- and fourteen-year-old daughters, both of whom are wonderful kids. He's overprotective, nosey, and has no idea why this should, or does, bother them.

"I have no idea," I say, laughing as I take the napkin from my lap and set it on the table.

The waiter returns the payment folio to Darren. He quickly signs his name on the credit card slip then slaps it closed. "Well?" he says, "How about we head to the hotel bar?"

"Sounds great. I was actually going to head there to meet Blake."

"Oh?" Darren asks as he puts his coat on.

"I told him I'd buy him a drink tonight."

"Will I be intruding then?"

"Never."

"Onward then." He holds his hand out for me to lead the way.

On our walk back to the hotel we run into Tate on the street.

"Movie?" I ask.

"Yep."

When we travel, Tate always catches a movie or two. Once, I offered to go with him, but he politely declined.

"Was it any good?" I ask.

"Nope," he says.

"Then I won't even ask about it. But what I will ask is if you'd like to join Blake and us for a drink in the bar."

"You know me, I'll never turn down a drink."

The hotel bar is posh but small. Blake hasn't arrived yet, so we find four stools at the bar. I place an order for myself and Blake, hoping he still drinks a Collins.

Within two minutes of sitting down, Darren, who makes friends wherever he goes, is deep in conversation with the bartender, Bill, about local spirits.

Leaning close to me, so no one else hears, Tate asks, "Everything good with Blake?"

"Yes, why do you ask?" I say.

He lifts a lazy shoulder in an answer.

"Tate?" I urge.

"I remember a while back, he looked interested, that's all. I haven't seen him around you since then, but he always perks up at your name." He takes a drink of his Scotch then slowly sets it down. "Then, of course, there's that photo that's made its way around the net today."

"Photo?" I ask, confused.

Tate looks over my shoulder, indicating something beyond me, just as I hear Blake say, "Hey guys."

I swivel in my chair to see Blake looking quite hand-some. He's changed from this morning into a well-cut oatmeal-colored sweater, and his blond hair is styled per-fectly. His blue eyes beam happiness at me.

"Hope you don't mind," I say and pat the chair next to me indicating for him to sit. "I picked up these two along the way." I tap the drink at his spot. "Ordered you a Collins. Did I remember right?"

Sitting down slowly, as if perhaps in pain, he says, "You did."

I imagine Blake's knees are quite sore, and they're prob-ably five shades of black and purple now. He makes no mention of them, though, and the next thing I know, we're swept into Darren and Bill's conversation. I listen, but at the same time, I'm distracted by Tate's comment about the circulating photo. Is it an old one unearthed from those accidental dates? Could it be something worse? Although, what really could it be?

An hour later the suspense of this mystery photo is killing me. I have to see it. I excuse myself, and head for the bathroom. It's only when I close the door to the stall that I realize I left my purse hanging on the back of my barstool with my phone in it. Frustrated with myself, I return to the bar. Since it would look weird to slip off again, I'll have to wait to see this picture until I get back to my hotel room.

After three solid drinks, I say to the bartender, Bill, "I've got to cash out. I'll take the tab for everyone."

"It's only nine," Darren says.

"Darren," I say, "I haven't exactly gotten back to eating normally yet, as you saw, so I can tell you I've reached my max for tonight."

"Are you—"

I hold up a hand, and say, "I'm fine, but I best stop now. Besides, I'm exhausted. You boys are welcome to stay, of course. In fact, Bill, can you leave the tab open and add it to my room?"

"Sure," Bill says.

"Actually," Blake says, "I think I'm done for the night too."

Tate leans back in his chair. "I'm ready to get some sleep myself."

"Ah, fine," Darren says. "I'll be responsible too."

After I pay, we all head for the elevators. Tate presses the button for the fourth floor, Darren the sixteenth, and then Blake the fourteenth. At the first stop, Tate gives me a sideways glance, and says, "Night," as he gets off.

On the fourteenth floor, Blake holds the door for me to go first. We amble down the hall toward our rooms. At first, I thought it was just his knees he hurt, but he's moving in a way that makes me wonder if his back hurts too.

"How are the knees?" I ask.

"They're fine."

"Are you sure you didn't hurt anything else when we fell?"

He looks sweetly at me and pats my back. "No, really, I'm fine. I think my old age is just showing. Thanks for your concern."

We stop at my door where I dig out the key from the inside zipper of my purse. I slip it into the lock and press down on the door handle.

"Take good care of yourself tonight," I say.

"I will," he says. "Thanks for the drink. It was fun."

"Anytime."

"You know, I owe you now."

"For what?"

"For taking care of me. Cleaning my blood, picking rocks out of my knees, and bandaging me up."

"Please, it was nothing. Thanks again, for your support that day."

Blake nods shyly, eyes still on me. "Nyla? May I ask you something?"

"Of course."

Blake shoves his hands into his pockets and looks down to his feet. "Before, like a year ago, we went out a few times." He looks back to me. "We had a good time, I thought. But then things stopped suddenly. Did I do anything to upset or offend you?"

"No. Not at all," I say. "I had a good time with you. It's that I was starting to see someone about that time."

"Gavin?"

I nod yes.

"I just wanted to be sure, since we're working together more closely now, that I didn't do anything."

"No. You're a great guy."

As Blake turns to walk away, he says, "Thanks, Nyla. You're a great woman. You have a good night."

I watch him walk down the hall and turn the corner to his room. Then as I push my door, it weightlessly flies open. I stumble into the room with a startled screech and into Gavin's arms. He looks down at me with a sexy, world-stopping grin.

"It's just me," he says, his arms tighten protectively. "Sorry, love, I didn't mean—"

There is a THUMP, THUMP on my door.

"Nyla?" Blake yells.

"I'm fine," I holler as I turn and open the door. Blake looks past me to Gavin, and I step to the side and invite him in. "I was startled."

"It was supposed to be a good surprise," Gavin says, playfully.

I place my hand on Gavin's forearm. "It is, really. Blake, this is my fiancé, Gavin. And this is Blake, sportswriter and our new sideline reporter."

Gavin's shoulders draw back as he extends his hand and says, "Good to finally meet you."

"Yes, good to meet you as well," Blake says. "Now that I know you're safe, Nyla, I'll see you in the morning."

I close the door behind Blake, lock the bolt, then flip the safety latch. When I turn to face Gavin his world-stopping grin is gone. Instead, one eye is squinted, and his lips are pulled to the side.

When I book a hotel, I always add Gavin's name to the reservation. That way if he can join me at any point in my trip, he can always get a key. He's never shown up, though, without telling me first.

"You seriously scared the crap out of me, Gavin."

"I'm sorry, it was supposed to be a surprise," he says. "But it appears to have brought out the fact that you have a co-worker who very much wants to protect you. Among other things, I fear."

"I think you'd protect any female you were on the road with too."

Gavin sets his hand on his hip and begins to pace. His shoulders swell with a full breath. "I heard your entire conversation from the moment you cracked the door. I have ten-thousand alpha male things swirling in my head, and I'm trying really hard to calm down."

I nod, but don't say anything. I'm shocked Gavin listened to our conversation and even more so that it seems to have set something off in him. I replay the conversation in my head. It seems platonic enough, though, there was the question of our accidental dates. Still, it bothers me that Gavin may not trust me.

"A photo made it to my inbox today," Gavin says.

"To your inbox?" I ask.

"I have your name flagged so when you're mentioned anywhere, it's delivered directly to my inbox. I have one for myself as well, though I rarely get a notice on me. Your name, on the other hand, gives my inbox a workout some days. Especially today."

"It did?"

"There are photos."

"I haven't seen them, but Tate mentioned it when we were all having drinks."

"Tate? Was he with you tonight too?"

"Yes, he and Darren."

Gavin finally stops pacing, picks up his phone from the table, and after a few taps hands it to me. There is a series of three shots from this afternoon. One just after Blake and I fell, him on me. The second, as he pushes off of me. And the third, as he helps me up.

"Gavin. This looks worse than it was. I went for a walk today, and that turned into a run."

"You ran?"

"Yes. And I was listening to my music. Blake tapped my shoulder, and I turned to see who it was. The next thing I knew, we were falling. He saved me from hitting the ground. You should see his knees, and I think he hurt his back."

Gavin taps the phone screen hard. "Do you not see the way he is looking at you in those photos?"

I look at his phone again. "He's worried that's all."

Gavin grunts and shakes his head as if clear it. "I wasn't that worried about it. Irritated, yes. I mean, sure, I felt like I should protect what's mine."

"Me?"

"Yes, you. But after the conversation I overheard between you two." He points roughly at the door. "Nyla? What's going on?"

I tell him about the day my mother passed away. I leave no details out, even though he flinches with irritation when I tell him Blake held me while I cried.

"I owed him a drink, and it was long overdue," I say.

"All right, but, you dated him? I didn't know that."

"No." I hold up a finger like a correcting school teacher. "I accidentally went on a few dates with him."

Gavin sets his hands on his hips and hinges forward. "I have no idea how that's possible. How does one end up on an accidental date."

"On the road, I usually have dinner with colleagues. That's all I thought it was at first. Then I realized—it's hard to explain, Gavin. And it doesn't matter. It's history, and I'm happily engaged."

I look over my handsome man, still in his work clothes. A crisp white shirt rolled to his elbows, navy vest, and pinstripe pants. His shoes are off next to the side of the couch, but his socks are still on, apple-red with martini glasses on them.

A smitten smile lightens Gavin's face. "When you look at me like that, love, do you know what it does to me?"

"Did you go straight to the airport from work?" I ask.

"I packed my bag this morning, so I could go straight to the airport after work. That was way before those pictures made it to my inbox. I couldn't wait another day to see you."

I set his phone down on the bedside table, and ask, "You just wanted to see me?" Then I begin to move to him.

Gavin's feet stay planted, and suddenly he looks nervous. "Ummm, n-n-no," he stammers.

On Monday he said he needs me to make the first move, and even though I'm as nervous as our first time, I do. I press my chest to his and lightly skim my lips along the side of his neck.

"Nice socks," I whisper.

"That outfit," he says.

I look down at my chest as I lift it higher. "You like my shirt?"

"Yes, and that skirt. It hugs your ass perfectly."

"It accidentally made it into my bag."

Gavin grips the collar of my blouse and moves like he's going to rip it off.

I grab his wrists and say, "What are you doing?"

"Ripping this off."

"What do you think this is? Some steamy romance novel? Unbutton it properly."

He whimpers but listens. With his thick fingers, he tries to work the top button free, but after a few short seconds, he bites out, "Why the hell are they so difficult?"

"You're shaking," I say.

"I'm nervous. Can you please just undo them?"

He grabs the collar again, but I pull away.

"Don't you dare, this is one of my favorite shirts."

"You are killing me. Please."

I undo the top button. "Haven't you always," then the second, "told me that you're a very patient man, Mr. Boston? You've waited all this time, what's a few extra minutes to let me properly unbutton my shirt?"

Luckily I wore a nice bra, though it's beige and nothing special. Had I known Gavin was coming, I would have packed my sexy white one, and put on lace panties instead of these cotton ones.

My shirt half open, I ask, "Is this why you're here?"

Gavin watches my hands like an animal half-crazed from deprivation. "This and so many more reasons. I don't think you'll ever understand."

"Why is that?"

His emerald eyes refocus on mine. "The intensity with which you pull me to you, there is nothing like it."

"Like the sun?" I joke.

"No, Nyla. There is space between the sun and her planets. She always keeps them at a fixed distance. You. You're an entirely different kind of star. You pull me in. All the way."

I unhook the last button, and Gavin grabs the edges of my shirt and yanks it off. Then my skirt. He catches the edge of my thong.

"Don't you dare," I say.

"Why? I've never gotten to rip anything before," his hand tightens on my thong, "and I really feel like I need to rip something."

"This isn't the movies they won't just rip."

"Let's try."

I make a "tsk-tsk," then slowly turn. I slip the thong from my body. Then unhook my bra. When I turn back around Gavin is naked too.

"Quick man," I say.

"Touch me," he says.

"What part?"

He points to his lips. "Start here, but don't stop."

I kiss his lips and slide my hands up his obliques, where I feel his muscles quiver. "You like that?" I trail my lips down his neck, shoulder, then I begin to move lower, but he catches my elbow.

"It's already going to be embarrassingly fast. If you do that . . ."

"I don't mind."

"I do because I want something else right now."

"However you'd like it, handsome."

Careful of my leg, Gavin sweeps me up and lays me on the bed. His hand squeezes the back of his neck as he looks down at me. I feel more beautiful than I have in months.

"You're ready for me? Because you know once I start—" I slide my legs apart, and he lays down between them. "I'm afraid I'll hurt you." He nuzzles my neck. "You know I'll stop if you need to, right?"

"You won't hurt me."

Slow, juicy kisses along my collarbone as his hand traces the curve of my hip, ribs, breast, neck. Then slowly he slides into me. I feel his trepidation even though his eyes are wide, lids flutter.

"I've missed you," he says. "You're so warm, and, Nyla, I love the way we feel together. I've needed this."

I've only begun to climax when Gavin stills and pulses inside me. His forehead falls to mine. A curse, equal parts amazement and frustration, hisses from his lip.

"I told you," he says, "it would be embarrassingly fast."

I cup his face, kiss him. "You should never be embarrassed with me."

"Nearly two months, a near-death experience, and this is what I bring to you." He pulls out of me and slides down my body.

I grip his hair in my fist to stop his descent. "No."

"Let me—"

"Not right now. I'm satisfied. I enjoyed it."

"You didn't finish, which means it doesn't matter how it felt." He pulls my nipple between his teeth and looks up to me with hooded eyes.

"Remember," I say, "it isn't about the destination, but rather the journey."

"Right. Is that what you tell yourself on the race track?"

"I guess, perhaps, there are exceptions to that. But right now, Gavin, I just want to lay in your arms. I want that more than anything."

"I don't think you understand, I need to help you finish. I want to show you how much I love you. I need you to know . . ."

There is a piece of his self-worth tied up in his eyes, in this job, so I open my hand. Gavin's hair falls from my fingers. His lips touch every inch of my skin as he makes his way down my body. Then his warm breath floats over my thighs as he says, "I couldn't wait any longer knowing you wanted me too." He looks up to my eyes. "You do, right?"

# CHAPTER 24

 *S*ex, it changes a woman, but love, it changes her even more. There's a healthy blood flow in my cheeks that no amount of blush has been able to re-create. My lips that were deflated with little lines around the inside edges are now plump. The scar along my cheek which had been a ghostly white is pink; I don't know why, but I like it.

The bathroom door opens without a warning knock, and Gavin walks in. He places his hands on the counter, framing my hips, and runs the tip of his nose along the curve of my ear.

He looks at me in the reflection of the mirror. "You were taking a long time," he says.

"Sorry," I reply. "Bathroom is all yours."

He flashes his silly, I'm-so-comfortable-with-you noth-ing-matters grin. "Don't leave."

The toilet is blocked from the counter by a wall, but no door. As he uses the restroom, I laugh inwardly. Is it silly that I even missed this? He flushes the toilet and walks back around the wall. I slide over so he can wash his hands.

"What exactly did you need me to stay in here for?" I ask.

Gavin shakes the water from his hands but doesn't bother to dry them. "It would be a shame to let this large tub go to waste." He sits on the edge of it and turns the water on. There are little bottles laid out on a towel folded like a fan. He opens the second one he picks up then pours the whole thing into the stream of water.

Over the last few weeks, when I never once saw Gavin hard, I was concerned . . . do these new scars on my body turn him off? Perhaps now that he's had to care for my body, he won't be able to see me as a sexual woman. Are the whittled curves of my body unattractive? Or, is the oppressive sadness I carry too much for him?

Now, all of these concerns are gone. Head to toe, Gavin's muscles are relaxed. His cock is a satisfied weight between his thighs, but already it shows he'll be ready for more soon. A million people can tell me how beautiful I look, but the only opinion that matters is Gavin's.

"What are you looking at?" he asks.

My eyes jump up to his.

"Nothing."

He looks down to exactly where my eyes had been, then winks at me. "Ready?" He turns the water off and gets in. "Come on."

The tub is oversized for one, but not sized for two. And Gavin, a big guy as he is, takes up most of it.

"There is no—"

He holds out his hand, presses his thighs to the sides of the tub, and pats the water between them. When he looks at me like this, there is nothing I can do but listen.

I step into the water, then he sets his hands on the top curve of my backside and glides me down between his legs.

"There," he says. "We fit."

"Tightly, yes."

"Good thing you like to be close to me."

"Just me?"

"Yes. Because I love to be close to you."

The bubble bath Gavin poured in has swollen to a thick layer that looks like whipped frosting.

"When I bought my old house in Portland," I say, "it was the claw-foot tub that sold it to me. I used to take baths every single weekend before we started dating. I'd set a glass of wine on the old, wooden stool next to the tub along with a stack of magazines. The water would be cold by the time I got out."

"Funny. Have you ever used the tub at the house?"

"Once when you worked late this summer. I think I'll start taking long bubble baths again."

"Can I join you?"

"Anytime. I appreciate you coming tonight, Gavin."

He makes a deep, grumbly agreement.

"Not like that," I say. "Although I liked that too."

"Thank you for receiving my intrusion well. I wasn't confident in my decision based on how badly you wanted to leave Monday. But frankly it left me feeling so, I don't know what the right word is, scared maybe. I needed assurance."

"Of what?"

"That you'd still want me."

"Funny, I needed the same."

"How could you ever question my desire for you? Sometimes I wonder if I might drive you crazy with how much I want to be around you, and to help you."

"Gavin, you know I love you, right?"

"Yes."

"Do you trust me?"

Gavin's arms wrap my chest, squishing the mound of bubbles away. "Of course I do."

"I mean, like . . . completely. Is there any part of you that doesn't? Be honest."

"Have I done something that makes you think I don't trust you?"

"That day, when you told me you might be sick, I pushed you away when you needed me. And these last few weeks, they've been hard. I wondered if perhaps things have changed for you."

"That was painful, Nyla. To be honest, it was the most hurt I've ever been by someone."

"Ever?"

"I love you with everything I am. Because of that, rejection from you on any level hurts. It's all right, though."

"It isn't."

"I went insane and scared you. I'm sure if I'd been calmer and talked with you, things would have gone differently."

"What made you go insane, Gavin?"

"I promised if I ever got sick again, I'd let you go. But I can't. Cancer I can deal with, but not losing you. You're stuck now. No matter what. There is something I can promise you, though."

I try to say, "What?" but I fail. He brings his hands to my cheeks and wipes them with his wet thumbs.

"I'll make every day of your life, our life together, worth it. I will be worth the risk. Some days I wonder how I can possibly be enough for you. How just an average guy like me will be worth the risk, but damn, Nyla, I'm really trying. You're 100 percent—"

"Happily smitten, in love with you."

"That sounds better than what I was going to say. Stuck. I love you so much it consumes me, Nyla. It makes me want to be the best version of myself."

I brace my feet against the end of the tub so I can turn to kiss him. The movement instantly begins to harden his cock.

"I fear I might wear you out before the night is over," I say.

"Did I awaken the lioness?" he says into my ear.

"No, Gavin, you roared her back to life."

His hands dive below the bubbles sliding along my belly until they arrive at their destination between my legs.

"That feels good," I say. "But faster, maybe. Please."

"Mmm, no." He sucks my earlobe, and with his mouth still full, he adds, "Don't worry."

"I'm not worried, I just want to—"

"Relax."

His fingers move in an irregular, torturous pattern. Occasionally he intersperses it with the rhythm we both know gets me off in sixty-seconds flat. I try to push his hand away, to take over, but he's much stronger than me. And really, I don't want to fight how good it all feels.

"Just relax and let me try this," he says.

"Gaavvvin."

"You don't always have to be in control of everything, even yourself."

Intense, focused, and determined have all been used to describe me. I know these seemingly nice words are at times used to drop a hint: just let go. But you don't become an elite athlete or thrive in the world of journalism by being soft, or letting go. Relentless focus, consistency, and above all, being in control is how I've accomplished things. But is there a time to surrender? Is there a space to be softer? With Gavin, could I surrender it all? And, if I did, what would I find?

"There you go," Gavin whispers in my ear. "Does it feel good, to let go?"

"It's scary, but this, this feels good."

Air rushes into me, and my body stills.

"There you are," Gavin says.

"Here. I. Am. Yes."

Before, I'd always had a level of control when I came. But as I unravel now—entirely out of my control—I try to let myself be here; in the throes of total release.

It feels like nothing I've let myself experience before.

But, it's scary.

•••

After Gavin double checks the lock, the alarm on his phone, and turns out the lights, he slides into bed next to me. He snugs me close to him, my head on his shoulder. The tips of his fingers move lazily across the front of my thigh.

"I feel like a whole new woman," I say. "Like I've taken a super drug."

"You definitely took a lot," he says proudly, "I wasn't too rough, was I?"

"I might be sore tomorrow, but in a good way."

On the nightstand, the glowing blue lights of the bedside clock show 2:28 a.m. I need to sleep; tomorrow is a busy day. I'm wide awake, though, and my body is on high alert, hopeful he'll do something to me once more.

"Nyla," Gavin whispers.

"Yes?"

"Do others know you're completely taken?"

"What do you mean?"

"I trust you, Nyla. It's him I'm worried about. The way he was looking at you in those photos, and I heard the hope in his voice when you were talking. It said, 'invite me in.'"

"Noooo, nooo."

Gavin shifts away from me and clicks on the bedside lamp. Propping himself up on the headboard, he looks at me seriously. "He did, and I can tell you know it too."

"We can't control other people's reactions to us, Gavin. If I got jealous every time I saw a woman's jaw come unhinged when you walked passed, I'd have gone insane by now."

"This is different."

"Is it?"

"You work with him now. In fact, he'll get to see you more than me sometimes."

I sit up and face him, place my hand over his heart. "I have no interest in anyone except you. I've never done anything, and never will, that violates your trust." Gavin takes my hand, kisses the inside of my wrist, and pulls me to him. I kiss over his heart, then say, "I'm yours, body and soul."

"And I'm yours," Gavin says.

"We can't doubt each other. It can tear people apart."

"Fine," he says, gruffly.

"No, not fine. Do you trust me?"

"Yes."

I pull away from him and look into his eyes. "Do you?"

He looks at me wordlessly so long that I'm worried he's going to say he doesn't. With each passing heartbeat my shoulders inch up to my ears. When at last he says, "Yes, I do," the tension in my neck eases. Then he adds, "These last several weeks have been tough, though. It didn't shake my trust in you, as much as it's left me doubting myself."

"Why would you doubt yourself?"

He begins to work the edge of the sheet in his hand as he rolls his lips between his teeth. "You deserve more than me." I open my mouth to interrupt him—to protest this insane statement—but he covers my mouth with two fingers, and continues, "I need to be with you and touch you intimately to feel secure with you. Without that these last few weeks, and the way you've retreated away from me, well . . . do you understand?"

I shake my head no like an involuntary vibration, as I say, "You haven't even been interested in me."

"How would you know?"

I glance down at the sheet, where just below is his member that got quite a workout tonight.

Gavin says, "Do you want to hear how sick I am?"

"What?"

"Even when you were cut-up, bruised, crying, I wanted to touch you." His face bunches in disgust as he closes his eyes. "When I helped you shower, I imagined things that turned me off so I wouldn't get hard, and even then it was really challenging. It isn't easy to control, you know. Sometimes I had to rush or keep you from looking at me just because, well . . . What I really wanted was you, every single second. Even on your really horrible days, I felt desperate to be in you. Man, I'm a sick husband."

He opens his eyes cautiously as if he's about to see something he shouldn't.

I straddle him, wrap my hands behind his neck, and bring my forehead to his. "You called yourself my husband."

"Yes, about that." Gavin brings my engagement ring to his lips. "I can't wait until after football season. With everything that's happened, I need to marry you. Now."

"Elopement?" I ask.

"I'm not sure that's what it would qualify as, but call it what you'd like."

Gavin and I originally wanted a simple wedding, but once we began to plan it quickly swelled into a major event. We booked the winery where we had our first date, perfect for an outdoor August wedding. Then we lined up a caterer, photographer, and DJ. I bought a dress, he purchased a new tux.

The very thought of re-coordinating this wedding makes my head spin. It's too much for me right now, I've only begun to regain my footing in life. But instead of telling Gavin this, I say, "Okay. We can talk to Brad at the winery and see what's the next date he has open. Then we'll coordinate everything else."

"I already checked with Brad, they're booked this weekend," Gavin says.

"This weekend? Well of course they are."

"But our home in Maui, it's available. Will you marry me this weekend? We'll keep it simple."

"I like simple."

"Yeah?" His eyes light with excitement. "I already threw it past my family and yours, and of course Trace and Linda. Everyone is ready to purchase flights, they just need our go ahead."

I giggle in a carefree way. "Just hop on a plane to Maui and get hitched?"

"Please don't make me wait any longer."

"Sounds amazing to me. Sure! Let's do it!"

With a sweet smile, he tucks my hair behind my ear, and says, "Mrs. Boston."

"I may have hit my head in that accident, but I do recall that conversation. I'm keeping my name."

"Maybe on paper you are, but not in my mind." Gavin switches the lamp off. "Tomorrow I'll email everyone. I've already booked us on flights from here to Maui on Friday. We leave bright and early."

"Betting on a yes, were you?"

"You have no idea. Send Mia an email with everything you need from the house, and she'll bring it. She and Kevin are going ahead of us to get a few things lined up."

"What about return flights?"

"I haven't gotten that far yet. But I'll go with you wherever you are next week. Then we'll take our big honeymoon after the season when you can squeeze me in for a couple of weeks."

I nearly say that right after the football season ends, I go straight into filming *Behind the Sport*. But I stop myself and consider how this man has bent and twisted to be with me. It isn't just today. He's traveled on countless occasions. A couple of times he was only able to fly out for dinner and stay the night before catching an early flight the next morning.

I've never surprised Gavin on one of his business trips. Never have I accompanied him on one. He adds all of his trips to my calendar, though. Silent requests to be a part of his world too.

Sometimes I wonder if he deserves more than me.

# CHAPTER 25

*I*'m not sure what it is about our Maui house, but when I step through the door, my body relaxes as if the weight of the world has been lifted. It smells of fresh ocean air, and today there is a twist of orange from a three-wick candle that's lit on the white-marble island. Lined up next to the front door are several pairs of shoes. There is a sweater laid neatly over an arm of the couch.

Months ago, when I first walked into here, it was bare aside from the mattress in the master bedroom and a couch in here. Now it's fully furnished in soft fabrics and textiles that reflect the environment around the house—tans, greens, blues. Thankfully, unlike me, Gavin has an eye for design. When I shop, I find things I like, but I can't picture it in the house and discern if it works for the overall vision. Gavin, on the other hand, knows the moment he sees something if it works.

"Hello?" Gavin hollers.

When no one responds, I say, "They must be here somewhere. Let's go set the bags in our room, and then find them. They're probably outside."

As I follow Gavin down the hall to our bedroom, a swell of gratitude whooshes through my heart. In addition to his own carry-on and suitcase, he's lugging mine.

I peek into the first guest room. There is a playpen with a pack of diapers ripped open next to it, and an explosion of small clothes on the bed. Kevin and Mia have been here for two days. I asked Gavin what they were doing, but he wouldn't tell me. Neither would they.

In the second room, three suitcases are neatly lined up at the foot of the bed. Linda, Trace, and the kids arrived this morning. I'm not sure they'll all fit in here, but Linda said it would be okay.

Our bedroom is the last door at the end of the hall. Gavin sets our rolling luggage next to the dressers, then our carry-on bags on the bench at the end of the bed.

I go straight to the closet where I discretely stick the cane Gavin made me bring in the very back. I intend for it never to see the light of day again. There is another large suitcase in here, as well as two garment bags. Gavin and I sent Mia a list of things to pack on our behalf. I owe her big for this.

The sound of laughter flutters on the wind through an open window in the bathroom.

"Sounds like they're outside," Gavin says.

I turn to the door, but he quickly closes and locks it. He moves to me biting his bottom lip and already reaching for my shirt.

"Not right now," I say with a laugh.

"Come on, they don't even know we're here yet. How about a quickie? I'm good at those you know."

"Tonight, there will be plenty of time."

I grab a fistful of his shirt and lead him out of the bedroom as he groans in protest. We walk down the hall, through the large open living room, kitchen, and dining room. As soon as we step through the French doors to out back, we're met with a swell of applause, whoops, and "congratulations."

Kevin and Mia are here along with the Smiths, as I expected. Who I'm surprised to see—because we didn't know if or when they'd be able to make it—are Jax, Brooke, and Gavin's parents.

As Gavin takes my hand and leads me toward the group, he asks, "Are you all right?"

Words evade me, so I nod my head quickly and swipe a tear of joy tumbling down my cheek. I hug everyone like it's been years since I've seen them. Just as Kevin lets me go, a saucy voice from behind me says, "It's way too quiet out here to be a party."

I spin to see Ms. Marshall and Walter.

Her gray hair, which usually is pulled back into a loose ponytail, has been replaced by voluminous curls. They frame the strong bone structure of her face and impart a new youthfulness. Her aging clothes, always two sizes too large and ready for yard work, have been traded in for a pair of well-fitting yellow shorts, and an orange tank top.

"What?" Ms. Marshall says. "You didn't actually think I'd miss your wedding, did you?"

"But you said you didn't think you could make it work."

I called her the morning after Gavin and I decided to do this. When she told me she wouldn't be able to make it I worried it was because of the cost. A last-minute trip to Hawaii is spendy. I offered to pay for her travel, but she scoffed at such a suggestion. I have no idea what her financial situation is. She rarely buys anything, but I think it's more because there isn't anything she needs.

"I just wanted to surprise you," Ms. Marshall says. "Looks like it worked. You boys want to help Walter? We picked up the food. Bags and bags of food."

Ms. Marshall walks up to me and holds me by my upper arms for a brief moment before pulling me to her for a motherly hug. Her skin is soft and smooth like an old pearl.

"You look much better than the last time I saw you," she says. "Only a little limp I see, but other than that, you're standing on your own two feet."

"Much better," I say.

"Good, good," she says with a firm pat on my waist. "Wedding eve. Finally. Are you ready?"

"I think so."

Mia hands me a small, fishbowl-shaped glass filled with brown liquid, and says, "You think so? I hope you know so."

"I am. I'm ready." I take a sip of the drink. "Oh, this is good."

"It's a mai tai," Mia says.

"Careful, they're strong," Kathy says.

The men return with bags of takeout, enough to feed twice the amount of people here.

"I didn't realize it was going to be so much food," Trace says. "Thanks for picking it up, Ms. Marshall."

"My pleasure. Least I can do."

Our patio table has been extended to accommodate everyone. It's topped with a white tablecloth and covered in tea lights. I sit down in the chair Gavin pulls out for me. Trace sits across from us, and asks, "So are we going to rehearse anything tonight, or wing it tomorrow?"

Trace, who was ordained by the church of the internet this summer, is marrying us. Gavin and I aren't religious, and we want something simple and quick. We went over everything in July, and since it's so easy and it's just family here, I don't feel a need to practice.

"I think we got it," I say like we're old pros at this.

I look to Gavin for confirmation, but the moment our eyes meet his drop away, and he mumbles, "Yeah, tomorrow is fine."

I take Gavin's hand and shake it playfully. "Do you want to rehearse?"

"No, no. I mean we both know what we're doing, right?"

In my childhood home on the second floor, there is a hall of photos. It's a timeline of our family. It starts with my parent's wedding pictures. Then photos of Kevin and me on the days we were born. There are our school pictures; kindergarten through college graduation. Pictures of me atop every podium I'd ever stood on. Freeze-frame moments of me running where my legs are slightly blurry. Holidays. Vacations.

About three-quarters of the way down the hall, Lorenzo emerges into the montage. First, it was Christmas, all of us gathered around the tree. There's a photo of me in my princess, snow-white wedding dress with my handsome groom. Then, as if a flip is switched, he disappears from all of the photos. No gradual exit.

After my mother died, we never hung another photo, and we never took one down. It was her masterpiece, and with her exit, in some ways it felt complete. However, I have been tempted to slip a new photo in, one of Gavin and I, to show he, too, is a part of our family.

At Richard and Kathy's house, photos are sprinkled throughout like a random collection. Pandora is not in a single one.

Sometimes I'm hit with the reminder that I'll always be Gavin's second wife. It feels like I've come in behind a racer I know I should have beaten. It makes my belly flip, my skin crawl, knowing he once promised her what he's about to promise me. I've never asked Gavin about his first wedding. Was it big? Did she wear a white gown, too? Was he happy? More than anything, though, what I really wonder is when he said I do, did he really think it would be forever?

•••

Last night was the first time I slept in our Maui bed without Gavin. I tossed and turned a good portion of the night because no matter how I lay, I couldn't get comfortable. My mind wasn't running as it does for some the night before their wedding. Instead, mine was calm, almost thoughtless. I missed the weight of him in the bed, the way our skin regularly touches through the night. It's a bittersweet thing to know the comfort of his presence is so soothing to me.

Gavin and I didn't exactly agree to it, but keeping with tradition we were separated shortly after dinner yesterday. The guys went to a fancy hotel with a bar on the beach where you can sink your toes into the sand while you order your drink. "It's not a bachelor party," Kevin said, but Trace followed that up with, "Doesn't mean we won't drink like it's one!" All of us ladies, and kids, of course, stayed here at the house.

"You in there, sunshine?" Ms. Marshall says through my closed bedroom door.

"Goooood morning," Linda sings.

"Are you up?" Mia asks.

"I'm up and ready for the day," I call back even though the covers are still tucked up to my chin.

The door swings open and in walk the three women. Ms. Marshall, whom I've never seen in a dress, looks particularly radiant with her gray hair pinned into a French roll and a butter-cream yellow sundress. Mia and Linda are also ready for the day.

"What the hell are you doing," Ms. Marshall says as she pulls the covers off me.

Thankfully I actually wore pajamas to bed.

"Your groom will be here in two hours," Mia says.

I sit up and yawn. "It doesn't take that long to get ready."

"Well, hurry and get up so we can help you into your dress," Mia says. "I'm dying to see it."

"Look at it. You hauled it all the way from Portland. And it's a simple dress, I don't think I'll be needing any help into it."

"No, I want to see it on you for the first time, or as you put it on."

"And here," Linda sets a white silk bag down, "is your special lacy lingerie. I wasn't as polite as Mia, I looked at it. Poor guy is going to have an actual heart attack, you know that?"

I realized only after Mia left Portland that I forgot to have her grab my wedding day lingerie. Linda was kind enough to stop by the house and get it for me.

"I didn't want him to forget his wedding night. And since he's had this package several times, I figured I had to do something to make it different."

"Why do women think things like that?" Ms. Marshall peeks into the bag. "Men would never think to dress their willy up just because you've seen it thousands of times."

"Hey," Linda taps her chin, "that's very true. Trace has never offered to get dressed up, yet he happily gives me something new every Christmas and Valentine's Day."

"You should get him one of those G-strings," Ms. Marshall says. "I've seen one that looks like an alligator for the—"

"Got it," I say, as mental images conjure in my head that I try to shake loose.

Rania lets out a scream pitched high enough to shatter glass, and Mia turns for the door.

"We'll leave you to it," Linda says. "T minus two hours."

Ms. Marshall taps an invisible watch on her wrist. "I'm putting money on it that your groom is early. He didn't seem happy to be rushed out of here last night."

Linda closes the door behind her and Ms. Marshall.

I go about my routine: get dressed in my workout clothes, drink a bottle of water, and stretch out on my yoga mat. As I draw my knee to my chest, my hands close over the gnarly scars on my shin and startle me. I wonder how long it will take for me to be used to them.

I roll up the mat and then go to the front door where I slip on my running shoes.

"Runaway bride?" Ms. Marshall says.

"Nyla!" Mia snaps as she bounces Rania on her hip. "Where are you going?"

"I need to go for a run."

"I don't think you have time," Linda says.

All three women look doubtfully at me.

"It doesn't take me long to get ready," I say.

"It's your wedding day. It will take longer," Mia presses.

"I don't think so. Besides, I really need to get a run in."

The room falls silent, even the baby. I take a few steps back and put my hand on the doorknob.

"I promise, I'll be ready right on time. Besides, when have I ever been late for anything?"

"Well," Mia says, "There was this one really horrible time you were late."

All three women's eyes are filled with concern. Despite the sun pouring in through the windows, an icy mist wraps my bones. The bottom of my feet itch, though, and there is only one way to fix it. So, I do what I need, and run.

# CHAPTER 26

When I return home, a woman wearing a white chef jacket and hair pulled into a tight bun on the top of her head, is hard at work in the kitchen. There are pots on the stove, sheet pans on the counter, and she's whipping something in a stainless steel bowl.

"Hello," she says. "Nyla?"

"Yes."

"Congratulations! I'm Anna, I'm doing the food for your wedding this afternoon. Your friends are out back."

"Thank you. I'm actually going to go get ready, so I'm not late."

She smiles as if she understands, and says, "It isn't the day to be late, is it?"

I go down the hall to our bedroom, where I lock the door behind me, take my clothes off, and get into the shower. I stand in the stream of water, arms wrapped around my middle. It feels like someone is using my stomach for a pincushion. Is it possible to be scared and excited at the same time? And is it okay?

As I tip my hair back into the stream of water and close my eyes, I see Lorenzo. I wasn't nervous when I married him, only excited. There was, however, a time that day when I was nervous. I should open my eyes, run away from these past memories, but I don't want to. So I keep my eyes closed and allow myself to be yanked back in time.

•••

Lorenzo nuzzles his cheek against mine, and whispers into my ear, "Why does everyone like to watch the first dance?"

I'm so nervous I can't even look up from his shoulder. I hate to dance, and I'm terrible at it.

"Tradition," I say, and step on his toe. "Sorry, I'm horrible at this."

He steps back away from me, lifts my arm, and spins me three times before he pulls me back in. He smiles smugly as if to say, *see you are good at this*.

"Of course, tradition," he says. "And what other traditions do we have left?"

"You know what's next," I say. "We've been planning this for a year."

His eyes lower to my lips, and his tongue slides across his. "I'd really like to fast forward to my favorite tradition."

"And what's that?" I ask.

"Over the threshold and into the bedroom. This really is a beautiful dress, but the laces in the back look like a Chinese finger trap. It might take me half of the night to get you out of it. Is there a quick-release button I don't know about."

"Unfortunately not."

"It's a husband torture device, is it? Don't worry, I'll gladly put up with any torture if you're the reward."

Lorenzo pulls me into his chest, where I close my eyes and follow his lead. Before him my life was good, but with him, it's unbelievable. Everything we do together is more fun, even my runs. People always said I could win gold, and while that's what I was always striving for, it wasn't until I met Lorenzo that I knew for sure I could.

Over the threshold into the presidential suite, Lorenzo carries me, eyes on mine as if this is something we must never forget. On the white comforter is a heart made from rose petals. There's a bottle of Champagne in a silver ice bucket and two flutes on the coffee table. It's Pop's favorite brand, no doubt his kind gesture.

Lorenzo opens the bottle, shooting the cork into the roof (luckily none of the liquid is lost), and says, "A toast." He fills the glasses, hands me one, and says, "To eighty years of wedded bliss, at least."

"Eighty? That will make me more than a hundred."

"One-hundred and one, actually. Me, one-hundred and three."

Lorenzo leads me over to the couch where he sits down and pats the spot next to him. "Take a seat, wife. I've got to get that Chinese finger trap off of you."

I comply like a good wife and sink slowly onto the couch. He angles me so that he can begin to work the back laces.

He curses below his breath, and asks, "You did this on purpose?"

"Nooo." He nibbles the side of my neck until I laugh. "I liked the back because it's so pretty and intricate. It's my favorite part."

"My least," he says flatly. "Why oh why? How many layers are there? Don't laugh. If you keep laughing, I'm going to hike the skirt up and take you because I'm more than ready. Actually, I'm aching right now."

I stand, look over my shoulder at him. "I'm all yours."

He's a vision in his black tux, sky-blue tie, and his curly black hair clipped close to his scalp.

"Nyla," he exhales. "No, sit back down."

"Go ahead," I purr.

He can't hide that he's ready, it's evident in the strain of the fabric. It might not be as apparent to him, but I'm ready as well.

"Your fingers," I say, "working over my back for the last fifteen minutes have . . ."

"What?" he says with lust.

"You know."

"I can't, Nyla. It wouldn't be proper. It's your wedding dress. That would make me an ani—"

I begin to work the back of my dress up, though it's not easy with all the layers.

"It's just us, Lorenzo. It only matters if it turns us on. It only matters if it is what we want. Do you know what I want?"

Dress hiked up, the lace of my panties on full display I turn to face my husband. His eyes skitter from the apex of my legs up to my eyes.

"What?" he says.

"You. Come on, Renz, since when have you ever been one to hesitate?"

"You're so beautiful, Nyla, that sometimes it makes me hesitate because I'm not sure why you agreed to even date me."

It isn't often that Lorenzo shows vulnerability, but when he does, I want to assure him that I'll move the world to keep him safe.

I drop the skirt of my dress, which makes him whimper, "No." Then I grasp the lapels of his tux and guide him to his feet.

"Am I dreaming?" he asks.

"I don't know," I say. "I thought my finger trap was a nightmare."

My joke is lost on him. He turns me around and works my skirt up. On his knees he pulls my garter off, then my stockings, and lastly the sweet, little lace panties. I place my hands against the wall to brace myself.

"You're sure this is how you want me to take you for the first time as my wife?" he asks.

"I'm not sure whose rules you feel the need to follow. But remember, we're married. We make our rules."

The soft material of his tux brushes against my ass as he works himself free.

"You are my wife," he says with pure amazement as he slowly eases into me. "We get to do this every day for the rest of our lives." He caresses my backside, thighs, shoulders. "The future is ours ... anything we want."

"Yes," I say and push back into him. "Anything."

•••

Sometimes I feel he's here. Sometimes I feel like I'm not alone. They're just memories, right? But I swear Lorenzo's lips are pressed to my neck and then they trail over my body as if he's everywhere at once. Are those his fingers on my hips? They must be. My body and even more scarily, my mind—both oblivious to time—ready for him. The pressure between my thighs mounts until it's painful, like a balloon that must be deflated before it explodes, but I refuse to touch myself.

It would be wrong to do this today, on my wedding day, to touch myself while fantasizing of Lorenzo. I'm ashamed to admit, there's been a time or two I have, even since I've been with Gavin.

I turn the water on cold, press my hands to the wall, and plunge my head below it.

There's a knock, knock on my door, followed by Mia's excited voice, "Are you dry and decent in there?"

"No," I choke out.

I'm neither dry nor decent. Guilt floods me. Not so much for the fact that I've already had a wedding day, that my husband took me still in my dress, or that I remember how amazing he felt, today of all days. I feel guilty for not feeling everything I did then, and for what I've lost along the way. The raw trust I had in my husband. The belief that he could keep me safe from anything. The bone-deep knowledge that with him we could do anything.

I wonder if Gavin realizes that though I've stitched myself together, I am not healed; I'm not sure I ever will be. Does he understand how losing Lorenzo wounded me? Does he know that I'm a coward? That I threw away my talent because I didn't believe in myself alone. Does he know I'll never be as good as I was the first time I got married?

"We're running short of time, princess," Ms. Marshall says. "Coming in." She opens the door just as I press a towel to my chest. "That was an awfully guilty sounding 'No.' Dare I ask?"

"You really shouldn't."

Mia's eyes are wide with assumption. "Guys are here," she says.

Relief floods me, but it's quickly followed by a rise of panic as if I've been caught in a naughty position by my husband. Was he in the house when I was thinking of . . .

"Are you okay?" Mia asks.

"Yeah. Fine."

"You're rather, flush."

"Oh, you are." Ms. Marshall winks at me. "A little tap-tap beforehand is good. No blush needed."

Mia's mouth drops open. "Oh dear! I thought I was bad."

"Your lawn man wants to know if he can come back here," Ms. Marshall says. "I suppose he'd like to mow something."

"What did I miss?" Mia says. "Lawn man."

Ms. Marshall pretends to a push lawn mower. "Ah the early days, you remember that?"

"Yes, I do."

"Good, Gavin does too. He's too polite to say it, but I think he wanted to mow you that night."

"Ohhhh," Mia says, then snorts a laugh that turns to all-out hysterics.

"Can I come in?" Gavin says beyond the door.

"No!" Mia yells to Gavin, then reaches for Ms. Marshall, and as she gently guides her out of the room, she says to me, "You have exactly fifteen minutes."

"Or else what?" Ms. Marshall asks.

"I don't know, and you aren't helping."

Alone again but not, I can feel the hum of Gavin's energy. There is a soft knock at the door.

"Yes?" I say.

"Don't you dare!" Mia yells.

"I'm not," Gavin says on the other side of the door. "I just want to tell her something."

"Can you not wait fifteen minutes?"

"No, actually I can't. Those jerks wouldn't even let me call her this morning. Nyla?"

"Yes, Gavin."

"I love you."

"I love you too."

"You have exactly ten minutes before I bust this door down."

"Fifteen."

"Not anymore. I'm waiting."

It takes me exactly five minutes to put on my make-up: eyeliner, mascara, and lipstick. Ms. Marshall is right, I don't need any blush.

I slip my sexy lingerie from the silk bag on to the bed. I pull the white, lace teddy on and adjust my breasts. In it, I feel so vixenish that I want to open the door to show Gavin right now. I'd like to bring him in here and have my way with him. But I resist the urge and go to the closet to get my wedding dress. I've only unzipped the gray garment bag a quarter of the way when I see what a terrible mistake I've made.

# CHAPTER 27

*I* groan, "Oh no."

"Oh no, what?" Gavin asks loudly through the bedroom door, then knocks. "Nyla, can I come in?"

"No, Gavin! Everything is fine!"

I hear the sound of rushing feet in the hall, then Mia says, "Oh no what? Back off, Gavin. Go back to the living room. Coming in, Nyla." She opens the door quickly and slams it shut just as fast. "What's wrong? Damn, that teddy is going to send Gavin over the edge."

"Can I see?" Gavin's lips must be very close to the door because his words are muffled but nearly as loud as if he were in here.

"Nyla?" Mia says. "You look like you've seen a ghost. What's wrong?"

I unzip the garment bag the rest of the way and pull the dress out. "This isn't my wedding dress."

"What? Your instructions said the gray garment bag in the back of your closet. This was the only gray garment bag."

"You got exactly what I asked for. This is my error. My wedding dress is in my office where I hung it the day I picked it up, just before . . . it's my mistake."

When I bought this cream lace dress with the blush silk underlay from the vintage shop, I swore it had been fashioned for me. It followed every curve of my body, even the length was just right. As I trace a piece of the lace, I wonder how it's possible that it's even prettier than I remember.

Mia runs her hands along the side of it. "It's soft like silk. Stunning. Are you sure it's not your wedding dress? Because it sure looks like it should be."

Quietly I say, "This is the dress I wore to the gala that Gavin and I went to last year." I run my hands over the teddy I have on, realizing this will not work under this dress. "I can't wear this because the back is completely open. I don't even have the right bra for it."

"What did you wear before?"

"A stick-cup bra."

"Can you go braless? Put band-aids over your nipples."

"Do what?"

"Oh, actually I have these little nipple petals."

"What?"

Mia holds her hand up like she's been struck with a good idea. "I'll be right back," she says as she runs to the door. She opens it a crack, and snaps, "Gavin, get back. Back. She isn't ready."

I take the teddy off and slip on a pair of white lace underwear; nothing special, but they'll have to do. Slowly, I sit on the edge of the bed and stare at the dress.

I remember the night of the gala with Gavin clearly. He was so handsome in his tux. The whole night he swept me off my feet. His attention was on me as if I were a deserving queen. He made me feel so at ease in his arms that I danced for the first time since my wedding. I wanted to let myself fall for him, but unfortunately, despite how amazing our night was, it didn't end well. I broke off what was just beginning because not only was he a cancer sur-vivor—something that hit too close to my heart—but he'd been married to Pandora, a woman I wanted nothing in common with.

I'm not sure if this dress being here, despite how much I love it, is a good or bad omen.

Mia returns a few minutes later with two nude-color, rubber things that look like flowers.

"Are nipples showing through a dress obscene?" I ask.

"In your wedding photos," Mia says, "I don't think you want that."

I place one of the petals over my nipple and press it, then the other. Nipples hid, I look like I'm ready for an edited photo shoot. As I slip the dress on it floats into place over my hips.

"Shall I zip you in?" Mia asks.

"No. Thank you though."

The zipper starts at the fullest part of my backside and is secured by three pearl buttons. Across the back, just below my shoulder blades, is a delicate tract of lace which is also secured by three buttons. I'm able to fasten all but the top two buttons between my shoulder blades.

"You sure I can't get that for you?" Mia asks.

I turn to face her. "No. That's okay."

Wondrously, she says, "Wow. He's going to melt. He has no idea how lucky he is, Nyla."

When I say, "I'm ready for Gavin," I feel the conviction in the core of not just my body, but my heart.

Mia shrugs. "Kinky game of dressing each other? So you know what to take off later?"

"This dress holds some memories."

Mia opens the door, steps out, and says, "Your turn, big boy."

Gavin steps into the room wearing a navy blue suit, sans jacket, with an ivory bow tie. He closes the door, then turns to face me. His eyes fall down me as he says, "I fell in love with you in that dress," like he's admitting something he shouldn't.

"It was an accident."

"What was?"

"This isn't my wedding dress. I asked Mia to grab the wrong garment bag."

"I think it was supposed to be, love."

I turn my back to him. "Would you mind? Helping me, here?"

His fingers trail along the muscles of my back as if it's the first time he's been allowed to touch me.

"That night," he says, "when you asked me to do this, I nearly fainted."

"You did not," I say.

"Really. And that night when you asked me to undo them, and then walked away, I spent the next ten minutes while you were changing upstairs—"

I turn quickly, just as he's working the second button into place. He looks over my face, shakes his head, and turns me back around to finish securing my dress.

"I'm a respectable guy, love, I wasn't doing that. I spent the next ten minutes taking deep breaths so that I wouldn't look like a guy with only one thing on my mind."

"Funny, when I came downstairs I thought you were contemplating something important."

"It was important. What would you have thought if you'd found me at full attention? Thank god you hadn't turned back to me after I unbuttoned you because it happened that quickly."

"And now?" I ask, slowly turning back. I press my hips to him and feel the change.

"Unless you're going to let me lift your dress for a quickie, you best not do that."

"I wouldn't be opposed. We've done a good job making up for lost time this week, but there is still more to be done."

A sudden swell of voices comes up the hall from the living room. The familiar voices of Gavin's family greeting mine.

Gavin smiles wistfully, and I say, "Maybe we'll have to wait."

"Please," Gavin says, "Let's go get married and eat dinner with these wonderful people who flew out here to be with us as quickly as possible."

"Quickly?"

"I want to get right back here because that dress, well, I've had a few fantasies that involve you in it. Ones I'd like to make a reality."

I run my tongue along my upper lip, and ask, "Fantasies that have to do with this dress?"

"Yes." A corner of his mouth lifts. "There are so many fantasies I want to make a reality with you."

"Haven't we done quite a bit of that?"

"We've only begun to scratch the surface of the things I'd like to do."

"You do know," I trail a finger down the side of his neck and into the collar of his shirt, "I'll do anything with you."

"Anything?" he asks as if testing me.

"Absolutely," I reply, without a doubt.

Gavin and I walk out of our room, down the hall, and into the living room where everyone is gathered.

"There she is," Kathy says. "Stunning, Nyla. And you, son, you look so . . . oh, you two." She opens her bag on the table and pulls out a box wrapped in silver paper. "I know this is last-minute, Nyla."

A hush falls over our small group, even the chef stops in her preparations. Aware of all eyes on me, I unwrap the box and pull off the lid. Inside is a silver chain on the end of which is an oval opal. Flecked with yellow, purple, and pink, it looks like a holographic image of another galaxy.

"The last three women to become a Boston have worn this on their wedding day," Kathy says. "We think it's good luck."

I hand Gavin the necklace and sweep my hair to the side as I turn around. The opal sits two inches below the hollow of my neck, a perfect placement with the neckline of my dress.

"Thank you, Kathy. It's an honor to join the family."

"It is perfect with your dress," she says.

A tingle runs through my body, lifting the hair on my arm despite the warm weather. This beautiful opal would not have matched my original wedding dress. But with this vintage one, it's perfect. As it was meant to be, I'm sure.

"I'm ready!" Emma announces as she bounds down the hall. She has on a white flower girl dress, her hair braided into a halo around her head, and she's wearing little white flip-flops.

Behind her, Linda wears a sundress that reminds me of the pink sunsets here, and her beautiful blond hair is braided to match her daughter's. "Is that the dress from the gala?" she asks.

"Yes. I poorly communicated which gray bag to grab."

"No. Things have a way of working out just the way they're supposed to. If I'm correct, I'd say Gavin would agree with that." She winks at him as if there is an inside meaning, but I leave well enough alone.

Together, we all leave the house and walk toward the beach. Emma happily tosses flower petals into the air and onto the ground. Alex tightly grips the box with our wedding bands, and every few seconds looks over his shoulder to check for Gavin and me.

When we reach the sand, Gavin pauses and looks at his wingtips. "I didn't plan this well, did I?"

"I love those wingtips," I say.

"I know you do, that's why I wore them. But they're not great for a sandy beach."

"We could go barefoot?"

Gavin kneels down and unties the blue laces of his shoes and removes his socks. He unfastens the buckles of my shoes and slips them from my feet while I steady myself with a hand on his shoulder. We leave them on a rock next to each other.

"They look cute together," Gavin says.

"I think you look cute barefoot in your suit on the beach."

I touch the opal on my neck and try to ask the question without saying a word.

"No," Gavin says. "My mom didn't ask . . . her, to wear it. She never was welcomed as a Boston woman."

I begin to walk, but Gavin pulls my hand.

"You are the only woman I've ever been in love with."

I'd like to dismiss the declaration, but his eyes assure me it's true. I'm sure he's loved before, but I am the only one he's loved like this. While I'd like to tell him he's the only one I've ever loved, too, I can't. When I walked down the aisle before, I was so in love with Lorenzo that I swore I'd never love anyone else. In some ways, I'm glad I was wrong.

Gavin and I walk across the shifting sands of the beach to the edge of the ocean. With no chairs or order to follow, our family gathers around us in a circle. We're lucky to have one person in our life that is willing to drop everything for us, but to be blessed by this entire tribe is something else.

As Gavin and I recite our vows, he looks at me like a man seeing the expanse of the universe for the very first time. It's how I feel too. He's a gift from the stars that I never imagined I'd be lucky enough to have. I'm enthralled by the way his emerald eyes sparkle, the way his fuller bottom lip begs to be kissed, and how his body moves mine in ways I've never experienced before. He's changed the very essence of who I am, and he's been my rock when I thought I couldn't survive the transformation.

When Trace pronounces us husband and wife, Gavin stares at my lips for a moment before he kisses me. It's sweet, gentle, and quite proper. So unlike how he usually kisses me, but with our family close and all eyes on us, it's perfect.

"Ladies and gentlemen," Trace says with raised arms like he's delivering a sermon, "may I present to you, Mrs. Nyla Tripple-Boston and Mr. Gavin Boston."

Gavin laughs as if a joke has been made and rolls his eyes.

I nod, and say, "Mrs. Nyla Tripple-Boston. But you can call me Mrs. Boston if you'd like."

"If you're joking you best tell me before I allow myself to get excited," Gavin says.

"For work, I'll still go by Tripple, but on paper, with family, everywhere else, I'm yours. Well, even with work I am, too, but I just, well it isn't—"

He pulls me to his chest and dips me back.

"No explanation needed, Mrs. Nyla Tripple-Boston."

He kisses me in the way he really shouldn't in front of our family, but I don't care. I give into him, to us, and as I release all fear, I choose to live bravely.

# CHAPTER 28

*I* slip on a pair of dark, fitted jeans, a thick purple and gray flannel, and the leather work boots I ordered special for this occasion. As I walk out of the bedroom, I grab my wedding ring from my bedside table and slip it on. I've been Mrs. Nyla Tripple-Boston for over four months now. For the first time in our entire relationship, I've taken time off to be here to support Gavin and his work.

"I'm ready," I say as I round the corner into Gavin's office and see he's on the phone. "Sorry," I add in a whisper.

A grin consumes his face as his eyes sweep over my body, and he stands from his desk. He's ready for work, though not in his standard office attire. Today he's dressed for a job site: a fisherman-style, navy sweater with the Boston Smith Company logo embroidered on the chest, straight-leg jeans, and a pair of work boots similar to mine, only larger and worn.

Gavin grabs my hand, kisses my temple and leads me to the front door where he holds up a finger to indicate, "one minute," and goes into the kitchen. When he returns, he's off the phone and has a thermal mug in each hand.

"Sorry about that, beautiful. Coffee to go, Mrs. Boston." He hands me one of the thermal mugs, which also has their company logo laser engraved into the powder blue coating. "You like our matching boots?"

"Very much, we could totally do a Jack and Jill ad for them." I point at a box on the entry table. "What's in that?"

Gavin smirks. "Something for you."

"For me?"

He opens the flaps and ceremoniously lifts out a flo-rescent-purple hard hat. He turns it to the side to show that it, too, has the company's logo. "They're required on the job site."

"Purple?"

"I want you to be easy to spot. Not that you actually need this for me to find you."

"It's perfect. Thank you." I put it on, lift my chin. "Well?"

"I didn't know a hard hat could be sexy."

"Imagine me in just this," I tap the hat, "and the boots."

"I better not at this moment. Later, however, instead of making me imagine it, how about you show me?"

"If you're lucky. I like your sweater."

"Do you?" He looks down at the logo and runs his hand over it. "I think Trace went a little over the top with the branding." He lifts his mug as evidence. "And you should see our jackets."

"Our?"

"Yep."

Gavin sets his mug on the table next to the door and opens the coat closet. He grabs an orange jacket with the company's name embroidered on the front. He slips it on one of my arms, I switch my coffee to the other hand, and he puts it on me the rest of the way.

"Wow, this is a really nice jacket," I say.

Gavin zips it all the way up to my nose and pulls the hood up. "I got the warmest one they had. This is what ice climbers wear. And the down liner is removable. I see that smile, you must be warm."

"How can you possibly see my smile?" I ask into the collar.

"The top of your cheeks round and your eyes crinkle a little."

"Crinkle?"

Gavin unzips the jacket and pulls back the hood, and gives me a quick kiss. Then he puts on his company jacket.

"Looking good, Mr. Boston."

"You should see me with a hard hat on," he says.

I bite my lip to keep from saying anything, and he laughs at me.

"We better go," he says, "before your dirty thoughts make it out of your mouth, and I haul you back into our bedroom."

"Yes, we can't be late when you're the star of the show."

I open the door, but Gavin puts his hand against it and pushes it shut. The humor in his eyes fades to a tender longing.

"Thank you again for making this week work for me," he says. "I know it's asking a lot of you."

"You do know," I say. "That you're worth it. Right?"

"I hope so," he says.

•••

Gavin turns off Yamhill at the worksite and slowly drives through an opening in the chain-link fence. We park behind Trace's truck which is exactly like Gavin's, only white. Linda hops out of the passenger side and waves at me.

Trace walks up to Gavin's side as he gets out, and asks, "Where are the magnets, man?"

"Forgot," Gavin says like a kid caught. He opens the back door and from a plastic sleeve pulls out two large, square sheets. He sticks one on his door and then comes around to my side and sticks it on.

"Looks good," I say.

"I refuse to keep them on all of the time like Trace. If I cut someone off, I might get an angry call at the office." Gavin offers the crook of his arm to me. "Are you ready, Mrs. Boston?"

Proudly I take his arm. "I am."

The groundbreaking event has attracted quite the crowd. Some in jeans ready to work, others in suits, and a few with cameras. Many of them turn to Gavin, offering him a friendly hello while others do so nervously; it's clear he's the man in charge here.

Something like stage nerves threatens to turn my legs into jelly. I've never represented Gavin like this. While this fact is shameful for a woman that's now his wife, I'm not sure how I should act. Is my usual head-held-high, ready-to-take-on-any-man attitude appropriate, or should I be softer?

As we walk toward the elevator, Gavin snugs my hand in the crook of his elbow tighter to his waist, and he leans to me. "What's wrong?" he asks.

"Wrong?"

"You've gone stiff."

"I wasn't sure if I'm supposed to be a proper architect's wife."

"What's a proper architect's wife?"

"I don't know, actually. I'm so used to being me, I'm not sure how I am supposed to represent you."

"Be you. I'd never ask you to change for me."

We step onto the elevator. While it's a solid, temporary structure with enclosed sides, something about it feels unsafe. We descend into the hole where we unload some distance below street level.

I look around the open space, at the rusted rebar, and feel a tinge of sadness for the person, whoever they are, whose dream failed. Funny how one person's tragedy can make room for another person's vision. I find it awe-inspiring that Gavin has repeatedly stepped in and picked up the pieces of someone's shattered dreams and brought them back to life. His home, this hole in the ground, and then, of course, there is me.

"The man has arrived," Alvis, Gavin's assistant, says.

"Don't let Trace hear you say that," Gavin replies.

Alvis pushes up his signature over-sized, gray-rimmed glasses. They make his large eyes look even more prominent, and accent his defined jaw and nose. He wears a company-issued jacket like Gavin's, but two sizes smaller, a pair of jeans, and black work boots.

"Looking sharp, Alvis," I say.

Trace's assistant, Marcy, joins us. She wears her hair in a snug, low ponytail, and no makeup except for bright pink lipstick. She's more serious than Alvis, which is good because Trace is at times a more serious person than Gavin.

"Morning, Nyla. Sorry I didn't say hi up there," Trace says and points to the street where our trucks are. "I was distracted by the fact that your husband can't seem to keep his company magnets on his truck. Anyway, great show last week."

"Thank you," I say.

Leaning toward me as if I have all the secrets, he asks, "What team do you think will make it all the way this year?"

I shake my head. "I can't. No favorites for me."

"Do you know this guy is killing us all in fantasy?" Trace says as he gives Gavin a light punch in the arm.

Gavin grins proudly and adjusts the collar of his coat.

"You can't help him, Nyla," Trace says. "That isn't fair."

I hold my hands up. "I'm not."

"With as much as you two talk about sports, that gives him an unfair advantage."

"Hey, he makes a lot of good points too. Granted I do know the game better." I bump Gavin with my elbow.

"No arguments on that point," Gavin says.

"But he's his own fantasy genius."

We all walk across the pit to a large group of people where Hank Johnson, the mayor of Portland, says, "There they are!"

His eye sockets are so large that you see the whites all around the iris. It gives him a sort of manic look, but he's got a warmness about him that reminds me of a cartoon character. He reaches behind him for a woman who turns to us, her eyes landing directly on Gavin.

"Patricia, dear," Hank says. "Trace and Gavin are here."

She has long blond hair, piercing blue eyes, and red lipstick that matches her trench coat. It's the kind that makes you wonder if anything is on under it.

"The men of the hour," she says as she shakes Trace's hand quickly, then reaches for Gavin's. She holds onto him longer. "Good to see you, gentlemen."

"And these two ladies are their wives," Hank says. "It's great to see you again, Linda. Nyla, do you remember me?"

"I do, sir," I say.

"We met right after you," he grips his forehead deep in thought, "you'd just won your hundredth gold."

I'm not sure sometimes if correcting people's errors or exaggerations like this is polite because it can come off as bragging. But I do feel uncomfortable about it, like a teacher over calculating your test score when you don't deserve it.

"Such a sight to see you run," Hank continues. "How's that leg working for you now?"

"Good as new," I say.

He claps once. "Joy. What a joy. Perhaps we could get you out to headline a charity run soon then."

"I'd be happy to."

"She's a keeper," he says to Gavin.

"That's why I married her."

"Patricia," she says, extending her hand to me.

I shake her hand. "It's very nice to meet you."

"You as well," she says, then draws half of her lip between her teeth. "Perhaps we can talk more, tonight, at dinner. You're coming, right?"

"I believe we all are."

"Fabulous. The chef is cooking up a storm at the house as we speak."

"Braised beef short ribs," Hank says with a pat on his belly, which looks like he has a bowling ball under his shirt.

"But you're a vegetarian, Nyla, am I right?" Patricia asks.

"Yes."

"Never fear," she winks, "I've got you taken care of as well."

"I forgot the shovels," Gavin says with a snap of his fingers. "Nyla, may I have your assistance?"

"Happy too," I say.

"May I help as well?" Alvis asks.

"No, I think Nyla and I got it. Thank you."

I follow Gavin, who moves quickly, back to the elevator. When the doors close, I say, "Please tell me it wasn't just me."

He makes an annoyed sound in the back of his throat. "She and Hank have something of an open relationship. Of course not publicly known."

"I'd bet not."

The corners of his mouth pull down as if turned off. "She has politely propositioned me a few different times."

"Politely?"

Gavin sweeps his arms for me to exit the elevator as the doors open. When I don't move, he presses his hand to my lower back and guides me out. He lowers his head next to my ear and pulls me close by wrapping an arm around my shoulders, then slides it down to my waist.

Images I could do without float through my brain. Her perfect red lips on Gavin's neck. Him looking down at her trench coat as she pulls it open.

"I declined," Gavin says.

"Thank god," I whisper.

"Did you doubt that?"

"I imagine you'd have said something if you had. Don't put it past her to proposition you again. I doubt you being married will deter her."

"Actually, you might be more worried about yourself."

Gavin reaches into the back of the truck. He pulls out two shiny, gold-tipped shovels.

"Will you take these two?" he asks.

"Wow, fancy."

He retrieves four more, two in each hand. "Yes, they are."

"Aren't you worried they'll get dirty?"

"They're shovels, don't worry about it. Anyways, when I saw her last, you were working, she came over to me and said, 'Your wife, quite pretty.' Then she grinned at me like she wanted a bit of you too."

"Shut up!"

"Powerful people don't know where their power ends sometimes."

"What did you say? Please tell me you said something."

We step back onto the elevator, then Gavin turns to face me and says, "I told her, 'You're welcome to hit on me every time we see each other, knowing you'll never get anywhere, but you hit on my wife, and you'll find I'm not always so nice.'"

"No, you didn't. Why didn't you tell me?"

"Honestly, I didn't think about it, and when I saw her just now, I was hoping it would be a non-issue."

"Maybe your determined statement turned her on."

"Sadly you might be right. You're mine, though. Remember that."

"I don't share," I say.

"Me either."

The elevator doors open to Alvis who quite helpfully takes the shovels from me. "Everyone is ready," he says.

There are at least fifty people gathered around as Hank gives his speech. He talks about how this structure will strengthen the Portland economy and how Boston Smith is a pillar of the community.

At his side, Patricia lets her eyes slide over the crowd. She's a trained trophy wife if I've ever seen one. It isn't until we make eye contact for the third time that it hits me. I know what's so familiar about her. Even the size of her, tiny and yet when you look at her she seems so much bigger: Pandora Person. They could easily be sisters.

A photographer works to put us all in an orderly fashion. She positions me next to Gavin, who is directly at the center with Trace on his other side. To my left are Hank and his wife. I glance to the side, and she smiles at me.

"I'm one happy man," Gavin says as he beams. "Dreams come true, you know that? I have been dreaming of this skyscraper since I was a kid." He lowers his lips to my ear. "But having the most beautiful wife in the world to share it all with, makes it better than I expected."

When I was a kid, I had dreams too. I wanted those gold medals. I sat on the floor watching the Games, and would say, "One day, Pop," and he'd always tell me, "I believe it." I was a young teen when I decided I'd make my name as a runner. First, I wanted to be the best at the school. Then the district, and then the state. College scholarships. National championships. All the while I was chasing the ultimate dream of gold medals.

Outside I looked unstoppable, and though I never lost a race, I was often scared that maybe I couldn't compete against the world. Then I met Lorenzo, and everything fell into place like self-honing puzzle pieces. He believed in me so much that it banished those little threads of doubt that could have been my undoing. Even though he wasn't a runner, he trained me like no one else could. He knew my body, the way my feet landed, and how my muscles worked intimately.

Lorenzo had dreams too. He wanted to write a novel, a great epic. But he let my dream become ours. Year after year he took jobs that paid the bills and spent all of his free time training me.

When cancer stole my husband, it crushed me, and I gave up everything we built together.

As I sink the golden shovel into the damp dirt to signify the beginning of Gavin's dream, I admire his tenacity. No matter how low the hardest of days drove him, how lonely his days got, he kept working for what he wanted.

I wonder, did I abandon my dream because I was afraid? Did I turn my back on a life that made me happy so I wouldn't have to process my loss? Did I keep Lorenzo from his dreams?

Flashes from a half dozen cameras blind me, but I keep my eyes open and lift my lips into a bright smile. I stand my full height, put one hand on my hip and the other around Gavin as he pulls me tightly to him. This isn't my dream, but for some reason, it feels just as rewarding. I wonder, is this how Lorenzo felt? I never did ask him why . . . why he let my dreams become more important than his.

# CHAPTER 29

After the groundbreaking ceremony, as Gavin and I head back to the elevator, he's stopped by a man. With his bushy beard, sharp cheekbones, and overall size, he reminds me of a lumberjack.

"This is Justin," Gavin says. "Best superintendent."

"It's great to finally meet you," Justin says with a firm handshake. "I seem to always miss you at your house."

"Oh?" I ask.

"Justin is in our fantasy league," Gavin says, "and sometimes comes over to watch football."

Recalling the many mentions of Justin's name, I say, "Ah yes, I'm connecting it all now. It is terrific to finally meet you too."

"I'm sorry to interrupt," Justin says. "Do you have time for a few questions, Gavin?"

"Do you mind?" Gavin asks me.

"Not at all," I say, and slip away.

The construction crew is getting their day underway now. Loud machines roar to life, people holler, and the rhythmic sound of hammers makes it all sound efficient.

As I walk around the perimeter of the site, taking it all in, I'm careful to stay out of the way.

Even with all of this going on around me, my eyes keep returning to my husband. He's the kind of guy that people notice. I've never seen Gavin in this environment before. I try not to be obvious as I watch him with fascination. He's in a circle with Justin, three other men, and a woman. Like us, they're dressed in company coats, flannels, jeans, and work boots. Their clothes, however, show they're the people who actually do the hard work: mud-splattered boots with creases along the toes, and jeans faded two shades lighter at the thighs and knees. They all watch Gavin talk, his arms moving animatedly, as if what he has to say genuinely matters.

Gavin says he doesn't like the spotlight, and while he doesn't in a showy way, he has no problem using it to get people to buy into his vision, to listen when he wants. It takes finesse, showmanship even. The fact that he emanates a solid calm certainly helps. Even from this distance, despite that I can't hear him, I'd pick up a hammer for him and help build this building too. He's destined for greatness far beyond what we see here.

"Excuse me," a sweet voice says, snapping my attention from Gavin. "Mrs. Tripple-Boston, I'm Samantha Lee, photojournalist for *Portland Life Monthly*."

She looks like a woman from the fifties with flawless skin, a high ponytail curled at the end, and a soft smile. As she adjusts what seems to be a heavy bag on her shoulder, she shakes my hand.

"Nice to meet you," I say.

She looks past me, and says, "Hello, Gavin."

"Good morning." Gavin sets his hand on my waist. "Nyla, Samantha is the photojournalist I told you about."

Boston Smith hired Samantha, a respected architectural photographer, to document the construction of the Yamhill building. Gavin was excited when she agreed to the project.

"Gavin showed me some of your work. It's amazing," I say.

"Thank you," she replies. "I'm very excited about this project. I also wanted to toss another one at the two of you. I'm working on the design issue for *Portland Life Monthly*. Rumor has it that you've got a gem on a large piece of property that you've restored."

"It really is," I say proudly. "Gavin did all of the work. It's exquisite. Every detail."

"I hired help here and there," Gavin says with a bit of shyness.

"He's modest," I say.

I look back to Samantha who's watching us like a photographer who's been looking for the perfect moment, and just found it.

"Design issue?" I say, encouraging her to continue.

"I'm wondering if we could feature your property."

Gavin looks down to me as if wanting to check my response, and says, "I don't know."

"It's a lot to ask, I know," Samantha says. "And we'd want to interview you two. They want to feature the inhabitants this year. Paint an idea about life in the house. No pressure. Really. But if you're interested, you know how to reach me."

"Yes," Gavin says. "We'll talk about it and let you know."

"Thank you for considering it. Great to meet you, Nyla. I'm sure I'll see you both soon."

As she walks away from us, I look up to the street level and see Oliver. He lifts his phone and points to it. I pull mine out and see a text message from him. "If you have a sec, Michelle will be right back. She'd love to meet you."

I give him a thumbs up and stuff my phone back in my pocket.

"Are we going to visit with Oliver?" Gavin asks.

"If you're all done here?"

"I am. We have just enough time to get changed, among other things, at home before we head to Hank's house."

"Enough time for what?"

Gavin and I return to the street level, where we cross Yamhill Street to Director's Park. It's a city block covered in gray-white bricks. On the far end is a life-sized chess board with three-foot game pieces. On this side is a half-moon-shaped fountain. There is no water in it during the winter, but in the summer it's filled with children at play.

At a bistro table sit Oliver and a gorgeous woman. She has shoulder-length hair that reminds me of gold, even the way the sun shines on it. Her large princess-like eyes watch us unblinking as we approach.

"Hello," I say.

"Hey!" Oliver stands to hug me, then shakes Gavin's hand. "Nyla, Gavin, I'd like you to meet Michelle, my fiancée."

Excitedly, I say, "What? When?"

"New Year's Day," Oliver says.

"Congratulations," Gavin says.

"Yes, congratulations indeed," I add.

Oliver and I worked together weekly for two months following the accident. Once I returned to work, however, I was available only on the weekends, and with those in high demand, time began to lapse. Then there were holidays, which made December and January impossible.

Still, Oliver checks in on me at least three times a week. He offers workout ideas, encouragement, and reminds me that soon we'll have to get back to training. In fact, he emailed last night asking if we could get back at it this Saturday.

With his crooked smile, Oliver asks, "Did you get my email?"

"I did," I say.

"I know you don't need PT anymore," Oliver says. "That much is obvious. But Perry was insistent I get you running again."

"I'm running."

"Fast?"

"No, not fast."

"It's fast," Gavin says.

I'm not even close to how fast I used to be, even on my casual runs. It's disappointing. Somedays I'd like to push my limits, but I don't. What if I hurt myself?

"Come on, Nyla," Oliver says. "Remember what you wanted?"

I remember everything I've ever wanted, and I remember everything I abandoned because I was scared.

Feeling a new determination, I say, "Okay, Saturday."

"Yes!" Oliver holds his hand up for a high five. "Okay. Good. I'm happy to hear that. And get that schedule back to me, or we'll lose two months again."

"You'll have it by the end of day tomorrow."

Michelle waves to someone up the street.

As Oliver waves to them, too, he says, "We're meeting my future in-laws to look at a few wedding venues. Starting with that one. It's on the second floor."

"It's a gorgeous ballroom," Michelle says.

"Have fun," I say.

Gavin and I head back to the worksite. At the corner, we stop when the MAX train rings its bell signaling it's about to move. As we wait, I stuff my hands into my coat pocket and bunch my shoulders to feel warmer.

Gavin puts his arm around me. "Are you all right?"

"Yeah. Why?"

"You look like you're thinking so hard it hurts."

After the train passes, we cross the street and get back into the truck. As we drive home, I watch the people out of the window. Business people in suits, tourists with open maps, musicians on street corners with buckets to collect coins.

All I think about is Saturday with Oliver. Under his watchful and trained eye, I feel safe. With him, I'll be able to open up my stride and see how fast I can run. As excited as I am, I'm scared I'll be disappointed in myself.

"What's on your mind?" Gavin asks, concerned.

I look away from everything rushing past me, to my husband. Nothing about Saturday is as important as today. Not my old dreams or my current fears. What matters today—on this dream-come-true day—is Gavin.

"Nothing, handsome." I lift up the truck's center console that separates the bench seat, then I unbuckle my seatbelt and slide next to him. As I slide my hands around his upper arm and lay my head on his shoulder, I say, "Everything is perfect. I'm so proud of you."

•••

Gavin follows me down the hall into our bedroom. As soon as we cross the threshold, he catches my arms and pulls me to his chest.

"Hey there, tiger," I say.

In my back pocket, my phone vibrates, but I ignore it because Gavin begins to devour my neck. He works to unbutton my shirt, yanks it off, tosses it aside, and then does the same with my bra. Then he lowers his head to my chest. I can't focus on what he's doing because my phone won't stop going off. This may be the call I've been waiting for. While I'm here, I'm not exactly off work. With Gavin's mouth working my nipple, I try to discreetly slip the phone from my pocket and peek at the screen.

Gavin snatches it from me, and says, "Oh no, you don't." Then he lobs it, and it arcs across the room like a softball pitch. It lands on our bed and bounces onto the floor.

I twist away from Gavin, and though he tightens his grip on my arm, I pull hard enough that I slip from his hold. Breasts bouncing, I hurry across the room and pick it up.

"The screen is cracked," I moan as my shoulders round forward.

Gavin pinches the bridge of his nose and closes his eyes. "I meant for it to land on the bed. Not the floor. I'll replace it."

"When?" I spin, pick up my shirt from the floor and press it to my chest. "I leave in the morning. And we don't have time for this. We're supposed to be at Hank and Patricia's for dinner in ninety minutes. I have to get ready. Damn it. And now I have this to get taken care of." I hold up my phone frustrated.

Gavin swipes it from my hand. "It's just the screen protector that's cracked. We'll stop on the way and get it fixed. I'm sorry. But talk about an ego blow, my wife checks her phone while I'm trying to have sex with her."

"I've been waiting for an important injury report!"

"There is always something important. Isn't there?"

He moves past me, sets my phone on the bed, and goes into the closet. I follow him and watch shamelessly as he quickly undresses and stuffs his clothes into the laundry basket. Naked, cock half at attention, he faces me. Raw hurt in his eyes, hands balled at his sides.

"Sometimes," I say, "I wonder why you put up with me. I shouldn't be working. I took the day off to be with you. You might not believe me, but I haven't even thought about work for the last few hours until that text came in." I drop the shirt from my chest, then slip my pants off. "I won't check my phone again the rest of the night. I'm not even going to think about work."

"Are you going to watch the game tonight?"

"It's Tuesday, there is no game."

"So I'm safe."

"There is one game I'd like to play tonight," I say.

"Yeah?"

I love the way Gavin's eyelids lower a quarter of the way when he wants me. It's then, despite how flawed I am, I know he wants me too. I'll never understand why he loves me so much. I wish I weren't so selfish, that I could be everything he deserves. But perhaps, I can try.

I kiss the scar on the left side of his chest, the one used for his port. Then my lips dance across his pecs to the other scar, this one used for his PICC line. They remind me, once again, that little else matters aside from us.

Gavin threads a hand into my hair while the other brushes along the scar on my cheek.

"What game are we playing?" Gavin asks.

"I'm going to see how many times I can make you come in one night. I've got a record to beat."

"Wait . . . is this actually something you've kept track of?"

"I've noticed."

"Nyla?"

"I'm a sports fan. I like numbers."

"And scores."

"I call it stats. I'd like to improve mine tonight."

I sink to my knees as my hand trails his belly, then his thighs.

"You . . . you are something else," Gavin says as if he approves of my plan. His hand slaps the top of his dresser and lets out an animalistic sound. "We'll be late," he warns as though testing me. "I won't have time to get your screen fixed."

Gavin's mouth falls open, his eyes on mine, and I agree with what is not spoken: nothing else matters.

# CHAPTER 30

$\mathcal{T}$he six-foot, wrought iron fence edged by even taller bushes keep the golf-course-like grounds of Hank and Patricia's house private. In the center of the property, the white mansion has not a speck of dust or a cobweb.

As Gavin and I walk up the front steps, a man dressed in casual chinos with a yellow plaid shirt opens the enormous front door. "Welcome, Mr. and Mrs. Boston?" he says.

Gavin inclines his head in greeting. "Thank you."

The man steps to the side for us to enter. Inside the entry, warmth wraps us despite its vast size. On a large table, a vase is overflowing with white roses.

"May I take your coats?" the man asks.

Gavin helps me from my purple peacoat. Then he removes his black wool coat.

I turn to where the sound of laughter dances down the hall. Linda's I recognize, and though the other is new to my ears, I'm certain it's Patricia's. I'm not sure what to expect from her, but between Gavin's warning and my observations, I think it could be an interesting night.

"They're just down there," the man says to us.

Gavin puts his hand on the small of my back. As we walk down the hall, he leans close to my ear to say, "You wore that dress to tease me."

"What?"

"That dress, it's one of my favorites."

I feign surprise. "I didn't know that. But did you know, that is my favorite suit of yours?"

Tonight my husband has opted for a charcoal pinstripe suit with a crisp white shirt, and brown leather wingtips. The suit hugs the lines of this body and accentuates what I love most about him—everything.

Just before we enter the room, Gavin stops me. "Ninety minutes, then say you're tired."

"Me? Why not you?"

"It's always more believable when it's the woman."

"I'll do it, but only because I've got a stat I'm well on my way to improving." I look down to his hips.

"Don't worry," he kisses my earlobe, "I'll rise to the occasion."

Patricia appears in the doorway and says, "There you are! Oh sorry. I didn't mean to startle you."

She has a pretty smile that's friendly with an edge of seduction. The gold metallic dress she has on sparkles like her hair and leaves no question as to the assets she likes to highlight. In some ways, I have to admit that I admire her raw, bubbly sexual energy.

"Come on in," Patricia says as she threads her arm into mine and pulls me away from Gavin. "We've been waiting for you."

In the sitting room, four large couches face each other in a square with a thick glass table in the middle. The crackle of the wood-burning fireplace is relaxing.

"I apologize for being late. I dropped my phone and had to stop and get it fixed because I head out tomorrow," I say. "You know how the world is now. Can't go a day without the phone."

"Oh goodness," Patricia says. "I could, but that guy," she points to her husband, "sure can't."

Hank, he's handsome in an old-school way with his retro brown suit that stops at the ankles. He watches his wife move across the room to a well-stocked bar cart like he can't wait to have what she's serving.

Linda pats the spot next to her on the couch and flashes her bright, infectious smile. She leans close to me, and whispers, "Right, broken phone. You should see yourself."

"Me?" I ask alarmed.

"You. Well, and Gavin."

Gavin, who is standing next to Hank and Trace already in conversation, does look rather happy.

"Newlyweds," Linda says like it's the reason.

"I'm working the bar, just like my college days," Patricia says. "What's your drink of choice, Nyla and Gavin?"

"A manhattan, please," I say.

"Same as my wife," Gavin adds.

"You've got some catching up to do," Hank says to Gavin as he lifts his drink. He looks over to his wife. "She's amazing. There isn't anything she can't make."

Patricia moves the drink shaker like a maraca, then pours the brown liquid into a heavy-bottom cocktail glass. After adding two cherries in each, she brings one to me and the second to Gavin. Hank plants a kiss on her cheek and leads her to the couch across from Linda and I. As she sits next to her husband, her plunging neckline threatens to spill her large breasts.

Gavin sits next to me and sets his hand high on my thigh. His touch makes my breath hitch, and for a brief moment, my eyes close. Perhaps I can fake being tired in less than ninety minutes.

Hank lifts his glass. "A toast to the brilliant team at Boston Smith. Here's to many more great Portland buildings."

"Here, here," Trace says. "To many." He tosses back the rest of his drink. Just as he begins to set it on the table, Patricia grabs it and carries it off to the bar cart.

"Gavin," Hank says. "Trace was just letting me in on your aspirations to develop the waterfront east of the city further."

"That's the plan. Though we'll see how permits, investors, and such go."

"Seeing how we need more housing, I'm certain we can work with you. Investors, that's never a problem for you, I'm sure."

I have no idea what plans Hank is talking about, and though I want to ask Gavin, I stop myself. I don't want to seem like an out of touch wife, especially in the company of these two super wives.

Linda, she's the best wife I've ever seen. She's at every event Gavin and Trace have. How often have I talked with Gavin and he says, "I've got a business meeting tonight, Trace and Linda will be there." She's always got the kids taken care of. On top of this, Trace is permanently smitten with her. And what's even more amazing is she always seems present and listening with two ears.

If I'm honest, about twenty-five percent of the time, perhaps more, my mind drifts to work. Even at the most inopportune times. Like today. Hence the cracked screen protector.

Patricia, while she's clearly got a wandering eye, is quite attentive to her husband. She's got this hostess thing down pat. About the only thing I know how to host well is a sports game. Throw out a bunch of chips, dip, and frozen appetizers that I baked, then call it good. Any other event though, I never find the rhythm to it.

"Okay boys, no more work," Patricia says.

Hank puts his arm around his wife and leans back on the couch. "You're right, dear. Nyla, I've been looking forward to hearing more about your status."

He lifts his chin to look over the table and at my leg. I run my hand along the scars as if trying to warm them. Sometimes on a cold night, it feels like a million little needles delving below the raised skin. Other times, just thinking of them does too.

"Good as new," I say. "I'm 100 percent."

"Really?" Patricia asks.

"Perhaps, not 100, but close."

"I heard," Hank says, "that you're doing a second season of *Behind the Sport*."

"Yep. After we get back from our belated honeymoon, I'll be off again to start filming."

"Honeymoon," Patricia says brightly. "Where to?"

"Italy," Gavin answers.

Patricia presses her hand to her chest. "Oh, so romantic."

"So between reporting and the TV show, when do you find time to relax?" Hank says.

"I don't think she ever stops," Linda says. "She's the busiest woman I've ever met."

"No," I say, "Not the busiest."

"It's Nyla's nature," Gavin says. "She moves a million miles a second and can do three things at once. It's how she gets it all done. The two months she had to sit around after the accident had her going stir-crazy."

"Wouldn't anyone," Patricia says. "Add wifely duties now into your mix and goodness." She waves a hand in the air. "Makes me crazy just thinking of it. It's all I can do to keep up with this guy." She pats Hank's knee. "At least the kids are older now, so it's a little easier. But even with teenagers I'm lucky to find time to listen to my own thoughts."

"Tell me about it," Linda says.

"How old are yours again?" Patricia asks.

"Eleven and six. It's finally starting to ease up. But I swear some days I feel like I might drop and not get back up again."

"You're an amazing mom," I say to Linda.

"Thank you."

"Nyla," Patricia says, "you've managed to make a remarkable career in a man's world. What's it like?"

"It's full of men," I joke.

"Yes, it is," Patricia purrs as she leans in my direction with a suggestive eye. "Bet that was crazy before you got married. All those hot athletes to date and all."

"I never mix work and personal life," I say.

"Strong woman. I'm not sure I'd even try and resist." She raises her glass. "After all, life is short."

•••

Two hours later Trace and Linda say they need to get home because of the sitter. We take this opportunity to head out, too, myself saying how tired I am.

Walking ahead of Linda and me, Gavin is deep in conversation with Trace.

"That Patricia . . ." Linda says. "She's nice, right?"

"Seemed so. You don't like her?"

"It's not that. It's just that she bears an uncanny resemblance to . . ." Linda gnaws on her lip. "Pandora. Even the way she's so sexually confident. Like no one would turn her down. And not so discrete about the wandering eye," she says as if implying something else, then adds quickly, "Though I don't think Patricia would do anything."

"Wait." I reach for Linda and gently pull at her wrist to slow our pace. Once there's more distance between the guys and us, I ask, "Did . . . Pandora?"

Her mouth opens, but she looks too pained to say anything.

Gavin and Linda grew up together, their mothers being good friends. While she and I have become close, I don't think she'd ever do anything that she thought would betray him. Certain things should come directly from the person who experienced them anyways.

"It's fine," I say. "You don't have to say anything. Gavin and I've never talked about her or them. Not much anyway."

Having come together later in life, both Gavin and I experienced full lives before one another. There's still so much he doesn't know about me, things I'm not sure he'll ever need to. I know it's the same for Gavin. They aren't secrets so much as they are things that don't need to be said.

This though, the little hint of infidelity, explains some of Gavin's insecurities and the way, at times, I see he has to work hard to wrangle them.

"The baby, though?" I ask.

Linda shrugs. "I never trusted her. Gavin, I think he felt obligated and didn't want to admit what was going on. He was also ready for that part of life. It was a confusing time for him."

Trace turns back and says to Linda, "You coming, babe?"

Gavin lifts his arm for me, and I walk straight to his side and wrap my arm tightly around him. I press my hand over his chest and lift onto my toes to kiss his cheek.

"Have a great trip," Trace says.

"Thanks," I say. "And congratulations on everything. I'm proud of you two."

Gavin and I get into our truck. Once he starts the engine, I set the automatic climate control to the warmest setting and check that my seat warmer is on high.

Everything tonight went fine with Patricia. In fact, once you get used to her blunt sexual nature you realize it isn't personal, it's just her. What I can't seem to shake from my head is Pandora.

"What are you thinking about?" Gavin asks.

"Oh, nothing."

"It's something. You're chewing on the inside of your lower left lip, which means you're thinking hard."

"Does Patricia remind you of someone?" I ask.

"Yes. I noticed that the first time I met her." He grips the steering wheel tighter. "She's nicer than Pandora, though."

I'm curious about it all. Why did Gavin—my big, strong, confident man—put up with it? How long did he know? How does it affect him now? Then again, most of me doesn't want to know. It will probably just make me angry.

# CHAPTER 31

$\mathscr{A}$s I step outside to the passenger pickup area of the Portland airport, I pull the collar of my jacket tight around my neck. It's cold, but not freezing like it was earlier this week for the groundbreaking ceremony. I weave my way up the sidewalk around people bundled in coats and dodge piles of luggage.

When I see Gavin leaned against his truck, one hand in the pocket of his jeans and the other scrolling through his phone, my feet slow. He doesn't even have a jacket on, only a sweater that's the color of milk chocolate.

As if sensing my presence, Gavin looks over to me and grins. He pushes off his truck and walks my way.

"Why are you just standing there?" he asks.

I look down at my still feet and can't think of a good explanation. "You made me stop in my tracks."

With his hand bracing the back of my head, he kisses me as he slips the bag from my shoulder. Then he grabs the handle of my suitcase. While Gavin puts my bags in the back of the truck, I hop into the front. On the center console is a bouquet of flowers wrapped in craft paper.

The silver-dollar shaped eucalyptus has filled the truck with its invigorating, clean scent. I gently touch the soft petal of a blooming lily.

"For Ms. Marshall?" I ask Gavin as he gets in.

Gavin reaches for a paper bag on the floorboard and sets it in my lap. "That is for Ms. Marshall." He picks up the flowers and hands them to me. "These are for you."

"Always a charmer, aren't you?"

Ms. Marshall invited us to dinner tonight. Even though this weekend is jam-packed, I couldn't turn down the offer. I haven't had time to sit and chat with her in months, and I miss her.

Gavin checks his mirror, then pulls into the flow of traffic. "I've already called Ms. Marshall with an update on time," he says. "She said she expected it and not to worry."

"I'd told her that with my flight getting in at six, and of course afternoon traffic, that I wasn't sure what time we'd actually be there. My flight being a half-hour late didn't help either."

Gavin takes my hand, turns it over, and kisses the inside of my wrist. "I really missed you this week."

"What? I was only gone two nights."

"I think it was from the bliss of our extra time together."

"That should make you miss me less."

"You think so? No, actually it makes me want you home more. You don't miss me when you're gone?"

"It worries me, actually, how much I miss you."

"Worries?"

"Your a hard guy not to miss, handsome."

Before Gavin, traveling never lost its luster. Weekends were an interruption to what I loved most, being on the road and sports. The longer we're together, though, the harder it is to leave, and the more I seem to miss him when

I'm gone. Admitting that to myself feels like a weakness, so I'm not sure I'll ever tell anyone else.

Gavin pulls up to the curb in between my old house and Ms. Marshall's. There is now a white, picket fence between the two properties. In my old driveway are two small electric vehicles parked nose to tail. I don't miss living here, but I do miss having Ms. Marshall as my neighbor. She was always there when I needed to talk, and even when I didn't know I needed to.

I begin to open the door, but Gavin reaches for my hand, and says, "Nyla. What worries you about missing me?"

"I can't explain it, Gavin."

He grips my chin between his index finger and thumb and turns my face up to his. "I'm not missing something, am I?"

I turn my face, kiss his palm, and say. "No, you're not missing anything, Gavin. You're the best husband."

"I'm trying. And you're a phenomenal wife, Nyla. You do know that, don't you?"

I wonder what Gavin thinks a good wife is. I certainly don't fulfill the ideals; in fact, I don't even come close. There's little hope I'll ever be a great hostess, I put my career ahead of everything, and nothing about our relationship is fifty-fifty; Gavin works harder for us than I do. I've told myself these things are okay for us, that we're different, I'm different. But this week, at the mayor's house, when I learned Gavin has aspirations to develop along the waterfront, I was reminded once again that I've fallen short on too many basic duties. I should know what he dreams about, and I should be around to support his dreams. Shouldn't I?

Sadly Gavin says, "Hmm. We'll have to talk about this later."

We walk the narrow pathway to Ms. Marshall's house. The daphnes she planted last year not only survived their first winter, but now are covered in fragrant white blooms. However, the one planted on our property line has been moved into her yard, probably to clear the path for the fence.

We climb the three steps of the wooden pink-painted porch. Gavin opens the screen door, then I knock.

"I got it," Walter says as he opens the door. "Hello. Come on in."

"Smells amazing," Gavin says as he closes the door.

"She's been in there creating some gourmet dinner all afternoon."

"Well," Ms. Marshall says, coming out of the kitchen, "I had a reason to cook."

She reaches out for me, but before her arms make it to me, I snatch her hand clad with an enormous, solitaire diamond. "Ms. Marshall! Is that a—" I look to Walter smiling like a man on top of the world. "Congratulations!"

Ms. Marshall waves me off, almost embarrassed, as she says, "Thanks. If he wants to put up with me. He can have me."

I laugh, though I feel a sharp stab in the center of my throat. She's joking, but her words sum up how I treat my relationship with Gavin. If he wants to put up with me—my absentee status, my lack of attention to our relationship, my not knowing everything he wants—he can have me. Even I know he deserves better. Why on earth has he settled for me?

Gavin hands Ms. Marshall the paper bag wrapped bottle.

She opens it and pulls out a beautiful, blue bottle of Bombay Sapphire gin. "You're a keeper," Ms. Marshall says to Gavin. "Everyone usually wants to give the old lady wine, but you know what the good stuff is, and my favorite."

She waves for us to follow her back down the hall to the kitchen, and says, "You've got a good husband, Nyla. You're a lucky woman."

"No truer words have ever been spoken," I say.

Gavin pulls me to his side and says so everyone can hear, "It's me that's the lucky one."

•••

After dinner, Walter makes Ms. Marshall and I drinks with the gin Gavin brought. Then he tells us to go sit in the living room while he and Gavin clean up. Ms. Marshall doesn't argue, so I don't either.

I sit on the love seat across from Ms. Marshall and curl my legs around me. It's like she's aging backward. Every time I see her she looks younger, more put together yet still herself.

"Getting engaged and glowing like a woman who's figured it all out," I say.

Ms. Marshall shrugs. "He begged me. What was I supposed to say?"

"Yes, because he makes you happy."

"Just taking a little of my own advice that I dished out to you a while back." She waves her hand across her body. "And not letting things go to waste."

At dinner, Ms. Marshall and Walter told us that while he's slowly migrated here for the past couple of months, last weekend he officially moved in. The house has been cleaned out. It's less cluttered and smells fresh. Sprinkled throughout are new things. This love seat, a side table, and a few framed photos of people I've never seen before.

"Are these his kids?" I reach for a silver frame on the end table. The photo is of three adults who appear to be my age.

"That's an old photo. Jenny has since had that baby, and three more."

"That's a lot of kids."

In the picture, Jenny is pregnant. She has fair skin with hair so blond it's nearly white. Her eyes are so light you'd think there is no color. It sounds plain, though she's anything but. Her brothers, with darker hair and eyes, look like her, only masculine.

"What about the boys? Do they have children too?"

"The oldest, who is the shorter one there, Matt, has one on the way. And Mel, the youngest, tallest, and best looking, I don't see him getting married any time soon. But, it wouldn't surprise me if he's got a few dozen running around that he doesn't know about."

"How do you get along with them?"

"It was a little awkward at first. Their mom held a special place in the family and is missed. But they're welcoming. Mostly I think they're glad to see Walter happy.

I hold up the photo and point to Jenny's pregnant belly. "You're going to be a grandma then. Times five."

"I still want one from you."

"Yes, but you already have five. You don't need another to get lost in the mix."

"I promise, it won't get lost in the mix."

I set the frame back carefully just like it was.

"I know it's an annoying question," I say. "Everyone wants to know what's next, but I have to ask. Will you have a big wedding?"

"We'll have a wedding. We're thinking sometime this summer. But as for how big it will be, I'm not sure. Marriage, it looks good on you, Nyla. You're always glowing now. And when you look at Gavin, you get this little grin like you are forever smitten. You two are good for each other."

I nod yes.

"So I know everyone always wants to know, 'what's next?'" Ms. Marshall says imitating the way I'd just said it. "But when will you start that family?"

"We already are a family."

"When will you grow it?"

"Ahhh, you know. That is not in our plan actually."

"You've got to be—" Something in the kitchen drops making a loud clatter. "You two okay in there?"

"Fine. We're fine," Gavin calls back.

Ms. Marshall pulls her lips to the side. "Should we believe them?"

"Yeah, because I don't really want to get up," I say.

"Good point. Anyways. I heard Linda, not too long ago, ask Gavin a similar question to what I just asked you. And he said as soon as Nyla is ready."

"He did, did he?"

"So, not in your plan, as in your and Gavin's, or in your plan, as in you?"

"Hmm."

"Hmmm, is right."

"It's complicated."

"It always is."

"You see. We're busy people. You have no idea the hours Gavin works. And me, I'm gone at least half of the time."

"I bet you're gone more than that."

"You're right. I just don't think kids are a good idea for us. You know when you start things like that you have to change your whole life. And who has to change the most, the mom. I can't. Too much to do."

"I've seen him with kids. Some men aren't cut out to be fathers. Don't want it. Others want to be, and absolutely should be."

"Maybe, in this case, it's that the woman isn't cut out for it."

"I felt the same way before I had my daughter. I've also seen you with kids, and you, too, are meant to be a mother."

"Are you going to come over and watch them?"

"I'd be happy to, anytime. I volunteer. Come now. They only disrupt life for a few years, but offer a lifetime of fun and joy."

"Not sure I can afford a few years disrupted."

Ms. Marshall leans forward, folds her hands together, and eyes me skeptically. "What aren't you telling me?"

"How can you always read my mind?"

She studies my face. I'd like to duck away so that she can't see anything in me.

"I'd assumed with you and Lorenzo that not having kids was a choice? But I'm sensing something else. Are you not able to?"

As far as I know, no one knows about Gavin's infertility but me. He asked me to never say anything. And I won't.

"Did the doctors say there is no possible way?" Ms. Marshall presses.

I lift a shoulder in an indifferent answer.

"Do you still have ovaries and a uterus?"

"Yes."

"Mmm-hmm. Well, miracles happen, right? You could get one. I bet you two are like bunnies. Keep doing it like that, and you'll increase the chance."

"Ms. Marshall!"

"Blushin' like a virgin."

"Alrighty," Walter's voice reaches us before he makes it into the room. "Do the beautiful ladies need refills? Bev, yours looks empty. Nyla?"

I drain the rest of mine and hand it to him.

"Bev," I say. "Sounds so strange to hear someone call you by your first name."

"What will be even stranger is that when I get married, I won't be Ms. Marshall anymore."

"You'll always be Ms. Marshall to me."

Gavin sits on the love seat next to me. "What are you two ladies talking about?"

"Nothing," I say firmly and give Ms. Marshall a don't-you-dare eye.

She winks at me and settles back into the couch.

Gavin reaches for the same silver frame I picked up earlier. "Beautiful family," Gavin says when Walter returns to the room.

"Thank you," Walter says. He hands Ms. Marshall and me our drinks then sits next to her. "And since that photo, my daughter has had four kids. My older son, the one on the right there, has one on the way."

Gavin stares at the photo a few moments before he sets it carefully back on the table.

I love this man with all my heart, and even though I know he deserves a woman that will give him the world and the family he wants, I want to keep him. And each day that I do, I feel even more selfish.

# CHAPTER 32

*W*hen I moved in, Gavin built my dream office for me. It has light lavender walls and natural wood, built-in bookshelves. My desk, made by Gavin's cousin, Stephan, is a substantial six feet wide and four feet deep, with hand-carved vines and flowers on the legs. On the wall across from my desk are three large paintings. They're each of the same emerald-headed hummingbird at different stages of flight. Lorenzo found them at an outdoor art fair near our home on Bainbridge Island. Sometimes I'll sit here and stare at them, and when I do, I remember a time when I had it all figured out, and I never doubted myself.

Finally done with my last phone call, I wrap up my work for the day and close my laptop. I open my office door, and I'm greeted by the robust laughter of Gavin and Oliver. I follow it to the kitchen, where they're leaned against opposite counters drinking glasses of water and talking, both with enormous smiles on their faces.

Gavin is dressed ready to work outside: jeans, a thick red flannel, and a black knit hat. He only wears hats like this when practicality calls for it because he says they're what hipsters wear now.

"Sorry to keep you waiting," I say to Oliver.

He sets his glass down. "I was early. It didn't take as long as I thought to get here."

"I'm ready if you are."

Oliver grabs his jacket from the barstool and puts it on. His clothes are a combination of silver and black high tech workout gear designed for go anywhere, do anything workouts.

The three of us walk out of the front door and across the courtyard. This large building used to all be Gavin's workshop until he split it in two; half for him, and half for the gym. Aside from a couple of favors he called into contractor friends, he did most of the renovation himself.

As Gavin opens the door to his shop, he says, "Have a good workout."

Oliver follows me into the gym where he lets out a long whistle, and a few "wows," as he walks around the space. Weights, treadmill, elliptical, stair climber, exercise mats, medicine balls, and more. You name it, Gavin bought it.

"Talk about state of the art," Oliver says and claps his hands. "Let's get started."

"What's the plan for today?" I ask.

"Upper body and arms." He grins like he's about to put me through the wringer. "Then let's get out for a real run."

I follow Oliver's every instruction. Warm-ups, stretches, and then weights. He pushes me harder than I have in years, and it makes me realize how easy I've been on myself.

With shaky arms, and sweat-soaked clothes, I grit and give every last bit I have to complete the last bench press. Triumphantly I say, "Fifteen!"

"One more!" Oliver says.

"What the! No! You said fifteen. I counted. That was the last one. I can't possibly."

He places his hand below the bar relieving some of the weight, but not all of it. His square jaw sets, his eyes narrow, and he says, "Don't wimp out on me. You can do this."

The full weight of the bar settles back into my hands as Oliver slips his hand away. I'm not sure I believe that I have one more in me, but I feel safe enough with him here to try.

I put all of my mental focus in my arms. I swear I hear the tiny tears in my muscles as they shred. It's always fascinated me that the way we get stronger is by our muscles ripping apart and rebuilding.

My arms are only halfway to pushing the weights back up, but my body begins to shake, and I screw my eyes shut. "Damn it, I—"

"Look at me," Oliver says calmly. He doesn't have to say anything, I see it in his eyes: *I believe in you.*

I scream like a woman sacrificing herself, then, finally, my arms are straight. Oliver takes the bar from me, the sudden weightlessness is jarring. I'm in so much pain, and yet it feels so good.

"Now that is how it's done," Oliver says. "Ready to run?"

"If I didn't know better, I'd say you're trying to break me."

"I'm just trying to remind you of what you already know. That you're a woman who can't be broken."

There's a distinct similarity between Oliver and Lorenzo, but we've spent so much time together now that I rarely notice it. Moments like this though—when he looks at me like he knows I'm something special, with eyes so firm and kind at the same time—my breath is stolen. I wonder if Oliver knows he looks like Lorenzo.

"I'd like to run outside since it's a nice day," I say.

We put our coats back on, then jog slowly down Appleton Way. At the main road, we turn right. This is an older area where sidewalks begin and end unexpectedly. Sometimes we can run side by side, other times Oliver slips behind me without a word and allows me to keep the pace.

A couple of miles in, Oliver glides back alongside me, and asks, "Are you slowing down?"

"No," I say, and push my legs harder. "But I'm not at a six-minute mile either."

"This isn't even close. And I bet in your day you could beat that six minutes."

"I used to be really fast."

I loved to sprint. I'd float over the earth, arms pumping like the engine, and legs like a propeller. For those quick, yet eternal moments, that was all that mattered.

"You do know the six-minute mile was an arbitrary number that Perry tossed out," Oliver says. "It isn't the real goal."

"It isn't?" I say with the ragged breath of an untrained runner. "What is the real goal then? Tell me what it is, and I'll crush it."

"What do you think you could do?"

My thighs ache, my lungs burn. Even though I'm close to empty, if I push through, a second wind will kick in. It's funny, this stage of the run, it's as if the body wants to convince you it's done, when in fact it's got so much more left.

"Well. . ." I say, "I don't know."

"I've been trying to think of ways to measure your improvement. And while I know you like a long leisurely run, what do you really love?"

"To run fast."

"Maybe we should do some sprint trials and work to improve them. Measure your improvement that way. I think you'd have more fun."

I slow down until I stop.

Oliver takes a few more steps before he turns back. "What's wrong?" he asks.

An idea begins to form, and then it's as if it leaps from my head into the world, and I swear I see holographic-like images all around me. It's my past; me running, Lorenzo coaching me, and us . . . happy.

"Nyla?" Oliver says. "What's wrong? Are you okay?"

I shake my head vigorously and hold up my index finger to quiet him.

The past fades into what I think is something new, a future perhaps. That's me I see, the now me, but my hair is longer. I'm wearing black running shorts and a purple top. Behind me is Gavin, Oliver, and I swear I see Lorenzo too. And, I'm on a track.

"Nyla!" Oliver's voice bursts through the images. He moves in front of me and puts his hands on my shoulders. "What's wrong?"

The weight of his hands on me is grounding. I turn my face up to him, his breath warm on my forehead, and say, "Sprints."

"Okay." Oliver's concerned face relaxes. "Sprints. We'll work on making those faster."

For months, no years, what I've wanted has been difficult to answer because there's been no clear or easy answer.

Suddenly, however, I feel more sure about this than I have anything in a very long time. Well, almost anything.

Oliver smiles cautiously. "I don't know what's going on right now, Nyla. You've bit your lip so hard you're bleeding, but you're smiling like I've never seen before, and I can't help but smile too."

Lorenzo knew my body in a way that few people will ever know another's. He knew how my hips moved, the way I pronated my foot, and if I lifted my hands high enough. He knew the flow of my breath. "I see it in the shape of your lips," he'd say.

When he died, I said I needed my runs to be for me. The truth is, my competitions had become ours, Lorenzo and mine, and in a way, they'd become so intimate I couldn't bring myself to share it with someone else.

Something has changed now, though.

I plea, "Train me."

"I am."

"No. Train me to be the best again."

"I must be missing something."

My body is overheating with energy that must be cooled. I unzip my coat desperate for the chilly winter air.

"Oliver. I need more."

"More what?"

"Gold."

Oliver looks over my body carefully as if analyzing its possibilities then into my eyes. "Nyla," he says, "tell me exactly what you want."

"I want you to get me in the best shape of my life so I can bring home gold."

"You want to come out of retirement? Make a comeback?"

"Yes."

"I'm sure you know what kind of commitment that will take."

"You do know how many medals I have, don't you?"

"Yes, actually, I know exactly how many medals you have, championships you have won, I even know your damn school records. But you do understand that getting back into that shape is different from growing into it like you did before? But, I know you can do it. Do you really want to work with me to do this?"

"Yes."

"Well," he laughs with excited hysterics, "when did you decide this?"

"Just now."

"Wait. You just decided to do this enormous, crazy thing."

"I've wanted it for a very long time. I need this."

"Do you have any idea—"

"I can do it."

"I know you can, Nyla."

I press my pleading hands to the center of my chest. "Please say yes, Oliver."

"Yes. Of course, yes. But while I'm a good trainer and this is right up my alley, you could do with a real sprinting coach too. Who was yours before?"

"My husband, Lorenzo."

"Ah."

"But I know just who to ask."

"Okay. Team Tripple Threat building in process."

"But you can do it? With everything you have going on?"

"I'm fully on board, but we'll need to look at schedules when we get back to your house. The occasional session we agreed to by email won't work."

"Thank you for believing in me so quickly."

"I have no doubt you'll do it. None whatsoever. You've got a fire in your eyes that I've only seen with a couple of athletes, and they are the best in the world too. Come on, let's go plan world domination."

Silently, we jog back up the hill. We get to Appleton Way just as Gavin's truck does. He stops, and I go to the driver side door as he rolls down the window. He's changed into a white, long-sleeved shirt and is freshly showered.

"Where are you off to?" I ask.

"Your brother called and is bringing you a surprise, so I invited him and the family to dinner. Then, not even five minutes later, Trace called to invite us to dinner, so I invited them too. I need to get groceries to make dinner for everyone."

"Sounds fun."

"You two have been at it for a while now. Don't wear yourselves out."

"We're done. Just heading back. I'll be ready when you get back to help cook."

I step onto the sideboard of the truck and kiss Gavin. After he turns and heads down the hill, Oliver and I resume our jog back up Appleton Way.

Back in the warmth of the house, I grab my computer from the office and then sit next to Oliver on the couch. He's already pulled his calendar up on his phone.

"At a minimum," Oliver says, "We need to meet weekly. Twice would be better. Ideally, even more. Especially as we get closer to races. What's up with this?" He points to April on the computer screen. "I don't see you for five weeks?"

"I'm going on a belated honeymoon, and then as soon as I'm back, I leave for work."

He gives me a look that says you gotta work with me here. "I'm not here for you to make excuses to. But I am going to hold you to it. This goal you have requires this to be as important to you as anything. Maybe more."

"I understand. Let me look over this more tonight and see what else I can shift or eliminate to make more time."

"Sounds good." Oliver shoves his phone into his jacket pocket. "I've got to head out. Wedding planning. Cake testing."

"The best part," I say. "Well, not the best part."

I walk Oliver to the door and open it for him.

A smile consumes his face. "Holy shit, Nyla. You're going to be the 'it' woman again. Do you realize that? No matter what, just coming back from retirement after all you've been through, it's going to change your life. You ready for that? What does Gavin think?"

I shift my feet as I nervously admit, "He doesn't know."

"You've been talking about it with him though, right? As you've been thinking about this."

"This is seriously new, so no, I haven't talked with him. I will tonight."

Oliver's mouth drops open. "Shit, Nyla. When you said you just decided, I didn't realize that meant you hadn't even talked to him."

"I haven't talked to anyone about it. I just now realized it's what I want."

"He's never been with you while you're training, has he?" Oliver says quietly.

"No."

"Be careful, Nyla. Sports can consume an athlete. And without careful attention, it can devour an athlete's life."

# CHAPTER 33

*My* schedule is a puzzle with too many pieces for the container in which it's supposed to fit. I've gone over my calendar so many times in the last hour that my eyes hurt. Production for *Behind the Sport* is nearly impossible to shift because it requires several of us for each meeting and shoot, so if I reschedule I affect everyone, including the timeline for the show. Next summer, when football season starts again, there is no moving any of those dates around. To top it off, Gavin left a note here on my desk with three dates on it. On the top, he wrote, "Would you join me for these trips, please? Your Loving Husband, Gavin."

"Hey," Gavin says as he walks through the door of my office.

I turn down the music as I say, "Sorry, I didn't hear you come in."

Gavin walks over and sits on the edge of my desk. He gestures to his note with a tip of his head. "Please tell me these will work. I scheduled them around what you put on our calendar, and it was not easy."

"What are the trips for?"

"Meetings with investors."

I lean forward on my desk and set my chin in my hand. "What for?"

"Building on the waterfront won't be cheap. Which means I have to convince a few people that I'm worth the risk. It sure would help to have my beautiful wife there to keep my confidence up. To take to dinner meetings. And for," he traces the outline of my lips, "nightly entertainment."

"Entertainment? Are you going to entertain me?"

"Yes. Those dates work all right? I know it will be tight with the show's schedule. One of them I think you'll have to leave early from."

I pull the paper closer to me and look at the three dates. He's asked me to dedicate nine days to his business, his travel.

"What's wrong?" Gavin asks.

"I need to talk to you about something."

He settles back on my desk slightly askew, one foot off the ground, and folds his broad hands together. "I'm listening."

"I'm not even sure where to start, Gavin. So I'll say it plainly and then do my best to explain it."

He sits frozen. I keep focused on his beautiful, emerald eyes. How I love him to the depth that I do, I don't think I'll ever understand.

"I'm going to start training again and run competitively. I want to win again. Championships, titles, gold."

"Um, all right." His face scrunches in confusion, and he scratches his temple. "Ahhh." A disbelieving laugh puffs out as air through his nose. "You said that after you said it plain, you'd explain. Please do."

"I know it's a lot to think about. It will take a lot of time."

"Yeah! Time you don't—" Gavin stands and walks a few paces away, then he folds his arms over his chest and shakes his head. When he finally looks at me again, there is a pain so deep in his eyes that I fear I've made a mistake. The hard thing is, I can't quite decide where my mistake began. Was it when I turned my back on a career that not only I, but my family sacrificed for? Was it when I tried to reinvent myself as a sports reporter, willing to rise to the top at the expense of a personal life? Perhaps it was when I met Gavin and just assumed he'd work into my schedule. Or was it just now, in making a decision this big without first figuring out how I'd make it work.

"You do realize," Gavin says, "I can't say a damn thing here without sounding like an asshole, right? Well," he throws his hands up in the air, "except, congratulations. I'm proud of you. I am. But damn, Nyla." He grabs the paper with his travel dates from the desk and crumbles it in his hand. "We don't spend enough time together to maintain a healthy, long-term relationship as it is. You can hardly squeeze me in. How have you magically made time to do this?"

"I haven't figured it out yet."

"Simple equation here, Nyla. We aren't building a sky-scraper. You have a limited number of hours in a week, where do you invest your time? And in what order of importance do you assign it all?"

"I'd never ask you if I am ahead of your career."

"That's because you've never had to wonder. Have you? Tell me one time that I was late for anything with you. Tell me one time I canceled on you." He cocks his ear in my direction, but we both know I have nothing to say. "No? Not one? That's funny because I have dozens of examples."

"I'm sorry."

"I'm not asking, never have, to be the most important thing to you. But I don't want to be a casualty of your ambitions. And I suppose Oliver is going to help with all this. So you'll need to make more time for *him*."

"He's making time for me."

"Aren't we all. That's great it sounds like he already knows."

I'm afraid to say anything else. It feels like I'm in a car on a cliff and the slightest movement, even a word or breath, will send it into the canyon.

As I say, "Yes," I feel things begin to tumble.

Gavin's nostrils flare and his eyes tighten. "Just what I want, my wife spending less time with me, and more time with her first-husband-look-alike. Yeah, don't think I didn't notice, or that your whole family hasn't noticed. It's just that no one wanted to say anything to you." I open my mouth, but before I can say anything, he adds, "Don't deny it."

"Okay, so he does! But I didn't plan that! And it doesn't even matter. I'm a married woman. Happily. I wouldn't change a thing about that."

He holds a very frustrated hand up to stop me from talking, and though it infuriates me, I press my lips together.

"So, Tripple Threat what's gonna give? What are you willing to sacrifice to be the best in the world again?"

"I'll figure it out. I will. I always do."

Gavin nods in agreement, and in the silence that follows his shoulders soften like a man who's given up.

"I am proud of you, for being willing to do this," he says. "I'm just . . . I know the cost will be steep."

He turns to leave the room, and I shoot from my chair, grab the sleeve of his shirt, and step in front of him.

"I'll give up everything else," I say, "but I won't give up us."

"That might sound romantic, Nyla, but I'm not sure I could live with myself knowing that you gave up the things that really make you happy for me. Running, your work, those are the things that truly make you happy. And as much as I want you, what I want more is for you to be happy."

When he tries to step around me, I place my hands onto his chest. I want him to say he won't give up on me either.

Frantically, I say, "I stopped competing when Lorenzo died because at first I just needed to run for me. It makes me happy, physically and mentally. But then I was afraid to run competitively without him. I never thought I'd find another coach, and I never tried.

"So I threw myself into reporting. I made it my life. The travel and irregular rhythm of the job made me happy because I never had to think of me. There was no pressure to train again like people would expect because there wasn't time. And while I was around people all the time, I didn't have to build close relationships and let them see me. All my weaknesses."

My chin begins to shake, and the corners of my eyes sting.

"The accident threw me for a loop. I was depressed. With Pop gone, I feel like the air around me is a little empty. And it wasn't the work so much as it was moving again and having a purpose to my days that made me feel happy again.

"Returning to work, though, I was so sad without you, and then you showed up." A smile on my face lightens the pressure I feel, softens the panic. "This relationship makes me happy. You make me happy, Gavin. Running and competing makes me happy too. I'm sorry I don't have it all figured out. But I'm trying. Don't give up on me, though. I'll be a better wife, I swear."

Gavin brushes his thumb over the scar on my cheek and kisses my lips lightly.

"Handsome?"

"Yes?"

"Will you help me figure out how to make it all work?"

"I'm not a miracle worker. I can try, though."

"Promise not to give up on me, on us."

"Never, love. Never."

Gavin pulls me into his chest and wraps his arms around me. I feel safe, like this might all work out.

The sound of crunching gravel tells me that a car is close.

"You're going to have to go to our bedroom," Gavin says. "Don't come out until I come to get you."

"Why?"

"Your brother is bringing something for you, like I said earlier. And don't peek out of the bedroom windows either. Go, quick."

I go to our bedroom, grab my phone from my nightstand, and sit in the leather chair.

It's the playoffs this week, so there is no game on Thursday. I still have to travel to L.A., though. I have several meetings for *Behind the Sport*. Also, Darren and I will be appearing on several shows to talk about the upcoming games. I need to see him before then, and not at work.

I text Darren, "Will you meet me at the track, Tuesday morning?"

Before I've even set my phone down, Darren responds, "Early morning workout? Sounds good. But remember, I've got old knees."

Gavin opens our bedroom door, shuts it behind him, and goes into our closet. He comes out with a sheer scarf of mine. He rolls it as he walks behind me, then lowers it over my eyes.

I jerk my head back. "What are you doing?"

"You can't see the surprise."

He puts the scarf over my eyes and ties it in place.

"Can you see anything?"

"Just a little light."

He leads me out of our bedroom, straight down the hall, and judging by the distance and the fact that we turn right, back into my office. I hear the shuffle of feet, the sweet coo of Rania. Gavin adjusts the direction I face, then moves behind me and unties the scarf.

There, in front of the hummingbird photos from Lorenzo is Pop's worn leather recliner. Tears spring from my eyes, and I press my hands to my lips.

Everyone is here. Kevin, Mia, Trace, Linda, and the kids. All watching me.

"You said you wanted it," Kevin says.

"Yes. So much. Thank you."

"Well then, Pop's red chair is yours. He'd be happy that you've got it."

"Red?" Linda says.

I sit in the chair and run my hands along the large rounded arms. "When mom had it reupholstered, Pop said the new leather was too red, so we jokingly called it the red chair."

"And, you'll never believe this," Kevin says. "When we took the back off the chair to move it, this rattled out."

He hands me a silver pen engraved with Samuel Tripple. It was a gift from Mom to him when he started his company. Soon after she passed, he lost it. It devastated him.

"The pen was in his chair?" I ask.

"There is no way he'd have found it. He'd be happy to know his favorite chair and pen are in your office."

"Thank you."

Alex, not interested in the old chair, wanders over to the bookshelf. He stops at the shelf with the three mahogany boxes and lifts the lid of one. He closes it quickly, making a high-pitched snap.

"Alex!" Linda whisper-yells.

Alex looks at Linda with round eyes. "Sorry," he says to her, then to me, "Are those your medals?"

"Yep."

"Wow! Can I look at them?"

I get up from Pop's chair. "Sure." I open the largest box, which contains my individual medals. I lift one out and slip in on Alex. He touches it like a rare treasure.

Emma rushes up to me and says, "Can I have one?"

"You can wear it, but you can't have it," I say and carefully put one around her little neck.

She bounces over to Linda. "Look, mama."

Linda kneels down and puts her hands on Emma's shoulders. "Very, very careful with that. Please. Nyla, this is very nice of you, but can you please take them off my children?" She keeps her hands on Emma. "They're capable of destroying anything, and I wouldn't put it past them to destroy these priceless and irreplaceable items."

"It's gold, Mom, what could go wrong?" Alex says.

"Now, take them off now," Linda says in a rush.

Gently I remove the one from Alex, and Gavin takes the one from Emma. Linda lets out a sound of relief.

"So," Gavin says to me. "Now might be a good time to share your news."

"News?" Mia says.

"Oh, I don't know," I say to Gavin. "It's kinda early, isn't it?"

"Perhaps too early to tell the world, but not family."

"You're pregnant!" Mia screeches.

"No," I look at Gavin squarely, "that isn't it."

"Probably not," he concurs.

"Well then, what's the news?" Mia says, her disappointment obvious.

"I'm going to start running again," I say.

"I thought you were already running again," Kevin says.

"I'm going to compete again."

"Like compete, compete?" Mia asks.

I bump my fist into the air playfully. "Go for gold."

Kevin claps his hands together. "That's wonderful, Nyla. You have no clue how much Dad wanted you to run again. He's probably dancing in heaven."

"Are you serious?" I ask.

"He just never wanted you to feel pressured. I mean, we all got why you stopped. But we hoped it was only a break before the return to greatness."

"You're going to be the poster woman for the comeback queen," Mia adds.

"Totally," Linda says. "The media is going to come after you. You'll just love that won't you, Gavin."

"Oh, yeah," he says dryly.

I slip my arms around his waist. "It won't be a big deal."

Kevin says, "Right. Won't be a big deal at all. You tell yourself that."

Gavin's enthusiasm melts, and he swallows hard enough that I hear the squishy sound in his throat. "I hadn't considered any of that," he says in a low voice.

I hug him tightly. "It will be okay."

I never wanted to be in the spotlight; it's just that the things I've come to love required that of me. While Lorenzo didn't want to be famous, he wasn't bothered by attention or crowds. Perhaps it was because he'd been an athlete who competed both in college and at the Games, so he understood how it all worked.

Gavin, though, is very different. So is this relationship and where I'm at in life. I've got a lot to figure out. How will I balance what I need with Gavin's needs? Is there a way to make room for everything, or will I have to let something go? Even with all these questions, there are a few things I know for sure. No matter what I choose or decisions we make, my marriage is a top priority. And no matter how the spotlight shines, I will protect Gavin.

# CHAPTER 34

$\mathcal{O}$n Tuesday morning, Darren and I arrive at the same time. The track is a unique blue color that reminds me of the inside of a thunder egg. Like us, there are others here seizing the morning: three men run a steady pace together, a few speed walkers with hips that move like dancers, and a woman who looks very serious about her pace.

Darren and I begin to walk the outer edge of the track slowly. He bumps my arm with his shoulder, and asks, "Why the track today?" as if he suspects something. "Aren't you more of a trail or city runner now?"

Occasionally Darren and I meet up for morning walks. We don't ever run together because years of playing professional football took a toll on his knees and other body parts.

"I have something to ask you, actually," I say.

"Anything."

"Anything?"

"Yep, I'll do anything you need. Now stop looking so nervous and ask me already."

I stop and face him. The words, "Will you be my running coach?" fly from my mouth as if they must be released quickly.

Darren's eyes dart to the right then left, as a smile grows on his face. Then, as if he thinks someone is playing a joke, he says, "What are you talking about?"

"I want to compete again."

"Tripple Threat Nyla." He shakes his finger at me. "I knew you weren't done. Always knew it." He laughs and looks around the track. "Coming home, are you?"

I nod. "Say yes?"

Darren waves me off and resumes our leisurely pace, this time I follow his lead.

"You don't need me to tell you how to run," he says. "You've done it on your own for years."

"You're one of the best sprinters of all time, Darren."

"Stop," he says as if he doesn't really want me to.

"Seriously, if you hadn't chosen football you'd have been winning gold medals too."

"Ah, shucks. Who knows, right? We all take paths. But really, you want my help?"

"Yes."

He strokes a beard he doesn't have, then finally asks, "What do you propose?"

"I need a new team because as you know, Lorenzo was my coach. Oliver, who Perry hired for my PT, is a sports trainer, and he's agreed to train me. But I need you to help me with my form."

"Come on, Nyla. What could I possibly add? You still hold world records, woman. Honestly, I don't feel good enough for the job."

I grab his arm to stop him and look him in the eyes. "You always talk about how players could run more efficiently.

You see those details other coaches miss, ones I have to slow tapes down to see."

"You really think I could help make you faster?"

"I want to set new records, and that means I've got to get in the best shape of my life and be a better runner than I was before. I need you. I'll fly here, to you, every couple weeks."

"I don't know. Maybe the family and I can visit you in Portland?"

I grip his forearm excitedly. "We'd love that! We have lots of room. And I'll make it worth your while."

"You don't need to pay me because I don't need any more money."

"I will."

"No. Absolutely not. I won't take one penny."

"I'll pay for your travel and stuff."

He shakes his head no.

"You make the rules, anything if you'll be my running coach."

He squeezes his lips together as he looks down at my shoes. "Are we starting right away? Is that why we're here?"

"I was only trying to set the mood."

"Mood set, Tripple. Okay, you've got me. I'm completely on board with this comeback."

I beam like a woman that's just won the lottery. Because I have. In a short time, I've aligned an epic team. Oliver has quickly come to understand me in a way few others have. Standing here with me is one of the greatest runners of all time and my good friend. And most importantly, back home, I have a husband that will always stand behind me.

"And just what does your fine man, Gavin, think of this?" He asks.

"It was a shocker at first," I admit.

"Ohhhhh boy, I bet it was. I'm sure living with you is a bit intense and crazy anyway."

"Hey!" I slap at his chest.

He laughs, vibrant and full, then as it fades, he continues, "But living with an athlete that's chasing a goal is nuts. And you, of all people, going back to greatness. His world is going to be rocked."

"It won't be that different."

All humor drains from Darren. "Best not to kid yourself, or him. Be honest right up front that everything changes. Priorities change. And once you tell the world, you'll be saddled with the responsibility to show people that a comeback at any age is possible. Plus, the media loves you, and that will affect both you and Gavin."

Darren looks over my body as if assessing a piece of mechanical equipment, then turns and begins to walk again.

"You know what," Darren says. "I need a hat." He makes a gesture with his fingers as if tapping the bill of his desired hat.

"A hat?"

"That says coach. In big block letters."

I begin to laugh.

"And a shirt." He rubs his hand across his chest. "That says coach."

"Anything else?"

"A jacket for when we're in that cold ass city of yours."

"That says coach?"

He nods approval.

"You want a whistle too?"

"Yep. And I need a bike."

"A bike?"

"I can't run anymore! You know this, Tripple. I have to keep up with you on longer runs so I can yell at you."

"Are you going to be a mean coach?"

"Nope, but I sure as hell won't let you lose. It's gold or nothing. That's all I'm on board for."

"Okay, gold."

He points to his head, and says, "Hat," then his chest, "shirt and jacket."

"A bicycle and whistle," I say.

"There we go. That's all I want." Darren plants his feet and lifts his chin like a commander in the navy. "What are you waiting for? I can't coach something I don't see."

"Ready?"

His seriousness busts into his easy self, and he slaps my back. "Let's go, Tripple!"

"Are you going to call me Tripple now?

"Nyla everywhere else, but coaches call their players by their last name."

"Yes, Coach."

He claps his hands like he's rallying the troops. "All right then, Tripple. Let's go!"

Darren's enthusiasm catches the attention of a group of men jogging past us.

"Not you," Darren says to them, then points to me, "her. Let's go, Tripple. You gonna let these slowpokes actually pass you?"

"Coach, they aren't part of this."

"Sure they are."

One guy turns and jogs backward with his buddies. "You wanna race?" he asks me.

He's taller than Darren, though half as wide and has the look of a professor. I'd bet he's at least ten years younger than me.

Darren laughs as if what the man said was really funny. "Oh, son, you don't want to embarrass yourself today."

"I don't know, I'm pretty fast."

"Do you have any idea who you're talking to?" Darren says.

I smile tightly. "Coach, come on, this isn't the field."

There's a twinkle in Darren's eyes that says he knows exactly where he's at.

The man walks back to me and extends his hand. "Matt," he says.

"Nyla."

"I'm up for a friendly race if you are. But I'll warn you, I ran in college."

"Yeah? Me too."

"Come on, it will be fun."

His buddies move to the side of the track, and one chants, "Matt, Matt, Matt."

"How far are we going?" Darren asks.

"I haven't even warmed up," I say. "I don't want to pull anything I'm just—"

"You got this," Darren says and winks at me. "It's okay if you lose."

"Don't worry," Matt says, "I won't make the loss too painful."

Matt's comment gives me pause to take stock of how I feel. Nervous? Yes. Determined? Hell, yes.

"One lap?" Darren asks.

"Easy," Matt says.

Matt looks me up and down, his eyes linger on my thighs. These are what you get when you're a sprinter.

"Are we ready?" Darren asks.

We aren't that official about it. There are no blocks, so we both take a more casual stance, like kids on the play-ground about to race.

"Set," Darren says.

I tuck my chin, ears alert.

"Go."

Going out for a run, that's easy. A race? It's hard. It isn't just that I feel the spot in my bone that's recently repaired itself. Nor is it the fact that while I'm in good shape, I'm not in race shape. What's really tough is I hear him; Lorenzo's voice fills my head as if he's right here next to me. *Drive hard out of the gate. Don't hold back. Float, not too much and not too little. Come off that bend, you know, like they did around the moon in that movie. You got this, Nyla.*

I used to think I couldn't race without Lorenzo here, but as I hear his deep voice immortalized between my ears, I know I can. I hope his voice never fades.

My nostrils flare, body desperate for more oxygen. This is where races are won. When the gas inside is gone, and all that's left is heart.

I cross the finish line, and though around me there is silence, I hear Lorenzo, *Like you never left.*

As I ease into a jog, I look back for Matt and see him cross the line. If this had been a real race, I'd have crushed it.

After a cooldown lap around the track, I jog to Darren. His face is flat like a poker player, but then his lips break into a disbelieving grin that rounds his cheeks.

Near the starting line, Matt is hinged over, hands on his knees. When he sees me approach he stands up like he's got a stitch in his side. "Injury, really?"

"It's true. I was in a car accident at the end of the summer."

"Walk away without a scratch?"

I turn my face and point to my cheek then stretch out my leg like a ballerina. The patchwork of scars sparkles under the bright morning sun. "Plenty," I say. "But obviously nothing that will slow me down."

"Where did you run?" Matt asks.

"U of O."

"What's your name again?"

"Nyla."

"Tripple Threat Nyla," Darren says as if introducing a rapper.

His friends haven't a clue, but there's a faint recognition on Matt's face that turns into a head shake, and he says, "You've got to be kidding me. I can't believe I didn't connect the dots. And wait," he points to Darren, "are you, Dryer?"

"Just call me coach."

Matt looks at me with question.

"Yes, Darren Dryer. And how about you, where did you go?"

"I graduated from Texas a couple years ago."

"I'm sure you were good, then." I wink.

"Yeah, except I just got my ass kicked by an injured woman that's a lot older than me."

"Hey, don't you ever talk to a woman about her age," Darren barks.

"I meant it as a compliment." Matt presses his hands to his heart. "A compliment, honestly." He extends his hand to me. "You look like you're training for something."

I lift a shoulder and say, "Life."

"Good luck with that." Matt walks backward toward his friends until he bumps into one of them, and then he turns around. He calls back over his shoulder, "Good luck, Tripple Threat."

Darren throws his arm around my shoulder, and says, "You've gotten sloppy. It's like you're a recreational runner."

"That's why you're here."

"It's gonna be amazing. The Tripple-Dryer-Big Guy team."

"You mean, Oliver?"

"Sure, you think he'll like it?"

"His last name is Buckle."

"Who knew. Buckle. Okay, fine. The Tripple-Dryer-Buckle team. He needs a jacket too."

"That says coach?" I ask.

 Darren holds up two fingers.

"That says coach two?"

"Yep!"

"You got it."

As I walk alongside Darren, victory hums in my veins. This little race meant nothing, but it reminds me of why I love to do it: I'm addicted to the win.

# CHAPTER 35

As the sun says goodnight to the moon, I slip from our warm bed into the cool morning air. For a few stolen moments, I admire my husband. His long, dark-haired leg sticks out of the sheets. After a week here in Italy, the skin between his eyes has smoothed, and he seems more relaxed.

I dress quietly in my running gear and tiptoe to the bedroom door.

"I don't know if I'm inspired or irritated by your dedication," Gavin says, his voice slow and sleepy.

I turn back to him. "You should be very impressed by my dedication."

"Why's that?"

I look at him as if he should know.

"Oh, yeah." His laugh turns into a cough. "That, I am impressed by. I'd be even more impressed if you were dedicated enough to lie in bed with me for a whole day."

"We'll miss the beautiful countryside if we do that."

"I didn't come here for the countryside."

"No?"

"I came here so I'd get you all to myself and there would be no distractions."

"I don't know, I find you rather distracting when I'm trying to look at the hills and pretty grapevines."

"I'm the only kind of distraction I want you to have. One day, Nyla, that's what I want on this vacation. A whole day in bed watching movies, cooking in the kitchen, and touching you."

"I have to run," I say. "When I get back, we'll spend the rest of the day touching. Promise."

He makes a disapproving groan. "You know, before you made this insane decision, you wouldn't have argued with me."

As Gavin turns onto his back, the covers twirl around him like soft serve ice cream. I walk back to the edge of the bed and trail my fingers across his hips to a part of him that is awake and ready for something. He catches my wrist and warns me with his eyes.

"I want all of you," he says.

"You've got all I have to give." I pull my hand back, lower my lips to the spot where my fingers were, and kiss gently. He reaches for my head, but I evade him. "I'll be back soon."

As I hurry away, Gavin moves to get up and yells after me, "That's not what marriage is about!"

While I'd prefer to go back into the bedroom, to let Gavin catch me before I get to the door, I can't. I promised not just my two coaches, but myself that I'd stay on top of my training while here. As I slip my feet into my shoes and quickly tie them, Gavin—nude and very ready—comes down the hall.

"Nyla Tripple-Boston! Get back here, or you'll get it twice as hard when you get back!"

As I open the front door, I reply, "That actually makes me want to wait," then quickly leave. Gavin may be brave enough to open the front door and pull me back in, so I immediately jog away.

Gavin and I spent the first week of our honeymoon in Rome where he marveled at the architecture, and I admired him as he explained everything he knew to me. Even when I had no idea what he was talking about, his excitement enthralled me.

Yesterday we drove here, Buonconvento, through the beautiful countryside. We're staying at a seven-hundred-year-old restored village which has several villas, common areas, and restaurants. Gavin rented one of the private dwellings, and although it's far too big for just the two of us, I appreciate the room to roam and the patio out back. Especially since we'll be here for another two weeks.

I run the outskirt of the property then weave between the brick buildings until, finally, I'm done. On the top of a small hill, I take a seat on the bright green grass. I look up my assigned leg routine from Oliver on my phone and commit it to memory. When I go to set it aside, a text message comes in from Darren.

Gavin and I agreed to a nearly electronic free honeymoon. We're only to use our phones to get ahold of each other, and for me to keep track of my workouts. We keep our phones on silent and let every call go to voicemail.

Not able to resist the curiosity, I check Darren's message. "Tell Gavin not to hate me. But you have to check your email. Let me know ASAP."

As I tap the envelope on my screen to bring up my inbox, I feel like a cheater. I sift through hundreds of emails until I come to the one from Darren with a subject line that says, "MUST READ NOW. TIME SENSITIVE." Inside I read,

"Stanley Smart interview to announce your return, which date works best?" There are three date choices, along with some additional information.

Aside from my family and a few friends, my return has not been shared. I'd considered a social media post in the next few weeks, but it looks like Darren has other plans. I'm sure this interview required him to pull a few strings.

"Book it," I write back to Darren. Then I gather my things, stand from the grass, and head to the on-site gym.

I don't have to tell Gavin about the tiny violation of our agreement, but I don't want to purposefully hide it from him. This announcement, especially on Stanley's high profile show, will affect us both.

When I ran competitively before, the public quickly became swept up in the budding relationship between Lorenzo and me. People devoured the college sweetheart storyline, the coach and athlete angle, the golden couple label. It wouldn't have been my first choice, but the two of us were used to it. But when Lorenzo got sick, I detested the attention and the way people became obsessed with us.

Last year after the gala, rumors swirled about who Gavin was. The snarky comparisons between him and Lorenzo made me sick. Thankfully, it only lasted a couple of days, and it was mostly on social media and websites.

Now, though, with my soon-to-be-public return, what's going to happen? I keep telling myself I'll be able to protect Gavin, to keep it all private. But will I? And how exactly should I prepare Gavin?

I open the door to the gym and step in. The first thing I notice is a perfect, and familiar, round ass in navy gym shorts. Gavin clears his throat, which makes my eyes snap up to him looking at me in the mirror.

His lips curl like a man who's about to get exactly what he wants. "Love," he says. "You look a little . . ." he drags his hands down the side of his stubbled jaw as he turns to face me. "I don't know, what do you think?"

"It's a damn good thing you're my husband."

"Is it?"

"Because the immediate thought that came to mind when I saw you would have made me an adulteress."

"Just a thought?"

"If you only knew."

"Surprising, since it seemed so easy for you to run away from me an hour ago."

"I promise you, it wasn't easy, handsome."

"Well, I hate to tell you this, but you're done for the day."

I shake my head no. "I've got to finish. If I don't, I'll feel guilty all day."

Gavin stalks over to me. "I guarantee you won't feel guilty about missing a moment of your workout. You'll definitely get it."

Gavin licks his lips and places his hand on my ass, then guides me directly back to the exit. When I step back outside, I break into a run, and although Gavin tries to snag me, he misses.

With an irritated laugh, Gavin calls, "Get back here."

"If you beat me to the villa," I say. "I'll do something extra special for you."

"How extra special?" he asks as we run past another couple out for a leisurely morning walk.

I slow a fraction and say, "Groom's choice."

Gavin picks up his speed, and as he passes me says, "It will be extra, extra special then, love."

He reaches the front door first and unlocks it. As he pushes it open for me, he asks, "Did you let me win?"

"Nahhhh."

He steps in behind me, kicks the doors shut, and pulls me to him.

"I've never seen you lift weights," I say as he strips me.

"You left me very . . . I needed to get out of here and blow some steam off."

He grabs his shirt by the back of the neck and pulls it off over his head. Then in one motion, he removes his shorts and boxers.

"Looks like you didn't blow everything," I say.

"No." Gavin wraps his hand into my hair. "But you're about to."

•••

I step out of the shower and wrap a towel around my body, then dry my hair as much as possible with another. From below the sink, I grab a blow-dryer, plug it in, and turn it on.

Gavin saunters toward me, a drunk grin on his face, and leans against the bathroom doorjamb. "I'll be right back."

I stick out my lower lip. "Where are you going?"

"Oh what, now you don't want me to leave?"

"Okay, lesson learned. I'll never walk away again. Wait for me?"

He gives me a quick kiss. "I'll be just a few minutes."

I finish getting ready then head to the back porch. I've yet to see anyone walk by, and there isn't another villa in sight. Knee-high terra-cotta pots filled with pink flowers line the stone patio. There are several pieces of wrought iron furniture with thick, tan cushions including two loungers and a table that can seat eight. I grab one of the loungers below an arbor and pull it into the sun. Then I lay down on my belly and prop myself up on my arms to read.

Only ten pages in, Gavin returns. He hands me a coffee then sits down next to me in the curve of my hip. From a small paper bag, he pulls out a white box that he opens and holds out to me. Inside is a variety of Italian pastries.

"Is that a cornetto?" I ask.

Gavin sets the pastry on a napkin and places it next to my hand.

"How's the book?" Gavin asks.

"Good so far." I take a bite of my cornetto. "And this is amazing."

We eat in silence. Off in the distance, I hear the chatter of people, but it's so faint it still feels like we're alone in this little corner of the earth.

I sit up and straddle Gavin from the back. Against my cheek and breasts, the muscles of his back are firm. I slide my hands up his arms below the sleeves of his shirt.

"Darren sent me a text message earlier," I say.

"That was not the comment I was expecting with the way you're touching me."

"Hear me out here, because you'll be pleased when I'm done."

"All right."

"Darren said I had to check my email."

He twists to look at me, rolls his eyes, and shakes his head. "We must always do what the coaches say."

"I could just not tell you."

He motions with the lift of his chin for me to continue.

"He got me an interview with Stanley Smart."

"Is that his real name?"

"I think so. Anyways, a full spotlight on his show."

"I'm sure that wasn't hard considering his show is on your network."

"It's still a big deal."

"Love, I know it is. I didn't mean anything by that. Tell me more."

"They want me to run a time trial after the interview."

He looks at me over his shoulder.

"What?" I say. "Don't look at me like that."

"Like what?" he asks, annoyed.

"Like you're trying to decide if you approve of this."

"I approve of it, not that you need my approval anyway. I'm irritated you broke the biggest promise we made about this trip. No work."

"No more, I promise."

"Right."

"I swear. And do you know how I'm going to make it up to you?"

"No. How?"

I wrap my arms around his waist. "For forty-eight hours, I am all yours. I won't look at my phone for a workout, and I won't even go on a run. You'll be sick of seeing me."

Gavin runs his hands along my thighs as my lips dance across his shoulder blades. "Oh, love," he says, "that will never happen."

I'm not sure I'll ever get enough of Gavin. I love the way he is on his own and what we are together. Sometimes a jolt of pain reminds me of how horrible it is to lose this connection, and though it warns me to keep some distance, I can't, I won't. I'm too far gone, and I want every moment of this life we have together.

# CHAPTER 36

Gavin stands, holds his hand out to me, and leads me from the sunny patio back into our villa. In the living room next to the coffee table is a familiar item, but I don't believe my eyes.

"What is that?" I ask.

"You know what it is," Gavin says.

"That's your guitar, Gavin. But why is it here? How did it get here?"

"I shipped it a week before we left."

Shocked, I say, "You shipped your favorite guitar? Why did you ship it?"

One side of Gavin's mouth lifts into a shy smile, his eyes full of love.

He owns three guitars. One he bought in high school that he proclaims is cheap, but can't seem to part with, even though he never uses it. He has another that he calls an investment from his twenties, which again I've never seen him play. Then there is this one, his favorite. It was a gift from Jax as a thank you for writing the words to the hit song that brought him stardom.

"I wrote you a song as your wedding present, but I wanted to wait until we were here, on our honeymoon, to give it to you." He takes a seat on the couch, and I watch fascinated as he unloads the guitar from the case and begins to tune it. "I can't take all of the credit. I mostly wrote the words, but Jax helped me tweak them with his musician magic. He, of course, wrote the music. You look so nervous."

"I've never had anyone write me a song, Gavin."

"Well, I wrote 'Mystery Girl' for you, I just didn't know it at the time."

Weak in the knees, I say, "But writing one with me in mind, that's about as flattering as it gets."

Gavin looks at the frets of his guitar as if checking they're still there. "Now we know why musicians always get the ladies."

"You're my musician."

"One-hundred percent."

"And my architect."

"Yes."

I sit on the couch next to Gavin, cross my legs, and turn to face him. He adjusts so that he, too, is facing me.

"Ready?" he asks.

"Yes."

"I haven't warmed up, so go easy on me. I'm gonna start with 'Mystery Girl' to get the nerves out."

"You can't possibly be nervous, it's just me."

He strums the chords of "Mystery Girl" several times before he flows into the beginning of the song. When Gavin sings it in his gravelly rock voice, it's done with all the emotions it was designed for.

*"I had no idea at the time,*
*How or why I stayed alive,*
*But, I think it is for you, my mystery girl.*

*For you, all the reasons I survived."*

Gavin changes chords, his fingers dancing in a way I've never seen before for this new tune. It echoes "Mystery Girl," as if they go together, but it's completely different. He looks at me, raw love and trust, as he sings again.

*"I never believed in my ability to see the future,*
*Until you, love.*
*I never believed the universe had plans,*
*Until you, love.*
*I never believed in true love,*
*Until you, when you became my love."*

There are many days I worry that I'll never be all Gavin deserves. On the nights I'm away, when the bed next to him is empty, I think of all the women who would give up everything for a human like him. And yet, he is mine.

Gavin reaches over his guitar and wipes the pad of his thumb over my cheek, then the other. "Please tell me those are good tears," he says.

I nod yes vigorously, then he sets the guitar in the case and opens his arms to me. Curled into the protection of his body, my favorite place in the entire world, I know that whatever bombs drop on us in life, we'll survive.

We spend the afternoon enthralled in our deep connection. We talk, make love slowly and fast, and we spend time in each other's arms. After a brief nap, we wake to the magic of the night sky blooming.

"Are you hungry?" Gavin asks.

"Yes."

"Let me cook for you."

In the kitchen, he pats a spot on the island. "I want you right here so I can look at you."

I hop up on the counter. "Tell me, Mr. Boston, what do you dream about in life?"

He fills a pot with water, then as he turns to put it on the stove, he cocks a grin, and says, "You're sitting right there."

"No. What do you want? Yamhill. The waterfront. What else?"

"I want to leave my mark on architecture. To build beautiful things that stand the test of time. Structures that someday, a long, long time from now, people will look at and marvel that something like that was built. And when they read about the building and the man who designed it, they'll find he had the greatest muse in the world's fastest runner."

"My artist."

"Yes, yours."

"What about you, Nyla Tripple-Boston. What do you want?"

"To win more races. To inspire women. I want to do more charity work."

"That's all?" he teases. "Too bad you're an underachiever."

Gavin moves about the kitchen gathering the things for our dinner. "Is there more?"

"Yes."

"Are they bad things?"

"No. What makes you think that?"

"You look like, well, like you don't think you should tell me."

I place my hands on my knees and sit up straight. As if I'm admitting as sin, I say, "I want to make more time for you. To sleep next to you more. Maybe most nights."

"Why is that so hard to say?"

"Because to want more with you that means I'll have to give up things I've worked hard for. Us strong women . . . we aren't supposed to give up things or change life for a man. It's disgraceful to all the women who came before, and worked hard so we wouldn't have to give up things for a guy."

Gavin looks at me a moment wordless until the water behind him boils, rattling the lid. He turns, picks up the container of pasta, and dumps it in. During the few minutes it takes the fresh pasta to cook, he moves about the kitchen efficiently. After he drains the water, he puts the pasta into a bowl and adds olive oil, Parmesan, and fresh basil.

Gavin sets it all on the table, then comes to stand in front of me. He lays his hands on top of my thighs, and says, "The women that came before you worked so you'd have the choices that every human deserves. If you make that choice because you want it, that's all that matters. If you make it, or don't make it, because you feel you're supposed to, then the revolution has been missed."

Gavin kisses my cheek and then helps me from the counter. I follow his lead to the dining room where he pulls out a chair for me. He pushes me in, then sits across from me.

"Nyla, I want to build our lives together. Even the separate pieces. You run, I'll cheer you on. I'll build, and you come to my groundbreaking ceremonies and ribbon cuttings. There are parts of our lives and even pieces of ourselves that we need to agree on and do together. Not because we are obliged to, but because we want to experience things together."

"Thank you for always giving freely in our relationship, Gavin."

"It's my pleasure."

"I want to give more to our relationship too."

"You don't ever give yourself enough credit for anything you do."

"I want more time with you, though. And I know you've done everything you can, there is nothing more you can give. I'm ready to shift things in my career, and not just by running again."

"What are you thinking?"

"I'm going to keep on with *Behind the Sport*. But I think I'll need to resign from co-hosting Thursdays and limit the amount I write."

"Do you feel that will give you enough time to train?"

"I think so. Don't get me wrong, it will still be crazy. But I think it's doable."

Gavin twirls pasta around the tines of his fork. "Have you thought about how much longer you want to run for?"

"No, I haven't thought that far ahead. It's funny. When I think of the future, I see the few things in the distance, but I can't really define how to get there."

"What else do you see in the distance?"

"You."

"That's good."

I take a bite of the pasta, and my eyes roll back. The tender fettuccine and nutty Parmesan melt in my mouth.

"How can just pasta be so good?" I ask.

"It's my water boiling skills."

"It is."

Gavin winks at me, then leans across the table and kisses me quickly. "What else do you see out there?"

"I know you want kids, Gavin."

"I know you hate talking about kids, Nyla. I wasn't trying to lead you there."

"It just scares the crap out of me. The idea of having them now."

"But I can still see you want them too."

"I can't while I'm running. But maybe after, we could adopt."

"Would you want to adopt a baby?"

"Maybe. But there are also older kids that need good parents."

"Please, before I'm fifty," he says with a hint of playfulness. Then he hooks a thumb over his shoulder and adds, "I want those kids outta the house before I'm seventy."

"Oh, gosh."

"You laugh, but I'm serious. Once I hit fifty, kid or not, I'm pulling the plug on that one."

"Okay, okay. Noted."

When I was young, I never thought about having a family. Once I started to date Lorenzo, though, I knew I wanted one with him. We dreamed freely about a growing family, even made decisions based on the future kids we envisioned.

With Gavin, I've been afraid to dream about a lot of things because I'm scared of everything I can't predict or control in the future.

"Gavin, I know it would take a miracle, but if I could have your baby, I would right now."

He lowers his fork down on to his plate as if it's a detonator. "Really?"

"Yes. As much as it scares me, and it would be insanely tight with races, I'd do it. Could you get retested when we get back?"

He shakes his head yes in cautious agreement. "Of course."

"And I'll get the IUD out. If it's meant to be, then it will. And if not, that's okay. We'll adopt in a few years. Way, way before you're fifty."

Gavin reaches across the table, takes my hand, and says, "Love, I believe in miracles." Then he turns it over and kisses the inside of my wrist.

# CHAPTER 37

When Darren told me the network wanted to do my big interview and time trial at Hayward Field, it sounded like the right place to do it. Still, I was nervous about coming here because I haven't been back since I lost Lorenzo. These weren't just my stomping grounds, they were his, ours.

As I walk along the sidewalk to the track entrance, Gavin holds my hand.

"You look amazing," Gavin says.

He's told me this three times now, twice on the drive down from Portland, but I appreciate his tender attention.

"Is that because this is your favorite?" I ask and run my hand along the royal-blue pencil skirt.

"That, and everything."

I slip my hand up Gavin's arm and snuggle in tight to him. "Thanks for coming."

"I wouldn't miss it, or any race in the future. Promise."

We pause at the grass-green front gates topped with a sign that reads, "Hayward Field." The raised, metal letters cast a shadow on the tan background like a sundial.

"Ready?" Gavin asks.

"As I'll ever be."

It isn't like coming home, but it does feel like a place I once lived. I drink in the bright terra-cotta color track, the spectator seating which seems bigger than I remember, and the electronic billboard that reads, "Welcome back Tripple-Threat."

"I remember watching you on TV," Gavin says. "It feels surreal to be here with you," he looks down to me, "and that you're my wife."

"Stuck with me for life," I say.

"Definitely not stuck. Blessed. Lucky. And more."

"Kid!" Perry sets a hand on my shoulder, and I turn into his arms for a hug.

He holds me at an arm's distance and looks me over like a dad ready to see his daughter do something great. His gray hair is thinner on top than the last time I saw him, and I hate to admit it, but he looks older too.

I'm grateful for his fatherly presence, though it reminds me of that empty space in my heart, which makes me miss Pop even more. I open my eyes wide to dry a threatening tear.

"You look like you're the fastest woman in the world," Perry says.

"Not quite there," I say, "but soon, I will be."

Shortly after Gavin and I returned from our honeymoon, I flew out to meet with Perry and share the change in my career plans. He said, "I expected the news to be big since you called an in-person meeting. To tell you the truth, from a network perspective, this isn't great. But from the personal side, I couldn't be more proud. I'll be there for all your races, kid."

Today, Perry flew in from California. He only has a couple of hours to spare since he's en route to New York. I told him he didn't have to come, but he wanted to.

"Good to see you, too, Gavin," Perry says. "Looks like you've been taking good care of our runner here."

"She's been taking good care of me," Gavin says as his eyes look beyond us and he points over my shoulder.

Three formidable-looking men walk through the green gates: Darren, Oliver, and Tate.

"What on earth!" I say, stumbling back and laughing. "Tate!"

"You didn't think I'd leave it up to these hacks," he points to the camera crew setting up on the green grass in the center of the field, "to get the best shot of your return to greatness did you?"

"No."

"Besides that, I had to be here for this. So I hopped on the flight with Darren this morning."

"Thank you."

"What do you think, Nyla?" Darren says. He puffs his chest, tips the brim of his hat, and turns to show me his back. They are all purple, my signature running color, with Coach printed in big block letters.

"Do you like them?" I ask.

"They're exactly what I wanted. Although I wasn't too sure about the purple. But I think it looks good on me."

"Where's my coach gear?" Oliver asks.

"I ordered them both at the same time, but later than I wanted. You should have yours, though," I say to Oliver.

"Really?"

"Yes, and they say coach as well. I'll check on the order later."

"I haven't checked my post box in a couple of weeks."

"Then you probably have them."

"This is quite an entourage," Stanley says from behind me.

Stanley Smart has the kind of voice you hear in movie trailers, and the serious tone matches the way he looks. The deep creases along his forehead never go away, even when he cracks a faint smile.

He started his career as a college football coach, and at some point in his late forties, he made the transition to sports journalism. He's been on every network, but he landed his weekly, one-hour show on the American Sports Television last year. He interviews today's best of the best athletes and covers the big headlines.

"I'm a lucky lady to have such support," I say.

"Indeed," Stanley replies.

He knows Perry and Darren well, but he looks at Tate as if he's trying to place him.

"Cameraman for AST, but I've been around for years. I think we've met before."

"Yes, good to see you again. And this must be Oliver, trainer extraordinaire."

"I like that title," Oliver says.

"And Gavin Boston." Stanley looks at him as if impressed. "Good to meet you too. We are ready, Nyla, if you are."

My decision to compete again has not been made public yet. The resignation from co-hosting Thursdays, however, has. It has prompted interesting speculation, most of which revolves around me being pregnant. I'm not, though, and according to Gavin's doctors, I never will be.

I sit in the chair next to Stanley and adjust my blouse, smooth my skirt, and cross my legs. I've been on camera thousands of times, but I still get nervous, especially when I'm the one being interviewed. If I had it my way, I'd quietly compete, no need for interviews. However, it doesn't work like that.

"Mrs. Nyla Tripple," Stanley begins. "Thank you for joining me today."

"I am thrilled to be here. Thank you for having me."

"Now, for those of you who don't know Nyla, and how could you not, let me tell you about this woman. For the last few years, she has made her mark in sports journalism. In addition to co-hosting Thursday football, you co-produce and host *Behind the Sport*, not to mention all of the other reporting you do. Nyla, it's been an interesting nine months for you, hasn't it?"

"Yes. Very."

"Last August, just days before your wedding, you and your father were in a head-on collision with a drunk driver. You lost your father, sustained extensive internal injuries, and broke your leg."

An invisible string slices through my throat making it impossible to say a thing, so I nod.

"Did it scare you?"

"Of—" I clear my throat to strengthen my voice. "Of course it did. Losing my father, though, was the hardest part of it all."

"You were close?"

"Very, very close."

"I'm sorry for your loss."

"Thank you."

"You made a miraculous, quick recovery and returned to your post as co-host only a couple of months after the accident."

"I love my work, and I needed to get back at it."

"And you married."

I'm still going to do my best to keep Gavin out of the public eye, but I can't, and won't, pretend he doesn't exist.

"Yes. The weekend after I returned to work."

"Lucky man."

"Actually, it's lucky me. He makes me incredibly happy."

"And your big news just keeps coming, doesn't it? Because you recently announced you've resigned your post as co-host. There are whispers that you're expecting."

"I'm not sure why everyone is so obsessed with knowing if I am pregnant. But to set the record straight, the answer is no."

"Tell me then, what led to this announcement. Are you making time for newlywed life?"

"That, and other things. After the accident, I sat down and took a look at my priorities. There are only so many hours in a day, and I needed to make some hard decisions."

"Now, with all this newfound time, what are you going to do?"

I smile and glance down at my wedding band. "I'm making room for my marriage, yes, to be home. I was on the road so much that sometimes I forgot I had an actual home."

"Wow!"

"Yeah." I shift in my seat, change the cross of my legs. "Enjoying my husband isn't the only reason I need to be home more, though. I've decided to come out of retirement and run competitively. My body, head, they're telling me I've still got a few good years left in me."

"How many?"

"Who knows."

Stanley grins, and those deep creases on his forehead soften as much as I've ever seen. "Welcome back, Tripple

Threat. Now, you are older, and you've been in retirement for five years. That's a lot to come back from."

"Older, not old, Stanley."

"You don't have the same coach as you did before," Stanley lowers his chin, his eyes glance at the grass, "do you?"

I glance off camera and see the men—Darren, Oliver, and Gavin—who have all, in their own way, filled pieces of the void left by Lorenzo. He'd be pleased to know it took so many men to fill his shoes.

•••

"Great interview, Nyla," Stanley says as he removes his microphone.

I stand from the chair, and say, "Thank you, Stanley, for your help and being here today."

"You'll do great. But you already know that, don't you?"

"I've basically bet my life on it. There is no other option."

On the other side of the cameras, Gavin stands with his feet hip distance apart, arms crossed over his chest watching me like a man who's just purchased something he's proud of.

I walk in his direction, and when he opens his arms for me, I pick up my pace and allow him to absorb me into my favorite spot in the whole world.

"I didn't embarrass you, did I?" I ask.

"By saying you loved your amazing husband? Hmmm. Let me think on that."

I lift my face, kiss his jaw, and say, "I really do love you."

"I love you too." Gavin lifts his chin. "Who's that?"

I turn in his arms and see the legendary photographer Sam Franca, better known as Franca. She has a gift for capturing people's personalities as much as their bodies. I've never seen a photo of hers that hasn't moved me.

The editor at *American Sports Journal* contacted me when he got wind of my impending announcement today. He asked if I'd write a featured spread on myself, and said he'd send the best photographer he could.

Franca's muscular arms in her spaghetti-strapped top are intimidating. If she weren't sizing me up with an artist's eye, I'd be nervous.

She tips her head for me to follow her and, keeping hold of Gavin's hand, we do. We go to a spot on the field where the stands are in the background.

Franca twists her hair into a messy bun as three assistants, all with different equipment, surround her like she's a rock star about to perform. She takes her camera from one of them. "I want you to use those curves, that beautiful face. Everything. Slip the heels off, then the skirt, and shirt. But don't go at it like a strip show, save that for your big guy." She slaps Gavin's chest like he must agree with her. "Here you're pulling off the layers, all those layers, and showing who you really are."

Below this professional outfit are my running clothes. High-tech fabric that fits like a second skin. Franca sent me an email instructing me to layer it all. I thought it would be so I could change quickly given our limited time on the field. I had no idea this is what she planned.

"Then," Franca continues, "I want to get some of you lacing up your running shoes."

"Got it," I say.

"I'm going to do a few test shots first," she says.

I stand in place while Franca and her team make adjustments to light reflectors. An assistant turns on a fan, creating a gentle breeze that pushes my hair back from my face.

"Ready when you are, Nyla," Franca says.

I swallow the stage nerves that try to escape up along my throat, but they climb even harder.

"Pretend it's just him," Franca says with a hip gesture to Gavin.

"I thought you didn't want those kinds of shots," I say.

Franca laughs and says to Gavin, "She's a handful, isn't she."

"Something like that," he says.

I slip one high heel off and set my foot into the grass, which is cool despite the warmth of the June afternoon. I'd once sat on this grass across from Lorenzo. It's where we began, the dynamic duo of wife and husband, runner, and coach. Strange that I'm here again beginning anew with a completely different team.

I reach behind my waist, unzip the skirt and let it fall to the earth. Franca calls out compliments as she moves around me. She tells me when to look at her, and when to look away. It's when she says, "Look at Gavin," and I do, that everything falls away, and it's just us.

I unbutton my cream blouse, one by one, and let it fall from my arms. Now, in my running clothes which hide nothing, I feel more like myself than I have in years. Here—entirely on display, Franca clicking away, and my eyes on Gavin—I've never felt so vulnerable and yet powerful in front of the camera.

"A couple with him," Franca says as a direction, not a question.

My Gavin would typically protest, but for some reason, he strides right over to me and follows Franca's cues as if he's a professional model hired to work with me today.

"You're my goddess. You know that, right?" Gavin says.

"And you, you're my god," I say. "You know that, right?"

"Okay, you two are seriously so hot you just burned my camera."

Something about the comment seems to bust Gavin back into reality and the reserved man he usually is slips back into place.

An hour later, after additional photos with Darren and Oliver, I'm on the terra-cotta color track. I bounce up and down, shake my arms and legs, walk back and forth. There are dozens of eyes on me and several cameras, so I do what I do best and slip into race mode. I shut everything out, squat down, and press my fingers on the track. With my eyes closed, I imagine what the race will look like, and how victory will feel.

Darren kneels down in front of me. "Ready?"

"More than, Coach."

I set my feet into the blocks.

"No pressure," Darren says.

"Lie."

"It's you against yourself."

"Are you asking for another world record?"

"Today, Tripple, I'm just asking you to come close. Make sure they know you're back."

"Racer, on your mark," an official calls.

I lift my knees from the track.

Fear is knocking, but I refuse to answer the door.

Systematically, I ready my muscles like a machine firing, energy builds.

Bam!

When I push off the blocks, there is a split second where I feel like I'm flying. A few moments when I forget that there is anyone else here. And then I know exactly where I am. My legs settle into the rhythm. Lorenzo's voice is not gone, but it is no longer the only one I hear in my head shouting adjustments. It's no longer the only one I hear telling me that I can do this; he is still here, though.

It's funny to cross the finish line alone with no one here to compete against except myself. I hinge at my hips, hands on my knees. Sweat drips down the side of my face, to my nose, and onto the track.

Darren walks up beside me. "You almost beat her."

"Who?"

"Yourself."

"You do know," I stand up tall, "that I'm going to soon. Right?"

"Tripple, we all know it. That's why we're here. To see greatness evolve from a new beginning."

# CHAPTER 38

"Hey there, sleepyhead," Gavin says as he opens his truck door. "We're almost home, I'm just grabbing the mail real quick here."

It takes a few moments for me to orient myself. We're at the beginning of our street, Appleton Way, and I'm still in my running gear.

Gavin gets back into the truck and hands me the stack of mail. "Sleep well?"

"I guess," I say and rub my eyes with the back of my wrists.

"You were asleep before we pulled out of the parking lot. Do you still want everyone to come over?"

"Yes, of course." I yawn. "That sounds good."

"Are you sure?"

"Yeah, I just need to shower and wake up. I might need a cup of coffee too."

"I'll put a pot on once we get inside. Your brother called a little bit ago and said they'll be here soon. He has something for you and wants a few minutes before everyone comes over. Is that all right? Or should I call him back and say you need to rest?"

Yesterday Mia told me she and Kevin have begun to go through everything in my childhood home. They've been so busy, and so have I, that we haven't been able to make time to work on it sooner. No one has even gone into my parent's room. In fact, they've been sleeping in Kevin's old room, and Rania has been in mine. I suppose if they want to stay long-term as they said, it's time to get it done.

I can't imagine what Kevin has for me. All I wanted was Pop's chair, which he delivered a few months ago. Sometimes, when I'm sitting at my desk, I look up and see the old thing shine in the afternoon sun, and I swear Pop is there.

"No, it's all right. He probably has some of Pop's stuff to give me."

I organize the mail in my lap into a nice neat pile. Then I begin to thumb through it. "There is a ton of mail here, when did we last check it?" I ask.

"Yesterday," Gavin says.

I flip to the last letter in the pile and see Lorenzo Garcia neatly printed with the address on Appleton Way. It's been so long since I've seen his name on anything. A strange, almost out-of-body excitement, floods me as if he might actually still exist for me to deliver it to. But when I notice the return address is from QFC, nausea overwhelms me. I press my fingers to my lips as if it might block the rising bile.

"Earth to Nyla," Gavin says.

I press the envelope with Lorenzo's name against the others and hold them against my belly.

"Yeah?" I say, my heart hammering so hard in my chest, I feel faint.

"I said, dinner choice is up to you. We can order in or make something."

"Okay."

"Okay, what?" Gavin puts the truck into park and reaches over to shake my knee.

I stammer, "Umm, uh, you know, why don't you pick? My brain is tired from everything today. No more decisions left in me."

His eyes narrow suspiciously as he reaches for the stack of mail in my lap. It's his thing. Every day he checks it, sorts it, and takes care of what needs to be done.

Quickly I pull it all away and say, "I got it."

"I'll take it and go through it while the coffee brews," Gavin says. "You can get your shower."

Panic crawls up me like a cat scaling a vertical wall. I press the mail stack to my chest and get out of the truck. "Actually, Gav, would you grab my bag? So much stuff. I'll get my shoes. And then, you know, I don't need coffee right now."

"No?"

Gavin watches me as I walk around the front of the truck. He looks at the mail pressed to my chest, and says, "I'm happy to make you coffee. I could use a cup myself after that boring drive with no one to talk to."

"Sorry about that," rushes from me.

"Hey, I was kidding. Are you all right? You're pale."

He reaches for me, but I evade him by walking toward the front door. As he unlocks it, I bite my lip and cling to the stack.

"Do you want to lie down?" he asks.

I need to get Gavin's mind off the concern that something is wrong with me and the curiosity of this mail clutched to my chest. I really shouldn't, because I promised myself I wouldn't use my body to distract him anymore, but right now calls for desperate measures.

"I'm not tired, actually," I say. "How about you meet me in the shower."

One corner of his mouth curls up. "That would be better than coffee."

Gavin sets my bag down, then reaches for me so quickly that I startle, and the mail falls from my arms and scatters across the floor. He takes my face in his hands. "On the field today I wanted to take you so badly." He kisses me like a determined man, hands slide all over my body.

My breath pumps harder than it did on the racetrack earlier. I'm dizzy. I open my eyes to see Gavin's are closed. I turn my head, and as he works his lips across my jaw, I try to locate Lorenzo's letter among the mess of mail. Why is there so much today?

I push him back and let my head fall to the side as if I feel amazing. I've never faked feeling good, and I feel horrible for this.

"Gav, handsome, why don't you go get the water warmed up. I'll pick these up and be right behind you."

"Leave them," he says and tries to pull me down the hall.

"No, no. If people come, I don't want them to slip on all of these. Go get the water started."

I drop to my knees. It's a frantic game of fifty-two card pick up. So much mail! Under rugs, and mats, wedged between the wood floor and baseboards. But I don't see the one I'm looking for.

Gavin begins to crouch down to help, and just as I'm about to tell him no, the doorbell rings.

"Kevin is really early," Gavin says irritated.

I lunge for the last letter sticking out from the mat in front of the door and say, "I'll get it." Mail clutched to my chest, I open the door. "Hey, guys!"

"Our champion!" Kevin says triumphantly in a sing-song voice.

"Oh, babe, that is horrible," Mia says.

"Ah, come on. How about Gavin. You got a good voice, give it a shot."

"Nah, you're doing well," Gavin says behind me. "Nyla, it looks like you missed one."

I turn as Gavin squats down. There is a letter below the entry table all alone and in plain sight with Lorenzo's name on display. He discreetly turns it over as he picks it up, stands, and holds it out to me.

"How'd it go?" Kevin asks.

Gavin cocks his head to the side.

"Good," I say brightly. "It all went great!"

"Do you want coffee now instead?" Gavin asks me.

"Please."

"Anyone else?"

"No, thanks," Kevin says.

"Sure," Mia says. Rania begins to mumble something that sounds like "ya, ya, ya," and Mia says, "None for you little one. Wow, Nyla, that's a lot of mail."

"Yep, big mail day. You know, I'll go put these down and sort through them later."

"All right," Gavin says. "Toss them on my desk."

"Yes, I will."

I knew the day I met Gavin that we both had secrets. After all, we'd lived a whole life before each other. I figured, if they didn't impact us now, there was no obligation to tell them. Now, though, I really wonder if anything should be kept a secret.

# CHAPTER 39

*O*n Gavin's office, I set the stack of mail on the corner of his desk like it's a grenade with the pin pulled. I snag the envelope addressed to Lorenzo. Of course, these running shorts have no pockets, so I slip it up the front of my shirt and tuck it in my waistband.

Like a spy, I carefully tiptoe to the office door and check to see if they've all gone into the kitchen. Clear. I exit the room, take a few silent leaps, and go into my office. I close the door gently and pull the letter out.

Lorenzo Garcia and this address on Appleton Way, I don't even know how that happened. In the top left corner is the logo for Quantum Fertility Clinic: simple black, block letters of QFC.

At my desk, I grab a letter opener that looks like a golden dagger from the drawer. I stick it below the sealed flap and slowly, silently drag it across.

When Lorenzo was diagnosed with cancer, one of the first things we were told to do was bank his sperm. I never thought about what I'd do if it survived him because that wasn't supposed to happen.

After Lorenzo passed away, a bill from QFC arrived. I called the company and told the friendly woman on the phone it was no longer needed, and she said she'd send me the paperwork to be signed. When the papers arrived I sat with them on the bed I'd once shared with Lorenzo and drank wine straight from the bottle. The documents were straightforward and only needed a couple of signatures. But to authorize the destruction of the last remaining pieces of Lorenzo seemed like I was committing a crime, a murder. And I couldn't bring myself to do it.

Instead of having it destroyed, I called and paid for another five years of storage just so I wouldn't have to deal with it again anytime soon. I'd hoped I would be stronger the next time.

We never told anyone we banked, and no one asked.

This is my secret. Mine and Lorenzo's.

I'm much stronger now than the last time I had this decision to make. It's time to finally let Lorenzo go. I'm in love with Gavin, our life together, and whatever the future has for us. And for the first time, possibly ever, I don't feel guilty for being entirely grateful for what we have today.

What am I obliged to tell Gavin, though, and what does he have a right to know? I'm sure he saw Lorenzo's name, and it's possible he knows what QFC is too. He also banked, although I'm not sure where.

I slip the paper from the envelope and unfold it. Every crinkle is as loud as a dinner bell. It's sure to draw attention, which will cause me to be caught red-handed. I glance up at the door, my eyes lingering for a moment on the handle, then I look down to the generic, white paper in my hand. The bold letters across the top reads, "Confirmation of Payment," and not bill as I expected. Confused, I scan the document all the way down to the bottom where it reads, "Name on card: Gavin Boston."

"Nyla?" Kevin hollers, making me jump.

"Yeah!" I call back, and scan the receipt again, though this time it's challenging to read it because my hand is shaking.

My office door swings open, and Kevin says, "Hey, Ny. I've got something for you."

I draw a steadying breath and manage to stand firm on my feet.

"Thought I should give it to you before everyone gets here," he adds.

I turn the confirmation of payment over, set it on my desk, and put an old copy of an *American Sports Journal* on it.

"Here," Kevin says.

He holds out a lilac, business-sized envelope. My name, written in dark purple with the elegant slant usually credited to a woman, punches my gut. I haven't seen Lorenzo's handwriting in years.

Suddenly, it looks like I see everything from the bottom of the ocean.

"This might not be the best time to give this to you," Kevin says, "given the celebration and all, but I found it a couple hours ago, and I don't feel right keeping it from you."

I take the letter slowly without looking up to my brother. Gently, I trace the letters with my finger.

"I'm not sure if you know this," Kevin says, "but Dad's car was totaled. Actually, I know you know that. What you may not know is the back seat was pushed up and surprisingly intact. Laid across it was Dad's suit coat. The police gave it to us. Mia didn't know what to do with it, so she hung it in his closet. Today, finally, I started to go through his clothes. When I moved the jacket, I felt this in the inside pocket. Mia said she didn't notice it before. That day, it was a blur."

A sharp squeak manages to make its way through my pressed lips.

"Are you mad?" Kevin asks. "It was an accident."

"Do you know whose handwriting that is?" I whisper.

"Yes," Kevin says, quietly. "It's Lorenzo's."

His name echos between my ears. I close my eyes and take three deep breaths.

"Nyla?" Gavin calls.

I look at my brother and the envelope, then freeze. Do I hide it? Is this a new secret? When Gavin rounds the corner into my office, I slip the letter below the magazine, atop the receipt. My brother's confused expression is enough to make me feel like a liar.

Gavin hands me a gold-rimmed, black coffee mug. "Your coffee, splash of half-and-half." His happy-natured face falls. "What's wrong?"

"Nothing." I sniff and wipe the wetness from my face. When did the tears start?

"I'd just tell him, Nyla," Kevin says.

It's the stress of the day . . . right? It couldn't possibly be that I've promised truth and loyalty, and yet I'm not as truthful as I should be. Why do I continuously fail this man?

Gavin's eyes implore me. "Tell me what?"

"I need more time," I say sharply and turn to get a tissue from the table behind my desk. My shorts catch a corner of the magazine sticking off my desk, sending it and everything I've tried to hide below, tumbling to the floor.

Kevin can't see the mess behind my desk, laid out at my feet, but Gavin can. The receipt for Quantum Fertility Clinic is face up. The lilac envelope, which proudly displays my name so beautifully I kind of hate it. The magazine, now face down, displays an ad for *Behind the Sport*; a photo of me in the middle of a football field, and I look like I've finally figured it all out.

"Just tell him, Nyla," Kevin says. "It isn't something worth hiding."

Everything starts out as information, maybe even knowledge. It isn't transformed into a secret until we choose to keep it to ourselves, even when we know it should be shared. I never set out to have secrets. I don't want them. But someplace along the line, I've found myself with so many that I've lost track.

Gavin sets his coffee mug on my desk and squats down. He sweeps the papers back below the magazine and stands with them in his hand. "You do know," he whispers as the corners of his eyes slide down toward his cheeks, "you can tell me, anything."

*To be continued . . .*

# WITH ENDLESS GRATITUDE

Writing a book includes endless hours with a scratch pad drafting, and behind a computer screen typing, deleting, and re-writing. To do this every day—transform ideas in my head into a book—is a dream come true.

Sean and Sarah, thank you for reading the early draft of this book and combing through pages and pages that at times, made no sense.

Emily, my editor and dear friend, what a privilege it is to work with you. Thank you for your invaluable feedback, corrections, and teaching.

To my first readers, Cecilia, Kacy, and Pam thank you for helping me polish the manuscript.

My dear daughter, being your mother is one of my greatest joys. Thank you for your patience and constant cheering on.

To my husband, Sean, I love our life together. Thank you for your unwavering belief in me, boundless love, and your willingness to read and edit no matter how busy you are.

Lastly, to you, my reader, it is for you I write. Thank you for sharing your time with me.

# ABOUT THE AUTHOR

Nicole is the author of the Bravely trilogy. Read more of her work and learn about her upcoming releases at NicoleDwigans.com.

When not writing, Nicole loves to spend time with family and friends, explore the world, and read.

She resides in Beaverton, Oregon, with her husband, daughter, Brutus Maximus (the Chihuahua), and Minnie (the lab+basset hound).

To stay in touch with Nicole, sign up for her VIP list at NicoleDwigans.com. She welcomes your feedback and book recommendations at Nicole@NicoleDwigans.com.

NicoleDwigans.com
Instagram: NicoleDwigans
Facebook: NicoleDwigansAuthor
Pinterest: NicoleDwigansAuthor